MY ENEMY'S ENEMY

BAEN BOOKS by ROBERT BUETTNER

MY ENEMY'S ENEMY

ROBERT BUETTNER

MY ENEMY'S ENEMY

This is a work of fiction. All the characters and events portrayed in this book are fictional, and any resemblance to real people or incidents is purely coincidental.

A Baen Books Original

Baen Publishing Enterprises
P.O. Box 1403
Riverdale, NY 10471
www.baen.com

ISBN: 978-1-4814-8405-3

Cover art by Kurt Miller

First printing, June 2019

Distributed by Simon & Schuster
1230 Avenue of the Americas
New York, NY 10020

Library of Congress Cataloging-in-Publication Data

Names: Buettner, Robert, author.
Title: My enemy's enemy / Robert Buettner.
Description: Riverdale, NY : Baen, [2019]
Identifiers: LCCN 2019004490 | ISBN 9781481484053 (trade paperback)
Subjects: | BISAC: FICTION / Science Fiction / General. | FICTION / Thrillers. | FICTION / Technological. | GSAFD: Science Fiction. | Suspense fiction.
Classification: LCC PS3602.U344 M93 2019 | DDC 813/.6--dc23
LC record available at https://lccn.loc.gov/2019004490

Pages by Joy Freeman (www.pagesbyjoy.com)
Printed in the United States of America

10 9 8 7 6 5 4 3 2 1

For Charlotte

In Memoriam
Richard E. Papenbrock
1945–2017

Husband, father, friend, devoted civil servant,
and Docent, National Museum of the U.S. Air Force,
Wright-Patterson Air Force Base, Dayton, Ohio

My Enemy's Enemy is a work of fiction. All characters and events portrayed in it are fictional, and any resemblance to real people or incidents is purely coincidental. Particularly, certain elements of contemporary U.S. and foreign security procedures, and of intelligence sources and methods, are deliberately misleading. Names of a handful of real places, organizations, and job titles have been changed.

However, background aeronautic, biographic, chronologic, geographic, historic, legal, medical, and technologic facts are true. Especially the most disturbing facts about Nazi Germany and World War II.

Statements and positions attributed to historic figures are accurate. Those figures' interactions with fictional characters are necessarily extrapolated, based on the consensus of historical sources.

My Enemy's Enemy

In August 1942, driven by émigrés like Albert Einstein, America's Manhattan Project began building the uranium fission bomb that destroyed Hiroshima three years later.

However, as U.S. work began Manhattan Project physicist Leona Woods said *Germany* "led the civilized world of physics in every aspect." Also, four years earlier in 1938, Germany had already annexed Czechoslovakia's Sudetenland, securing vast uranium reserves, and nuclear fission of uranium was first observed, not by émigrés in America but by Otto Hahn and Fritz Strassmann in Berlin.

The Third Reich in its twelve years built mankind's first interstate highways; hosted, televised, and won the Olympic games; deployed mankind's first jet and rocket aircraft, cruise missiles, and smart bombs; and launched ballistic missiles to the edge of space. The Third Reich also murdered two-thirds of conquered Europe's "undesirables," six million of whom were Jews, yet managed to hide it.

But history says the Nazis built no atom bomb because Werner Heisenberg, the physicist they scorned as "The White Jew," told them it was too hard?

Contents

MY ENEMY'S ENEMY

PROLOGUE

One if by sea.

—Common misquote of *Paul Revere's Ride*,
by Henry Wadsworth Longfellow

PROLOGUE

"IS IT TRAUMATIC WHEN AN OFFICER KILLS A PERSON?"

It was the third sympathetic-but-awkward question that Timmonsville, South Carolina, police officer Leon Rollins' front-seat passenger had posed. So, despite the cruiser's AC, Leon sweated as he drove southeast from Timmonsville.

Leon's momma had taught him that patience was a virtue. But college sophomore criminal justice major Becka Forsyth, all one hundred eleven freckle-faced pounds of her, apparently didn't sweat, was as white as Leon wasn't, and was sorely testing his patience.

Leon shrugged. "No Timmonsville officer has killed a person since I've been wearing this uniform." He didn't say that watching a friend killed was more traumatic than killing an enemy. He had experienced both too often, when he had worn a different uniform.

This July 4 holiday weekend morning, Timmonsville's five officers were spread wide, racking up holiday pay directing traffic at fun runs and parades.

Becka reached out and fiddled with the shotgun locked to the dash.

Leon said, "Please don't screw with that."

Leon regretted flexing his "Ride-alongs-in-back" rule for a college kid who actually *appreciated* the police. Besides, all they were doing was driving to question a witness who lived out in the county, who had last night seen kids downtown, tagging the Dollar General store's windows.

3

The quiet two-lane Leon and Becka now traveled, South Carolina State Highway 403, was also the Cale Yarborough Highway, named after the NASCAR driver who was the town's most venerated native son. On a wooded stretch a mile north of the highway's intersection with Interstate 95 they approached a spanking new white delivery van pulled off on the opposite northbound shoulder.

An apparently male silhouette was visible through the van's bug-splattered windscreen in the van's passenger seat. The driver's side door was open and the driver's seat unoccupied. A dark-skinned, but not African American, male wearing a bright red ball cap, with its purchase tag still attached and flapping in the breeze, stood alongside the van apparently staring at its hood.

Leon slowed the cruiser as it drew even with the van. The man, with his back to them, waved a circled thumb-and-forefinger "okay" as he trotted thirty feet to the wood line. There he unzipped, turned his back, and took a leak.

Leon flicked his eyes to the rearview as he kept rolling past the van. A half mile further, he spun the cruiser around in the Floyd's Convenience Exxon parking lot, just before the interstate ramps, and drove slowly back toward the van.

Becka straightened. "What's up?"

"What did you notice back there?"

"Oh. Not his dick, if that's what you mean. The van's brand new. Maybe fresh off the boat from the port at Brunswick, down by Savannah."

"Why would you think that?"

"It's a Horangi Bruiser. The Horangi plant in west Georgia only builds SUVs and sedans. Bruisers are imported from South Korea. Sometimes they drive them to the dealerships instead of trucking them. If a dealer doesn't have enough cars coming in to fill a transporter. Probably did come up the freeway. Because the van's grille and the windshield have way more bug splatter than you'd expect from low-speed in-town driving."

Leon raised his eyebrows. Maybe the criminal justice system could use more bright college kids like Becka.

He said, "And?"

"He was wearing a brand-new Georgia Bulldog hat. That's not a capital crime, even in South Carolina." She pointed back toward the convenience store. "They probably sell every hat in the SEC there. He probably just turned the wrong direction onto a road he'd never been on before. He looked like a Mexican newcomer. But even citizens make that mistake."

Leon nodded. "True. But let's assume you're right. Those two drove that van up the interstate from Brunswick. Stopped at a gas station and bought something. Then turned the wrong way to get back on the freeway. Everybody *has* done that. But how many people who did that didn't already use the gas station bathroom, while they were in there?"

Becka shrugged. "When you gotta go, you gotta go. Peeing by the side of the road's not a capital crime either, at least in my family."

Leon said, "The Georgia plate on the back of the van's so old and dirty I couldn't read it in the rearview when we passed. Not a cardboard manufacturer's or dealer's tag."

"Then why didn't you stop back there?"

"Didn't want to spook 'em." And I needed a second to weigh whether stopping at Floyd's, and kicking out my civilian, was worth the risk of them getting away.

Becka said, "Now what?"

Leon pointed at the screen mounted to the console between them. "When I'm close enough to read the tag, I'll run it. By the way, my life-experienced eyeballs tell me he's a 'newcomer,' alright. But from someplace that ends in 'stan,' not Mexico."

"That's profiling."

"Damn right. Becka, like you said, nothing we saw is a capital crime. But it's something worth a second look. Good police work starts with noticing things that are just a little off."

By the time they stopped behind the van, Leon knew that the tag should have been on a two-year-old blue Horangi Bruiser registered to a pet grooming business outside Savannah, not on a shiny new white Bruiser. Something was more than a little off.

Becka said, "Now you call for backup?"

"This is Timmonsville. This morning I am the backup." He pointed at the separate radio he could use to request assistance from the Highway Patrol. "So, now—"

The driver wearing the Georgia cap hopped out of the van, then walked back along its side toward them, smiling and waving. In addition to the cap, he wore jeans, a zipped-up windbreaker two sizes too big on a warm day, and cheap joggers. The outfit looked like it had been on a shelf in a Walmart a day earlier.

Leon kept his eyes on the driver, while he felt for, then lifted, the loudspeaker mic. He heard his own words boom, "Sir, please step back inside the vehicle."

The driver raised both hands and shook them above his head. "Is okay! All empty! I show you!"

Leon hissed, "Fuck!" He thumbed the mic again. "Sir, please get back inside the vehicle! Immediately!"

The man ignored the order, stepped around to the van's rear and flung open its doors.

The van's rear compartment was as shiny white, and as empty, as the inside of a floor model fridge at Home Depot.

Becka said, "Well, so much for the twenty-five underage sex slaves hypothesis."

Leon adjusted his gear, flicked on his bodycam, and reached for his cap.

Becka said, "Let *me* go talk to him."

Leon peered at the driver. The man remained beside the van's open rear doors, shifting foot to foot.

He thumbed the mic again. "Get back inside the damn van!" Leon turned to Becka. "What? No!"

"Leon, female interventions with immigrants escalate to confrontation thirty percent less often than male interventions."

"They teach that at college?"

"No. I follow @ProgressiveLawEnforcement. Leon, just because you're a hammer doesn't mean every citizen is a nail."

He turned his face away and muttered, "Jesus Christ."

He *definitely* should have locked her in the backseat cage.

Slam.

She was out the door, smiling, waving to the guy, and tugging on her TPD Ride-along souvenir blue ball cap. In that instant Leon realized that, in her navy blue polo and slacks, she looked way too much like a cop.

"Dammit!" Leon opened his door, climbed out, then sheltered behind it. He peered around the window frame, right hand resting on the Glock holstered at his waist.

Becka crossed half the twenty yards that separated the two vehicles when the van's passenger door flew open.

The passenger was out in a heartbeat, his movements professionally economic, the rifle instantly apparent.

"Gun! Becka! Gun!"

From ten feet away, the passenger raised the rifle to his shoulder and shot her through the head, twice.

She had been so focused on the driver that she probably never even saw it coming. That was a blessing. Two rounds. AK-47. Blood. Bone chips and brain tissue sprayed like shrapnel. It was fucking Helmand Province all over again.

Leon fired once, struck the big passenger with the rifle in the shoulder. The impact only knocked the guy back one step.

Both of them charged him.

"Allahu Akbar!"

Well, of course. What the hell else had he expected on a deserted road in the prime terrorist target of Timmonsville, South Carolina?

He concentrated his fire on the wounded one, even though he was farther away, because his AK was powerful enough to shred the cruiser's door like it was cardboard. Finally, the guy dropped to his knees, then flopped face down on the asphalt.

The unarmed guy had closed to within five yards.

Leon shot until empty.

It wasn't clear whether the guy pressed a detonator concealed in one fist, or whether the final round Leon fired detonated the vest beneath the man's too-big jacket.

Leon, teeth gritted as he lay in the hospital bed, thumbed the button on the pain med dispenser so hard that his fist trembled. The damn machine had cut him off, so he squeezed the nurse call button.

The duty nurse, carrying a syringe on a tray, bustled in faster than a morbidly obese sixty-something white divorcee should have been able to.

Leon shook his head.

Why did it seem like half of every hospital's staff, who of all people ought to know better, looked more like a heart attack waiting to happen than their patients did? Maybe they hadn't spent enough time starving through Parris Island Basic at Gunny Cobb's "voluntary" Fat Man's Table.

She consulted the analogue watch pinned to her scrub top, over her presumably laboring heart. "You're due, Hon."

She plugged the syringe into the IV bag port suspended above his left arm, flicked the syringe's barrel with a fingernail, then said, "You're gonna need these. There's more federal people on the way up to visit with you."

"What flavor this time?"

"The flavor that don't tell you what flavor they are. And Yankees to boot."

The head Yankee of the pair shuffled in. Old, bald, skinny, and white, he wore black-rimmed glasses. They were big and thick enough to be safety goggles. He had sweated through his shirt, and carried his suit coat, with his tie stuffed in the pocket. Welcome to South Carolina.

The woman with him was half his age, and still wore her suit jacket, which fit over athletic shoulders. She wore her jacket, Leon assumed, more because the bulge beneath it at her waist announced "pistol in a belt holster" than because she didn't feel the heat.

Her eyes, brown and lovely in a café au lait face, darted around the room, just like the eyes he saw in his bathroom mirror every morning. Like she had learned the hard way that the only safe place was the one you had already left in one piece.

Goggle Man said, "Thank you for seeing me, Officer Rollins."

Leon turned his head toward the catheter tube that tethered him to the IV bag on the stand alongside his bed, and at the vacant space beneath the bedsheet. The cruiser's door behind which he had sheltered had saved his life, but had not saved his exposed lower left leg.

Leon said, "I had a choice? Just so you know, DHS and the bureau already debriefed my ass off."

Goggle Man nodded. "I do know. I read the transcripts on the plane. My focus is different."

"What focus is that?"

"You saw combat. In the Marine Corps in Afghanistan. And you indicated you assumed immediately that the two men who you shot were Arabic, or at least Muslim—"

"Seriously? *That's* what you're here about? I didn't shoot them because I wanted to violate their civil rights. Or get some back for my friends. I shot them because they were trying to kill me. And because they blew an innocent kid's head off. It might surprise you to know I'm quite sensitive to the civil rights challenges of being a minority in America."

"That's not what I'm here about at all. There's not much left of the one who wore the body bomb. Anything about him suggest a connection to East Asia? Manner of dress? Documents, or vocabulary neither Arabic or English?"

Leon turned his eyes to the ceiling. "I think his clothes were made over there. Like everybody else's clothes."

"Just the two? Nobody escaped into the woods?"

"Read. My. Bodycam. There was no mysterious Chinaman." Leon turned to the pretty lady who was packing. "Is this guy for real?"

She turned her head and stared out the window.

Goggle Man said, "Your Ride-along passenger, Ms. Forsyth, worked for Georgia Power?"

"She was a criminal justice major, interning for the summer with security at Vogtle."

He nodded. "The nuclear power plant northwest of Savannah."

"Was there a question in there I missed?"

"Any reason to believe she had been exposed to radiation?"

"I think she sat in a chair at the plant monitoring security cam screens. She was a *kid* on a Ride-along. Her aunt is a clerk for the city of Timmonsville. Becka was visiting for the holiday weekend."

Leon turned his face away from the pair of them. As tears filled his eyes, he whispered, "And now she's dead. Because of me. Charge me with whatever you want. Or tell me what it *is* that you want. And tell me what she died for. Or leave me be."

Leon swallowed, heard a phone ping, and when he turned his face back he saw that the old man had bent toward the woman, while she displayed a phone screen to him.

The old man stiffened, like he had been stabbed in the back. "I'm sorry, Officer Rollins. I genuinely am. I didn't come here to add to your grief. I wish you the best, and I thank you for your service. And I wish I could tell you more. But I can't. Something has come up." Goggle Man turned, and left without another word.

As the woman followed him out, she turned and looked back at Leon. He could have sworn her brown eyes glistened.

Ten minutes, and one happy button click, later the female suit returned, alone.

She closed the door behind her, plucked the TV remote from

the bedside table, switched to a music channel and upped the volume.

Leon said, "Where's your asshole partner?"

"He's not my partner, he's my responsibility. And something really did suddenly come up. I handed him off to the other person in my detail, who's driving him to reboard his plane."

She removed her jacket, folded it, then hung it over the back of the room's chair.

Leon nodded toward the pistol she wore on her trousers' belt, a .357 Sig Sauer. "What are you, then? The muscle? Come back to cuff me to the bed so I can't flee?"

"If that's what turns you on, Marine." She smiled. "He's not really an asshole, just out of his comfort zone. He understands suborbital mechanics, and throw weights, and gaseous diffusion enrichment. He doesn't understand people who've lost limbs and friends in the suck."

Leon stared past her. "But *you* do?"

Unsmiling, she unbuttoned the left cuff of her starched white blouse, then rolled her sleeve up to her elbow.

Maybe she really *was* the muscle, come to beat the crap out of him.

She said, "I came back here because one percent of us do ninety-nine percent of America's bleeding. Sometimes we bleed wearing one uniform, then we come home and bleed again wearing another. Sometimes we come back home, then bleed again, but the government says we have to do it wearing a suit, as a civilian. Then the ninety-nine percent thank us for our service while they tell their kids not to play with ours, because our service changes us in ways that make them uncomfortable. I can't make that right for you. Or for me. But I can give you the straight answers your sacrifice has earned."

He stared at the sunken place in the sheet, below his knee, where his leg had been until the other day. "How would you know what I've sacrificed?"

She swung her left leg up onto the bed and tugged her trouser cuff up, displaying a shoe, laced over a thin black sock, and above that a silver metal tube prosthesis. "Helmand Province, 2010." Then she turned up her left forearm and pointed at an Oreo-sized eagle and anchor tattoo on it. "Parris Island, 2006. *Semper fi*, Sergeant Rollins." She sat side-saddle on the bed's end then poked a finger at him. "*Semper fi* or not, after I leave here, you will forget this conversation happened. If any living soul ever hears one syllable of what I'm about to tell you, I will hunt you down and saw off your other leg. Then your nuts. Before they lock me up or shoot me. Are we clear, Sergeant?"

Foggy as he was, he stiffened. "Clear enough, ma'am." Civilian muscle or not she still *sounded* like a Marine officer.

She said, "The pair you and your partner pulled up behind were Islamic radicals who had infiltrated the United States. I'm guessing you got that at 'Allahu Akbar.' But not just any Islamic radicals. They matched the bigger one's DNA to an Egyptian elite operator called the Crocodile. They've Hellfired him, and somebody who they think is his brother, without result, three times. They think the brothers split up, then dropped off everybody's radar, six months ago in Yemen.

"The Horangi Bruiser van, that was probably stalling out on the two of them, was being hauled from the port at Brunswick to Horangi's plant in western Georgia. For Horangi's annual national dealer show-and-tell. It's a standard van. But with an experimental fuel cell drivetrain. It's a trade secret, and it stalls a lot. The two you shot hijacked the van off a one car flatbed, then shot the transport driver through the head. They hid his body, and the flatbed, in the woods."

Leon turned his eyes to the ceiling. "His bad luck. And ours. You think they were planning to plow the van through a crowd in Atlanta?"

She shook her head. "Waste the terrorist equivalent of SEAL Team Six on a suicide mission that any radicalized U.S. citizen could accomplish with the family car? My protectee, the former physics professor, would call that an inefficient conversion of mass into energy."

He frowned again at her pistol. "Since when does the U.S. hire civilian bodyguards for physics professors?"

"Since the Israelis assassinated four of the Iranian nuclear weapons program's top civilian scientists, inside Iran. That started in 2010. It changed the rules of the game."

"I didn't even know there was a game."

"Well, there is. And somebody just broke *all* the rules."

"Nuclear?" He nodded. "The Vogtle plant. They were going to crash the van into a nuclear reactor?"

She shook her head. "The reason he asked about your passenger's radiation exposure was because, with her employment history, it was at least possible she might have experienced an anomalous exposure. The medical examiner was curious enough that he checked her body with a Geiger counter. She was clean. But the body next to her, the guy you shot, autopsied at between three and six grays exposure."

"That's a lot?"

"Three to six grays? His hair would've fallen out in another week. And before that, he would have been so sick he wouldn't have given a shit. Three crew members on the ship that brought the van from South Korea to Savannah did develop radiation sickness symptoms. One died."

"The van? The van was radioactive?"

"The van was deactivated where it sat, in the police impound lot yesterday. After they cleared a fifteen-mile radius, on the pretext of a hazmat spill."

"Deactivated?"

"By a robot. That didn't care how many grays it absorbed. The bot's been moved to temporary storage at the Savannah River National Laboratory in Georgia, along with the van, and the bomb."

"No. There was no bomb in that van. It was empty. I saw it myself."

"The bomb wasn't *in* the van. It was *built into* the van."

He swallowed. "Wait. The guy blew himself up twenty yards from that van. The nuke was a dud?"

She shook her head. "His boss, the Crocodile, had the activating plug in his pocket. They would have inserted the plug when they got closer to their target."

"Target? Where do you think—?"

"The smartphone the guy also had in his pocket was providing turn-by-turn directions to Ford's Theater in Washington. A symbolically significant ground zero. Located centrally enough between the White House, the Capitol, and the Supreme Court that even a twenty-kiloton ground burst would waste them all. And on the Fourth of fucking July."

"Jesus!" Leon clicked the happy button again.

"They're sure *he* wasn't involved. The rest is complicated. We're sure the van originated on the Korean Peninsula. We're sure the

North Koreans are still too unsophisticated to deploy an ICBM we can't defeat. Much less a reliable nuke small enough to fit on an ICBM, yet. Now we're sure they *are* capable of custom-building a clunkier, larger, Hiroshima-style enriched-uranium device, that could be made to look like part of a vehicle drivetrain. As long as the device was built into a big fat drivetrain package so unique that no ordinary mechanic or inspector would know what it should look like anyway.

"The radiation sickness we think resulted from physical contact with manufacturing residue. U-235 doesn't emit anything close to the radiation plutonium does. The DPRK's human intelligence network in South Korea is deep enough, and ruthless enough, to slip a doctored van, or components used to doctor a van, into the South. Then onto a ship, outbound to the U.S."

"*To* the U.S. is easy. *Into* the U.S. is hard."

She shook her head. "Our best defense against terrorist contraband is the *perception* you just expressed. But three trillion dollars' worth of stuff enters the U.S. every year. Most of it by sea, through over three hundred ports. We can't check it all.

"We concentrate on stuff from funky places, with crappy port security, where people don't like us. South Korea's our friend. Horangi's a good corporate citizen. It employs thousands of car-building U.S. citizens. It was transferring a vehicle from one of its factories to another, in its own ship, with legitimate business reasons to bypass normal vehicle prep, customs, and security procedures."

"But they hijacked the van."

"Exactly. The two suicide bombers didn't risk getting caught at the port, where security was tight. They just stole the van back later, in the hinterlands, where 'homeland security' is just cops like you. The United States was very lucky the cop happened to *be* you."

She continued, "By the way, a hazmat truck caught fire. You stopped to help. It exploded. The truck's driver and your Ride-along passenger were killed. You were wounded. Sad. Tragic. End of story. Got it? Leon, the U.S. doesn't want to advertise how close this call was. Like my protectee says, if you want to drop a single nuke on the U.S. the surest way is 'one if by sea.'"

"The line is 'One if by *land*.'"

She shrugged. "In 1776, maybe. Sending a message about attacking the United States is more complicated now."

"Meaning what?"

"Meaning when somebody test-fires missiles into the Sea of Japan, the United States sends a proportionally responsive message. When somebody beheads an American journalist in the Middle East, the United States sends a proportionally responsive message. When somebody delivers a viable nuclear weapon into the continental United States, that would have glassed central Washington while the President was congratulating Girl Scouts in the Rose Garden, and with seven hundred thousand extra people in the kill zone for the National Mall Fireworks, we send a different message."

"Send it to who?"

"To the only alliance in the world crazy enough to try it. An Islamic splinter faction, so schizophrenic it can't decide whether it's Shia or Sunni, that would have been glad to claim credit for the whole operation. And a North Korean infrastructure that was delusional enough to think that we'd accept that version, even though we would have eventually found North Korea's fingerprints all over this."

Leon swallowed. "We're at war?"

"Not war like you and I bled in. And not for long. My protectee, like lots of scientists, is a dove. He insisted on a face-to-face with you to nail down the Korean connection, before the U.S. acted. He's on his way back to D.C. because the hawks decided, an hour ago, that they already had the connection nailed down. I think they just sent him down here so they wouldn't have to keep arguing with him."

"You're saying—?"

"As we speak, the biggest shitstorm of drone, B-2, and cruise missile strikes, electronic warfare and cyber warfare, conventional military and paramilitary operations, and covert ops, in the history of shitstorms is preempting North Korea's conventional weapons capability along the DMZ, destroying its strategic missile capabilities in place, and decapitating and paralyzing its infrastructure, from the top down."

Leon frowned as he shook his head. "But everybody knows—"

She smiled. "That we're powerless to prevent North Korea from inflicting massive civilian casualties in Seoul during the first hour of a war? Leon, the U.S. conceals from our enemies what we actually *can* do just as effectively as we conceal from our enemies what we actually *can't* do. Civilian casualties in Seoul are projected under one hundred. And we're simultaneously waxing every suspected Islamic radical we're tracking that ever looked cross-eyed at an American, no matter where they are."

"But—"

"But nothing. Our friends and enemies around the world are being quietly told that if the risk, collateral damage, violations of sovereignty, and secrecy make them uncomfortable, they should thank us for responding with conventional weapons instead of nukes. *This* time. But that in the event of a recurrence, the unpublicized policy of the United States shall be to respond immediately and in kind against any nation even suspected of complicity. And that if they don't like it, they can go fuck themselves."

"That's insane."

"My protectee doesn't say 'insane.' He says, 'rash and irresponsible.' He threatened to resign over the policy when they discussed it. I think they'll fire him before he gets the chance to quit.

"But Leon, my brother, and his kids, live in D.C. You and your partner saved their lives. And the lives of maybe a *million* innocent people like them. It probably wouldn't sound rash or irresponsible to any of them. The "war on terror" didn't end today, after twenty years. But today its rules changed.

"I thought you deserved to know that. Because, rumors aside, probably nobody else with a clearance below Top Secret ever will."

The two of them sat silent, as though straining to hear distant explosions.

Finally, she stood, slipped back into her jacket, and turned to leave.

Leon called after her. "Hey, you got a name? Maybe after I get out of here you and I could—"

She turned in the doorway. "Ginger. But you can call me Lieutenant. Like my husband and my kids do. They got used to the leg. So did I. So will you, Leon. I swear."

She blew him a kiss, then left him staring at the empty hallway.

Leon stared up at the ceiling.

America had just responded, to a single nuke that *almost* destroyed an American city, by escalating its response up to the conventional-warfare Mother of All Covert Shit Storms.

With North Korea gone as the last truly rogue nuke supplier, and with the terror organizations willing and able to use nukes decimated, this "One by Sea" was surely the last nuclear bomb that could, or would, be smuggled into the U.S.

But if, in the future, somehow, somewhere, somebody did get hold of a nuke, then set it off inside America, we were going to nuke the crap out of the prime suspect then ask questions later. And the remaining prime suspects were nation-states that could, and would, nuke us back.

Leon rolled his head back and forth on the pillow and whispered, "Son of a bitch."

Then, like the good Marine he would be until the day he died, he set about sucking it up, carrying on, and forgetting what he had just heard.

PART I

My enemy's enemy is my friend.
—Variously attributed Indo-Aryan
proverb dating from 150 B.C.

One

THE SHEIK'S BODYGUARD PEERED DOWN THE HILLSIDE THROUGH Waziristan's thin, gray morning twilight, then pointed with his rifle. "The Asp! He made it!"

Propped up in his favorite wooden chair, beneath the mud brick house's wooden front canopy, the Sheik leaned forward for a closer look. To improve his view of the frigid, dun-colored landscape he cupped one hand above his eyes. Today his fingers trembled as much from excitement as from the cold and the palsy. On clear winter days like this one, the canopy allowed him to enjoy fresh air, while it shielded his ever-more wrinkled hide from the sun.

The canopy also, his younger protectors insisted, hid him from the down-peering eyes of the satellites and the robot planes. Those could identify him by his height, as revealed by the length of his shadow, and by the walking stick upon which he now relied. Then his enemies could murder him by pressing a button. He didn't doubt that the Americans were clever enough, and vicious enough, to do it. But he doubted that the Americans considered him worth looking for any longer.

His entourage no longer bothered to shuttle him back and forth across the nominal border between the region that had been Pakistan's Tribal Areas and Afghanistan's equally sympathetic southern border provinces. And the entourage, itself, was not merely shrunken but was comprised of trusted veterans too old and untried recruits too young. In the aftermath of the Great Blow's failure Islam, *his* Islam, the only *true* Islam, had become impotent.

Six months earlier something—no one was, even now, sure exactly what—had gone wrong in a distant place called Brunswick, in the United States.

And in the following days and weeks Islam's soldiers had been struck down with unprecedented suddenness and viciousness. True Islam's voices had fallen silent around the globe, overwhelmed by false preachers of moderation and cowardice, who called themselves faithful. Not only the Sunni Islamic majority, but even the less resolute among the Shia, had been seduced by the West's depredations and cowed by its power. And today those charlatans controlled Islam's future.

Financial and technical benefactors, private and governmental, had been overcautious in the best of times. Now they shunned true believers as though they had become lepers.

On the slope below the Sheik two guides, rifles slung across their torsos, escorted a third man. He sprang from boulder to boulder up the hillside as though weightless. The Asp resembled the Egyptian Cobra from which he took his nom de guerre. Born on the Nile's banks, quick, deadly, cunning, and equally at home in water as on the land. The Asp had traveled his long and circuitous journey's last kilometers by night, even though the protection darkness offered was pitiful against the Great Satan's eyes in the sky.

The Sheik sat back, brow furrowed, crossed his arms, and awaited the arrival of True Islam's last hope.

The Sheik watched the Asp as they sat together on the woven rug that softened the house's earth floor, and drank tea.

The Asp was the second son of a Cairo physician who had been a colleague of the Sheik, in the days when both had practiced medicine. The Asp resembled, to Egyptian eyes at least, his Peruvian mother. The Asp's dark eyes and beard, and his wiry, athletic, body, reminded the Sheik of himself in youth. But the Asp's complexion was somehow darker, his features less sharp and prominent, his eyes rounder, and his stature shorter. Those more widely traveled than the Sheik had said that the Asp could pass for a Mexican gardener. The Sheik hoped so.

The Sheik said, "You are breathing heavily."

The Asp nodded. "It's just the altitude."

"Is the North Sea as cold as they say?"

The Asp smiled and wrapped himself with his arms, panto-miming a shiver. "In the water, yes."

They spoke, one to another, the colloquial but cultured Arabic of the upper-class Egyptians they were.

The Asp continued, "But when one is dry, and appropriately clothed, the North Sea's disamenities are no more severe than the disamenities of this place." He shrugged. "When you instructed us all to disperse and await your call, I went to work where there was work to be found. But I long for the Red Sea."

"And I long for the warm spring in Cairo."

"Perhaps we will both return. When the apricots are in season."

The Sheik smiled, as much because the Asp remembered and honored the old colloquialism as at the expression itself. Apricots were never in season, in the way pigs never flew, and Hell never froze.

The Asp's smile faded.

The Sheik scratched his white beard. "You believe Islam—real Islam, not the westernized rubbish peddled on the television—has become like the apricots?"

The Asp shifted on the rug, frowned. "I believe apricots can-not flourish in a drought."

The Sheik motioned to his assistant to bring the manila envelope and remove it from its protective plastic bag. The Sheik caressed it, then handed it across to the Asp. "You read English. Behold the rain."

Twenty minutes later, the Asp tapped the papers together against the floor, slid them back into the envelope, and frowned.

The Sheik said, "You're an engineer. Is it possible?"

The Asp shook his head. "An engineering degree does not make an engineer. And my degree is not in that kind of engi-neering, in any case. As for possibility, the date on the document is old enough that you should have had time to investigate this. You wouldn't have dragged me here from Amsterdam if you had disproved this. So, may I ask what you've learned since you received it?"

The Sheik shook his head. "What I have learned in my life is that when a thing seems too good to be true, it generally is. This stank in the way bait stinks. The sort of cleverly disguised deception of which the Jew is fondest. Besides, at the time we received it we presumed the Great Blow was the better option. Therefore, I elected to set it aside."

The Asp narrowed his eyes. "Then why have you now reached out to me? Surely I haven't traveled from Amsterdam to Pakistan to render a layman's opinion on this document's aroma?"

The Sheik said, "You speak English. And some Spanish, I believe."

"I could not pass for British, let alone American. And never for a Spaniard, if you're suggesting—"

"I am not suggesting. I am pointing out that you possess unique talents and skills required to confirm and exploit this opportunity."

The Asp snorted. "The talents and skills required to exploit this opportunity, assuming it is *not* a Jew trap, are equivalent to those the Prophet used to split the Moon. If you want a miracle-worker I suggest you inquire whether He is available."

The Asp's response was blasphemous, theologically unsound, and shockingly disrespectful of authority. But it underscored that he possessed the independence, the audacity, indeed the Westernness, this task would require.

From childhood, the Asp had always competed with his older sibling's size and strength. He had compensated with daring and imagination, tempered and assisted by tenacity and careful planning. It was the moment to invoke the Asp's special connection to this project.

The Sheik raised one finger. "The Prophet did not split the Moon. God in his greatness did. God may choose any man as his messenger. He chose the Crocodile to strike the Great Blow. He and another soldier died in the attempt, unmourned among the infidels. Does your irreverence extend so far as to dishonor your own brother's sacrifice?"

The Asp sat back, stunned, his jaw agape.

His reaction surprised the Sheik. Operational security had restricted the details of the Great Blow. But surely the Asp had suspected his older brother's role, if not his fate? Both had chosen names of creatures of their native Nile Valley. The Crocodile more powerful of build, more gregarious, than his slender, silent younger brother. But both had survived close-run calls, had lost friends, and had shed their own blood and the blood of infidels, all in Islam's name. Both were highly regarded fighters. Both knew the risks and rewards.

Tears formed in the younger man's eyes. Whether of shock, sorrow, or pride the Sheik could not read.

Finally, the Asp blinked, swallowed, then bowed his head and whispered. "Please accept my most sincere apology, Sheik. I am honored you have selected me for the team that will pursue this opportunity."

The Sheik smiled and shook his head. "There is no team. You will operate alone. And with unfettered discretion."

The Asp stiffened and shook his head. "No one man could accomplish this undertaking."

The Sheik raised his palm. "The mouse passes easily between the stones of a wall that the camel cannot break through."

The whole truth was rather more complicated than the Sheik chose to reveal. The Sheik was sending a mouse because that was all he had left. The personnel available since the post-Brunswick bloodbaths had dwindled. The maimed, the simple-minded, and the too-old and too-young, were all that remained of the Sheik's army today.

Many in the West superimposed their own egalitarian ideals on jihad, presuming it was waged by impoverished dimwits, plucked like fish from an inexhaustible sea of peasants and motivated by a dearth of wealth, or by a desire to redistribute it. This pleased the Sheik, for a self-deluding enemy was an easily defeated enemy.

But the Asp, like his martyred brother, the Crocodile, resembled elite knights, rather than rabble. Born of good family, and personally known to the Sheik since childhood, they were university-educated and multilingual. They were skilled in the use of weapons and explosives, blooded in battle. And, most importantly, dedicated to God. The Asp was not merely a knight. He was the *last* knight that remained on True Islam's chess board.

The Asp at last responded to the assignment with which the Sheik had tasked him.

The younger man said, "Just me? A small army would find this undertaking challenging."

The Sheik said, "If this document is accurate, the two most difficult obstacles to success are already overcome." He crooked an oft-broken finger at his bodyguard, who brought the knapsack and placed it between the Sheik and the Asp.

The Sheik laid his palm on its canvas. "Also, this will in many ways be more useful than an army. The wealth packaged inside, in various fungible commodities and currencies, represents virtually every rupee's worth of value that we have been able to scrape together over the past six months.

"Inside you will also find a list of persons and institutions. We believe each of them remain either loyal enough, or mercenary enough, to sell you the various travel and other documents you may require. Also, to procure and provide apparatus and information not readily available. Commit the list to memory then destroy it."

The Asp nodded, tucked the manila envelope back into its plastic Ziploc, and then into the knapsack. "How will I communicate my plans and my progress to you?"

The Sheik shook his head. "You will not. Your autonomy and anonymity will be your sturdiest shield. Even when our ranks were filled with soldiers I trusted, we were too often compromised by secrets unkept. Today I trust no one. I counsel you to do the same. Your success will be the only report I need. And it will announce itself not only to me, but to the world."

The Asp inclined his head. "As you wish." He gathered himself to stand.

The Sheik reached out and tugged the younger man's sleeve. "Your eagerness is admirable. But sit. We will pray. We will dine together and talk of your family. And of better times past and to come. You will sleep. Then tonight you will begin."

The full moon had risen by the time the Asp shrugged the pack onto his shoulders.

The Sheik, with his bodyguard's assistance, rose and walked with the younger man as he took his leave.

Outside, the wind blew thin and cold, and the Asp assisted the Sheik, one strong hand supporting him beneath one elbow. The older man picked his way, using his walking stick for balance. The going was easier than it could have been, because the bright moon's light illuminated each rock and pitfall, and even cast faint shadows.

They traveled together the few steps to the end of the tiny, open flat upon which the house had been constructed. Beyond, the downslope became steep and rocky.

The younger man paused there, turned, and embraced the Sheik. "I don't even know where to begin. Especially alone."

The Sheik patted the Asp's shoulder. "No man is alone when he goes with God." The Sheik pointed his stick at the Moon. "This is his sign to you. You carry with you the hope of the world against the darkness. God will illuminate your path always."

Then the Sheik frowned, looked around, and spotted one of the two soldiers who had escorted the Asp up from the valley trail during the previous night. They would escort him down, as well. The man dozed, his back against a boulder, his rifle across his knees.

The Sheik called, "Yusef! Our guest is about to leave!"

The man sprang to his feet. "Yes, Sheik!"

The Sheik called again, "Where is Ali?"

The sentry looked around, then shrugged. "Perhaps he has gone to piss, Sheik."

The Asp's eyes met the Sheik's as the younger man's fingers tightened around his elbow.

Without a word, the Asp spun around and ran, headlong and stumbling, down the slope.

The Asp had put perhaps thirty meters distance between the house, and himself.

Then, for an eye's blink, the Sheik saw the missile. Black, as it crossed the Moon's white face, it was scarcely larger than a young olive tree's trunk. It streaked above his head, then struck the house, ten meters behind him.

The warhead's explosion, a red thunderclap, flung the Sheik through the air. Stone and timber, blasted from the house, battered him and caused him to tumble.

In his life's final instants, the Sheik glimpsed the Asp, also tumbling. Limp, as a mountain goat shot through its heart, Islam's last hope plunged toward the valley's floor.

A boulder rushed up at the Sheik.

Before his skull struck it, with an arrow's swiftness, he relaxed his body and awaited his entry into Paradise. His sole anxiety was whether the Asp would greet him there.

Two

THE ASP SOMERSAULTED DOWN THE CANYON'S STEEP, BOULDER-studded slope as he realized what had happened.

The younger of the two fighters, who had guided the Asp across the final kilometers to the Sheik's refuge, had been a traitor. A new recruit, he had rebuilt ranks decimated by the bloodbath that followed the Great Blow's failure, but had therefore been sloppily vetted. The traitor had revealed himself by his too-coincident absence, as the drone's missile approached. The traitor had doubtless managed to inform his true masters, whether Paki, American, or British, that the Sheik's encampment awaited the arrival of a "high value" target.

This, in turn, told the Asp that the Sheik's headquarters had been surveilled by the Americans' malignant eyes in the sky for months. The Sheik, now a shadow of the threat he had been, had been allowed to remain. As bait, that would eventually draw in fighters like the Asp. All of whom had dispersed after the Great Blow failed, in order to survive the Great Satan's retribution.

As the Asp tumbled, he threw up an arm, shielding his head. His forearm struck a boulder so sharply that he heard bone snap.

After seconds that seemed to last a lifetime, he came to rest on the V-shaped canyon's narrow floor. He lay, conscious and on his back, shocked by centimeters-deep frigid water that coursed around him. In winter the torrent that had, over centuries, carved the canyon was just a trickle. It remained unfrozen only because it flowed so swiftly.

A hundred meters above him, the explosion's smoke drifted.

Aglow with orange flecks of still-burning debris, it likely contained bits of the Sheik, himself.

No. The Sheik had not been vaporized. He had been alongside the Asp, meters from the house, in the instants before the missile struck. The force of the blast had undoubtedly killed him. But it had also left a body, which the drone would be able to identify.

The Asp's flight reflex had placed him in the sheltered lee of the canyon's downslope. And saved his life.

The Asp thought of the Sheik's broken body, sprawled somewhere on this mountainside. And he realized that he remained in danger. Even as the smoke dissipated, the invisible drone circled above, a mindless, unrelenting vulture. Its distant masters would momentarily re-task it to assess the strike's results. They would count and identify bodies, and determine whether usable informational materials might be salvaged from the debris.

More importantly, they would task the drone to locate survivors, then fire again.

Ten meters from him, the stream in its meandering had undercut rock and left behind a meter-wide ledge perhaps three meters long that overhung the water.

He tried to move and the pain in his broken forearm struck him like lightning. His left ankle shrieked, more likely twisted and sprained than fractured, but he could not stand, much less run.

The flecks of glowing debris burned out into ash. They drifted down, and sizzled against his bloody cheeks like hot gray snow. He had just seconds.

Teeth gritted, he rolled onto his belly, then dragged himself to the ledge. His damaged arm and leg were useless baggage. He realized that the opening beneath the rock was too narrow to fit under while wearing the knapsack, which remained on his back. He wriggled out of it, then wedged himself, face up and fully concealed, beneath the ledge. Then he dragged the pack in behind him.

The space between his nose's tip and the ledge's undersurface was perhaps a handspan. It was as though he was already sealed in his coffin.

It would not have been enough to play dead in the stream. So long as he lived, his body heat would silhouette him on overhead thermal imagery. He would be easily distinguished from a corpse, which would quickly cool to its surroundings' temperature.

Fleeing, and so becoming a moving target, meant certain death. But weakened by injuries, freezing as the water coursed around him and sucked away his body heat, staying put was scarcely better.

However, as the Sheik had said, his cause was just. God was with him. God had spared him from the blast, and now from the drone's further predation.

The fog of shock, and the numbing anesthesia of the freezing water, mercifully dulled his pain. As consciousness faded he realized that if God chose to bring rain, or snow, and flood this stream, he would drown, trapped beneath this ledge.

Had God spared him from the blast to serve a greater purpose? Or merely to grant him a peaceful death? Soon enough the Asp would learn which.

He tugged the knapsack close against his torso for insulation, then closed his eyes.

Seven weeks after the Asp had evaded the Paki damage assessment party, sent overland for on-ground evaluation of the drone strike, his ankle merely throbbed.

The twelve-hundred-kilometer journey from Pakistan's former Tribal Areas to the port of Karachi could be covered by automobile in one or two long days. But security, not speed, was his priority. And he required intervals of rest to heal. He relied more upon local buses than upon the sometimes policed trains. Even though True Islam still had many friends in Pakistan, not least among those who enforced its laws.

A friendly orthopedist, who treated the infection created when the Asp had amputated his own, frostbitten, left small toe, had dismissed the broken arm as a closed fracture of the ulnar shaft. It was, he had said, an injury familiar to Paki physicians. It occurred when common thieves, and also demonstrators, shielded their faces from nightsticks swung by the police. The orthopedist had also amputated another frostbitten toe from the Asp's left foot.

Today the healed "night-stick fracture" remained fragile enough that the Asp towed his rolling suitcase using his uninjured arm. A slight limp, caused by his diminished left foot, remained for the moment. It would, God willing, heal soon enough.

This part of Karachi's East Wharf, along Chinna Creek, smelled of rot and creosote in the humid sea air. But its pavement made for easier walking than the rocky mountain trails he had sometimes resorted to during his journey.

Still, he paused fifty meters from the freighter's gangway, both winded and to assess the unexpected next obstacle to his progress.

The Quran counseled patience and frugality's virtues. But the primary reason he had avoided air travel was to avoid the heightened security that accompanied it.

He had already purchased two serviceable false passports, from a forger in Karachi. Based on the first of these, and on one-way passage paid in full, and in cash, he had been issued a passenger's port photo ID. The tag allowed him to pass onto this wharf. His pass would allow him to do the same at intermediate ports of call, if he chose.

The bereted public servant who loitered at the gangway's base was a cargo inspector. He had no reason or jurisdiction to interfere with a passenger, properly documented or not. But he wore a walkie-talkie on his broad belt. The Asp had no desire to contest his authority and invite scrutiny.

As at most ports, vessels that called at Karachi carried, in addition to freight, a handful of passengers. He had booked passage on this break-bulk forty thousand DWT vessel because of its unflattering online photos of its three passenger cabins.

More particularly, he had booked it because those photos probably accounted for the fact that all three cabins remained un-booked, just one day before sailing. His voyage's purpose was not to make new friends among fellow passengers.

Sailing time was in one hour. The cargo inspector no doubt reasoned that the ship's sole passenger would be along directly.

The Asp donned plain-glass reading spectacles, extracted his leather-bound copy of the Quran from his case's front pocket, and approached the gangway with the book open, as though he were reading.

When he reached the gangway, he flashed his photo ID, suspended from the lanyard he wore around his neck.

The cargo inspector stepped between the Asp and the gangway.

The Asp stopped, heart pounding, and looked up at the inspector's mustachioed frown. "Is there a problem, Inspector?"

The cargo inspector didn't answer. He simply pointed toward the Asp's Quran. "That is a beautiful edition. May I admire it more closely?"

The Asp handed it across.

When the inspector returned the book, the rupee notes that had formed his bookmark were gone.

It was a silly dance, but an ordinary one outside the First World. Minor government officials were routinely paid less than living wages. They were expected to make up the difference by extracting gratuities. For doing the things that the law required them to do anyway. More enterprising officials, like this one, extracted a bit extra, for not doing things that were none of their business in the first place.

For the Asp, this exercise's upshot was reassurance that, during this adventure, forgers' shortcomings could usually be remediated by folding money.

Suitably compensated, the cargo inspector smiled. "First freighter voyage?"

"Yes."

"Do you speak Chinese?"

The Asp shook his head.

The inspector jerked a thumb at the rust-streaked black hull that rose behind him. "The captain speaks no Urdu or Pashto. Don't be alarmed when he demands your passport. It's normal. He'll return it to you when you leave the ship in Shanghai."

"I know."

When the Asp disembarked in Shanghai, he would destroy this set of identity documents anyway. He would depart Shanghai with new documents better suited to the roles he intended to assume. Commercial hubs like Shanghai hosted expansive communities of competent, reliable providers and modifiers of documents, stolen or forged. Several such providers appeared on the Sheik's list.

According to what the Asp had read online before booking this cabin, *none* of this vessel's crew spoke Urdu or Pashto. Another privacy bonus.

The cargo inspector smiled once more and snapped off a salute as he left. "May God grant you gentle seas, fair winds, and a successful journey."

Seas, winds, and unflattering photos aside, the Asp's cabin was a plain but clean metal box. So many years removed from his upper-class childhood, he now found the accommodation sinfully luxurious.

A single bed, dressed in white Egyptian cotton, would be changed weekly. A rectangular porthole, and en suite bathing facilities, would pamper him as he healed. And he would rebuild his strength in the ship's "gymnasium," a space scarcely bigger than a market stall in the Khan-el-Khalili.

He removed his laptop from his wheeled case, then plugged it in to charge at the cabin's small writing desk. Freighters offered passengers no internet connection, and he would have avoided one's insecurity anyway.

He faced toward Mecca, removed his prayer rug from his bag, prostrated himself on the cabin floor, and completed the afternoon prayer.

After prayers, the cabin's deck plates shuddered beneath his feet as the ship's engines stirred. He sat at the desk, started up the laptop, then scrolled through the reading list of two hundred fifty-six books and videos that he had downloaded.

He needed no book to teach him that Islam's enemies were the Jew, and the Godless states the Jew manipulated. What he needed to know more about were the Jews' other enemies. One enemy in particular. Because this quest, upon which he was embarked, depended on the proposition that the enemy of one's enemy was one's friend.

The twenty-one-day voyage to Shanghai afforded him the gift of time to understand the past. The past was immutable, but without understanding it he could not confirm which truth confronted him in the present. Nor could he utilize that truth to devise a plan to shape the future in a manner pleasing to God.

He selected an appropriate volume, then studied until aches in his leg and forearm broke his concentration. He pushed his chair back, stretched, and peered out his porthole at the darkness that had fallen.

Facts were necessary. So, too, historians' opinions. And maps, black-and-white photographs, and jerky, grainy newsreel films, viewed on a laptop's screen. The Asp's study of such things, and thereafter his action taken, based upon it all, would, God willing, bring forth God's great fist.

But the Asp wished that, instead of darkness, he could see back through time to where it had begun. In the decadent tumult of the Weimar Republic.

PART II

I still [in 1974] wear the Iron Cross with diamonds Hitler gave me... The real guilt [is] that we lost.

—Hanna Reitsch, "Germany's Amelia Earhart." Presented a poison vial by Adolf Hitler, in his bunker April 26, 1945. Died August 24, 1979.

If some day we are compelled to leave the scene of history, we will slam the door so hard that the universe will shake.

—Joseph Goebbels, German Minister of Propaganda. Appointed successor Chancellor of Germany by Hitler, April 30, 1945. Cremated the following day in the bunker's courtyard. Alongside his wife, after they poisoned their six children, then themselves.

Three

"I CAN'T *BELIEVE* THEY IGNORED A DUESENBERG!" RACHEL BERG-
man's brother, Jacob, snapped his eyes away from the two flappers
on the sidewalk. Pouting, he clenched his hands on the steering
wheel as he drove.

Rachel peered over her shoulder at the girls receding behind
them. They were older than she was, probably twenty, but affected
the same cloche hat, spit curls, and short hem uniform that she
did. An odd way, it suddenly struck her, for 1928's modern woman
to assert her individuality and independence.

She rolled her eyes at her big brother. "What they ignored
was a pimple-faced eighteen-year-old Jew driving his uncle's car.
Jacob, the thing that interests or disinterests a modern woman
about an automobile is its driver."

To be fair, Uncle Max's pale gray dreadnought interested
the very devil out of Rachel Bergman. Not so much because it
did turn most heads, or because it smoothed Munich's ancient
cobbles into silk, but because it was as American as The Great
Gatsby.

Jacob snorted. "You weren't old enough to drink beer until
this morning. What does a sixteen-year-old child know about
what interests a modern woman?"

"I know that the modern woman we dropped off Uncle Max
to meet is a gentile, a divorcee, who bobs her hair, and carries
cocaine powder in her compact so she can sprinkle it on the
mirror. Also she will probably sleep with him after dinner, to
get her loan approved."

"What?"

"Mother told Father when they didn't know I was listening. Mother did *not* approve."

Jacob parked the Duesy a block from the beer hall, helped her from the car, and they walked together as the dusk deepened.

He said, "You know this is still blackmail under the law. Blood relation to the victims is no excuse."

"Jacob don't be an idiot. You're not a lawyer yet. You're escorting your sister out for beer on her sixteenth birthday. Uncle Max snuck you out under Father's nose the same way on *your* sixteenth birthday."

"And you threatened that you would tell Father that he did."

"I did *not*. I merely suggested the three of us ask Father whether his daughter and son should be treated equally."

"Equally? Ha! Hell will freeze before Father lets me get away with half what you do."

"No."

"Yes! You've been getting away with everything for so long that you think you always will. You think that mere reality can never defeat you."

Rachel narrowed her eyes. "Are you saying there's something *wrong* with that?"

The Hofbräuhaus am Platzl had stood unchanged in Munich for so many centuries that Mozart had drunk beer in it. But Rachel had never been inside before. She would have preferred a smoky jazz cabaret, like the one where Uncle Max and his divorcee were drinking gin, and doing whatever one did with cocaine powder. But hard liquor remained, officially at least, years in a sixteen-year-old's future.

The Hofbrau's vaulted plaster ceilings, painted with floral murals, canopied a pillared cavern of a hall that on busy nights accommodated three thousand. Early on this June weeknight a few hundred scattered customers dotted the benches that lined the cavern's long wooden tables.

Not that the place was quiet. A lederhosen-clad brass band, on a central, elevated stage belted out Bavarian drinking music. So loudly that the lager rippled in the glass steins of customers seated near the stage.

Jacob led her past the stage, found them an empty table away from the noise, and after they sat asked, "What did Father say to Mother when she tattled about Uncle Max's divorcee?"

Rachel scowled and growled, imitating Sheldon Bergman. "Well, *someone* has to examine her collateral."

Her brother laughed.

A pigtailed blonde bar maid with blacksmith's biceps dropped off two liter steins of lager, from the eight she carried.

Jacob and Rachel clinked steins, then he sipped.

Rachel gulped, then she looked away and blinked, so her brother couldn't see her eyes water. A sip would have been more prudent.

Jacob furrowed his brow. "You swill that stuff like you've done it before. Has somebody been examining *your* collateral?"

She raised her chin. "This is 1928. Men don't tell women how to drink beer. Or with whom to drink it. You're stodgier than Father."

They sat and listened while the music blared and thumped.

Bavaria was home. It was charming and beautiful. It was also as old and boring as the smiling fat men playing old-fashioned music on the stage.

Today she was old enough to drink beer. With the law's blessing, if not her father's. Soon enough she would enter university. That *would* require her father's blessing. Or at least his pocketbook. America, rude and an ocean away, was out of the question. Even, or perhaps especially, for Father's little princess.

But today, Berlin's cabarets crackled with America's wicked electricity. People said Berlin was now "the sexual capital of Europe." But Father wouldn't even let her drink beer, when the law itself said it was perfectly fine. To let her leave home for *anywhere* was going to be difficult enough.

Jacob said, "Father's not 'stodgy,' he's responsible. Like any good banker. Uncle Max can afford his Duesenberg because Father moved the bank's assets out of Marks at the beginning of the war, before the government decided to just print money to finance it."

"Finance *this*." Rachel wagged her head. "Collateral *that*. You and Father can be such... Jews."

"It's not a disease, you know." He narrowed his eyes at her. "Sometimes I wonder whether you are the least Jewish Jew in Europe. Or merely still a rebellious child, Rachel. Do you understand what Germany's endured since the war? What Jews have endured since the Pharaohs? And how much better off our family, and the bank's depositors, whether gentile or Jew, have been than most Germans? Because of Father's prudence, and humanity, and common sense. Because he's 'such a Jew.'"

"Don't patronize me, Jacob." She shouted to be heard over the tuba as she stabbed a finger into her brother's chest. "I'll tell you what I understand. I understand Versailles wasn't a treaty. It was the public stoning of an entire nation, by other nations that were no better. Followed by armed robbery and a gang rape."

Jacob leaned close and whispered, "Rachel! If you expect to be treated as a lady, don't shout about gang rape."

A passing, mustachioed man, whose right arm ended in a stump at the wrist, leaned toward them. When he did, the two tiny medals pinned to his loden jacket swung from their ribbons.

He nodded. "*That's* the truth, young lady!"

She felt the warmth and tingle of her first beer, and stuck her tongue out, little sister to big brother. "*He* knows a lady! And I know the truth. When I was eight, I saw the Bolsheviks beat people in the streets. So hard that blood spattered the lamp posts. I heard the gunfire. And the screams. And the sirens. Before I was twelve, I saw two more revolutions fail. I saw the government print paper marks by the bushel to pay the Versailles reparations. The same country—" she pointed at the one-handed veteran's back, "—for which that man gave his *hand*, devalued his life savings. Until they were too worthless to buy his family one loaf of bread. We let the French steal the Ruhr from us at gunpoint, because Versailles denied us guns to defend our own land.

"Jacob, Germany's been in the toilet for most of my life. And most of Germany blames it all on Jew bankers."

"No. Not 'most of Germany.' The National Socialists *tried* to blame the economy, and the war, on us. They also tried to start a revolution in a beer hall. The Nazis who weren't shot got thrown in jail for their trouble. Today the economy's booming. Rachel, the Nazis won less than three percent in the elections last month. From now on they're irrelevant. And so are their ideas."

"Father disagrees. Father told Mother that now Hitler's out of jail he's soft-pedaling the Jew baiting, and the violence. That he's saying that the good times are a house of cards, built on loans from American banks. And that the American stock market is a bigger house of cards. It will crash. And when it crashes, the Americans will call their loans. And Germany will crash, too."

"Well, Father and Hitler happen to be right about the economy. And Hitler's the only politician with the guts to predict the big, roaring party's going to end badly."

She shrugged. "Father says it's not guts, it's opportunism. That politicians change their convictions like honest people change their underwear."

Jacob shrugged back. "Sure. But when the markets crash, and Germany's in the toilet again, Hitler will look like Nostradamus. And nobody will care about his dirty underwear. You know, he could be chancellor by 1933."

"That ranting pipsqueak?" She sniffed Jacob's empty stein. "Was there cocaine powder in your beer?"

Jacob cocked his head at the ceiling. "If the Nazis really have matured from thugs into political dealmakers, a coalition government might be fine, compared to gridlock. Speaking of unsavory deal making..." He turned to her with puppy eyes.

Rachel tipped her stein, peered into it, and sighed. "I know. A deal is a deal. Yes, Lisl Schroeder is in my English literature club. Yes, I will introduce you to her. No, that will not get you anywhere."

"She's stuck up?"

"No. She's nice." Again, Rachel rolled her eyes at her idiot brother. "Jacob, she's a *gentile*. Mother will make Father cut off your inheritance. After Mother cuts off your penis."

"Bergman!"

The shout came from among a half-dozen young men wearing football kit. Their cleated boots' thunder echoed through the beer hall, as loud as the band.

Her brother waved them over, and they arrived, sweaty and muddy amid much backslapping and laughter.

Horowitz, a friend of Jacob's, smiled at her.

"Bergman, aren't you going to introduce us to your beautiful girlfriend?"

Someone said, "Don't introduce her to Winter if you expect to go home with her, Bergman."

Laughter.

Someone else said, "Here he comes!"

Another called to him, "What took you so long, my captain?"

"Somebody had to stay behind and pay off the referee for that penalty kick."

More laughter.

The team captain who waved as he trotted toward the group, holding a silver trophy cup aloft in one hand, was blond, stood taller than the rest, and was broad through the shoulders, where many football players were slight.

His eyes sparkled blue, his chin was strong and cleft, and his smile shone like the sun. Sweat sparkled on his forehead and he breathed heavily and rapidly, nostrils flared.

She shivered as she stared at him, and realized that she was holding her breath. He was the most beautiful human being Rachel Bergman had ever seen.

Jacob said to Horowitz, "She's not my girlfriend. She's my sister. Say hello to Horowitz, Rachel."

Someone said, "Bergman, has no one told you there are laws against seducing your sister?"

Even more laughter.

The beautiful human set the silver cup on the table, leaned across it, and smiled into her eyes. "Rachel. Miss Bergman. I'm Peter. Peter Winter. And if you were my sister, I would break the law."

The captain's teammates hooted, then dragged him and the trophy away across the hall to another table, at which more of their club already sat.

Rachel stared after them, and she was sure Peter Winter had turned and searched her out, and smiled, before he was consumed in the celebration's scrum.

Jacob said, "Sorry. Horowitz isn't a bad sort."

"What? Oh. Who is he?"

"I take it by 'he' you don't mean fat Horowitz. Peter Winter's the best fullback in Bavaria. Maybe in Germany. Shall I go over there and slap him, for getting fresh with my sister?"

"I may go slap him myself. On the behind."

"Rachel!"

"He just made a joke. And a clever one at that. He seems quite nice."

"For God's sake, he's nineteen."

"And I suppose you're going to point out that he's a gentile, and Mother and Father wouldn't approve."

"Not just *a* gentile."

"What?"

"His maternal uncle was one of the sixteen marchers who the police shot dead, around Hitler in the Odeonsplatz in the 1923 putsch. The Nazis call them their 'Blood Martyrs.' Pure blood is everything to them. That makes Peter National Socialist royalty."

Rachel's jaw dropped. "Him? One of those? Never!"

Jacob said, "I didn't say that. Peter's the kindest, most honorable fellow I know. I just reported his family tree, which is hardly his doing. But if Father's right about the Nazis, I suppose in politics Peter's family ties could be an advantage someday."

She rolled her eyes again. "God. He wants to be a politician? That's more disgusting than being a banker or a lawyer."

"Actually, it's even worse. He wants to be a physicist."

"He hardly looks bookish."

"Fullbacks rarely do. But I'm as good with numbers as Father is, and in calculus Peter not only left all the rest of us in the dust, by the end of term *he* was explaining differential equations and topology to our instructor. In the fall Peter's off to University, in Leipzig."

"Ugh. Bavaria without Alps. If he's so smart why not Berlin?"

"Apparently, all the very best physics people are fighting to get in to Leipzig now."

"Why?"

"There's a rising genius there, named Heisenberg. They say Einstein himself has already nominated Heisenberg for the Nobel Prize."

Rachel peered across the great hall, to the table where Peter Winter's teammates raised their steins, toasting their captain, who was too beautiful to be a physicist, and too honorable to be a Nazi. Suddenly Berlin seemed less important.

"Jacob, isn't Goethe Father's favorite author?"

"Father is a German to his core. By definition that makes Goethe his favorite author. Unlike one of us at this table. Who prefers Hemingway and Fitzgerald."

"Or, as Father calls them, my smut and rebellion peddlers."

"You know, Goethe attended the University of Leipzig. Be careful. When you argue your case for university with Father, don't even *mention* Leipzig, if you hope to sell him on Berlin. If he gets the idea in his head, he'll pack you off to Leipzig kicking and screaming. To get the smut and rebellion scrubbed out of *your* head."

"Jacob, you are the smartest person I know, but sometimes I think *your* head is a block of wood. If it's Father's idea to send me to study at Leipzig, and Peter Winter is there, too, neither of them can object to it, can they?"

Her brother smiled at her and shook his head slowly. "Poor Father. And poor Peter Winter. Any man who matches wits with you doesn't realize what he's gotten himself into. Until it's too late."

"Jacob, none of us ever realize what we've gotten ourselves into until it's too late. The secret is to find a way out once we do."

Four

"WHERE ARE YOU FROM, MY FRIEND?" THE MEXICAN, ONE THIN hand on his brown beer bottle, squinted through the empty bar's midday gloom, and across the table at the Asp.

The Asp stifled a frown that would betray his frustration at the question.

He had conducted his Shanghai business successfully, despite a forger who had tried to re-trade a deal, and was therefore now dead. He had then crossed the Pacific by freighter without further incident, from Shanghai to Lima, Peru.

Although his mother had been born in Peru, and what Spanish the Asp spoke he had learned from her, he had not stayed long in Lima.

By back roads, and through back doors, he had crossed Colombia's porous borders. Then the borders of Central America's jigsaw of nations. Until he arrived here in Ixtepec, north of the equally porous border that separated Guatemala from Mexico.

Behind the Asp lay thirty-five thousand excruciatingly slow, but impeccably secure, kilometers. He had spent hours in his onboard cabin, practicing his Spanish. He had kept his facial hair shaved down to a Mexican-style mustache. He had acquired, and wore, Mexican peasant clothes.

But now, after hearing the Asp speak just a few words in Spanish, this man had realized instantly that the Asp was not Mexican.

Two thousand kilometers—thirteen hundred *miles*, he reminded himself—still separated him from the United States' southern border. The closer he approached that border, the greater his risk became. His appearance was consistent with those around him here. But, with his accent, he dared not risk traveling without local assistance. Even though local assistance came with its own risks.

He answered the man. "I am from Peru."

"Ah." The man nodded. "I knew by your accent you weren't local. What brings you to Ixtepec?"

"I'm looking for a *Vaquero*." He used the word for "Cowboy." It was the title applied to recruiters, who filled the northbound migrant pipelines to America.

"Me?" The Mexican pointed a finger at his chest as he shook his head. "Assisting people who want to sneak into the United States is against the law."

"Of course." The Asp pointed through the bar's open door. "But the lady selling bread, on the plaza, suggested you might know of such a person."

The Cowboy smiled, and nodded. "Ah. My aunt. I am not in the business, of course. But as you are a friend of the family, perhaps I could provide hypothetical advice. You are alone?"

The Asp nodded. "Hypothetically, what service would such a person provide?"

"First the traveler needs a place upon the back of the beast."

"The beast?"

"The train that will transport you as far as Mexico City."

"First I must buy a railway ticket?"

The Cowboy shook his head. "It's a freight. As long as you are traveling under an organization's protection, the railroad personnel and the police along the way will not trouble you. It is safe, but it is not luxurious. Our clients ride on the car roofs, rain or shine."

"I am a simple man. That is quite satisfactory. What then?"

"In Mexico City, an organization's staff will provide comfortable accommodations, until you can transfer to a bus. The bus will take you to the border crossing point you select."

"What crossing point do you recommend?"

"Where do you want to settle in the States?"

"I need to get to Houston, initially."

"Do you fear water?"

The Asp wrinkled his forehead, pointed at the man's bottle. "Only in my beer."

The man threw back his head and laughed, then said, "In that case, it's easy. From east of Juarez, almost to the Gulf of Mexico, there never was, and never will be, the great wall you have heard of. The Rio Grande River, its canyons, and the Sonoran Desert through which the river flows, are wall enough. You will be assigned to a group that our affiliates will lead on foot to the crossing point. There all will cross the Rio Grande in inflatable boats."

"Your question about the water. The river is swift?"

The Cowboy shook his head. "Not at all. Most of our clients are families. They fear for the little ones."

The Asp hid a smile behind a cough. The transition from hypothetical advice to a negotiation between buyer and seller had been triggered by his single joke. "Boats? Doesn't that attract attention?"

Again, the Cowboy shook his head. "We employ *Chequadores* on the U.S. side. Our checkers are the best informed, and most vigilant, anywhere on the border. They know the border patrol's schedules perfectly. They know where the sensors, that detect footsteps and body heat, are located. They even know the schedules of the drones in the sky. Groups cross only when and where it is safe."

"How large are the groups?"

"Twenty or thirty, total. Families, mostly. Simple people. Very compatible with yourself. After the crossing, and a few hours additional walk, you will all be met, then moved to secure and comfortable accommodations in the States, until a group for Houston is assembled. Then you will be driven by car or truck to begin your new life."

The Asp frowned. "It seems that a large group, including mothers and children, would move slowly. And be easily spotted."

The Cowboy smiled, as he raised a finger. "Here is the reason we enjoy such a good reputation! That is of no concern! *Our* services are guaranteed. Even if you are apprehended, you will merely be returned across the border. We provide up to three additional attempts at no additional charge."

"Could I just hire a guide locally, up near the border?"

The man recoiled, eyes wide, as though bitten. "Hire a coyote at the border? My friend, unlike us they are all dishonest and violent criminals. Some smuggle drugs, even while they assist travelers like yourself. They abandon their clients to die in the desert at the first sniff of the border patrol. Or they slit their clients' throats, then rob their possessions."

"All of them do this?"

"Without exception."

"Shocking."

"Yet one hundred percent true. Also, while we pay taxes to the appropriate cartel, which insure your safe passage, you cannot be sure your border coyote has paid his. If you travel with one who has not paid, the cartels may kill you both. Or may kill your coyote, then leave you alone, to die horribly in the trackless desert."

"Even more shocking."

The Cowboy frowned as he shook his head. "Trust me, my friend, you don't want a border coyote."

"How much, then?"

"If you were Mexican, four thousand U.S. dollars from here to Houston, all inclusive. If you were Central American, six thousand. Clients from greater distances, like you, are more complicated. Ten thousand. All of these prices include our repeat guarantee. Payable in cash now."

"That seems high."

"If you were a chink, or a sand nigger, the fee would be even higher."

For an instant, the Asp didn't recognize the slang, but context left no doubt.

He said, "I have heard equivalent services are available for eight thousand." Failure to haggle might arouse suspicion.

The Cowboy shrugged. "You get what you pay for. Also, because we treat you as family, we offer flexible payment options. Others may not. You can pay one third now, one third before you board our transportation, from Mexico City for the border. The balance upon arrival at your final destination in the States, about to begin your new life. Most of our clients have their relatives here in Mexico wire the last two payments to us. After they telephone them and report their safe completion of each stage."

"Sadly, I have no relatives who could do that. May I just pay you now for the trip as far as Mexico City? Then we'll see how it goes."

The Cowboy's mouth corners turned down, as though he was

about to cry, as he shook his head slowly. "If you unbundle our services, our organization cannot guarantee you will obtain the better life you seek. Because you are like family to me already, I would prefer not to take your money on such a basis."

The Asp had entered the bar with no intention of involving himself in the conspicuous human cattle drives offered by over-acting hucksters like this one. But the Asp was, in fact, the very sort of "sand nigger" that the United States was most interested in interdicting. Anonymity, offered by blending in as just one simple, silent Mexican among many, during the kilometers between this little town and Mexico City, would be worth what it cost.

He slid the envelope across the table. The envelope contained fifteen hundred U.S. dollars. His research had showed that amount represented market value.

The Asp said to the smuggler of humans, "Of course you would prefer not to take it. But you *will* take it."

The Asp collected his pack from the seat alongside himself, then stepped from the idling pickup truck. Its driver sped away, to return eventually to Mexico City, where the Asp had hired him. The Asp stood alone in dusty, moonless darkness, on a winding dirt track that ran parallel to, and ten kilometers south of, the Rio Grande River.

According to his study, the Rio Grande, like the Nile, flowed through a desert. The Sonoran Desert south of the river was in the Mexican state of Coahuila. On the north side, the Sonoran Desert sprawled across the sparsely populated Big Bend region of the American state of Texas.

The silent gray and white desert in which he stood was rocky. Also scrub-dotted, unlike the orange sand sea of the Sahara he knew, that began just kilometers west of Cairo.

The scent of the truck's petrol exhaust, perhaps because it was like his father's straight-six Jag sedan's exhaust, reminded him of his brother's seventh birthday. Or perhaps it was this night, which like that one was perfectly cool and still.

On that night the Asp's parents had the servants pack a picnic, and then had given even the driver the night off. The Asp's father, himself, had driven them all out to the Pyramids, to mingle with the tourists for the Son et Lumière show. All because his brother liked the lights.

The Asp would celebrate no more birthdays with his brother, or his father and mother, in this life. The journey from that happier time and place had already been long and painful, and remained to be completed.

Ten minutes later another car, a Jeep SUV appointed like a limousine, approached. Handsome, in its blocky way, as the Jag had been in its curvaceous glory, the Jeep arrived at the rendezvous. It dropped off the guide, along with the large backpack that contained the inflatable boat.

The guide's greasy hair hung to his shoulders. He smelled of tobacco and sweat, and wore his shirt open. A gold crusader's cross dangled from a gold chain that encircled his neck.

Hands on his hips, he looked the Asp up and down, then pointed at the Asp's backpack. "You're taking that into the States with you?"

The Asp nodded. "You're charging me four times, to compensate for the three empty seats you usually fill. So there should be space."

"It's not a question of space. It's a question of what's in your bag. I'm already carrying a kilo and a half."

"You didn't say you transported drugs, as well as people." *And I didn't ask, because the people who told me about you already told me.*

"Listen, man. Coahuila is Los Zetas territory. I pay my taxes to the Z's. They let me freelance a kilo and a half every trip, because I kick up to them from my take."

They told me all of that, too. What attracted me to a drug smuggler, operating on the fringe of the Los Zetas cartel, is that, unlike a mere smuggler of peasants, a smuggler like you needs to avoid the Americans almost as badly as I do.

The Asp said to the guide, "I am carrying no drugs. I've brought my own water. Like I was told."

The guide pointed at the bulging pack. "That's a lot of water, friend."

"My personal belongings are in it, also."

The Asp had exchanged most of the diamonds, and almost all the gold, that the Sheik had issued to him, in Shanghai. The Latin American and United States currency which he had received for the gold and diamonds had been in small, easily spent denominations. So his pack now bulged.

The Asp knelt, unzipped his pack's front pocket, removed an envelope, and passed it to the guide. "Five thousand U.S. As agreed." He dug through the pack, then handed across more bills. "And another thousand. To compensate you for any anxiety my pack may cause you."

"Anxiety? If you're lying, and the Z's think I kicked up for a kilo and a half, but brought across more, they won't just kill me. The Z's will hack my corpse apart. Then send video of the pieces to my relatives." He slit open the envelope with the folding knife he carried, then counted the bills. Then he rubbed the additional bills between his thumb and forefinger as he cocked an eyebrow. "No drugs?"

The Roman Catholic supermajority which dominated the south half of this hemisphere was merely a geographically distinct branch of the tree from which sprouted Cairo's Coptic Christian underclass. The Asp had learned to hate the Copts. He had little doubt he could learn to hate their cousins in this hemisphere.

The Asp raised his palm. "I swear upon the grave of the sainted Virgin Mary." He hoped the reference was appropriate.

The coyote frowned. Then he squatted, with his back to the raft pack, shrugged into the pack's straps, and stood. "Whatever you say. From now on, keep up and shut up."

By the time the coyote led the Asp through the hundred-meter-wide brush and reed belt along the river's south bank, both the Asp and the guide had sweated through their shirts. Nourished by the Rio Grande's water and the silt it carried, the foliage offered both concealment and early warning of another's approach. Even the Asp could not pass silently through the dense vegetation. It was a cleverly selected spot to prepare for the river crossing.

Ten meters from the water's edge, the smuggler paused and dialed his phone. His sweat-damp face shone in the light and shadow painted by the phone's glow.

After moments, he nodded, then switched off the message from his lookouts. "We're clear. Let's go."

He unpacked the inflatable, then filled it using a foot-operated pump. With the Asp's assistance, he dragged the boat to the water's edge. They clambered aboard, then the current swept the boat downstream. The crossing itself took scant minutes, because the small boat was assisted by the current, which trended from the south bank toward the north bank. On the north bank, the river had carved a ten-meter-tall slope that would have to be climbed like a cliff, more than hiked up. Using a screwed-together plastic paddle, the coyote stroked first from one side of the tiny craft then the other.

Once they had set foot in America, the coyote's lack of urgency surprised the Asp.

He deflated, then buried the raft. Then he transferred the plastic heroin bags, and his drinking water, into a smaller pack that had been folded in with the inflatable.

The guide set a pace that the Asp matched only with difficulty. His strength and stamina were returning, but he never had been, never would be, the athlete his brother had been.

The Asp and the guide had consumed the water that each carried, while on the move. So the Asp's throat was dry and his muscles aching when, tiny and faint in the distance, a vehicle's headlights winked, then went dark.

The guide grunted, corrected course toward the rendezvous. At four-minute intervals the headlights winked again, for a single heartbeat.

The distance to the pickup vehicle had diminished to perhaps eight hundred meters.

The Asp's heart rate, already high, increased. It would be soon, or it would be never.

Ten paces later, the Asp began to question his ability to read human nature.

Then the guide said, "Damn! Stone in my boot."

He knelt, tugging at his right boot top with one hand, while he waved the Asp past with the other. "You keep on toward the car. I'll catch up."

Passing the kneeling guide on the man's left, the Asp withdrew his knife from his left trouser pocket, then flicked open its blade.

The Asp heard fabric whisper against fabric as the man stood, then rushed him from behind. The Asp saw, at the edge of his peripheral vision, the knife the man had withdrawn from his boot. He raised it, to slash the Asp's throat. The guide lunged for the Asp's backpack with his free hand.

The Asp was unsurprised by the attack. Mildly surprised by its clumsiness.

He sidestepped, then parried the guide's knife stroke with his own right forearm. The attacker's momentum carried him past the Asp. Then the Asp drove his own knife into the guide's side, above the kidney. The Asp twisted the blade, a wound that stifled the coyote's scream to a faint sigh.

The Asp barred his right arm across the man's throat, then wrenched out his blade and slashed the man's neck, from one carotid artery to the other. He hopped backward, avoiding the worst of the blood gush, and let the guide crumple on the rocky ground. There he bled out noiselessly.

The Asp had been sure the guide assumed that a client willing to pay far above the going rate to cross the border was running drugs on his own. He had been almost as sure that the man would therefore try to rob him of them, his fear of the cartel overbalanced by greed. The Asp had correctly presumed the man would strike after they crossed the river, when he was free of the inflatable boat. But his client was still burdened with his own pack, and also further fatigued by the long trek.

If the guide had simply performed his part of the bargain, the Asp would have relied on him to keep silent. There was honor among thieves. The Asp would then simply have vanished into the great American abyss. Just like thousands of Mexicans did each month.

Once the guide's attack had proven his untrustworthiness, killing him became not merely justifiable, but a necessary precaution.

The only true gamble had been that the guide did not carry a pistol. Or that, if he did, he would not use it, because a shot echoing in the desert might attract attention.

The Asp knelt, rolled the corpse onto its side, and retrieved from the man's pack the money he had paid the guide. He also removed one of the dead smuggler's plastic heroin bags. He released the body and it flopped back, face up, its dead eyes staring at the stars.

The Asp stood as the headlights winked again, a beacon drawing him deeper into America's dark heart. During his journey, so far, he had successfully relied on the presumption that others did not carry guns. But now he was in America. Here everyone, criminals, police, shopkeepers, women, children, carried guns everywhere. He would henceforth approach all Americans as though he were approaching one of the Nile cobras from which he had taken his nom de guerre.

He shook his head and sighed. American society's casual acceptance of violence disgusted him.

Astride the bloody corpse he had just created, the Asp cocked his head at the irony of his observation. Then he reminded himself that American violence was random, Godless bestiality. On the other hand, violence furthering God's purpose was simply a tool. As was the soldier who used it.

He grasped the guide's head by its hair, then, with his free hand's fingers, located the cartilaginous interval between two cervical vertebrae. The guide's hunting knife was notched along its spine. This created a saw-toothed edge, sharp and sturdy enough to cut brush, or to dismember game.

The Asp paused for breath when he had finished sawing. Then he re-gripped the guide's hair, and twisted. Cartilage popped, and the head tore loose, as easily as a roasted lamb's leg did. The head dangled by its hair from the Asp's fist, leaking like a broken melon in a paper sack.

He laid the head, eyes up, alongside the torso, then slit the heroin bag with the guide's knife. Squeezing the head's dead, but still-pliable cheeks, he poured white powder into the mouth until it mounded up between the dead man's lips, and streaked his face.

If the body were found before desert scavengers ravaged it, the presumption would be that, just as the guide had feared, the cartel had disciplined a freelance cheat.

The headlights winked again. The Asp stood, then circled wide to approach the vehicle from behind.

Five

THE ASP PAUSED, KNEELING TEN METERS BEHIND AND LEFT OF the car. It was parked, switched off, on a small rise facing southeast. Blocky in silhouette against the false dawn it was an enormous American Ford Expedition utility vehicle. More truck-like, and older, than the guide's Jeep had been, the vehicle had the all-wheel drive, stout suspension, and high ground clearance appropriate to its use far from any paved road.

If he simply took the car, he would be delayed by disposal of at least one additional body. Worse, he would have to navigate rugged, unfamiliar terrain in darkness until he found a road. A vehicle stranded in daylight due to a broken axle, or high-centered, would be difficult at best.

He knelt behind a saw-toothed cactus, outside the driver's sight lines. The driver's window, and the window on the passenger's side, were open, allowing the night breeze to flow through the car.

A girl, twenty or younger, sat alone behind the wheel. She tapped her palms on its rim, to the metallic whisper of music that leaked from white-corded earbuds she wore.

As he crept, crouching, along the car's flank he drew, then flicked open his knife. The dead man's knife was too bulky, and now also too incriminating. He had buried it along the way, along with the bloody, filthy dungarees and shirt he had changed from.

He advanced noiselessly, although the breeze in his face and the noise in her ears made stealth superfluous.

When he clapped one hand across her mouth, and pricked the blade against her throat, she stiffened. His hand muffled her squeal.

53

He whispered, in Spanish, "Relax. I'm not going to hurt you."

She froze for two breaths, then he felt her relax. He pulled the blade's tip away from her throat, then released his grip. She crabbed backward onto the car's center console, gasping and wide-eyed.

She tore her earbuds out, rubbed her throat, examined her fingers, found no blood. "You fucking psycho!"

She stared at him, cocked her head. "Where's Arturo?"

He stared back.

She pointed south. "He just left you out there, didn't he? He only does that when he's bringing in junk along with his clients. He was supposed to tell you to signal back to me with a flashlight."

"He didn't tell me."

"Somebody else is picking *him* up. *You* better not be carrying dope. My deal with him is to drive *illegals*. Period. He doesn't pay me enough to smuggle drugs."

Rather than test his "Peruvian" Spanish further, the Asp said in English, "I understand. He did leave me, and headed west. I didn't realize he was smuggling drugs. I'm not. I'm just an honest man, looking for honest work."

She raised her eyebrows, nodded, then replied in English. "With English that good, you won't be looking for work long. Where are the others?"

"There's just me."

"Fuck!" Perched on the console, her earbuds dangling, she slapped her palm on the dashboard so hard that dust rose.

"There's a problem?"

"Yes, there's a problem! Houston's a seventeen-hour round trip. With four passengers, I make money. Driving this gas pig, with one passenger, I barely cover expenses."

"How much does he pay you?"

"A lot less than you paid him. I'll bet on *that*."

Three hundred dollars was the portion of the Asp's fee that the coyote had told him represented transportation to Houston. The Asp doubted that the guide paid the girl more than one hundred fifty per head. And if "somebody" was nearby, awaiting Arturo's arrival, the Asp needed to leave this area quickly.

He counted hundred-dollar bills, then held them out to her. "How far will one thousand dollars get me?"

Her jaw dropped as she snatched the money and counted it herself. "For a thousand bucks, I'll drive you past Beyoncé's house."

"I don't understand."

"It's a joke. Rock stars live in California. Not crappy Houston. *Mi amigo*, there's a *lot* you don't understand about America." The girl slid back behind the wheel and nodded at the passenger's seat. "Climb in. Pay attention to every word I tell you. And by the time we get to Houston, you'll understand America better than George fuckin' Washington."

He woke, but remained motionless in the Expedition's passenger seat with his eyes closed. He realized that what had startled him was the sun's dazzle, as it sprang above the eastern horizon, toward which the girl drove.

She was still lecturing.

"—in fact, a lot of the big cities avoid asking. A big city cop who turns an undocumented Latino in to ICE will probably get a total ass chew from the mayor."

The Asp opened one eye, turned his head toward her.

In daylight, her complexion resembled his, but acne scars pocked her chubby cheeks. Her dark brown hair hung, uncovered, to her shoulders, and her lips and eyes were painted. Her legs and arms were bare, and her right arm tattooed, from wrist to shoulder, as though overgrown with black vines.

She said, "I crossed the Rio Grande with my family when I was eight. I've worked undocumented as a grocery cashier for six years. I've never been hassled."

He had assumed from her appearance that she was a prostitute. It didn't trouble him that Western men allowed their women to dress, and to paint themselves, like whores. In fact, he had passed hours in Amsterdam cafés sipping coffee, while watching them walk by on the sidewalk. It was just that the West seduced decent Islamic women to do likewise.

The highways here were concrete, wide, little different from those in northern Europe, really. Save that more of the cars were enormous American models, and the distances were marked in miles.

An hour's further driving and he began to realize America's vastness, in a way no map could teach. He and the girl had begun their drive eastward roughly halfway across the single state of Texas. They would remain in the same state for hours, and could have continued within the state for hours longer, if they continued east, or turned north beyond Houston. Texas was the largest of the continental United States. But there were fully forty-seven more.

Slaying so colossal a beast as the United States seemed impossible. Yet an elephant could be slain by a single bullet, no larger than a finger. He had now penetrated the beast's hide, and was free to circulate within its body. All he needed now was the bullet.

Ten minutes later the girl exited the highway. She stopped at an enormous box of a retail store that appeared to sell virtually everything. There was even a counter that sold pistols, rifles, and ammunition, alongside aisles displaying garden hoses, and children's playthings. The place was immaculate. Every shelf was neatly filled, and music purred from the ceiling.

In the early morning, the vast store was deserted, save for employees, all of whom were obese.

He purchased a smartphone, with prepaid network service, for cash. The polite male Negro who sold it did not appear to be carrying a pistol.

Meanwhile, the girl bought what she described as "road food," which they consumed as she drove. Once he removed the bacon from his sandwich, the remainder was warm, and tasty. The coffee was hot, although thin, and bland. After all he had endured, it failed to keep him awake.

The girl said, "You're *not* going to Arturo's safe house?"

The Asp shook his head. That had never been his plan, and now anything associated with Arturo the Coyote was out of the question.

"You got family here, already? Or do you want me to drop you at a motel?"

They had stopped again in central Houston, for natural relief and more watery coffee. Humid, flat, and punctuated by sleek skyscrapers, the city reminded him of the nouveau splendor of the Gulf States' capitals. Except that where the Gulf capitals had sand, Houston had fields of unkempt grass, littered with windblown trash. Houston, like those places, was a Babylon, built on a gulf's shores, and nourished by oil.

But in one important way all of those cities, from Houston to

Dubai, were unlike Old Europe's capitals. And that posed a problem. In Amsterdam, people moved unnoticed from place to place by tram, or on foot, or even by bicycle and canal boat. American cities sprawled, built on the assumption that everyone owned a car. Summoning and paying a car service or taxi, or renting a car, involved others in one's business. What public transport there was in America went from nowhere to nowhere with intermediate stops at nowhere still. Therefore, he had planned, from the beginning, to confront the issue of acquiring a vehicle sooner or later.

With the girl's question, sooner had arrived.

As they walked across sun-scorched asphalt from the restaurant back to the girl's car, he circled the vehicle. He squatted alongside, and examined each of the Ford's four enormous tires. It was equipped with a tow hitch, and the sun had faded its black paint. But its all-wheel drive mode, suspension, and engine, had performed perfectly during the drive across the desert, and on the highways.

Its front and rear Texas license plates matched, and were current. It was neither shabby enough to be stopped as a nuisance, nor flashy enough to appear out of place in the hands of a common Mexican. It had no navigation system, and was old. So most probably it could not be tracked by an embedded GPS chip. That was important. Changing phones, he had just confirmed, would be simple. Changing vehicles less so.

He asked, "What model year is your car?"

"It's not my car. It's my boyfriend's. 2010, I think."

The Asp thumbed his new phone, consulted an automobile selling application, then asked her, "Would he sell it?"

She shrugged. "He's a mechanic. Fixing up cars and reselling them is what he does. I get a different car every month. One month I got to drive a Mustang. That was awesome." She inclined her head. "But he keeps his business on the down-low."

"This is just what I'm looking for."

"Really?" She raised her eyebrows, then called on her phone. She spoke as she paced the parking lot. Two minutes later she held the phone against her chest, then said, "He's got a clean title to this one at his shop. And the plates are current, so you can drive on them for a while if you don't get caught. But getting a loan with no job, no driver's license, and no social? He says that could cause you trouble."

The Asp eyed his new phone's screen. "I'll pay retail plus a thousand. Cash."

Eyes wide, she whispered into the phone.

The Asp said, "If he has to see a driver's license and social security number, I have both. But I'd rather not show them to anyone if I don't have to."

The girl raised her palm. "Dude. You had him at 'cash.'"

One half hour later the girl drove the big Ford utility through a sparsely trafficked neighborhood of metal-box business buildings. She turned in through the open gate of one, then parked. A half dozen dust covered sedans, in various states of disrepair, were enclosed within a two-meter-high fence topped with concertina razor wire. The Asp followed the girl through the open overhead door of a steel-sided box garage.

The Asp blinked as his eyes adjusted from sunlight to shadow. From the garage's concrete floor a hydraulic lift grew like a greasy steel tree. Atop the lift perched a Japanese sedan. Three of the sedan's wheels had been removed and stacked at the lift's base, like cake layers.

A pneumatic wrench, wielded by a coverall-clad man, screeched as he removed the sedan's fourth wheel. He stacked it atop the other three, then wiped his hands with a rag as he walked to them.

He pecked the girl's cheek, then turned to the Asp, and said, "*Bienvenido a Los Estados Unidos!*"

The girl laughed. "English, baby. His is better than yours."

Her boyfriend smiled. "You'll like it up here, man. Keep your head down, work hard. You'll eat good and have money to send home." His complexion was as dark as hers, tattoos showing on his neck, above his coverall's collar. His cheeks were shaven, and his mustache black.

The boyfriend stepped to a desk, then dug through papers stacked on it, beside a dusty beige computer and monitor, then lifted one sheet.

He said, "Ah! Here we go. Fill this title in with the name on your license when you need to." He handed over another sheet. "This is a bill of sale. From the guy who sold it to me. I just filled it in, to you. But I didn't date it. If it's all the same to you, I don't exist." He put his arm around the girl. "Neither of us are documented."

"I understand. And you do not know me, either."

"Exactly. The last thing people like us want in this country is to get noticed. The plates came with the car. They don't expire for seven months. You shouldn't get stopped if you don't speed, or run a light, or hit something. But if you do get stopped, show 'em the title and bill of sale. Tell them you just bought the car, and you're on the way to the tag office. Okay?"

The Asp nodded. "What if I decide to cross the border? Into a different state?"

The girl and the boyfriend turned to each other, then laughed.

She said, "Just go. Any state's plates are good in any other state. If you *settle* in a different state, you're supposed to apply for new plates. But they won't stop you to check. Unless you're dumb enough to put a sign in your window that says, 'Tag Applied For.' Anglos don't much mind getting stopped and warned to get local tags. You mind."

The boyfriend said, "If you've really got a good license, in Texas the worst you'll get is a ticket, for no proof of insurance. A Houston cop might even just let you off with a warning."

"I understand. Thank you." The Asp handed the money across.

The boyfriend handed across the car's ignition key, on a wire ring attached to a paper tag. "Our pleasure."

The girl asked, "You need directions?"

The Asp raised his phone and smiled. "I should be able to find my way."

As he walked to the car, the girl called, "Good luck. It's been nice not knowing you."

It took the Asp twenty minutes searching online to determine which of the vendors that could provide the equipment he needed was nearest to him. He had chosen Houston for his destination because it boasted several similar vendors. The first might not stock everything he needed.

Browsing online, as long as one was not browsing for something like plastic explosive, was unlikely to trigger a second look in a vast universe of electronic traffic. But buying online, however convenient, left a trail.

The vendor's warehouse was enormous, but few of its customers actually visited its tiny showroom. The Asp browsed equipment displayed on racks and in glass cases until the counterman returned. He towed a four-wheeled cart, piled with the items the Asp had recited from memory.

As the Asp picked through the pile, the counterman squinted at the screen of the terminal on the counter, while he tapped a keyboard. He was white, middle aged, and balding, and he squinted over the top of his glasses at the screen. "We had everything on your list. Account?"

The Asp cupped a hand behind his ear. "Pardon me?"

"The company you're working for. Where do we bill this?"

Most of the Asp's list could have been purchased from a consumer shop. But he had chosen a retailer that catered to businesses and professionals, because several of the items no consumer retailer would carry.

He said, "I'll pay for it myself."

The clerk pursed his lips. "Really? This is gonna push thirty grand." Then he smiled and nodded. "Got it. You want the points. What card will you be using today?"

"I'll pay for it in cash."

The counterman puckered his lips and the Asp realized his error. Americans were rich, but they didn't pay cash for large purchases.

The Asp said, "The firm I'm working for prefers not to be identified with the project yet. I got an expense advance for this stuff."

The counterman nodded again, slowly. "Oo-kay. Cash and no questions works fine here."

The man tapped more keys. "Printed receipt or email?"

"Printed."

As the Asp paid the bill, the counterman's eyes widened at the stack of currency. The Asp realized that this man would remember this transaction, because it was outside his routine. Therefore, what he remembered had to lead in the wrong direction.

The counterman pointed at the high-piled cart. "You need help out with that?"

The Asp shook his head. "I can manage. But can you tell me the best way to get to the airport?"

"Which one? Hobby or Intercontinental?"

The Asp made a show of consulting his phone. "The one where I'd catch a flight to Barcelona."

"That's Intercontinental. Take a right out of our lot. Left at the third light, to the freeway. Then follow the signs."

Ten minutes later, the Asp returned from his second trip to the Ford. Even with both of the Expedition's rear seat rows folded flat, his extensive shopping list had filled the vehicle.

Its rear lift gate was centimeters short of latching, and had to be secured with twine that the Asp had begged from the counterman.

When the Asp reached the third traffic light, he turned right, instead of left as the counterman had instructed him.

If the counterman were ever asked to speculate where his anonymous customer had been headed, he would probably remember that the Asp was flying out of Houston, which was wrong. Perhaps to Barcelona. Which was wronger.

The Asp lay on his bed, in a room rented in a motel alongside the interstate highway. He had traveled north from Houston for three hours. He read the weekly local newspaper, published in the small town near the highway exit.

The girl had recommended this practice, whether on paper or by online editions. Such papers reported mundane information, like newcomers to communities, and local celebrations. Such information pointed the way to temporary jobs, such as furniture moving and clearing trash, for which Americans hired unskilled, temporary laborers, and paid in cash.

Mundane employment did not concern him. Fitting in to the middle of America concerned him greatly. Local newspapers provided guidance to custom, to local government procedures, and to manners of speech and behavior.

His motel room had two beds. The bed alongside the bed in which he lay was piled high with all the gear he had purchased in Houston. He had removed it all from the Expedition because otherwise the Ford's rear lift gate could not be fully closed and locked. When he tired of the small-town news he tossed the paper onto the mound of gear.

He had not planned to stop for the night, but learned that Americans often repaired their highways by night. That minimized inconvenience to commuting workers, but maximized inconvenience to someone who preferred to be seen as little as possible. He had also learned that, in America, driving at the posted speed limit was more conspicuous than racing along with the flow. But with each detail he learned, and each kilometer he traveled north of the Mexican border, he became less a potential terrorist, and more one quiet, undocumented Latino looking for work, in a sea of others just like him.

Too exhausted to sleep, he read again the document the Sheik had given him, so long ago, and so far away. Whether it was fact or fantasy the next days would reveal.

Then he opened the laptop resting on his stomach, scrolled through his reading list, and selected a title. At first, he had almost not downloaded the volume, thinking it was a joke book. Surely there was no such discipline as "Jewish Physics"?

Six

RACHEL AWOKE IN HER DRAPE-DARKENED BEDROOM AND STARED up at the ceiling's gilded plaster curlicues, lit by the morning light that leaked in above the valance. The previous night's embers glowed in the corniced fireplace. The embers struggled to warm the room against the chill, brought by the morning of January 31, 1933, to the Bavarian Alps. Her bedroom, and the country house to which the Bergman family fled on weekends and holidays to avoid Munich's grime and bustle, hadn't changed since her parents had the place built, when she was four.

Well, one thing had changed.

She rolled onto her side and buried her nose in the pillow next to hers, still warm, and redolent with the scent of shaving soap and new husband.

"Are you ready to greet your first morning as Mrs. Winter?" Peter Winter was already out of bed, standing next to the brocade-draped window, with one hand on the drawcord. Barefoot and bare chested in his pajama bottoms, he grinned at her in the half light.

She clutched the duvet and her negligee to her breasts and pantomimed a shiver. "Look at you. It's freezing in here. Will our children be half polar bear?"

"Better half beast than half gentile."

She blinked, and his smile faded. He returned to the bed, laid beside her propped on one elbow, then kissed her forehead. "Stupid joke. I'm sorry."

She shook her head. "No. Mother really did say that once. And worse. If she had lived to see her daughter married to a gentile, she would have locked herself in her bedroom and stayed there until we left for the train. She could be as stubborn as a goat."

"So you inherited more than her nose?"

"I am not!"

Rachel Bergman's mother had died three years earlier. As intolerant of gentiles as any Nazi was of Jews, the irony was that somewhere in Esther Bergman's lineage was a very un-Jewish ancestor. Who had passed on to Esther Bergman a turned-up button nose, and alabaster skin that contrasted spectacularly with her raven hair. Which Esther had, in turn, passed on to her daughter.

Rachel's mother had been the only one in the family unaware that her daughter was keeping company at university with a boy who was, as her father observed, "as Jewish as a pork knuckle."

Rachel smiled and threw back the duvet. Then she climbed across her day-old husband, stood barefoot on the cold stone floor while she fumbled with her slippers, and dropped them. When she bent, shivering, to retrieve them, Peter grabbed for her bare bottom and she hopped away.

She slid on her robe while she walked to the window, then turned to him. He sat on the bedside, hands clasped in his lap and feet dangling. Like a bad boy who still expected dessert, rather than like a newly titled Doctor of Physics.

After the civil wedding ceremony in Leipzig, and the train ride, it had been dark when Rudolph the driver had collected their party and luggage in Munich. And on the drive up into the Alps light snow was falling. So, Peter had yet to really see the place.

She took the drapery drawcord in her hand and crooked a finger at him. "Come stand here by me and I'll show you the best view in Bavaria."

He stood beside her, arm around her waist, and kissed her hair. "You already showed me the best view in Bavaria when you dropped your slippers."

Her room faced east, out across the house's forecourt. As she drew back the drapes, the sun shone above the jagged peaks at the valley's end. The sky was electric blue, and the land still, and gleaming white. Bare trees, as well as the evergreens, were frosted, as though sprinkled with diamonds. The hand of man was barely visible in the valley.

He whispered, "God. This place is magic."

As they stood together, silent, Milton the stable man led Willi, Father's black stallion, saddled and with breath steaming from his nostrils, across the ankle-deep snow into the forecourt.

Father, bundled against the cold, stepped out through the front doors a story below them. He tugged on gloves as he limped, right leg stiffened by the steel rod inside it, to his waiting horse. He spoke to Milton, patted his shoulder, then with a boost from the stable man swung up into the saddle.

Peter said, "Your father still rides?"

"Every day that he's in residence up here. Sometimes even in the parks down in the city. Regardless of weather or his physical limits. Obviously."

"How did he—?"

"When the war started, the army said he was too old to join the cavalry. Even though he was a champion equestrian. So, he commissioned a cavalry troop out of his own pocket, then trained recruits himself. Before the first class graduated, there was a jumping accident. According to Mother, Father's head injuries and depression frightened her worse than his leg. There were days when he said he would rather have died, charging the French trenches, than live with his failure to defend his homeland. The government awarded him a citation for his civilian service to the nation. But I think he still feels he did too little."

"Is he as hard on his children, and his customers, as he is on himself?"

"Don't ever tell Jacob I admitted it, but compared to him I get away with murder. Look who Father let me marry. Father's not hard on customers, especially if they're veterans. He reviews their loan applications personally. Even the worst risks get approved. I think that's why he's more hopeful about the Nazis than a sane Jew should be. Hitler was gassed at Ypres, you know."

"And all this time I thought Hitler was *born* a lunatic."

As they watched, Sheldon Bergman cantered his horse out across the snow, toward the rising sun. He rode leaning left, to compensate for the stiff right leg that extended from his mount's flank. The stallion's hooves kicked up snow. As horse and rider shrank in the distance, it appeared that they floated toward the peaks atop a cloud.

The sun climbed, the land further brightened, and the every-other-day delivery arrived. The village grocer, reins in hand, drove a jingling, red-painted sleigh, pulled by a grey mare. It negotiated the unplowed and unpaved road to the Bergman house better than the grocer's usual chugging van.

Traudl, who was both the cook and the wife of Rudolph the driver, bustled out. She hugged her husband's old army greatcoat around her thick middle, as she handed a steaming mug up to the grocer. He handed down a crate piled with produce, fresh fish, and the recent newspapers.

The isolated country house had been designed as the Bergman's island of respite from the modern world. Father had allowed a telephone line only after a decade. Mail was not delivered, but collected when, and if, staff went into town. Music was always available, from the conservatory's grand piano, or from the phonograph. Like most posh modern phonographs, its console included a sensitive radio receiver. But tuning in the news, rather than music, was frowned on.

Traudl and the grocer shared a laugh. Then, sleigh bells on the mare's harness a'jingle, he turned back toward town and vanished.

Peter shook his head. "You said it was a country weekend house. I expected a log cabin. Not a fairy castle. With twelve bedrooms, riding stables, a billiard room, a Rubens hung in the foyer, electric lights, and servants."

As she stepped toward the suite's bathroom she pointed at the bedroom door. "There should be a basket of firewood and a breakfast trolley to the left of my door. When I'm here at the house Rudolph leaves them as part of his morning rounds."

Peter wrinkled his forehead as he clicked on the bedside lamp. "Does he leave the electricity, too? Because I didn't see any power lines."

"In a way, he does. He fills up our generator's gasoline tank every morning."

Peter cocked his head. "The Bergmans make their own electricity? Why? One of the biggest hydroelectric stations in Germany is just over at Lake Walchen."

"Overhead lines would've spoiled the view. To muffle the noise, the generator's in an abandoned salt mining shaft under the house. Father says all south Bavaria is good for is views, silence, and salt mines. He had the telephone line buried, too."

"You do understand, Baroness Rothschild, that on an assistant physics professor's salary you won't be able to reshape the world to your whims, anymore. We won't be able to afford even a party line telephone."

"Oh, stop. I would happily live in a salt mine to be with you. Just pull the trolley in here while I make myself beautiful."

He poked his head out the door and called back. "There's wood. But *just* coffee." He dragged the linen-draped trolley into the room. "Can't we get dressed? And go down for breakfast?"

She glanced back from the bathroom doorway. "If that's what you're hungry for. Or when I finish in here I can show you the best view in Bavaria again."

On mornings like this one, Traudl served breakfast in the conservatory, where the glass walls and ceiling let in the sun, and the Alpine views.

Father, still wearing his riding jacket, sat at the lace-clothed table's head. His gray eyes peered at the other diners through pince-nez spectacles, clipped on his very Jewish nose. When Rachel was a child, he had led the table conversation, as German patriarchs did. Since his wife's death, he more and more followed the discussion, rather than led it.

At the table's foot Rachel's older brother, Jacob, attacked a soft-boiled egg.

At Father's left-hand Uncle Max slumped, red of eye and nose, bald, with a day's supply of unlit cigars bulging from his robe's breast pocket.

Across the table from Uncle Max sat the morning's only non-family guest. Fresh-faced, wavy haired, he was turned out for breakfast in jacket, white shirt, and tie.

Max Bergman was forty-two, but looked fifty-two. The guest was thirty-two, but looked twenty-two.

Uncle Max drew an unlit cigar, then stabbed it at the guest, who had been a civil witness to the marriage at the previous day's ceremony in Leipzig.

Uncle Max said, "Einstein's a Jew. So, this 'relativity' is 'Jewish Physics.' Lenard and Stark aren't, so their work is 'German Physics.' You're not a Jew, Professor Heisenberg, but your 'quantum mechanics' is also 'Jewish physics'? It's nonsense to me."

Werner Heisenberg smiled and shook his head, then lectured like the professor he was. "Nonsense, yes. But explicable. Max, before this century physics, like most sciences, investigated and explained the universe by hypothesis, followed by experiment. For example, Galileo hypothesized that gravity accelerates different masses at the same rate. Legend says that he proved this by dropping two identical balls, one filled with lead, and the other with soap, from the Tower of Pisa."

Heisenberg sipped from his cup. "But in this century, Einstein and others of us have proved hypotheses with mathematics. Then left the experiments to others."

Max said, "I don't need to place two balls on a table, then count them, to prove that one plus one equals two?"

Heisenberg nodded. "Relativity and Quantum Mechanics are as certain as one plus one equals two. Traditional experimental physicists, like Lenard and Stark, roll up their sleeves and experiment in the laboratory. They see theoretical physics as lazy, at best, and dishonest at worst."

Jacob looked up from his egg. "And Jews by nature are assumed to be both?"

Heisenberg said, "Jacob, you and I know that's rubbish. But professional courtesy bars a physicist who has not won a Nobel Prize from arguing the morals of those who have. And both Lenard and Stark have."

Peter, standing beside Rachel in the conservatory's doorway, waved a hand. "Werner, professional courtesy doesn't require endorsement of bigotry. And if the rest of us in the physics community keep pretending Lenard and Stark are arguing scientific method, we'll all pay for it, eventually."

Heisenberg, Jacob, Max, and Rachel's father turned to the new arrivals.

Her father's face softened when he saw her, and he and the rest of the men stood. She stepped around the table, kissed his cheek, then stood behind him as she pushed him back down into his chair.

As Uncle Max sat, he jerked a thumb at Peter and said to his brother, "This is your new son-in-law, Sheldon? He doesn't *sound* like a Nazi's nephew."

Rachel's father glared over his pince-nez at his younger brother. "Max, Peter is now part of our family. Professor Heisenberg is our guest. In my house, on this day, we celebrate the marriage of my daughter. *Your* niece. Today there will be no talk of Jews. There will be no talk of Nazis. Today, we are all Germans. On every day, we are all Germans." He peered around the room. "Do I make myself clear?"

Silence.

Traudl bustled in and refilled coffee cups.

Rachel's father looked around the table, then said, "Traudl, would you kindly go upstairs and be sure Rachel is out of bed? That girl must not sleep in on such a beautiful, sunny morning."

The silence deepened as everyone stared, open mouthed, and watched Rachel's father sip his coffee while his daughter stood close behind him.

Later that morning, Peter cleaned up in Rachel's bedroom, after Jacob took his new brother-in-law out for a ride. As Rachel descended the staircase, she heard Chopin being played on the conservatory piano. Heisenberg sat at the keyboard.

When he saw her he paused. "Sorry. Has my banging disturbed you?"

She shook her head. "You play beautifully. Peter says if the Nobel doesn't come through, you can survive by playing boogie-woogie piano. But Peter says the prize is certain when the 1932s are announced."

Heisenberg shrugged. "In physics only the speed of light is certain. I'll keep practicing." He smiled. "Peter asked me to play something at the little party this afternoon. Does his new bride have any requests?"

She shook her head. "You've already done so much for Peter—for *us*. He wouldn't marry me until he could support me. So, in hard times the assistantship means everything. I'm very grateful."

Heisenberg smiled again. "If you're so grateful then he didn't tell how little physicists are willing to work for."

"Oh, he did. Why do you think a physicist is our piano player?"

Heisenberg laughed, then glanced around the gilded room. "Rachel, your family could have afforded a symphony orchestra, not just a civil ceremony and a family dinner."

Rachel ran her hand along the antique Bechstein's ebony lid. "Yes. We're very fortunate. But the only family Peter has left is his grandmother, and she's too ill to travel. Marrying a gentile obviously doesn't bother the Bergman family anymore. My *mother* was the rabid Jewess. But Peter in a yarmulke would have been awkward for some of my mother's friends. And a banker's lavish wedding would have embarrassed my father, when his depositors are struggling through a depression."

Heisenberg nodded, lips pressed together. "Your father has a generous heart."

It was a tactful way for Peter's mentor to avoid mentioning her father's mental lapse.

She said, "So have you. Our wedding trip wouldn't be possible without my father's generosity. But also, not without the time off you granted Peter."

"Rachel, Peter worked harder for his doctorate than any student I've had. The time off between jobs wasn't a favor. He earned it. He needed it. And the job offer was purely selfish. I snapped him up before someone else did."

"The Depression hasn't hurt the market for physicists?"

Heisenberg shook his head. "Only for the bad ones. I've worked with Arnold Sommerfeld, Max Born, Niels Bohr. I now have the good luck to number many of the brightest young lights in physics among my graduate students. Peter visualizes abstract concepts as well as any of my mentors and colleagues, and as well as any of my students. And Peter sees the world practically, and clearly. Which, frankly, we theoreticians rarely do."

"I think practicality had less to do with staying than his pleasure working with you did."

Heisenberg shrugged. "But Peter won't stay long. The world won't let him. In physics, the future arrives earlier than in other professions. Peter's twenty-four. Einstein turned twenty-six in 1905, while working as a Swiss patent clerk pending his doctorate. In that year, Einstein published four papers. In the aggregate, they changed mankind's understanding of the universe forever. We call it Einstein's 'Miracle Year.' I was twenty-six when Quantum Mechanics came to me.

"At this moment, Peter Winter is even less known than Einstein was before his 'Miracle Year.' But one morning soon I will wake to find Peter gone. Perhaps to a chair of physics elsewhere. Perhaps to more practical and important things. And I will be overjoyed. A teacher's greatest reward is his students' success."

Jacob ran into the room from the foyer waving a folded newspaper. "The grocer brought yesterday's paper."

Rachel said, "He always does. Why are you whispering?"

"Father said no politics today."

Rachel said, "What's happened?"

"Hitler's chancellor. Hitler! On January thirtieth! Can you believe it?"

"Hitler? No. I can't. Jacob, give me that!" Rachel snatched the paper. Before she unfolded it, she said, "The Nazis didn't win a majority. Those buffoons in the Reichstag have done nothing but argue about forming a coalition government for months."

Heisenberg stood and read over her shoulder, eyes wide.

Peter trotted down the stairs, buttoning his jacket and raised his eyebrows when he saw them.

Uncle Max wandered in from the billiard room, still in his robe, and swirling brandy in a snifter. "What's the fuss?"

Jacob said, "The Nazis have taken over!"

Max said, "Oh. That. Not precisely. The president appoints the chancellor, and Hindenburg remains president. He appointed Hitler yesterday. But the cabinet will be drawn mostly from other parties. The *Communists* will have more ministers than Hitler will. If the Nazis expect to pass anything, they'll have to compromise. Life will go on in Germany without radical changes."

Peter said, "Unless something radical upsets the balance."

Rachel said, "And ruining this day for my father won't change anything in Berlin." Rachel took Peter's arm. "Therefore, we all have a marriage to celebrate. With no talk about politics. Then Mrs. Winter and her husband have a train to catch."

Rachel, wearing sandals, dark glasses, and a woolen sweater with slacks, sat on the ferry slip's planking and leaned back against her overstuffed trunk.

The view east toward Greece, across the azure Ionian Sea, was less spectacular than from the hilltop villa where she and Peter had passed the last month. But both they, and either of the views, were a world away from Germany. The locals grumbled that February on Zakynthos was cold and rainy. But, compared to the snows of Leipzig and Bavaria, the last month had seemed sun-drenched and warm.

Although a month with nothing on her mind but Peter, and what wine would best accompany dinner, would have been heaven anywhere.

Beside her Peter slouched, hat brim shading his eyes.

She ran her finger over his ear and whispered, "Are you asleep?"

"No. Just wondering why, now that this place is finally warming up, we're leaving. We get back to Leipzig on March second. Do you know how many days it snows in Leipzig in March?"

"Too many."

"It was your idea to get married as soon as Werner hired me."

"Because it was your idea not to sleep together out of wedlock. I would have been perfectly happy to live in sin. Everyone is doing it these days."

"Not exactly."

"Oh? Uncle Max—"

"Is hardly everyone. Which has been our good luck. Renting the villa would have cost my first year's salary."

"Thank Father, not Uncle Max. Father did a large favor for the Swiss banker who Max horse-traded for the loan of the villa. Uncle Max's talent lies in wheeling, dealing, cutting legal corners, twisting arms, and cashing in the favors Father's earned." She stretched. "Regardless, I have a modest proposal. Let's stay here. Forever."

"And live on what?"

"You're a theoretical physicist. You said Einstein developed his theory of general relativity by thinking in his bedroom for two weeks. You can mail your work to Werner. And the Swedes can mail you back your Nobel Prize."

"Einstein didn't have you in his bedroom."

"I'll inspire you."

"They don't give Nobel Prizes for that kind of inspiration."

Rachel peered at boats bobbing alongside the wharf. "Alright. I'll buy a fishing boat. I'll catch our dinner every day, while you think. After dinner, I'll join you in the bedroom and you can tell me everything you thought of. As long as it doesn't include other women."

"A fishing boat? When we came across on the ferry the sea was glass, and you still vomited over the rail."

"Very well. *You* catch our dinner. I'll buy a typewriter and create racy novels. If they're *really* trashy I'll make us a fortune." She propped herself on her elbow and turned to him. "Would it bother you if I worked?"

"Depends on the profession. Based on the last month, you could make a fortune as a call girl."

She slapped his chest. "Seriously, does it bother you that my family has money—"

"While my dowry is a doctorate in a field with no practical

application, and a dead Nazi uncle I wish had never existed? I would think the bothered party would be you." He stood.

"Are you going to rent our new villa?"

He shook his head. "To buy the ferry tickets. And there's a coffee stand over there that sells German papers. They'll relieve boredom on the train."

She stretched back so the sun warmed her face, waved her hand like Garbo, and sighed. "Bring me back an espresso, and I'll teach you a better way to relieve boredom on the train."

Peter was back in three minutes, taut and unsmiling.

She sat upright, and pushed her glasses up on her forehead. "No espresso? I suppose this means the honeymoon's over."

He handed the newspaper down to her as he said, "During the night on February twenty-seventh somebody set fire to the Reichstag building. The Nazis claim it was the Communists, and that it was part of an ongoing plot to trigger a revolution. Hindenburg's signed a decree suspending most of the constitution."

She stiffened.

Whatever the Weimar Republic's practical shortcomings, its constitution guaranteed civil liberties that even the American and French constitutions barely matched.

She said, "For how long?"

"That's unclear."

"Obviously the Nazis did it."

Peter shrugged. "Most people seem to accept that the Communists had a hand in the fire. Violent revolution *is* their portfolio. And at this point it hardly matters who did it." He frowned as, in the distance, the ferry's hoot announced its approach. "Rachel, *should* we stay here? Abroad, that is? Werner would write me a recommendation I'm sure. With it I could get a position anywhere. Even in your beloved America."

"He would. You could. And you would each cry for a week when you left. Don't be silly."

She held out her arm, and he pulled her up to stand alongside him. They stared at the sea.

Peter said, "The Nazis now have the power to arrogate more power. And they will. And when they have it, they'll use it. It could become uncomfortable at best, and deadly at worst, to be a German Jew."

"Spoken like a naive German gentile. Peter, it's *been* uncomfortable to be a Jew *anywhere* since Pharaoh kicked us out of Egypt. Even a Jew with a button nose, who can barely pronounce 'Hanukkah,' and whose married name is 'Winter.' I can survive it."

Peter placed his hands on her shoulders and turned her to face him. "Rachel, you think you can survive *anything.*"

"Because I *can.* Anything except choosing between my homeland and my family, and you."

Peter frowned. "You understand, that fire didn't just burn a building? Germany itself may go up in flames, literally and figuratively. And perhaps all of Europe before it's done."

Arm in arm they peered northeast across the blue Mediterranean toward mainland Europe.

She said, "All the more reason that staying abroad is out of the question. When your house is on fire you try to save it. You don't run away and let it burn."

"I expected you'd say that. I *hoped* you'd say that." He held up his hand, which was closed around something. "I went ahead and bought ferry tickets."

She opened his hand with her fingers and peeked at the pasteboards in his palm. "As long as you bought two. Because we're equal partners in this until the end."

Seven

AT A CONVENIENCE STORE'S COUNTER, ON A HEAVILY TRAFFICKED road near the interstate highway, the Asp prepaid forty-five dollars in cash, to refill the big Expedition's gasoline tank. He also paid most of a ten-dollar bill for a bag, into which the store clerk packed food, and a cup of coffee-flavored hot water the size of a small bucket.

"Have a nice day, man." The clerk's eyes returned to his smartphone's screen as soon as he handed the Asp the bag and his change.

"You too." The Asp smiled. He smiled not because he wished the clerk well, but because he had now driven north, and west, from Houston across the flat barrens of Oklahoma, Kansas, and now eastern Colorado. And every American he had encountered showed the same utter disinterest in him. No one in America knew, or cared, that he existed. It was a situation he intended to perpetuate.

The Asp turned toward the glass doors that led out to the warming morning, and to the canopied ranks of gasoline pumps. And his heart skipped.

His Expedition was parked broadside to him, at the pump nearest the doors. Behind his vehicle a blue-uniformed police woman knelt, studying the car's rear. She wore a Glock automatic pistol on her hip, and a radio microphone was clipped at her chest. Her patrol car, a white American SUV, with blue markings that identified her as a Denver Police Department officer, had parked behind the Expedition.

The boyfriend who sold him the big Ford had said the Texas license tags matched the vehicle and were current. The boyfriend had also said that driving with one state's tags in another state was lawful. Whether he had been a fool, or a liar, didn't matter.

The Asp could easily slip out the door and walk away. But that was no option. The gear he had purchased in Houston, and more importantly the funds with which to purchase more, were inside the car.

He could wait, and hope other duties would force her to leave. That was unlikely. American street police were said to react badly to a bribe, which would have routinely defused such a situation elsewhere. He dared not try that. But if he waited, and she radioed for additional officers, the odds against him would worsen.

Heart pounding, he pushed open the glass doors and approached her. Each step closer to her reduced the advantage her pistol gave her against the knife in his pocket.

He had closed the gap to two meters when she looked up at him. Eyes hidden behind dark glasses, her blonde hair was drawn back from her pale face.

He slid his free hand into his trousers pocket and gripped his knife.

She said, "This your Expedition?"

"Yes, Officer. Is anything wrong?"

She stood, hands on her hips. Her right hand rested on her holstered pistol.

He forced himself to breathe slowly as he measured angles and distances. There would be surveillance video. But there was nothing to be done about it.

She pointed down at the Expedition's rear bumper. "You drive all the way from Texas with all this stuff?"

He nodded, gripped the knife tighter. "Moving from Houston. Just got to town. If I find work, I'll get Colorado license tags."

She said, "This tie-down cord may have been snug when you left. But it's about worn through. Here, where it loops through the latch. You need to fix it, before you drive any further."

He exhaled. "I will. Thank you, Officer."

She smiled. "Spilling your stuff all over Federal Boulevard wouldn't help you, or the drivers behind you."

The speaker in the canopy above the Expedition clicked. "Pump One is on."

The police woman glanced up at the speaker. "That's you?"

He nodded.

She flicked her fingers to her cap's brim as she nodded to him. "Hope you enjoy Colorado. Most of us do." She turned, and walked back to her patrol vehicle.

He stood like a statue and felt the tension drain from his muscles.

The police woman hadn't asked for his papers, hadn't questioned him, hadn't inspected the contents of his vehicle, hadn't demanded money.

It was as the Mexican girl and her boyfriend had told him, after all. If you were polite and deferential, American police didn't "hassle" you.

He grasped the pump handle, lifted it, and realized that his hand still trembled.

"Hold it right there!" The police woman shouted, pointing at him. She stood sheltered behind her vehicle's open driver's door.

He felt a fool. Her disinterest had been a ruse, to allow her to withdraw, then engage him with her pistol from a safe distance.

He froze, felt adrenaline again crackle through him.

She called, "You picked up the diesel hose!"

He peered down at the green, rubber-shrouded nozzle, trembling in his hand. The other hose, still in its cradle, was shrouded in black.

He smiled, nodded, and waved at her with his free hand, while he replaced the green nozzle.

She smiled back, climbed into her vehicle, and closed its door.

He waited until the police woman pulled away into traffic before he picked up the gasoline nozzle, then began filling the Expedition's enormous tank.

He leaned against the car's fender, suddenly dizzy. That should not have been. He was accustomed to functioning under stress.

A van stopped at the pump alongside and he understood. The lettering on its side read "Mile High Plumbing." Houston, like Cairo, like Amsterdam, like most of the places where he had lived his life, was near sea level. But he had driven imperceptibly uphill for two days. Now, although he stood on a flat prairie, he had ascended the high plains of North America and stood one and one-half kilometers above sea level. He was breathing air as thin as the air in the Waziristan hills, where he had begun his quest.

He resecured the cord that held down the Expedition's rear lift gate, then returned to the interstate highway, and drove west.

In the near distance the foothills of the red-brown Front Range of the Rocky Mountains, mottled with green pines, loomed above the prairie and above Denver, the "Mile High City." Concealed for the moment behind the foothills, the Rockies themselves lay ahead.

The Expedition climbed for an hour, passing lumbering trucks, while being passed by powerful sedans, as the old SUV's engine labored in the ever-thinning air. Ahead lay the tunnel the Americans had bored through their continent's backbone. A road sign announced the Eisenhower Tunnel's elevation as eleven thousand thirteen feet above sea level.

After just a few days of temperatures displayed in degrees Fahrenheit, food and drink measured in pounds and ounces, and distances to cities shown in miles, and in feet remaining to road exits, he was thinking in the arcane units that demonstrated America's disdain for the rest of the world.

He had climbed from the "Mile High City" more than an additional mile. The air had become not merely thinner, but colder. Three to five degrees colder per thousand feet, to be precise. Therefore, while it had been sixty-eight degrees in Denver, here snow patches dotted shaded parts of the slopes, even in early June.

The tunnel was in fact two parallel tunnels, and as the westbound lanes' tunnel mouth swallowed him the thunder of surrounding traffic pressed on him in the confined space. The mountain mass above him rose an additional sixteen hundred feet, and the tunnel stretched on for nearly three miles, its western exit invisible. Then he was through, descending from the Continental Divide in sunlight. He had overcome another obstacle with ridiculous ease.

He had now driven two days at highway speeds. Yet the Pacific Ocean, and the rock stars' California mansions, remained a thousand miles further west. Behind him, to the east, the Atlantic and New York and Washington were even more distant. But no obstacle hindered his travel to any of them. State borders were recognizable only by signs welcoming visitors. The police cars of states and municipalities changed livery as he progressed. But the police in them remained equally indifferent to his passing.

The highway here snaked west through valleys, then up over mountain passes and again down, forty miles deeper into the

Rockies. He pulled off the interstate highway at the second exit for the resort town of Vail. North of Vail, he located the deserted, unpaved road he sought. It twisted further north, through pines and scrubland. The elevation at the Vail exit was less than nine thousand feet, and snow remained on the ground only in shaded patches.

By the time he exited the dirt road onto a trail, marked only by a single post as tall as a man, he had climbed again. The post was painted with red rings. Those, he realized, signaled not only the turn off, but snow depth during winter.

After a half mile, the trail entered a pine stand, then climbed acutely. The track was so boulder-strewn that the Expedition negotiated it at a pace little faster than walking speed.

Snow cover increased with altitude. Three times he stopped, then cleared drifted snow, using a broad, collapsible shovel. Twice he wrestled aside dead pines that had fallen and blocked the trail. The exertions at altitude dizzied him.

Dusk had deepened, to the point that he had turned on the Expedition's headlights, when the lights' beams reflected from a chest-high tubular metal gate. He crept the vehicle to within ten yards, left the lights on, and stepped from the car.

The twilight's frigidity stunned him as he walked to the gate. The thin fleece, that had been too warm in the Denver morning, was now inadequate.

The gate was the sort emplaced in livestock pen fences. It denied vehicle passage through a narrow gap in a rock ridge, and was wide enough that, when open, a vehicle could pass through. Its steel bore the rust of years, but massive bolts drilled deep into the granite at the hinges and latch remained sturdy.

As the Sheik's document described, the gate was secured at its latch by a padlock, as sturdy as the rock bolts. But the lock was rusted shut.

A warped, wooden sign, wired to the gate's top rail, announced, in faded red letters:

TRESPASSERS WILL BE SHOT
SURVIVORS WILL BE SHOT AGAIN

Shivering, breathless, but with no concern whatsoever of being shot, the Asp fetched from the Expedition bolt cutters, purchased in Denver along with the shovel. He cut the lock, then drove the

Expedition through, closed the gate, and replaced the lock with one of the sturdier replacements he had also purchased.

Beyond the gate, the trail climbed higher, through the pines.

By the time he reached the cabin, darkness was complete. He cut off the cabin door's lock, by the Expedition's headlights.

Using his phone's flashlight, he searched the cabin's interior, and found a lantern, fuel, and a blanket. Then he prostrated himself on the cabin's plank floor and prayed by the lantern's light, shivering, while just enough red remained in the sky for sunset prayers.

After prayers, he ate and drank from the supplies he had brought with him, and confirmed that his phone received no signal in this isolated spot. He wrapped himself in the blanket, then returned to the Expedition. In its confined space, and with judicious use of its heater, he would be warmer than in the cabin, and he could recharge his phone from the car's dashboard outlet.

He didn't bother to relock the cabin door. He had seen no other vehicle, or any other sign of permanent human habitation, on the last six miles of the dirt road before he reached the trail. From that point on, his isolation had been total.

Somewhere along the trail, as it wound east and up, the Expedition had crossed the boundary into the Eagles Nest Wilderness. The wilderness was a mountainous 133,000-acre preserve, set aside by the American government. Within the wilderness, visitors could "take only pictures and leave only footprints."

The cabin, and the trail, were an "inholding," property privately owned before the wilderness was created in 1976, and thereafter restricted from modern development. The government trail network in the wilderness led only to other, more scenic parts of the preserve. Neither hikers nor police were likely to visit this place.

He snugged the blanket around his shoulders, then reclined in the Expedition's front passenger seat. Exhilarated as he was by developments, he felt his eyelids droop with contented fatigue.

He fell asleep with the thought that he was now alone, buffered on all sides, safe from America. But America was not safe from him.

When first light woke him, he scrubbed fog from the Expedition's windows and examined his surroundings. The cabin, a one-room box built of cut logs, with small, grimy windows and a rudimentary stone fireplace, offered as much shelter as he would need.

He prioritized his further reconnaissance.

An outbuilding, situated three hundred yards upslope, was designated in the materials the Sheik had provided as a "workshop." Constructed of lumber covered with tar paper, it was even less enchanting than the cabin. Inspection of the workshop's contents would matter only if more immediate concerns resolved favorably.

Google Earth showed a third, more distant, building on the property, adjacent to a small alpine meadow. Accessible only by a barely noticeable trail, he would explore the building only when, and if, time permitted.

The cabin and workshop stood in cleared areas amid pines. As altitude increased, the familiar pine forest transitioned to twisted, stunted bristlecone pines. Those more resembled gray driftwood than living things.

As recounted in the document, the cabin had been built during the 1920s, by an unsuccessful gold prospector, at an elevation of eleven thousand six hundred feet. Situated just below the tree line, the pines still provided the cabin minimal shelter.

The workshop had been constructed during the 1950s, also amid pines.

Mere yards upslope from the workshop, even the bristlecones vanished. Above the tree line the slopes were as bleak, and as rockbound, as the Afghan mountains.

The insulated parka he shrugged into, and the wool cap and gloves, had seemed overprotective when he purchased them.

With gloved hands thrust in the parka's enormous pockets, he set out up the barren slope for a preliminary reconnaissance of Upper Pika Lake. The lake surface's altitude, according to topographic mapping accessed on the internet, was twelve thousand and two feet above sea level. The lake nestled in the lee of Pika Mountain's peak, which towered an additional one thousand twenty feet higher.

Like most high mountain lakes, Upper Pika was a tarn, simply water pooled in the bottom of a basin gouged and scraped from a mountain's flank by the freezing, thawing, and movement of a long-vanished alpine glacier. This tarn was neither fed nor drained by streams. Only pristine precipitation that fell on the tarn, and within the sloping cirque that surrounded it, replenished its waters.

The pika, a tiny rat from which the lake took its name, was one of the few animal species adapted to the arid, barren, frigid wasteland above tree line. Pikas survived hibernation by drinking their own urine. So, the Asp hardly expected Upper Pika Lake to be a flower-bordered alpine jewel from a travel video.

But when finally, head and limbs aching and lungs aflame, he topped the rocky ridge that rimmed the lake, then peered down at its surface, his heart sank.

Eight

THE ASP THOUGHT UPPER PIKA LAKE RESEMBLED A TEARDROP
that had been wept by God, when He had seen the bleakness
He had created.

The Asp stood atop a ridge at the teardrop's broad end. The
lake tapered away from him to a point, one and one-half miles
distant. To his left, Upper Pika Lake's south shore consisted of
a scree slope of angular boulders that had spalled off the sheer
thousand-foot cliff which formed Pika Mountain's north face.

The mountain's bulk shaded the lake from a sun that hung
low in the sky for all but two months of the year. Therefore,
even on this day, less than a week before the summer solstice,
the lake's surface remained a wind-scoured ice sheet.

He crabbed and slid down the steep, rock-strewn embankment to the lake's western shore. Then he extended one booted
foot, and tapped the ice, as tentatively as a child might. His foot
rebounded as though he had kicked iron.

Many other high lakes in these mountains were well studied,
and often visited, because they were convenient to roads or trails.
The sunlit ones thawed early. Wildflower-sprinkled meadows surrounded them. So the government stocked them for recreational
fishing. Upper Pika Lake was too high, too inaccessible, and too
plain, to have been studied, or visited, often.

Its depth, temperature, and fauna, if any, could only be
extrapolated from better-known examples. He had accordingly
prepared for a range of possibilities, including ice cover. But
among them ice cover was the least welcome.

He searched until he found a boulder weighing perhaps fifty pounds. He pried it from the frozen ground, then heaved it out onto the ice. It thunked the surface, but did not crack it, then skidded, spinning slowly until it stopped twenty yards from shore.

He returned to the Expedition, removed three items, tested each, then backpacked them up to the lake's western shore.

First, he reassembled the ice augur, a chest-tall battery-powered drill, used by ice fishermen to bore an eight-inch-diameter hole through lake ice. Near shore he cut through the ice with it, and confirmed his boulder experiment. Five inches of ice thickness would support his weight, but the augur would easily penetrate it.

Next, he assembled the costliest item he had purchased in Houston, a proton precession magnetometer. The model he had selected was a four-foot-long yellow tube, with handholds and a digital display screen on its back end, and a larger sensor tube on its front end.

The PPM measured minute disturbances in the Earth's magnetic field. Steel and other nonferrous metals created such disturbances, so treasure hunters and archeologists used PPMs to locate shipwrecks, and artifacts like anchors and cannons, on the sea floor. More familiarly to him, the oil industry used PPMs to find pipelines buried underground, or laid across the seabed.

The magnetometer he had chosen was watertight and neutrally buoyant, designed to be pushed through the water by a swimming diver. But the magnetometer's dry weight was light enough, and its sensitivity great enough, that a man could sling it over one shoulder, like a musette bag, then search with it.

He sat on the shore and peered across the ice. The Sheik's document fixed the point of interest roughly at the lake's widest point, which was two hundred yards east of the lake's west bank, where he now sat, and two thousand yards from the lake's western tip. A tarn, like a spoon, was likely deepest where it was widest. That, too, was consistent with the expectations the document created.

He defined a search grid by mentally noting distinctively colored and shaped boulders visible on the shore, connected the headphones that would announce a magnetic anomaly by a tone, slipped them over his head, then replaced his wool cap. When he switched the device on it blipped in his ears.

Pocketing a handful of pebbles, he set out across the ice through the cold, still morning.

Forty-five minutes later, stillness turned into howling wind. It forced him to slit his eyes, and he tugged the parka's hood up over his cap and the headphones that the cap covered. His onshore landmarks vanished in the fog of blown snow.

The cold seeped through the parka, and pessimistic fears seeped in with it. He was in the wrong place. The lake was too large to find the *right* place. The lake bottom was deeper than the PPM's range, which in this application was perhaps one hundred feet.

Or, worst of all, the Sheik's document was a figment of imagination, or a fraud of Satan and of Satan's Jew minions. He had traveled halfway around the world, and killed two men, for nothing. This entire exercise was a waste of the Asp's time, and of God's patience.

Suddenly the Asp stopped, then adjusted his headphones. Had he heard a tone? Or had the wind just changed pitch? He walked forward. The tone weakened. Backward. It strengthened. He reached into his pocket, plucked out a pebble, and dropped it at the spot. Then he walked at right angles to his previous line of march.

After ten minutes, three pebbles on the ice formed a triangle, fifty feet on each side. He walked to the triangle's center point, tipped the PPM up on end, and consulted the visual readout. The readout confirmed the tones. Within this triangle, the Earth's magnetic field was minutely disturbed.

That could be because the rocky lake bed at this spot was anomalously rich in nonferrous metallic minerals. It could be because the instrument was miscalibrated, or because he hadn't used it correctly. Or—he shivered inside his layered clothing, but not from cold—it could be something else.

He switched off the PPM, left it to mark the spot, returned to shore and slumped on its slope alongside the ice augur, gasping. At sea level, the morning's work would have tired him little more than a seaside jog.

Ten minutes later, he carried the augur, and the remaining equipment case, across the ice to the yellow PPM.

He positioned the augur's tip so it pricked the ice, leaned

his body weight on the machine's handles like a child riding a bicycle, then pressed the augur's trigger. Seconds later, God rewarded him with a mound of shaved ice and a neat, tubular hole eight inches in diameter. Lake water welled up through the hole, then spilled out across the ice's surface.

He repeated the process until he created an opening large enough to pass the item in the case that he had carried onto the ice.

He removed the underwater video camera, then connected it to the coiled, armored optical cable that would in turn connect to the monitor built in to the case.

He checked and adjusted the picture feed, then improvised. The camera comprised a trio of stubby yellow tubes that housed the camera proper, and two spotlights above it. It was designed to be held by a swimming diver, using the pistol grip that protruded from the camera's belly. The Asp looped and secured the cable with plastic ties, so the camera hung at right angles to it.

Then he switched on the camera lights and paid out the cable until the camera hung ten feet beneath the ice. The cable was one hundred fifty feet long, and alpine tarns like this one were rarely as deep as a hundred feet.

Twisting the cable in his hands, and shuffling his feet, he circled the hole in the ice. He watched the monitor image change as he panned the camera through three hundred sixty degrees.

As he expected, he saw nothing. Tarns like this one, seldom illuminated enough during a year to support photosynthesis, were often sterile. The water was so clear that the translucent ice ceiling scarcely darkened the view.

At thirty feet down, he panned again. Nothing had changed.

At fifty feet, the monitor image still showed nothing.

At sixty feet, he paused, and again panned the camera.

On the monitor, an object appeared, then vanished. The event so startled him that the cable slipped through his gloved fingers, and the camera dropped ten feet. The cable slacked, as though the camera had struck something. When the image stabilized, the monitor view showed just swirling sediment. He pulled up five feet of cable, then panned again, slower. He nearly lost grip again, when a shark's dorsal fin flashed out of the dimness, across the monitor screen, and disappeared.

He maneuvered the camera again. It was not a shark's fin, of course, but a stationary object, shaped like a fin, past which the camera had moved.

And that was as it should be.

His heart leapt.

He retrieved the camera, pulling hand over hand, and repacked it.

Then he faced east, and knelt on the ice for midday prayers. Concentration proved difficult. An exhausting, dangerous day lay ahead. But a joyous one.

He laid out all the gear from the Expedition on the cabin's floor.

The ice augur, camera, and magnetometer had proven to be wise purchases. The inflatable boat and expensive pole-mounted sonar had supported the alternative assumption that the lake would be thawed. They proved to be costly, irrelevant bulk.

The boxed kit of cheap wireless cameras, which he had bought to form an early warning perimeter, he would replace, unopened, in the Expedition. The kit transmitted its cameras' images via the internet, to a smartphone. With no cell service here, they were useless.

In hindsight, he should have expected ice. But his cold-water diving had been in the North Sea's salt water, which remained liquid down to twenty-eight degrees Fahrenheit. This freshwater lake's ice would thaw only above thirty-two degrees Fahrenheit.

That arcane mistake had cost only money.

If the Asp made mistakes in this operation's next phase, they could cripple or kill him.

The Asp sat stiffly on the ice of Upper Pika Lake alongside the hole he had cut earlier in the morning. He had expanded it, by successive augur borings, to manhole size. His cold-water wetsuit, eight millimeters thick through the torso, restricted his motion, and felt stifling in the dry, sunlit air. But, even with hood, gloves, and dive booties, it would be barely adequate to warm him in this water.

The afternoon sun, shining brilliantly through the thin air at twelve thousand feet, had crept above Pika Mountain.

He studied the plastic printed dive tables he had purchased, as a check against what the dive computer he would wear would tell him.

The thin air at altitude not only admitted brighter sunshine. It increased the danger of decompression sickness, "the bends."

Nitrogen gas in breathed air dissolved into a diver's tissues as he descended, as the air's pressure increased with water depth. When the diver ascended, the process reversed. If he ascended too fast, the nitrogen regassified within the diver's muscles and joints as painful, dangerous bubbles.

A single dive to sixty feet that began at sea level, and continued on bottom for the length of time it took to breathe most of a single tank of air, required a slow, but simple, ascent. As a young instructor, he had guided hundreds of nervous tourists to sixty feet beneath the Red Sea, then safely back to the surface, easily.

But the same dive to sixty feet, that began two and one-third *miles above* sea level, materially magnified the difference in pressure between depth and surface. That, in turn, magnified the volume of absorbed nitrogen that had to be slowly released from the tissues on the way to the surface.

To avoid the bends at altitude a diver had to spend less time at depth, so that less nitrogen was absorbed, and so that enough air remained to ascend at a safely slow speed.

He had performed hundreds of dives more complex, and more hazardous, than the one he was about to undertake. But never totally unsupported, as he was now. And supported or not, few divers had in fact been on bottom at twelve thousand feet elevation. He rechecked his calculations, then his equipment.

He adjusted his vest-like Buoyancy Control Device's straps, slipped on his fins, tugged his mask into place. Then he slipped in to the near-freezing water, descended to ten feet, and rechecked his equipment.

He had been apprehensive that, given his breathlessness at altitude, he would burn through his air supply in minutes. But once in the water he realized that the air he was now breathing was compressed to sea level pressure, and so contained more oxygen in a given volume.

He floated there, gorging on the oxygen banquet, compared to the starvation he had been experiencing the last few days. He clung with one gloved hand to the shot line. The shot line was a weighted cord, that he had fixed to the ice above, then had dropped through the manhole. It hung vertically, from the surface to the lake bottom, seventy feet below. Marked at ten-foot intervals, it offered an ascending diver a measure of his depth, and so a measure of his safe ascent rate.

The dive computer integrated into his breathing apparatus provided real-time warnings, so the shot line was redundant for that purpose.

But not for another purpose. He peered up at the ice's undersurface, a rippled, glowing, crystal ceiling. Contrary to urban legend, no "air gap" existed between a lake's ice cover, and the water upon which it floated. No mythic space where a lost swimmer, trapped beneath ice, could sneak a breath. Nor could a swimmer break through five inches of ice. A swimmer who could not find open water would die beneath this ice.

So, if he became disoriented, he could follow the shot line back up to the surface.

He descended without incident, sweeping the water with a dive light that was redundant in the clear dimness.

The "shark fin" tip appeared below him, lying flat on the lake bottom at a depth of seventy-one feet, ten feet away from the shot line's weighted bag. His bottom time was limited. So was his objective. He didn't pause to inspect the fin, beyond a quick hand swipe across its surface that confirmed its condition. This cold, still, sterile environment had neither corroded it, coated it with silt, nor encrusted it with organic matter.

The fin widened as he swam above it until, sixty feet from its tip, its width had increased to perhaps thirty feet, and it bulged upward.

He played the light across the bulge and found, as expected, two rectangular openings that faced toward the surface. The larger opening was sealed. The smaller opening, as wide as his shoulders and four feet long, was unobstructed. He shined his light into the opening, and found a narrow passage. It extended from the opening inside the great fin, and it appeared clear of obstruction.

Normally, a prudent diver, particularly one diving without a companion, would not enter an unfamiliar, confined space. But these circumstances were not normal. And, so far, everything he had expected to find he had found.

The passage appeared too narrow to be negotiated while wearing his tank and BCD. Even if the space proved large enough, the risk that his equipment could catch on, or entangle with, unseen obstructions was too great.

Therefore, he expended some of his limited time on bottom removing his tank and BCD. He grasped them and held them in front of himself as though they formed a swim practice kickboard. Then he swam through the opening and inched ahead through the dark passage. The passage opened into a wider, taller space after ten feet. Within two minutes his light revealed the object he sought, lying loose. He tucked it into the mesh collecting bag attached to his waist, then retraced his path. He shrugged back into his equipment, returned to the shot line, then ascended, with minutes to spare.

Back in the cabin he dried off, tended his equipment, and performed evening prayers.

Then he wiped dry the object he had salvaged and turned it in his hands, while he ate his evening meal. The object was the size and shape of a laptop computer, or of a slim, but oversized, textbook. He hefted it, tapped its exterior with a fingernail, then ran a small magnet over it. Stainless steel. The panel that gave access to its interior was hinged halfway along the case, not at the case's base, like a laptop computer would have been. Steel rings on both edges of the case, at the hinge line, appeared to be anchor points for a missing strap by which it could be carried.

Only the contents interested him. He pressed the release button on the case's side, and the lid clicked open. The papers and other items inside were arranged within an internal accordion file. They were, like the plasticine accordion file itself, dry and pristine. No perishable rubber seal had kept the case's interior watertight. The piece was simply machined with the extraordinary precision one expected in Swiss watches.

He ignored the pencils and other hard items, except for a red metal tube, the size of a small hand flashlight. This he removed from its clip, then tucked away in his back pack.

Finally, he lifted out the loose-bound sheaf of laminated papers and leafed through it. The graphics were clear enough, but the text, as he should have expected, required extensive additional attention, before it would mean anything to him. He placed the laminated sheets in his backpack, too, then snapped the case shut, and slipped it into his bulky coat's oversized side pocket.

He would need additional equipment, and many time-consuming tasks lay ahead.

One task, however, now required immediate attention. He knew that weariness begat carelessness. He also knew that timidity begat failure.

So, despite his exhaustion, he climbed into the Expedition, and drove down the mountain.

It was past midnight when the Expedition's headlights illuminated the sign announcing the interstate highway's intersection at Vail.

His phone's lodging app showed many warm beds available in the town, but he blinked away fatigue.

A portable illuminated sign beside the highway access ramp warned that repairs, west of Avon, would delay interstate highway traffic in both directions, between 10:00 p.m. and 5:00 a.m., throughout July. Within America, the government fastidiously warned Americans about trivial inconveniences.

About the genuine danger he posed, America's government told Americans nothing. Because America had no idea he was here.

He turned the Expedition westbound onto the interstate highway. The road closure didn't trouble him. He was only going as far as Avon.

Nine

AT TEN MINUTES PAST 2:00 A.M., FRANK LUCK LEANED HIS ACHING back against his Ford's tailgate. He sighed, and slowly peed an evening's worth of Coors Banquet into the weeds that bordered the parking lot. He limited his drinking to Saturday night dinners in Avon, partly because he didn't tolerate alcohol as well as he used to, and partly because he didn't tolerate what Avon had become since 1980, when he was twenty-two and peed like a racehorse.

Even in 1980, Avon had been less a ranchers' town than a bedroom community for maids, and busboys, and ski waxers, who worked the resorts up the interstate in Vail. But these days the tourists flooded up and over the Divide in greater numbers, even in summer. So, Avon had remade itself to their liking. Today Avon's bars served more craft ale than Coors and called themselves gastropubs.

But whatever Avon's bars called themselves, and their beer, they still closed at 2:00 a.m.

Frank zipped up his Levi's, then retrieved the six pack of Coors from the cooler in his pickup's bed box. Then he set off walking, to share a couple of them with someone else who understood that the difference between craft ale and Coors was only the price of the resulting urine.

Frank pushed open the unlocked glass front door, then crept into Bristlecone Senior Apartments' dim-lit lobby, past the worn plastic-covered couches and unattended reception desk, to the stairwell.

He tugged the dented fire door open, then climbed the stairs toward the room of Rosaria Martinez, his best friend's widow. The rusty steel stair treads creaked and the bulb in the stairwell's first-floor light remained burned out, as it had been for months. As old folks' homes went Bristlecone was no gastropub.

By the time he paused at the landing he was puffing. He pushed the stairwell door open a crack then peered down the barely lit corridor.

Frank wondered whether the people who came to places like this, to grow older and die, got used to the smell. Or whether it was the smell that killed them.

The corridor was empty, and snores and coughs leaked through the closed doors of the room-plus-bath apartments. He counted to the fourth door on the right, across from the corridor's linen closet. He stopped alongside a linen cart parked outside the closet door and cocked his head.

Rosie's door was ajar and her room's lights out. Normally she left it wide open, and waited up for him with the lights on.

From the dark a woman coughed. As he pushed the door open she wheezed, and rattled out a fit of coughs.

Finally she rasped a whisper, "Three blind mice."

"What? Rosie, you sound awful."

"Three blind mice!"

He stepped through the door, toward the bed in which she lay. From the corner of his eye he glimpsed a flash of motion.

Frank stiffened and turned.

A man stood, silent and silhouetted against the faint light. Frank realized he had been standing in the room, behind the door.

Frank pointed at the guy with his free hand. "You people need to take better care—"

The man lunged at Frank, his right hand thrusting, and a blade that he held glinted in the light.

Frank swung the six pack, clobbered the son of a bitch on his temple, and heard him blurt out a curse.

But the man just staggered sideways a step, recovered, and lunged with the knife again.

Frank jumped back, and the blade missed his gut by inches. He retreated into the corridor, swung the linen cart between himself and the man as the guy pursued him.

Frank Luck had won his share of bar fights. In recent years, his win percentage had dropped. He had two inches and forty pounds on this guy, but he was half Frank's age. It was summer, but he wore an oversized parka. Its sleeves were pushed up, and his bare forearms were muscular, like a jockey's. His skin was brown, and his eyes gleamed, black and unblinking, like a timber rattler's.

Frank carried a folding knife in his jeans pocket. But knife fighting with someone who seemed to know how to use one would be stupider than playing pool with a man who walked into the bar with his own cue.

The man circled Frank, eyes on the six pack that was Frank's only weapon.

Frank had heard Mexicans curse all his life. He had heard Arabs curse on the nightly news often enough. Snake Eyes, here, was as Mexican as falafel.

Frank shoved the linen cart at his opponent.

Snake Eyes stepped out of its path like a matador, smiling. But his long jacket caught on the cart's handle, as it rolled past. Something clattered from his pocket to the floor.

Eyes on Frank, Snake Eyes inched forward. With a toe he swept the flat metal object out of his path, and under the linen cart.

Frank heard distant footsteps, then flicked his eyes away from his adversary, toward the sound.

Snake Eyes seized the moment and spun.

His left foot slashed up and caught Frank flush on the point of his jaw. White light flashed behind Frank's eyes, then faded to blackness.

Ten

THE ASP STARED DOWN AT THE OLD MAN WHOM HE HAD KNOCKED unconscious, as the man lay faceup on the dim corridor's floor.

Gray haired and mustachioed, the man was dressed just as a film cowboy of the Wild West would dress. He wore ornate leather boots, blue jeans, and a wide-brimmed hat, which now rocked on its crown alongside his head. All that was missing was a holstered six-shooter on the man's hip.

The Asp sprang back into the old woman's room, held his palm above her nose and mouth, and felt the faintest respiration.

He gently pinched her nose with the fingers of his right hand, while he pressed his left palm across her mouth.

She was so frail that she barely stirred. It was over in seconds, though it felt like minutes. He wiped her face with his handkerchief, then turned to leave.

"Help!" The old cowboy on the corridor floor called out.

Before the old man could stir, the Asp stepped to him and returned him to unconsciousness with another head kick.

Fast footsteps approached from the stairwell up which the Asp had climbed. More footsteps sounded from the corridor's opposite end, around a corner. His escape routes were blocked, and within seconds, he would be seen.

He stepped across the hallway, entered the linen closet in front of which the cart had stood, then pulled the closet's door shut behind himself.

In the corridor, separated from him only by the unlocked

door's thickness, a pair of excited voices muttered, and he heard one voice phone for emergency assistance. Moments later they were joined by a third voice, female.

Ten minutes later the Asp remained standing in the closet's darkness. The thick parka already made him overwarm. His heart pounded, while the aromas of laundry soap and starch mingled in his nostrils.

He rubbed his temple, and winced at the tender lump already swelling there, due to the blow the old man had landed with the heavy carton he carried. If the Asp's older brother were here, he would mock his baby brother's incompetence.

The Asp closed his eyes in the darkness. Again he was a child, playing hide-and-seek in the sweltering summer heat, in the laundry and kitchen building behind the Zamalek house. Only the knife, now held ready in his hand, and the consequences if he were discovered, had changed.

A fourth voice sounded in the corridor, this one accompanied by occasional static and bursts of conversation. These, the Asp deduced, came from a policeman's radio.

At the sound, hair rose on the Asp's neck. Just as outside the filling station in Denver, he was instants away from confronting an adversary who outgunned him.

The fourth voice said, "Well, Frank Luck. I haven't seen you out cold, intoxicated, on a floor in three whole months."

The cowboy's voice said, "Dammit, Cody! That hippie provocateur—"

"Frank, he was a Democrat from New Jersey."

"That's what I said. And he coldcocked me."

"The bartender said you swung first. You know, an Eagle County Sheriff's Deputy has more significant miscreants to interrogate on Saturday nights than you."

"Did you see him?"

"Him? What I see is a drunk cowboy passed out on the floor. In an old folks' home. At two thirty in the morning. You okay, Frank?"

"Is *she* okay?"

One of the other voices said, "If he's talking about the woman in room two thirty-six, she's *dead*."

The Asp heard sounds of a scuffle.

The cowboy roared, "That son of a bitch!"

"Whoa, Frank! Lie back down. You smell like a brewery, and you had a fall. Your pupils are dilated like you've been concussed. A doctor probably should look you over. I expect they'll keep you overnight for observation."

"Doctor my ass! I'm fine."

"Okay. We'll see. Now, what happened? Start at the beginning."

"The beginning? I drove into town for Saturday dinner, like always. Had a beer."

"Oh?"

"Maybe I had several. There's no law against walking while under the influence."

"True."

Luck said, "After closing time, I walked over here to have a couple more beers with Rosie Martinez. Her kids sold the ranch after Carlito died. Then they parked her in this place four months ago. They never come to see her. So I come up once a week, after the bars close, and we talk."

The deputy said, "Hold up, Frank. What did you mean when you asked whether I saw a son of a bitch?"

Silence.

English was not the Asp's first language, but the pause between question and answer struck him as abnormal, and no doubt struck the policeman the same way.

Before Luck the Cowboy answered, murmurs, and the sound of shuffling feet, rose in the hallway. Undoubtedly the commotion had awakened other residents.

A female voice quavered. "Frankie! *Madre de Dios!*"

The old cowboy said, "Rosie?"

The policeman raised his voice, "You in there! Leave the decedent in the bed for a minute, and come out here."

"Yes, Deputy?" It was a different voice.

"If this lady standing beside me is Frank's friend Rosie Martinez, who's the lady in the bed there?"

"Eleanor Love. Like the card on the wall beside her door says."

The deputy asked, "You were the first one on the scene?"

"Yep. I'm the senior night attendant. I heard somebody yell for help. When I got here, this gentleman was flat on his back on the floor, right where he is now. Out cold. The six pack was on one side of him, and his hat on the other. Right where they are now. He's not one of our residents, so I called 9-1-1. And here you are."

"You didn't see anybody else?"

"Just the other night staff, when they showed up."

The policeman said, "Tell me about this Eleanor Love."

"Not much to tell. I didn't realize she had passed away until after I called for you."

"You don't seem shook up about it."

"Bristlecone's not a regulated nursing home. But it's not a seniors' health club either. She was listed as ninety-seven years old, when she moved in three months ago. She had one bad leg. But she could walk. She could attend to her own bodily functions. She was lucid enough to take care of herself, and order her meals. Our residents have to be able to do all that. But she went downhill. That's basically the only direction our residents go."

"Then why was she still here?"

"She probably wouldn't have been here after noon tomorrow. A doctor visits all the residents here, once a week. Her dementia had gotten worse lately. She just speaks—used to speak—gibberish, lately. We expected she'd go any time. Or the physician would send her out for hospitalization tomorrow. If she lasted that long."

"Any reason to think she was helped along?"

"No! No. I don't mean to sound like an asshole. But death is the rule here, not the exception. Our residents don't live here because they enjoy the mountain air. Mountain air's thin, and their lungs are generally shot. They live here because it's close to where they've lived all their lives. And because it's cheap, compared to full-on senior care."

The policeman said, "Had she been ill?"

The attendant said, "Ms. Love had had bouts of pulmonary edema—fluid buildup in the lungs. That's common here. She had a weak heart. That's common here, too. So FPE—Flash Pulmonary Edema—a sudden recurrence—certainly could've finished her. There's no sign she did anything but stop breathing in her sleep." The voice paused.

The Asp slightly relaxed his grip on his knife.

Perhaps his plan had not gone entirely awry.

The materials the Sheik had provided only gave the old woman's address.

That this place had proved so soft a target had been a bonus.

He had expected she would neither help him, nor put up a fight. He had come only to tie up a loose end.

It was now obvious that coming here, to silence her, had been an unnecessary blunder, and stupid. But it now appeared likely he would get away with it. It reaffirmed God's blessing on the Asp's mission.

In the corridor, the attendant spoke. "Deputy, you can't be thinking Frank, here—?"

The policeman said, "Wait. You *know* Frank?"

The attendant said, "Sure. I work this shift every Saturday. Frank visits Rosie every Saturday night, after the bars close. The two of them share a couple beers and chitchat. It's the highlight of Rosie's week."

"2:00 a.m. is visiting hours?"

The attendant said, "Official visiting hours end at 8:00 p.m. But our residents don't generally have the kind of family who visit at all. We don't lock the door, because somebody's usually on the front desk after eight, anyway."

"Usually?"

"The desk person's also supposed to do chores. Like empty the public area trash cans, and walk around the floors every couple hours. I mean, nobody sneaks in to a place like this. We keep most of the residents' valuables, and *all* the meds, locked up."

"You have a security camera on that front door?"

"No. The only security camera we have covers the safe closet on the lower level. That's where the valuables and the meds are locked up."

"Don't scrub that camera's record."

"Sure. We'll keep it."

"No other cameras?"

"Nope. Like I said."

The deputy said, "None of that explains why Frank is lying here in front of Eleanor Love's room, if he was coming to see Rosie Martinez."

The attendant said, "This is room two thirty-six. Rosie's room is *three* thirty-six. Right above this room. It's an easy mistake. The floors look alike. I've done it myself."

Another voice, young and female, said, "Sir, do we have to shut this area off or something?"

The deputy said, "There's no evidence of trauma or suicide.

She wasn't in the custody of law enforcement, or of a public institution. She was not in good health?"

The male voice said, "Like I told you, she was dying."

"And she'd been seen by your doctor here within the last thirty days?"

"Absolutely. And the doctor's due to visit again five hours from now, around breakfast time."

"Next of kin?"

"None listed. Her bill auto-payed out of her own bank account. She never had visitors."

"That checks all the statutory boxes I'm responsible for. Cause of death, and a decision whether to notify the county coroner, will be up to your doctor, when he gets here today. Anything beyond that will be up to the Eagle County District Attorney's Office." The deputy paused, then said, "Except for you, Frank. You never answered my question about whether I saw some son of a bitch."

Frank the Cowboy said, "Now that I think on it, Cody, I don't really remember. I think you and this fella got it right. I just happened to count floors wrong. Then I slipped on the floor, and picked a bad place to take a nap."

There was another silence, then the deputy said, "Nothing here says 'crime scene' to me. Unless you're lodging a complaint about Frank trespassing?"

"He wasn't, really. He was just a late guest."

The deputy said, "Alright."

The Cowboy said, "Then I can go home?"

The deputy said, "In your shape? Only if you walk. I'll give you a lift out to your place."

"I suppose you're confiscating my beer? As evidence?"

"Frank, Eagle County doesn't want your beer. Or your guns. Or your health plan. We just want you to go home, and sleep it off. Without another fistfight over the Second Amendment."

The Asp realized that he was sweating, and he was sweating because of the parka he wore in the confined space. He felt the parka's pocket, found it empty, and remembered. The steel case that he had kicked under the linen cart! Evidence! When it was discovered, the tidy story would unravel.

Twenty minutes later the corridor beyond the door had been silent for five minutes. The Asp cracked the linen closet's door and, after the closet's darkness, squinted against even the corridor's subdued night lighting. The only sounds were, once again, muffled snores.

The policeman was gone, presumably with the drunken cowboy in tow. The other doors along the again empty corridor were closed.

He opened the door of his hiding place, stepped into the corridor. Opposite the linen closet the door to the old woman's room had been closed.

He crept into the room's darkness, touched the woman's emaciated form, now covered head to foot by a sheet, and confirmed it was a corpse's familiar dead cold.

He returned to the linen cart. It remained exactly at the angle that he recalled it had been. He crouched, and felt beneath the cart for the steel case. When his fingers touched only floor tile, he flattened himself on his belly and peered into the inky shadow beneath the cart, then stood and moved the cart aside. Nothing remained on the floor space that the cart had covered.

He tiptoed back into the old woman's room, searched the room's drawers and closet, and found only a hairbrush, dentures, and clothing.

Then he padded to the staircase, and stood hands on hips on the landing, in the stairwell's dark silence, while he evaluated the new situation.

The steel case's loss, itself, was trivial. Only some of its contents mattered, and those remained safely in his possession. The old woman's silence was now guaranteed.

The sole problem remaining from the night's events was the fact that the drunken cowboy had seen his face, and possibly now possessed the steel case. Both circumstances jeopardized the Asp's greatest asset, his anonymity.

The Asp doubted that the Cowboy had genuinely forgotten what had happened, as he had told the policeman. However pleasant and gullible American police seemed, the Asp suspected that the Cowboy had his own reasons for withholding his recollection of their encounter.

The Cowboy unquestionably knew that the case had fallen on the floor during their scuffle. From his vantage, supine, on the floor, a mere turn of his head would have allowed him to see the case, although it remained out of sight of the policeman and the others. From his position on the floor, the Cowboy could easily have swept the case from beneath the cart, then concealed it on his person, while the policeman and employees conversed.

And the Cowboy had a reason to do so, because the case would unravel his denial if discovered, but would corroborate his tale of a phantom intruder, if in the future he chose to reveal the truth.

The Asp left the building, walked back to the spot where he had parked the Expedition, then sat in the driver's seat thumbing through the internet. Within seven minutes his inquiries led him to an address for one, and only one, Frank Luck, age sixty-two, of Eagle County, Colorado.

The address was barely fifteen minutes' drive from the Expedition's current location, and the satellite view of the small house and outbuildings among evergreens showed the nearest neighboring residence was a good half mile from it.

The Asp had no way of knowing how long it might take until the policeman delivered Luck to his home, then left him alone to sleep off his drunkenness. But the Asp was sure the policeman had other work to do.

A police encounter, no matter how unlikely, was too great a risk. To maximize the time buffer between the policeman's departure from Luck's residence and the Asp's own arrival, the Asp decided that thirty minutes of darkness would offer all the cover he needed.

He had now been awake, and under intense physical and mental stress, for nearly twenty-two hours. Those twenty-two hours had immeasurably changed the odds in his favor, once the matter of Frank Luck, and the missing steel case, was resolved.

The Asp set an alarm on his phone that would allow him to sleep, wake, drive, and arrive at Frank Luck's residence thirty minutes before local sunrise. Then he reclined the car's seat, and drifted off.

Eleven

FRANK LUCK LEANED, ARMS FOLDED, AGAINST ONE OF HIS FRONT-porch roof's stone support columns and watched until the sheriff's department SUV pulled away toward Avon. Frank unlocked his cabin's front door, walked to his kitchen table, then hung his jacket on his chair's back. Then he tugged out the flat metal case, which he had tucked into his belt at the small of his back, and sat.

He turned the thing in his hands, opened its lid, peered inside, and ran his fingers over the engraving he found there.

He raised his eyebrows, whistled, then stood and put on coffee.

As soon as he had glimpsed the thing beneath the linen cart, and remembered how it had gotten there, the simple thing to have done would have been to rake it out from under the linen cart, where Snake Eyes had kicked it, and hand it over to Cody.

But the longer Frank had listened to the deputy, the less sure Frank had been that telling all of the truth all of the time would set him free.

If the doctor, and the coroner, decided the old woman had died naturally, Frank would look like a stumblebum who couldn't hold his liquor. He'd been called worse.

But if they decided that somebody had murdered the old woman, after all? Then the last thing that Eagle County, and the district attorney, whose salary the county paid, wanted to announce was a violent, mysterious Arab, on the loose during summer tourist season.

So, the prime suspect would be a drunk cowboy who had gotten rowdy more than once in his life. And who had been found three yards from the body. It would also make evidence that tended to clear said cowboy, by corroborating his story, likely to vanish.

Coloradans like Frank Luck, who Frank believed included most Coloradans outside the People's Republic of Denver-Boulder, believed that the first person a man turned to for help, or for justice, was the person he saw in the mirror. And the last place he turned to, for *anything*, was the government.

Frank sat down at his desk, logged on to his desktop computer, then spent an informative hour on the internet. He blocked his appointments calendar for the next five days, poured the coffee into a thermos, and shut off his computer.

Then he phoned for an Uber to drop him in town, where he had parked his pickup.

He showered, packed a bag, and tucked the metal case into it. He also retrieved the lever-action Winchester, in its fringed leather sleeve, from the front closet, along with a box of ammunition.

After he tucked the ammunition into his bag, he carried the bag and the rifle onto the front porch, set them alongside the porch rocker, then sat and rocked in dark silence, broken only by the rocker's squeak.

Ten minutes later, a car's lights shone through the trees, on the road that led to his place. Moments later, the lights glared as the car turned off the road, then snaked up his driveway.

The Uber dropped Frank off, alongside his truck in Avon. He yawned in the false dawn, tucked his bag and the rifle behind the pickup's driver's seat, then started the engine.

Even in this, his busy season, Frank usually refused appointments Sunday mornings, while he slept off Saturday nights. But today he was up and at 'em, beginning a twenty-six-hour drive east. And it was still forty-five minutes before sunrise.

Twelve

CASSIDY GOODING'S PHONE TRILLED AGAIN, ECHOING IN THE empty employee locker room's 6:00 a.m. silence. She ran from the shower, snatched the phone from her locker's shelf, then peered at the screen as she answered.

"Merk?" She put her boss on speaker as she laid the phone on a bench and toweled her hair.

"Did I wake you, Cass?"

"Nope. Rode in this morning."

"You know cycling in the dark at rush hour's insane."

"So is stealing a wrecked P-38 from cannibals. But it worked out for you." She dropped her towel, turned in front of the locker room mirror, and wondered whether museum work had grown her twenty-five-year-old ass fat enough to tempt cannibals. "What's going on, Merk?"

Dr. Howard Merken said, "I'm running late. The van's lift stuck. Now I'm stuck in beltway traffic. I'm calling to give you a heads-up. I got an email a couple days ago. From a guy who wanted the foremost expert in America on pre–Cold War aviation, to evaluate an artifact. He may be arriving in D.C. this morning. So, I just emailed him *your* contact information. I told him you were the *second* foremost expert in America on pre–Cold War aviation. If he shows up, would you entertain him 'til I get there? My calendar says you and I are scheduled to spend the morning in the restoration hangar, reviewing the Horten. The three of us will just meet up there."

"What kind of artifact?"

"Your kind."

"Meaning what?"

"Meaning, a man who drives with two hands and no feet shouldn't talk and drive simultaneously." Somewhere, out in greater Washington's predawn gridlock, Merk cut the call.

Cass stuffed her helmet, cleats, jersey, and cycling shorts into her locker as goosebumps rose on her bare arms. And not from the morning chill.

Forty-five minutes later Cass perched on a stepladder in the restoration hangar. She peered down into the Horten Ho 229's seventy-five-year-old fuselage, using her phone's flashlight. As she looked, she dictated notes for the Horten's preservation team into her Bluetooth headset's microphone.

Her phone's voice ringtone trilled in her earpiece, so loudly that she nearly fell.

She flicked her phone to answer. "Hello?"

"Dr. Gooding? Frank Luck from Colorado here."

She cocked her head, then remembered Merk's mystery guest. "Yes. Dr. Merken told me you might call."

"That's me."

"You wrote you were headed this way."

"Just got in."

"Have you got your luggage?"

"I have."

"Did you fly in to Reagan?"

"Nope."

"That's perfect. *Don't* just tell the driver you want the National Air and Space Museum. If you do, you'll spend an hour in traffic. Then wind up in downtown Washington. Say you want the 'Udvar-Hazy *Annex* of the National Air and Space Museum.' The annex is actually right on the other side of the airport from the Dulles terminal. You'll be here in fifteen minutes."

"I am here. That's why I said it was Frank Luck here. This fella with the badge at the front door says your museum doesn't open 'til ten."

"Let me talk to him."

The voice changed. "Dr. Gooding, it's Ernie."

"Ernie, I'm literally up in the air just now. Can you escort Mr. Luck back to the Restoration Hangar Overlook? I'll meet you there."

"I'm not supposed to leave the desk, ma'am."

"Okay. Just point him across the Mezzanine Catwalk. I'll meet him at the *Enola Gay*, in five minutes. Tell him to look for the redhead in jeans, with the brow ring and the ink."

Ernie the guard said, "Ma'am, I can't turn him loose on the museum floor outside of opening hours. Could you come up front and sign for him?"

Cass rolled her eyes. "Does he have anything with him?"

"A canvas bag. He let me hand search it, but he wouldn't let it go."

She jumped the last two steps off the ladder onto the hangar floor. "I'm on my way."

Frank Luck from Colorado stood at the entry desk. A faded canvas gym bag dangled from his left hand, and he shifted, foot to foot, in his cowboy boots. Six feet of mustachioed, wrinkled leather stretched over barbed wire, he wore a broad-brimmed straw hat over bushy gray hair, denim jeans, and a denim jacket, over a checked shirt. His crystal blue eyes were bloodshot, and she guessed his age was sixty.

She extended her hand. "Cass Gooding, Mr. Luck. My pleasure."

He raised his eyebrows. "You're Doctor Gooding?"

"Doctor of aeronautical history, yes. Appendectomies are three doors down. Call me Cass."

He shook her hand. "Frank." He stretched and yawned.

"You've had a long trip, Frank." She pointed into the museum's barrel-vaulted aviation hangar and led the way toward it. "I'm working this morning in the Restoration Hangar, at the back of the museum. I have coffee there. We can talk. Dr. Merken is driving in now. He'll join us."

They turned onto the Mezzanine Catwalk.

Suspended between the aviation hangar's ground floor and second floor, the catwalk was a pedestrian bridge that bisected the vast enclosure, and from which many of the two hundred forty-plus air and spacecraft on display were visible.

As they walked, Frank Luck craned his neck at the aircraft displayed on the floor beneath them, and more aircraft suspended above, beside, and all around them, as though in flight.

Cass said, "First visit to the annex?"

"Yep."

"Is aviation your profession?"

He shook his head. "Never found much use for airplanes."

"Oh. What *is* your profession?"

"Ranching."

"Do you enjoy it?"

"These days I do."

"Oh." She smiled at her guest. "The ranching business is good these days, then?"

"Wouldn't know. Quit it ten years ago."

"Oh."

Halfway across the catwalk he stopped, staring at the silver, four-engined bomber pointed nose-first at them.

Elevated on stands above the floor below the catwalk, the plane's cockpit rested just beneath their eye level. A transparent panel, fixed to the catwalk's railing, separated them from the plane.

Frank Luck whistled softly.

She smiled. "For a man who doesn't know about airplanes, you just picked out the most controversial one in the place."

"Never said I didn't know about airplanes. Said ranchers don't have much use for 'em."

"Oh. Then what, in particular, caused you to react to the *Enola Gay*, here?"

"Human stupidity."

"You disagree with the U.S. decision to drop the A-bomb, then?"

"Didn't say that."

"Somehow, I felt that coming."

"I disagree with the stupid humans who blame a hunk of aluminum."

"Yes, vandals have attacked the plane. As a symbol of militarism, and human folly. That's why we've raised it on blocks, and shielded it behind glass."

"I suppose you've got a model of the bomb, too. Do they throw blood on *it*?"

"We do have one. But no, they don't. Which is odd. Because the bomb and the aircraft were very much a package deal. The *Enola Gay* was a 'Silverplate' variant B-29. One of a small number of aircraft modified to carry a five-ton atom bomb, high enough and far enough to cross a big enough swath of the Pacific to reach Japan. Or, if the war had developed differently, across a big swath of Europe, to reach Berlin. Without the bomb *and* the plane, history wouldn't look the way it does."

Frank shrugged. "I'd say history looks the way it does because folks write it later to fit what they want to prove."

"Are you this skeptical about everything?"

"Only the things that are wrong."

At the Restoration Hangar's door, she tapped in her code. When they entered, Luck's boot heels' clump echoed in the deserted space. Two stories above the hangar floor, a glass wall allowed museum visitors to look down on the aircraft restorations in progress.

Cass led him past incomplete aircraft, each ringed by a clutter of parts and equipment, like it was a nesting bird.

Behind a gray Sikorsky flying boat that had been stationed at Pearl Harbor on December 7, 1941, Cass stopped at the scaffolding-mounted cockpit section that she had been examining when Frank Luck had called her.

As the two of them arrived at the Horten, Merken's van rolled in through the hangar's outer door, then parked alongside the old jet's fuselage. They waited while he lowered himself in his wheelchair, on the van's whining lift, then rolled toward them.

Dr. Howard Merken, bald and pudgy, his sixty-something eyes smiling behind round wire-rimmed glasses, was a Doctor of Aeronautical Engineering. He was also Curator of Aircraft of the Smithsonian National Air and Space Museum.

Merken had spent his life chasing airplanes hidden in barns, crashed in jungles, and frozen in glaciers, until a plane crash had changed him, from a pilot-adventurer to a museum curator.

While he and Frank Luck shook hands, Cass poured three coffees from her thermos, which stood on a sawhorse-and-plywood work table.

Luck lifted a magazine off the table, flicked his eyes from the magazine cover to the Horten's rust-brown fuselage section, and read aloud, "Stealth Bomber That Almost Saved the Nazis!"

The magazine's cover illustrated an airborne Horten 229 jet, decked out in swastikas and iron crosses. The drawing resembled the worn prototype beside the three of them, which had been captured during World War II's final days.

The illustration depicted the Horten, flying alongside a contemporary U.S. Air Force B-2 Spirit stealth bomber. Like a pair of boomerangs, the two all-wing jets looked like siblings. Or like grandparent and child, the Horten smaller, and a half century older.

Cass smiled. "That article's clickbait on paper. It's true that the Ho 229 was years ahead of its time. It's true that all-wing design can reduce radar and heat signatures. It's true that an all-wing design can carry more payload, and fly farther. That's why the B-2 looks like it does. But the Ho 229 was a single-seat *fighter*, not a long-range bomber. Its stealth characteristics were incidental. And, we know today, imperfect."

Merk said, "Frank, what the Horten 229 was designed to do was fly faster and higher and farther than its competition. And it would have. But all that Germany could manage in the war's last days were plywood prototypes. This one's the sole survivor. Bugs, unfortunately, eat wood. We've spent years just trying to preserve what's left of it."

Frank Luck set the gym bag he carried onto the makeshift table. "Sounds like I brought this to the right folks."

Cass shrugged. "Maybe. I'm the assistant curator of mid-twentieth-century aircraft, here. My doctoral thesis was about German defense production, especially aircraft production, from 1930 through 1950. So, what've you got?"

Frank Luck unzipped the bag, then handed Cass a flat metal case, the size and shape of a thick laptop, or of a hardbacked textbook.

She wrinkled her forehead, hefted it, tapped its surface with a black-polished fingernail.

The old cowboy pointed at a latch button on the case's smooth side. "Open it and look inside the flap."

Engraved on the hinged flap's stainless-steel underside was a precise rendering of a swooping eagle, in three-quarter profile, that clutched a swastika in its talons.

Cass widened her eyes, as she ran her fingers across the insignia. Then she tugged a pencil from one of the case's interior loops, turned it in her fingers, passed the case to Merk, and said, "Hmm."

Merken looked up at her. "What do *you* make of it?"

She pursed her lips. "Me? Well, I understand why Frank brought it to us." She looked at their visitor. "As you obviously figured out, the engraving is the logo of the Luftwaffe during the Third Reich."

She traced her finger around the case's edge. "The proportions are like a rectangular briefcase, except the top flap is hinged on the narrow edge. As we describe things today, this case is arranged in portrait plan. Not the landscape plan of a conventional briefcase. These metal rings on the back would have been where a handle, presumably cloth or leather, would have attached. These internal pockets, with the pencils, and the plasticine protractor, and the steel dividers, are just where you would expect them to be."

"Expect them to be if it's *what*?"

Merk said, "Frank, what it *resembles* is a German military officer's map case. It's got Luftwaffe markings. So the officer would have been a flight officer, likely a pilot. It's taller than it is wide, so it could be slipped into place, alongside a pilot's seat, in a cockpit's close quarters. That would allow the pilot to keep maps, and navigation charts specific to the flight, near at hand. Also, documents like mission orders, and preflight checklists."

Cass pointed with the green pencil in her hand at the other pencils and implements tucked into the case's loops and pockets. "The pencils and drafting tools would be used to make notes, to do math, and to plot courses on the maps. Getting from point A to point B was complicated before GPS. These wooden pencils are Faber-Castells. Today, Faber-Castell pencils are made around the world. But the company started in Germany before the Napoleonic Wars."

Cass pointed at the pencil she held, at the manufacturer's name stamped on the varnished wood. "Based on condition, this pencil looks as new as the case looks. But this logo on the pencil tells a different story. Faber-Castell's logo was, and still is, a pair of jousting knights. But, in 1905, the company started imprinting its pencils with this 'set of scales' logo, instead. In the 1990s, Faber-Castell changed back to imprinting the jousting knights on its pencils.

"So, we can't say definitively that these are the right pencils. But we can say definitively that they aren't the *wrong* pencils. They don't *prove* anything, but—"

Merk said, "But they make *me* less suspicious that this object is just some neo-Nazi art project. The only design inconsistency is this empty clip. Map cases didn't have anything like it. But it's about the size to secure a small flashlight. That would have come in handy reading maps in a cockpit at night." He grimaced. "However . . ."

Frank said, "However what?"

Cass crossed her arms. "These map cases were mundane, utilitarian items, Frank. Thousands were made, but they rarely come up for sale, these days. Because they were made of leather, and leather rots. I've never seen, or even heard of, one made of metal. Let alone one made of stainless steel, and machined as precisely as a watertight Rolex chronometer."

Frank frowned. "You think it's fake, then?"

Merk said, "On the contrary, Frank. At least in my opinion. Fakes are made to fool buyers. Faking a leather map case in stainless steel would be as stupid as faking a Van Gogh using magic markers. But mostly what persuades me it's real is this case is so over-engineered."

Cass said, "In my doctoral thesis I wrote that 'there was no such thing as German engineering, there was only German over-engineering.' Germany's always made top-shelf stuff. Mercedes-Benz Cabriolets. Leica cameras. But German stuff has rarely been made simply or cheaply.

"German defense production in World War II was the same. One German Tiger tank could slaughter a half dozen American-designed Shermans. But Tigers were so complex to build, and to maintain, that only a couple thousand of them took the field. Against fifty thousand inferior Shermans, the Tigers were toast."

Merk said, "The V-2 rocket was a technical marvel. But the German rocket program cost Germany nearly half of the two billion dollars that the Manhattan Project cost the U.S. By comparison, a single B-29 could deliver ten times the explosives a V-2 could, carry them ten times farther, and do it again and again. And the unit cost of that single, reusable B-29 was less than a million dollars."

Cass said, "And after the war turned against Germany, it got worse. Companies peddled designs so overdone that they looked like fifteen-year-olds sketched them in study hall. The German economy was short of labor and materials to build the designs, anyway.

"The design projects' purpose was to keep company personnel at their drawing boards. So they wouldn't be conscripted, then slaughtered on the Russian front."

Merk said, "Internal Nazi politics made it worse. In a police state, ratting out your neighbor was expected. But Hitler's principal heirs apparent, *Reichsmarschall* Goering, the head of the Luftwaffe, and Himmler, *Reichsführer* of the SS, built competing little Reichs of their own. They ordered up secret pet projects left and right. Castles. Mansions. Archeological goose chases. And they got away with it. The Germans had plenty of bureaucrats auditing defense projects. But if a bureaucrat blew the whistle on the wrong stupid project, he might disappear."

Cass pointed at the Horten 229. "This is a good example. The Horten brothers were twenty-something self-taught glider build-ers. They joined the Air Force in the late thirties. They funded their glider building by operating a sketchy military unit they called *Sonderkommando Luft Drei*, 'Special Air Command Three.' When an auditor discovered it, and ordered them to stop, they just changed the name to 'Special Air Command Nine.' Then they started stamping all their documents 'Top Secret-General of the Air Force.' Nobody ever questioned their operation again."

Merk stretched open the accordion pockets of the map case in his lap by scissoring his fingers, then squinted inside.

Frank shook his head. "It's empty. I already looked."

Merk nodded. "Yep."

Cass snatched the case back from her boss, inverted it above the plywood desk, and shook it. "Spoken like two men who've never lost a receipt in a purse."

A yellowed square of slick paper, curled at its edges, slipped out of the case, fluttered like a leaf, then landed on the makeshift desk. It was a faded color photograph, of two men and two women.

Cass stared at the photograph as gooseflesh again rose on her arms.

Finally, Merk whispered, "I'll be damned!"

Thirteen

FRANK STARED AT THE PHOTOGRAPH, THEN LOOKED UP AT CASS and Merk. "Friends of yours?"

Cass stared at the four people in the old photo. They stood outdoors, shaded beneath a half-visible, bare-metal, riveted structure. The shorter of the two women, petite, with short blonde hair, wore a tailored white pants suit and flats. Face upturned, she pointed at the riveted object. The man who stood with her peered where she pointed.

Merk said, "Frank, that's Hanna Reitsch. Reitsch was to German aviation as Amelia Earhart was to American aviation. Earhart's a personal hero of mine, but, honestly, Reitsch was the more versatile and accomplished flyer."

Frank tapped with a wiry finger on the male figure who stood alongside Reitsch. "Is this guy who I think he is?"

Even though it was just a photograph, Cass shuddered as she stared at the bespectacled, professorial man. He wore the black death's head peaked cap, and black jodhpur-and-jackboots uniform, of the *Reichsführer* of the SS.

Merk nodded. "It's Heinrich Himmler. CEO of the Holocaust. Commander of the SS. Head of the Secret State Police—the *Gestapo*. Probably the second most powerful man in the Third Reich."

Cass said, "Also probably the creepiest."

Frank said, "What about the pair standing behind them?"

The man, tall, blonde and gorgeous, with a cleft chin and eyes that even in the faded photo were Aryan blue, wore a business suit. The woman, as tall for her gender as the man was for his, stood beside him and wore a pilot's coverall. In her left hand she held a leather flight helmet with attached goggles, along with the map case. She looked as blonde, blue eyed, and beautiful as the man.

Cass shook her head. "I have no clue who they were. But there's this map case in her hand, big as life."

Frank said, "Any guess where and when this was taken?"

Merk shrugged. "Where? No. When? Certainly *before* May 8, 1945. That's the day World War II ended in Europe. By that time Himmler and Reitsch were running for their lives, in different directions. Certainly, it was taken *after* mid-1943."

"How can you tell?" Frank asked.

Merk said, "In late 1942, Reitsch was test flying the Messerschmitt 163 Komet. The Komet was the first, and to this day the only, rocket plane flown in combat."

Merk jerked a thumb toward the main hangar. "We have one restored out there. The Komet looked like a bat out of hell, went like one, and was more dangerous to fly than one.

"Reitsch crashed so badly that she was hospitalized for five months. Among other injuries, she lost her nose. For the rest of her life, she wore a prosthetic. From the pictures I've seen, the wide, flat nose you see in this picture isn't the one Hanna's momma gave her."

Frank flipped the photo over, then stared at it and frowned. "Anybody read German?"

Merken rolled his chair forward, adjusted his glasses, then read aloud the penciled words, so faint they were barely legible, "'*Mit Hanna und Mein geliebter.*'"

Cass said, "'With Hanna and my beloved.'"

Frank said, "What do you make of that?"

Merken said, "Pilots routinely carry photos of their sweethearts and families when they fly. There are two pilots in this picture. The one who wrote this note was obviously not Hanna Reitsch."

Cass said, "Tens date tens. My interpretation is that the two hotties in the background were a couple."

Frank said, "Well, that's all interesting. But it doesn't give me the answer I need."

Merk said, "Me either. Frank, to me the most startling thing about this photograph is what these four people are standing underneath."

Frank leaned forward. "Is it an airplane wing?"

Merk nodded. "And a little more of an airplane. But show me, or Cass, a sample this large of any known aircraft, built between 1930 and 1950, and either of us will tell you its make and model. I can't identify this one." He looked up at Cass. "You?"

She shook her head, then said to Frank, "Where did you say you got this case?"

"I never said."

Cass exhaled. "Well, *could* ya' say?"

"I could."

"Well?"

"Let's just say I didn't buy it."

"Ah." Merk nodded. "You're looking for a pre-purchase appraisal. Factoring in the provenance that the photo supplies, you might be surprised what it could be worth."

"It's not mine to sell. But I didn't steal it."

Cass raised her eyebrows. "What does that mean?"

"Let's just say a fella left it behind. When I get back to Colorado, I'm gonna find him. Then we're gonna have a little talk. Because he's made my life complicated."

Merk said, "The National Air and Space Museum would like to talk to him, too. Frank, to an aeronautical historian the story of an aircraft, that nobody knew existed, is like buried treasure. And the trail that leads to *this* treasure starts where you acquired this case. Therefore, I have a modest proposal. Let Cass tag along with you to Colorado."

Cass let her jaw drop. "Excuse me?"

Frank said, "Never found much use for traveling companions."

Merken sat back. "Oh. Then you won't do it?"

Cass laid her palm on her boss's shoulder. "Wait for it."

"Never said I didn't *like* traveling companions. Just said I never found much use for 'em."

"Oh. Then Cass can accompany you?" Merk pulled his phone from his shirt's front pocket. "Have you booked a return flight?"

"Nope."

Merk worked his phone with both thumbs. "I'll check with travel, and see what flights have availability. Your ticket—both your tickets—will be on us, of course."

"That won't work."

"Oh, most certainly it will. All museum budgets are tight.

But I do have discretion to fund something like this. It's the least we can do for you."

"They won't let me check my Ford."

"Oh. I didn't realize—"

Cass bent toward Merken. "May I have a private word with you, Dr. Merken?"

Before Merk could answer, she wheeled his chair behind the Sikorsky.

She stood in front of him and spread her palms. "Merk? What the hell?"

"You're a promising historian. The analytical and archival skills displayed in your doctoral thesis are outstanding. But I hired you over equally qualified candidates because you expressed enthusiasm for field work. A *complete* historian does more than surf the internet and oversee static restorations."

"Exactly! You think I like counting termite burrows in a fuselage? Since I took this job, I've spent the price of three vacations and most of my spare time getting my private rotorcraft license."

"A recreational display of enthusiasm for helicopters is great. But it doesn't advance knowledge of twentieth-century aviation history. Which is your job."

"Well...Hanna Reitsch was the world's first real helicopter pilot."

"Reitsch may have been the German Amelia Earhart. But replicating one of her many skills doesn't address history's central question about her. She loved flying. She loved her homeland. But she flew for the Nazis, enthusiastically. Was she a naive patriot? Or did her loves cloud her judgment about their misdeeds?"

Cass rolled her eyes at her boss. "You're asking *me*? I've read all the source materials about Reitsch, and they're ambiguous."

"Exactly. If Reitsch is your passion, go beyond the written material and resolve the ambiguity. So history can guide the decisions of others who in the future face dilemmas like hers. Or pick *any* unsolved aviation mystery. Then get out there and solve it with field research!"

"'Field research' is swimming with sharks, to explore a lost B-24, a hundred fifty feet down in the Mediterranean. Like you did. 'Field research' is tomb raiding. *This* is a ride-along with Clint Eastwood's more annoying cousin."

Merken puffed out a breath. "You're overreacting."

"No, you are. That map case, and that photo, have survived for seventy years. They won't disappear tomorrow. There's no hurry."

"I'm sure the people who left the Horten prototype in a shed full of termites for half a century also thought there was no hurry." Merken frowned. "I'd prefer not to let Frank and his map case out of my sight." Merken spread his arms as he looked down at his legs. "But I don't have that option anymore."

Cass rolled her eyes. "You're guilting me? That's the best you got?"

"I'm not guilting you. I'm challenging you. You marshal and analyze internet and archival material better than any historian I've ever encountered. But unless a historian digs deeper than that, history may not tell the truth."

He rubbed his fingers across the old map case. "Cass, the urgency about preserving World War II history isn't loss of *things*. It's loss of the flesh-and-blood people who can tell those things' stories. Stories that teach us about individual human choices, made for better and for worse. In totality, those comprise history."

"Obviously."

"Cass, what's obvious is that the stories of World War II, that haven't already been told, may die tomorrow. Gone to the grave, with the people who lived them. It's an actuarial certainty that any of those stories left untold *will* die, before you turn thirty-five." He rotated the case in his hands. "When I touch a fuselage, or an object like this, I delude myself that I can feel the untold stories, and the choices. And I feel the stories in this case slipping away."

Cass heard knuckles rap hollow aluminum, turned, and saw Frank Luck standing alongside the Sikorsky flying boat.

Luck said, "Not my business, but I don't have to touch that steel briefcase to know something about the story that's inside it."

Cass said, "Oh, really? And will you share your insight, Frank?"

"The people in any story with Nazis in it got pushed into some choices for the worse."

Fourteen

AUGUST 1, 1935 WASN'T THE FIRST SUMMER DAY ON WHICH RACHEL
Bergman Winter had arrived at Munich Central Station. Much
about the platform was the same.

The sultry air smelled of coal smoke, and grease, and sweat.
The humidity wilted her hair under her broad-brimmed straw
hat, and made her dress, thin cotton that she wore with no slip,
cling to her damp thighs.

The hissing train alongside which she walked, that had carried her today from Leipzig, was as ordinary, and as grimy, as
a thousand other trains.

But, in the two years since she and Peter married, and the
Nazis had taken power, more had changed than was the same.

Her last name was Winter, now, and she clung not to her
father's hand, but to Peter's arm. They fought toward the terminal,
against an outrushing tide of tan and crimson.

Hitler Youth bands of beaming pre-teenaged boys snaked toward
their trains, outbound to countryside camping trip destinations.

Elbowing and teasing one another as they walked, they wore
identical billed caps, tan, flap-pocketed shirts, with crimson arm-
bands printed with swastika roundels, and black short pants and ker-
chiefs. Each boy carried a bedroll, and wore a dagger in a belt sheath.

The newspapers reported that, in the two years since the Nazis
came to power, Hitler Youth enrollment had grown to two million.

Rachel batted her eyes and said to Peter, "Darling, when I get
in the family way, how should we decorate the nursery? Hand
grenades if it's a girl, and a machine gun if it's a boy?"

"I know. But speaking as a former eleven-year-old boy, if someone offered me a uniform with a real dagger, and a holiday in the woods with my friends, I would have signed up in a minute. Because it sounded a great adventure. Not because I ached to pledge my allegiance 'til death to some grown-up."

"That's the point, isn't it? Condition them before they're old enough to know the difference?"

"Well, there is a competing view out there. When I was an eleven-year-old in Germany, during the postwar, too many boys spent their days stealing their family's daily bread, because otherwise there was none. Some people compare this and see wholesome outdoor camaraderie, and a welcome improvement over crime, poverty, and hopelessness. These boys *are* smiling."

"God, how can you stand being objective? It's so limiting. Is there anything in the universe to which you see no good side opposite the bad?"

"You. Every moment of every day I see how unambiguously lucky I am to wake up beside you."

Rachel rolled her eyes. "You are so full of crap." She hugged his arm tighter. "But never change."

At the platform's end she spotted her brother, Jacob, waving his flat cap at them as he ran to them.

She hugged him, then held him at arm's length. His face was pale beneath stubble, and bags bulged beneath his eyes.

She said, "We came as soon as we got Max's mysterious telegram. Is it Father?"

As Jacob led them through the station, he said over his shoulder, "No. Father's no worse. Perhaps a bit more confused, more of the time. As I wrote, he lives down at the country house all the time now. Traudl and Rudolph look after him, when I can't. Max runs the business here in Munich. As much as any Jew can still run a business in Germany these days."

"Then what is it? Don't you say dare 'nothing.' Because, Jacob, I know you. And you look like the very devil. Is it your engagement? Have you and Lisl had a falling-out?"

They reached Uncle Max's gray Duesenberg, and as Jacob and Peter loaded the bags in the car's trunk, Jacob frowned. "Not here. You'll understand it all when we get to Max's place."

✧   ✧   ✧

Max Bergman's flat was a balconied twelve-room, on the top floor of a four-story in Prince Regents Square, in Bogenhausen. Buildings in the area had become posher addresses after 1929, when the minor celebrity Adolf Hitler took a flat there.

Max's building's main doors were propped open, while workmen loaded crates and furniture into a van parked at the curb.

In the lobby, the movers had commandeered the lift, and Jacob led them up the stairs to the top floor.

At his flat's open front door Max Bergman stood, wearing a smoking jacket, with an unlit cigar in his mouth.

He hugged Rachel with one arm, and Peter with the other, as he led them and Jacob into his vestibule.

The apartment echoed, nearly bare.

Alongside flat wooden crates stacked on end, Max's beloved chrome and leather Bauhaus chairs stood in the center of the main room, beneath the chandelier.

Rachel said, "Uncle Max, what's going on?"

"We're moving to Lisbon."

"We? You? Why? No!"

Jacob said, "I told him no, too."

Rachel said, "I don't understand."

Her brother said, "I'll go first. For starters, you were right. My engagement's off. Lisl's family tolerated her engagement to a Jew, because I was a lawyer. But now that Jews can't practice in the courts, her father finds my prospects unacceptable."

"Then her father is an asshole. You two should elope."

Jacob said, "Rachel, Lisl agrees with him."

"What? Then Lisl's an even bigger asshole. I always thought you were too good for that blonde bitch anyway."

Jacob said, "Rachel, Lisl's your friend. You said she was nice."

"She was. Until she hurt my brother." Rachel paused. "But Jacob, how will moving to Portugal help you?"

"It won't. I'm not. I'm moving north, to Wetzlar. I'm taking a job as a janitor. Jews are still allowed to do that."

Rachel spread her palms, and her mouth hung open. "A *janitor*? For God's sake, Jacob! Why?"

"It's janitor's pay, but that's not the real job."

"I don't understand."

"It's with Leica."

"The expensive-camera company?"

Max shrugged. "If you're going to sweep floors, you might as well sweep floors for the best."

Jacob ignored his uncle and nodded at Rachel. "The Leitz family are gentiles. But, since the Nazis took over, they've been helping Jews emigrate from Germany. They give Jews phony jobs at their Leica stores overseas. That gets them exit papers they couldn't get otherwise."

"But Jews can't take money out with them."

"Exactly. When they arrive abroad, Leica gives them a new camera from store inventory, so they can 'promote the brand.' In America, a Leica will make a big down payment on a new Ford automobile, or buy a used one, outright. It's not a fortune, but it's a fresh start."

"The Nazis allow that?"

Jacob shrugged. "If they do have an idea what's going on, they're turning a blind eye. Leicas are popular exports, and Germany needs the foreign exchange."

"And you?"

"Every time the Nazis tighten the screws, more Jews beg to get on board the Leica express train. The Leitz family still have a camera company to run, so they're swamped. I'll help prepare papers, make the process more efficient, and hide it better. It's the kind of work I'd be doing as a lawyer, anyway. And I'll be doing some actual good. Which is why I went into law in the first place."

Rachel rounded on her uncle, hands on hips. "You, of all people, didn't put this altruistic idea into his head, did you, Max?"

Max raised his palms. "No! I swear! I told him it's noble. But breaking the law these days is more dangerous. Especially if you're a Jew."

Max held Rachel at arm's length, then blinked, his eyes glistening. "Rachel, I also told him that his father would be proud of him."

Rachel nodded, as tears flooded her eyes. For once, she couldn't speak.

Jacob hugged her, and pecked her cheek. "It will be fine, Rachel. We'll all be fine. I'll write you every week."

Ten minutes later, Rachel had waved from Max's balcony until Jacob, valise in hand, disappeared around a street corner, bound for the next train to Wetzlar.

She was proud of the choice her brother had made. But terrified that, because of it, she would never see him again.

Max closed the door on the last mover, who carried out the last crate. It contained a Gauguin, of which Rachel was fond, that Max had always insisted he found on the sidewalk.

The big apartment was still, and empty, except for telephones on the floors, and the cords that connected them to its walls.

Rachel pointed at the bare walls, and shook her head. "Why? And why Lisbon? And why on Earth do you think Peter, and I, and Father, would go with you?"

"Because things are changing for the worse in Germany. The Nazis are planning to rubber-stamp a new package of laws. At their party meeting, during the Nuremberg rally next month."

"I suppose you know this a month and a half early because Goebbels dropped a copy of these laws on the sidewalk?"

"Something like that."

Peter said, "What kind of laws?"

Max lit his cigar, puffed it until it glowed, then shrugged. "The Aryanization of businesses will become even more confiscatory. What little equity and control of Bank Bergman I've been able to finagle for the last few years, by colluding with gentiles I know, will be gone. The emigration tax on Jews will also rise rapidly. In a couple of years, it will cost a Jew ninety percent of net worth to cross the border. If the Jew is allowed to cross at all. Anyone subverting the tax by transferring money out of Germany will be declared an 'Economic Saboteur.' And punished as severely as an actual saboteur."

Peter said, "But you can get out with your possessions now?"

Max nodded. "Until these laws become public knowledge, forgery and bribery, in facilitation of harmless smuggling, will remain as affordable as ever inside Germany. Outside Germany, well, I've had friends of friends among the Frogs, the Spics, and the Portugueses, for years. They're expecting me to cross their borders with a truck, which they will not search, and with my Duesy, and with my household. Into France, at Strasbourg. Then out of France and into Spain, at Irun, then into Portugal, at Vilar Formoso."

"What?"

"Actually, the Duesy will change hands as soon as we cross the border into Portugal. From there to Lisbon, you two, and my brother, will have to ride in the back of the truck, instead of in style in the Duesy."

"Again, I don't understand."

"There's an official in Portugal who likes fast cars. He will get the Duesy. We will get necessary documents, and protection, that will enable us all to live as legal expatriates in Portugal. The cost of living is reasonable, the climate is agreeable, and the country is rigorously neutral. Most of the local wine is drinkable, and the port is incomparable."

Max relit his cigar. "However, if Peter finds a position outside Portugal, I've made sure that your exit is part of the deal."

Rachel shook her head. "Max, Peter is a junior academic. We understand and plan to make our life without accumulating wealth. Peter's not Jewish. So he's not in danger of losing his job in Germany for that reason. For his career in physics, the best star to remain attached to is Werner Heisenberg."

Peter nodded. "It's all just as Rachel says, Max. Besides, your brother—my father-in-law—won't thrive in an unfamiliar setting."

Rachel laid her hand atop Peter's. "Max, we appreciate your concern. But we're staying in Germany. And so is Father."

Max shook his head. "You don't understand. The economic penalties in these Nuremburg laws are the least of it."

Rachel said, "What?"

"The racial purity measures will forbid German citizens, who are defined as Germans having no more than one-eighth Jewish blood, from marrying, or being married to, a Jew. Extramarital relations with a Jew are similarly forbidden. In other words, a single Jewish grandparent disqualifies a person from fornicating with a German who has less than one Jewish grandparent. Jews may not employ, in their households, German female citizens of child-bearing age. Which is defined as less than forty-five. Apparently, hanky-panky with the help endangers the empire."

Peter sat, openmouthed. "Every bit of that is utter nonsense. People won't take it seriously."

"They may not take the ideas seriously. But violation penalties include prison at hard labor. People will take *those* seriously."

Rachel clutched Peter's hand tighter, as she shook her head. "No. No, no, no, Max."

Max said, "If there are silver linings, the first is that old Jews not in the work force, or out in public, are barely noticed.

Neither is property they own. So my brother probably won't be much affected, for now.

"Also, to look good to the world for the Berlin Olympics, the racial purity laws won't be enforced until after the games close in August 1936. That's why the time to get out is now. When nobody cares a damn. Right now. With me."

Rachel said, "A German citizen could be married to another German citizen? Or sleep with one, outside of marriage?"

Max puffed his cigar. "Certainly. In the latter case, of course, the usual risks of jealous husbands, pregnancy, venereal disease, and eternal damnation would still apply. Not that I speak from personal experience."

Rachel walked to the windows and stood looking out across Max's balcony, and across her hometown's rooftops. And beyond, to the thin, distant line of the Bavarian Alps, where her father was. She rested her forehead on the windowpane as she crossed her arms and thought.

Finally, Rachel turned and said, "Then it's simple."

Thirty minutes later, Rachel and Peter sat cross-legged on the bare plank floor, beneath Max Bergman's crystal chandelier. Behind Max's closed bedroom doors, they heard his muffled voice, as he spoke on the telephone.

Peter said, "This Lisl Schroeder, Jacob's former fiancé? You and Lisl were friends?"

Rachel shrugged. "We shared a passion for American English literature. The English language is much broader than boring German. And the American flavor of English is earthier. Hemingway even *swears*, and his sexual overtones are quite steamy. But Lisl and I weren't that close."

"Well, remind me to never get on your bad side. 'Blonde bitch'?"

"Two hours ago, you told me I didn't *have* a bad side."

"Two hours ago, you didn't need one."

Max flung open his bedroom door, then walked to them. His cigar was gone, and he held pages of notes.

He said, "Rachel, I think you're mad to do this."

"You think Jacob's mad to stay, too. But if he can stay and try to make a difference, Peter and I can do no less."

Max asked, "And how will you make this difference?"

Rachel said, "I'll find a way. I always find a way."

Max sighed. "I never was able to talk sense into your father or your mother, either. The irony of this is that, except for your mother and Jacob, the Bergmans may have been the least reverent Jews in Bavaria. But these laws bite us just as hard as they bite any Rabbi."

Max eased himself to the floor alongside them, grunting, then eyed his notes as he spoke.

"Fortunately, no announcements of your wedding appeared in the society pages. Or much of anywhere else. So, the beauty of German bureaucracy is that, if it's not down on paper, it didn't happen. A gentleman who has access to the Leipzig public records will cause all records of your civil marriage to disappear, in return for a late-model Duesenberg."

Rachel said, "Max, we can't let you—"

Her uncle waved her silent. "By fortunate coincidence, I have a late-model Duesy I don't need, if you two and my brother aren't driving it to the Portuguese border. My Portuguese friend is happy to accept cash instead. He's also happy to accept *less* cash, because the three of you won't require papers. Since you insist on staying here."

Peter blinked. "Max, that is—"

Max raised his palm. "Nothing. The *least* I can do for family." He stared hard at Rachel. "One member of which will disappear. Rachel Bergman will be presumed to have snuck out of Germany with her crooked uncle. Are you genuinely prepared for that, Rachel? To give up your identity?"

"Max, it was my idea."

"Well, your idea will require a few adjustments. If you're willing to take advice from an expert in the field."

"Alright."

"My forger recommends that you re-emerge as a gentile, obviously. Preferably a foreign national, legally in Germany. The papers are less familiar to anyone examining them. And it's harder to cross-check them against birth records in another country. Also, going home to visit provides an excuse to leave Germany, if things get too hot."

Rachel sat up straight, and smiled. "Foreign? How about American? I speak English like a native."

Max shook his head. "You also speak German like a native.

That has to be explained. So, you will need to be French, from Alsace. It's on the Rhine, but Alsace has only been French since Versailles."

"Oh."

Max paused and shuffled pages. "He thinks you two should be unmarried. The civil marriage process would require close inspection of documents. And the scrutiny will become more intense once the new laws are in place. Besides, a new marriage creates a new story. That has to be kept straight."

Rachel swallowed.

Peter laid a hand on her calf. "I don't like the idea, either."

Rachel covered Peter's hand with hers. "It's fine. What made us married in the first place wasn't some stupid government paper. And the lack of one doesn't make us less married."

Still, she turned away and stared out the window.

She drew a breath, then turned back, dry-eyed, to Max and said, "So, what's next?"

"You'll need photographs. The forger will arrange that. Everything is paid for, and I've dealt with him before. Don't let him gouge you for more. Obviously, you should change your appearance before you have photos taken. With your nose and complexion, blonde hair would be enough to eliminate any presumption you're a Jew. And it would probably prevent an old acquaintance from recognizing you crossing a street."

Rachel turned to Peter and flicked her eyebrows. "Lucky you. You can sleep with a saucy French blonde, and your wife won't even mind."

Peter frowned. "Blonde hair may prevent you from being recognized from across the street. But if anyone who knows us in Leipzig sees us together, things would be awkward."

Rachel said, "I thought about that. With Jacob gone, Father needs to hear a familiar voice and see a familiar face, besides Traudl's and Rudolph's."

"What are you saying?"

"I'll move down to the country place. No one in the village there would remember the little Bergman girl, much less pay attention to old Mr. Bergman's new, blonde French-German nurse, when she does the marketing."

Peter frowned deeper. "Live apart?"

"Not for long. You said Arnold Sommerfeld took *emeritus*

status in April. Everyone has known for years that Werner succeeding Arnold in the Physics chair at the University of Munich was Werner's dream job. And Arnold's preference.

"It's only a matter of a few months before Werner takes over, and brings his assistant with him. You said plan to host Christmas this December, here in Bavaria. Remember?"

"I know." Peter crossed his arms and shook his head. "But Rachel, I can't live apart from you. Not even for four months."

"You can. When you're lonely, just imagine me in my French nurse's outfit."

Fifteen

AFTER CASS'S ARGUMENT WITH HOWARD MERKEN, SHE, HOWARD, and Frank Luck returned to the Horten 229 project's makeshift planning desk.

Merken said to Cass, "So you agree this object is genuine?"

She nodded.

Merk said to her, "What do you make of the aircraft in the photograph?"

"Well, the opening faired in to the wing's leading edge is a jet intake."

"Agreed. But the jet's embedded, not mounted in a nacelle, like a Messerschmitt 262 or an Arado Blitz. Or even like the intakes on the Ho 229. And the aircraft sits too tall to be any of them, anyway. It's not a fighter, like the 262 or the 229. Fighter pilots climb in on top. Behind Himmler's left shoulder you can see an open belly hatch. Planes with *crews* need belly hatches. But if that hatch leads up into the crew compartment, why is the hatch in the wing undersurface?"

Cass tapped a finger on her upper lip as she nodded. "Because it's an all-wing design."

Frank turned to Cass as he pointed at the Horten's fuselage on its stand. "All wing? Like this rust bucket?"

Merk nodded. "But a lot of the brown color isn't rust, Frank. The Horten 229 was mostly plywood."

Cass said, "Partly because that was the Horten brothers' material of choice for their gliders. The rivets visible in the photograph show *this* plane's skin was aluminum."

133

"Aluminum's better?"

Cass shrugged. "Not necessarily. By the late nineteen thirties most new designs *were* aluminum. But some up-to-date designs were still built from wood. Howard Hughes built the Hercules— the 'Spruce Goose' flying boat—out of wood. The British built thousands of a twin-prop, plywood, fighter-bomber called the Mosquito. The Mosquito was the fastest thing in the sky when it entered service. By the end of the war it had been adapted to do everything from treetop-level bombing to aerial photo reconnaissance."

Merk said, "Frank, the Mosquito and the Ho 229 were built from wood mostly because aluminum was *scarce*. Both sides allocated what aluminum they had to operational aircraft. Aluminum wouldn't have been squandered on a design mock-up."

Cass said, "That's important, because it tells us that the plane in the photo was no mock-up."

Merk said, "Which begs the question, if the Germans built a large, operations-ready all-wing jet, how did it vanish from history without a trace?"

Frank shrugged. "Seems to me history's just the version of things folks agree on later."

Cass rolled her eyes. "And all these years I thought it was *Napoleon* who said that."

"Well, that just proves my point, doesn't it?"

Sixteen

THREE HOURS AFTER CASS HAD LEFT THE UDVAR-HAZY ANNEX
as a passenger in Frank Luck's pickup truck, she squirmed against
a booth's orange vinyl upholstery in a twangy-music truck-stop
restaurant.

Cass had grown up in the Silicon Valley, and gotten her
degrees at Harvard. So she was now somewhere in the middle
of a landscape that she had only looked down on, literally and
figuratively, from thirty thousand feet.

Luck had fueled his truck, which was so old that its side
windows were lowered by hand cranks.

The waitress delivered their meals, on crockery plates, and
left the check.

Cass reached for it, but Luck the Cowboy was quicker on
the draw.

Cass said, "You heard Dr. Merken. This trip is on us."

Luck shook his head. "I don't take government money."

"You wouldn't be. The Smithsonian's funded by its substantial
endowment, and public donations."

"For thirty cents on the dollar. Congress appropriates you the
other seventy cents. After Congress steals them from folks like
me. So this trip is on me, either way."

"Well. *I'm* not the government. I'm the anti-government."

"Figured that when you ordered a banana and a bottle of
water. Instead of real food."

"That's ideological profiling."

"Then turn me in to the ideology police. Catch a bus back to

Loony Town. And charge your ticket to all those public donations."
Luck twisted in his seat, and the vinyl squeaked as he drew an
enormous folding knife from his jeans' right pocket.

He flicked the knife open, then sawed at a slab of pink ham,
and white fat, bigger than a tablet. Over the slab, the waitress
had poured a gray mix of refined wheat flour, and animal fat,
that was thicker than motor oil.

Cass said, "You carry your own knife?"

"Every day. Better to have and not want than want and not
have. Everybody carries a knife."

"No. And why?"

"Restaurants have tough meat and dull knives."

"That's disgusting."

"The knife?"

"The meat. I'm vegan."

Luck snorted. "Bunch of hippie crap." He pointed his knife at
Cass's truck-stop banana, which was shriveled, and more brown
than yellow. "Bon appétit."

Ten minutes later, the waitress cleared their empty plates
while Cass sat silent and sideways, with her back pressed into
the booth's corner and her feet up on the vinyl.

Luck cleaned his knife with a white handkerchief, pocketed
both, then said, "What kind of plane do you think it was, exactly?"

She straightened in the booth. "If what we see in that photograph *was* a real plane, it's the only kind of plane that Germany
didn't really have lots of. Long-range heavy bombers."

"Why didn't they have them?"

"The German Air Force was designed to support ground
forces. Through a short, fast-moving ground war—blitzkrieg. Not
for strategic bombing over long distances, and for long wars."

"So they didn't care?"

Cass shook her head. "Oh, they *wanted* a long-range bomber.
Goering, the head of the Luftwaffe, had been blustering about
a transatlantic plane, to shut up the Americans, since 1938. The
big German manufacturers made proposals to him. But the plane
in the photograph, what I see of it, most resembles a design by
the Horten Brothers."

"Horten. Like the plane I saw this morning?"

Cass nodded. "But the Hortens were a garage-band startup.

Not a real, live aircraft manufacturer. At some point they drew up a design for a plane, called the Ho XVIIIA. It was basically a bigger Horten 229 'flying wing.' But with six jet engines instead of two. It would have been bigger, wing tip to wing tip, than a B-29, like the *Enola Gay*. Roughly the dimensions of that modern B-2 stealth bomber you saw in that magazine illustration."

"If the Nazis overdid everything, why would it surprise you if they built it?"

"Because the 'Amerika Bomber' didn't make strategic sense. To put enough TNT-on-target to affect the war's outcome, the Nazis would have needed *thousands* of transatlantic bombers. Too many planes, too many miles, too much fuel that was needed elsewhere."

"What if it was like you said about the B-29 and the A-bomb?"

"A package deal? Sure, then it would make sense. But Frank, the Nazis never seriously even *tried* to build an A-bomb. That's historic fact."

"I thought Napoleon and I agreed that historic fact is a bunch of crap."

A day later, as she drove west with Frank across Missouri, Cass switched Merken's incoming call onto her phone's speaker.

Merk said, "I've sent you a lead in response to Frank's question, that you texted. About the Nazi German nuclear weapons program. When I updated the *Enola Gay* narrative two years ago, I consulted several people."

"Which one's my best source?"

"Best? Wilmot Hoffman, no contest. He won the Albert Einstein Medal, for a historical essay about politics and the expatriate physics community during World War II. But he retired three months ago."

"Retired from what?"

"I'm not precisely sure. Technically, he was on MIT's physics faculty. But he had an advisory connection to the federal government, regarding nuclear weapons policy. That role seems to have occupied most of his time. And that role was classified. I had to incorporate his input without attribution. The email address I've sent you is his personal address. But I don't think he'll respond if you use it."

"Why not?"

"The word is his 'retirement' wasn't entirely voluntary. He's been described as a pacifist. I think he finally stepped in something once too often. Based on my conversations with him, I think he got fed up with Washington, and Washington got fed up with him."

Frank said, "My kind of guy."

Cass said, "If Frank likes him, I don't. Who else have you got?"

"Hoffman's your best bet."

"Why?"

"Because his expertise is most on-point. And he retired in Vail, Colorado. Google Earth says Vail is fifteen miles as the crow flies from the address you gave me for Frank's house. It's harder to ignore a human being on the doorstep than to ignore an email."

"That's it?"

Merken said, "No, actually, it's not. Another thought clicked, after you mentioned the De Havilland Mosquito to Frank. Last year I was out at the Air Force Museum at Wright-Patterson, in Dayton, for a meeting. An elderly gentleman was standing in front of the Mosquito they have on display, staring up at it, misty-eyed. The way the old vets do. And he was wearing an Army Air Forces lapel pin. I introduced myself."

"Naturally. You're were recruiting a docent."

"I'm always recruiting docents. Especially docents who have World War II stories to tell. Those get scarcer every day."

"So, what did he say?"

"I got him to write out his contact info. He seemed interested in *one* plywood plane, so I invited him to visit the Annex, and offered to show him *another*, the Horten, up close and personal. He scurried away like I'd offered him hemlock."

"The old vets usually can't wait to tell their stories."

"Exactly. For me, a red flag went up immediately. But there wasn't much to do about it, then or since. Now, though, it's at least worth another contact. If I can find his info, I'll call him."

The next day, somewhere in the flat middle of America between the Missouri River and the Rockies, Cass switched off her headset music, and tried again to connect with Frank Luck.

She peered out across the empty prairies and said, "I see why you quit ranching. It must be lonely out here."

Frank shook his head. "You say lonely. I say peaceful."

"Then what made you quit?"

"The bank that held the mortgage."

"Oh. I'm sorry. Is insolvency common in ranching?"

"There's two kinds of ranches. The kind that go broke, and the kind where the wife works in town, to cover the losses."

"You weren't married, then?"

"Once. Didn't take."

Cass smiled. "She got tired of too many three-word answers?"

Frank shook his head again. "I got tired of too many questions. So I ran her off."

He drove for thirty seconds, then said, "You plan on yakkin' the whole way?"

Cass jogged in place in her motel room, watching on the room's muted flat screen as people in Washington argued among themselves. They argued about issues that people like Frank Luck, who she had left in the motel bar, thought were a bunch of hippie crap.

She punched up Merk on her phone, then spoke into her headset while she jogged.

"Cass?"

"Yeah."

"Where are you?"

"In a motel. Elevation eight thousand feet."

"Thin air. Does that help the triathlon training?"

"No bike. No pool. No vegan-friendly dining. The best workout I got was holding my breath through the Eisenhower Tunnel. At the moment, I'm jogging in place in my room."

"Oh. What more has Frank Luck told you?"

"That he doesn't believe in telling anyone much. Except for life lessons. Veganism is hippie crap. There are two kinds of ranches. A dull knife cuts no ham. Merk, this is cruel and unusual punishment."

"Be patient. Remember what I've told you. 'Historians track unicorns one hoofprint at a time—'"

She sighed. "—even if they step in something unpleasant along the way."

She had counted this road trip's sole collateral benefit to be a break from Merken's incessant life lessons. That should have cut her advice overload down to her mother's bi-weekly texts about the inexorable ticking of a single woman's biological clock.

Instead, the incoming life lesson bombardment now emanated from three sides, not two. After Merk hung up, Cass sprinted in place for sixty seconds, holding her breath.

Seventeen

THE MORNING AFTER MERKEN'S PEP TALK, CASS'S HEAD NODDED as the pickup's brakes squealed. Frank stopped his truck in front of a house.

The glass-and-stone one-story's lawn was wild grass and wild flowers, with a "SOLD" sign in its middle. The house nestled on a pine-shaded cul-de-sac on Vail's outskirts. Vail turned out to be an upscale, ersatz, alpine ski village, complete with gingerbread storefronts, flowered window boxes, vegan-friendly restaurants, and ski shops that in summer rented bicycles.

In the house's driveway an elderly woman, wearing jeans, shirt, and a visor over her short gray hair loaded a Tiffany-style lamp into an SUV's rear compartment.

Cass hand-cranked her window down, then called, "Excuse me. I'm looking for Dr. Wilmot Hoffman."

The woman turned, then walked to Frank's pickup, while she tugged off gardening gloves. "So am I."

"Oh."

The woman, her face tanned and lined, extended a thin hand. "Velma Hoffman. I'm his wife. Except on fishing days. Which turns out to be most of them. Wilmot and I are supposed to go antique-swapping this afternoon. Why do *you* want to find him?"

"I'm Dr. Cassidy Gooding. I work at the National Air and Space Museum, and I've come out from Washington. I have a couple of questions to ask Dr. Hoffman. I tried to call and text him."

Hoffman's wife shook her head. "He doesn't answer those when

141

he's fishing." She slid her phone from her jeans and tapped its screen. "But I track his location. So they can recover his body if he winds up face down in some creek." She nodded. "Got him. Give me your address and I'll text you his current coordinates."

Hoffman's wife turned back to her SUV as she said, "When you find him, tell him if he's not back by noon I'm starting an affair with the gardener."

Frank parked the pickup four hundred yards from Wilmot Hoffman's location, as shown on Cass's phone.

Their path led first up a roadside embankment, covered with sharp-cut granite cobbles that scuffed her low-cut trainers as her ankles twisted.

Ahead of her, Frank sprang easily from rock to rock, in leather-soled cowboy boots, with high-stacked leather heels.

Cass puffed. "How the hell do you walk in those ridiculous things?"

Luck smiled back at her. "Cowpoke usually says that to his gal, on a date."

"*His* 'gal'? Is possessive, judgmental, sexism central to cowboy culture?"

"Don't know. I know working cowgirls and working cowboys wear the same boots. The heels keep their feet in the stirrups. And they all deserve the same pay for the same work."

"Oh."

"You date much?"

"What?"

"You can't prove it by my life, but the right cowgirl, and the right cowboy, can make a good life together. Maybe a young gal like you ought to spend less time looking for airplanes, and more time looking for the right young fella. Before all the good ones get taken."

Cass stopped dead, hands on hips and panting.

He stopped, then turned and looked back at her. "Altitude gettin' to you?"

"Too many life lessons gettin' to me. My mother already texts me those twice a week."

Cass charged up the slope, and as she passed Frank said, "You plan on yakkin' the whole way?"

✧   ✧   ✧

Four minutes after Cass and Frank topped the road embankment, they wound through pines and ferns.

Cass touched Frank's forearm. "Hoffman's a Ph.D. with a lefty bias. My boss has corresponded with him before. All things considered, it's best if I do all the talking. Okay?"

"Never really cared to do the talking."

"Right. My mother claims that, too."

They emerged from the pines alongside a stream twenty yards wide, its water so crystalline that Cass could count the stones and pebbles that paved its bed. Ten yards out from the stream's grassy bank an elderly man stood knee-deep, while the stream's water surged and sparkled around his rubberized bib waders.

His face was shaded against the mountain sun by a broad-brimmed canvas hat, and dark clip-on sun lenses covered black-framed glasses. The glasses were so thick and heavy that they could have been goggles.

They watched Goggle Man draw back the fishing rod he held, which looked thinner than Cass's index finger. He whipped the rod repeatedly, so that the green line curled from the rod's tip in a translucent crescent, until it settled atop the rippling water and floated downstream.

Cass crept down the grassy bank, until it gave way to jumbled rocks. She stood next to a soft-sided cooler balanced there. Visoring her palm over her eyes, she called, "Dr. Hoffman?"

He watched his line float, while he tugged a loop of it with his left hand. "Who's asking?"

"Dr. Hoffman, I'm Dr. Cassidy Gooding. I'm Assistant Curator of Mid-twentieth-century Aircraft at the National Air and Space Museum. You assisted us, when the Museum updated the descriptive materials for the *Enola Gay* exhibit."

"What do you want *now*?"

"I have questions about nuclear weapons."

"All sane people have questions about nuclear weapons. If I wanted to keep answering them, I wouldn't be *here*."

"Dr. Hoffman, I came all the way from Washington to research this."

"And I came all the way from Washington to learn to fish. Please leave me to do so."

"Crap." Cass took off her shoes and socks, rolled her jeans to her knees, then waded out into water so cold that it burned.

By the time she stood alongside Wilmot Hoffman she couldn't feel her toes.

She said, "Dr. Hoffman, please!"

He turned and looked her up and down as she shivered. "You're scaring the fish."

"Don't matter."

Cass and Hoffman turned to Frank. He squatted on his haunches, squinting at the stream while chewing a grass stalk.

Hoffman called, "What?"

"I'll bet you all the beer in this cooler that you haven't had a strike all morning. And you won't have one if you stay here all day."

Hoffman said, "How the hell would you know?"

Frank pointed at a compartmented clear plastic box full of tiny feathers that rested in the grass alongside the cooler. "You're throwin' Green Drake soft hackles. Gore Creek Drake hatch ended last week. There's a reason you're the only fool standing in this creek today."

Hoffman turned to Cass, then jerked his thumb at Frank. "Is Wild Bill with you?"

Cass stared up at the sky and sighed. "Dr. Hoffman, meet Mr. Frank Luck. He doesn't care to do the talking. Until he does."

Hoffman flipped up his dark lenses while he stared through his goggle glasses at Frank. "Frank Luck? Frank Luck from Avon?"

"Most days."

Hoffman grinned, then reeled in his line as he slogged to the creek's bank, clambered up to Frank, then pumped his hand.

Arms spread for balance, Cass picked her way back to shore across the creek bed's slippery stones. "Frank? What the hell?"

Hoffman said to Frank, "I've been trying to reach you for days."

Cass asked, "Why the hell would you want to reach *him*?"

"Mr. Luck, here, is the most sought-after fly-fishing guide in Central Colorado."

Cass stared openmouthed at Frank. "You said you were a rancher."

"You asked me what my profession was. Fishing's not a profession. Fishing is a way of life."

"Oh. Of course."

Wilmot Hoffman turned to Cass, beaming. "Why didn't you say you were with Frank in the first place?"

✦　　✦　　✦

Ten minutes later the three of them sat on the creek's bank in the sun drinking canned beer from Hoffman's cooler.

Frank said, "Wilmot, they say you used to be a nuclear physicist."

"They say right."

"Any good?"

Cass sighed. "Jesus, Frank. Wilmot taught at MIT. He won the Albert Einstein Medal."

Frank said, "Einstein? Know much about Nazis?"

Cass redirected the conversation. "Frank, what the hell is a Drake Hatch?"

Frank said, "Trout eat mayflies. Green Drake are a species of mayfly. In the summer mayfly eggs hatch. Different species, different times, different places, at different elevations. They grow from nymphs, to emerging adults, to adults, in a day or so."

He paused and sipped. "If you fish the right spot, at the right time, with a fly that matches the right stage of development, the trout are so busy snappin' at all those mayflies that they don't notice the one that's got a hook in it. 'Til it's too late. If it's the *wrong* spot and the *wrong* time, you're just drinkin' beer in the woods."

Hoffman leaned back, feet up on a boulder. "What does this have to do with Nazis?"

Cass said, "Frank, here, came across an artifact, that a colleague and I believe dates from World War II. It suggests that near the end of World War II the Nazis had actually built a small number of airworthy, long-range, heavy-lift jet bombers."

Hoffman said, "I'm not surprised. The Nazis never met a weapons system they didn't like."

"Well, that's the thing. The conventional wisdom is that there was *one* weapons system that they didn't like. The one that would've benefitted from a small number of long-range, heavy-lift bombers. And their failure to pursue that system may have cost them the war."

Hoffman smiled, nodded. "Ah, yes. The misbegotten *Uranverein*."

Frank said, "What?"

Cass said, "Long story, Frank. In 1938, Germany took over a strip of Czechoslovakia along the south German border, called the Sudetenland. Britain and France let them get away with it."

Hoffman said, "Mines in the Sudetenland happened to be

one of the world's principal sources of an obscure element, called uranium.

"Also in 1938, Otto Hahn and Fritz Strassmann, chemists in Berlin, bombarded uranium with neutrons. Some of it devolved into barium. They eventually realized that what had happened was that the bombardment split neutrons off the uranium nuclei. When the neutrons split off, the energy that held them in the nucleus was released.

"That discovery—nuclear fission—was so significant that Hahn and Strassmann won the Nobel Prize for it."

Cass sipped her beer. "At that time, Germany had already won more Nobels in physics and chemistry than any other nation on Earth. Scientists agreed that Germany led the world of physics in every aspect."

Hoffman said, "So, it was also assumed that Germany was way ahead of the world in the race to build a uranium fission bomb."

"I thought the Nazis chased away all their geniuses."

Hoffman said, "Einstein was visiting the U.S. when Hitler became chancellor, then he stayed abroad. Plenty of high-profile physicists who were Jewish, or rejected the Fascists' mistreatment of their Jewish colleagues, also emigrated from Axis Europe to the U.S."

Hoffman shook his head. "But, in total, eighty-five percent of scientists in Germany working in the nuclear-related fields stayed in Germany. Team Germany had a very deep bench."

Cass said, "Including maybe the world's most visible theoretical physicist after Einstein, Werner Heisenberg."

Wilmot nodded. "Heisenberg was so visible that, even though the Nazis called him 'The White Jew,' and suspected his loyalties, they eventually put him in charge of a research effort called the *Uranverein*, the 'Uranium Club.'"

Frank said, "A *club*? To build an A-bomb?"

"The Allies certainly thought that was the Uranium Club's mission. They took great risks to destroy Germany's sources of 'heavy water.' The Allies feared it would be used to modulate a nuclear chain reaction. They also almost assassinated Heisenberg."

Cass said, "When the war ended, the Allies realized that the 'Uranium Club' hadn't asked for, or gotten, much government funding. The club had mostly screwed around, trying to build a nuclear reactor."

Hoffman said, "In 1942, Heisenberg reported to Albert Speer, who ran defense production, that an A-bomb was too remote and too expensive."

Frank narrowed his eyes. "Your boy Heisenberg slow-played the Nazis?"

Hoffman frowned. "Physicists like me would like to *believe* he did. That one of our number had the courage to deliberately sabotage the Nazi bomb."

Cass said, "But history disproves that."

Wilmot nodded. "After Germany surrendered, the British held Heisenberg, and some others from the club, under house arrest."

Cass said, "At an English country house, called Farm Hall. British intelligence bugged the shit out of the place, during the months that the war continued against Japan. In August 1945, when Heisenberg and the rest of them heard about Hiroshima, they were astounded."

Wilmot said, "The Farm Hall Transcripts showed that the Germans had simply made fundamental theoretical errors from the get-go. They had variously overestimated the weight of uranium 235 that a fission bomb would require, by an order of magnitude. They had missed the boat, completely, on the suitability of graphite to modulate a sustained chain reaction.

"At best, the Uranium Club just didn't try very hard to help the Nazis. At worst, they were incompetents, and cowards, dodging the draft and saving their jobs, without a thought for saving the world."

Hoffman tipped up the last of his beer. "So, however obviously your exotic airplane appears to have been an A-bomb delivery vehicle, history tells us Germany had no A-bomb to deliver."

"Unless," Frank squinted into the creek's swift-flowing depths, "the Nazis were using your boy Heisenberg, and his club, like fly fishermen use mayflies."

Eighteen

PETER WINTER PRESSED HIS TELEPHONE'S HANDSET TO HIS EAR while he cradled the dial unit in his other hand. He paced back and forth, tethered to his flat's wall by the phone cord, and waited for the operator to connect his long-distance call.

While he paced, he peered out his walk-up garret's single window, and rested his eyes on Leipzig's familiar rooftops. He had occupied the same flat as a graduate student.

On September 17, 1939, the view from his window seemed to be the only thing in his life, and in Germany, that had not been turned upside down since graduate school.

Two weeks before, on September 1, 1939, the German army had invaded Poland. It was merely Hitler's latest experiment in foreign brinksmanship.

In 1936, Hitler had kicked the French out of the Rhineland. He had also "encouraged" German "volunteers" to aid his fellow Fascists in Spain's civil war. His "volunteers," the Condor Legion, did this by slaughtering civilians with sleek, new bombing airplanes. Airplanes that, according to the Versailles Treaty, Germany was forbidden to have built.

In 1938 Hitler merged Austria into Germany by holding a figurative pistol to Austria's head. Then he annexed the Czechoslovakian Sudetenland, by holding the same pistol to the heads of France and Great Britain.

But Hitler's Polish invasion had finally drawn declarations of war from the guarantors of Polish sovereignty, France and Great

Britain. Today, reports said the Russians had also attacked the prostrate Poles, from the east.

Already, it seemed like the Great War had been merely the first act of a baroque mourning play, interrupted only until the war's adversaries could blunder into the second act.

But, within Germany the play raced ahead without intermission. By 1936 the Nazis had tripled government investment. High speed automobile roadways had progressed, overnight, from bureaucratic fantasies to reality. Germany had not only won the Berlin Olympics' medal count, it had staged the games, and broadcast living pictures of them through the air by a revolutionary process called television. Ranks of men, shouldering gleaming new shovels, marched off to public works projects, all over Germany. Unemployment was down by two-thirds.

Citizens delighted by prosperity tolerated cartoonish laws that required them to greet one another on the street by saluting. Not even by simply saluting the Fatherland, but by hailing Hitler, himself.

However, for Peter the Nurembergs, and the other laws that cascaded before and after them, had been no delight. Germany's New Order had drowned his marriage, disqualified his brother-in-law from practicing law, and delivered the bank that Peter's father-in-law had built to a figurehead, "Aryan," manager.

Peter's Jewish colleagues across Germany were excluded from teaching positions. Heisenberg, himself, had been attacked in the Nazi newspapers. Werner had been accused not only of practicing the black art of theoretical physics, but of Jewish sympathies.

By the time the government cleared Heisenberg, Arnold Sommerfeld's Physics chair at the University of Munich, to which Werner had long been heir apparent, had passed instead to a lesser physicist.

As Heisenberg's career languished, so had his assistant's. In a field where the immortals made their names before they turned twenty-seven, Peter Winter remained anonymous at thirty-one.

Bad as times were for Peter, and for those close to him, they were far worse for other Jews, for gypsies, and for homosexuals. Since 1933, countless numbers of all those groups had silently disappeared into the prison that the Nazis built outside Munich at Dachau, which the Nazis euphemistically called a "camp." And by now members of those groups who remained at liberty were quietly disappearing to who-knew-where-else.

The operator's voice in Peter's ear said, "Dr. Winter, I will connect your call now."

With blonde Rachel achingly distant, hiding in plain sight in the Alps, the greatest change in Peter's living arrangements as a working physicist was his splurge on a private line telephone.

Although, in today's Germany, privacy could never be assumed. A telephone operator, a fearful or vengeful neighbor on a party line, to say nothing of a listening policeman, combined with a disloyal remark, could undo the lives of speaker and listener.

He listened for a click, a pause, anything that might betray an eavesdropper, but heard nothing.

"Peter!"

His heart skipped at the sound of Rachel's voice.

She said, "I miss you desperately."

"Yes. Miss Rachel, it's good to hear you as well."

She sighed, an eye roll in her voice. "You're being ridiculous. But all *right*. To what does our household owe the pleasure of your call, Dr. Winter?"

"Would you please advise Mr. Bergman that I will be arriving in Munich, on the late train from Leipzig?"

She squealed so loudly that he held the phone away from his ear until she stopped.

Then he said, "I would appreciate the opportunity to stop by and discuss the status of my prior accounts at the bank."

She said, "What happened?"

"Werner got called to a meeting in Berlin. So, I have a couple of days."

"Mr. Bergman is no longer actively involved at the bank. But he will be pleased to receive you at his country house. You'll stay here, of course, Doctor. Mr. Bergman will insist."

"If it won't inconvenience the household."

"Not at all. It will be my pleasure to make up your room personally. And so frequently that you won't sleep much. Rudolph will collect you at the station in Munich tonight. He'll be the one who scratches the crack in his ass with his right hand before he raises it and hails Hitler."

Peter squeezed the handset, said nothing.

She said. "All *right*. I get the message. But I can't wait."

Peter had set his packed case down, to slip on his coat, when knuckles rapped the flat's door.

He opened the door, and the taller of the two men who stood in the hallway said, "Dr. Peter Winter?"

It seemed to Peter that he felt blood freeze in his veins.

The pair wore black leather slouch hats, and overlong trench coats, with cloisonné swastika badges pinned in the lapels. It should have been ridiculous that an organization called the "*Secret State Police*" wore a non-uniform that every German had learned to spot—and to fear—from a city block away.

"Yes. I'm Peter Winter."

"Please come with us."

Rachel. If they hadn't already picked her up, he had to warn her.

Peter had never come close to a run-in with the law in his life, so he didn't know what police arrest procedures had been before the Nazis. But everybody in Germany knew that today police arrest procedures were whatever the police wanted them to be.

He pointed at his bag. "I was just leaving. On a business trip. May I phone and let them know I've been delayed?"

"I'm afraid that won't be possible, Doctor. But perhaps you should bring your bag."

"How long should I expect to be gone?"

"That's not up to us."

Peter sat in the middle of the closed, black Horch's rear seat, squeezed so close between the two secret policemen that he smelled the tobacco on them. The big car sped west from Leipzig, faster than he could think. He could beg a piss break, make a run for it. But then what? A fullback could always outrun a policeman, but could never outrun a bullet.

The Horch approached the road's intersection with the new, unlimited-speed highway that stretched north to Berlin. The car slowed, and a cold knot formed in his stomach.

The secret police interrogated suspects in the basement of its headquarters in Berlin. The mere address "8 Prince Albert Street" now terrified sane people.

Shortly after Max Bergman had relocated to Lisbon, without Peter, Rachel, and her father, denunciations of Werner Heisenberg had started in the Nazi press. He had been called a "White Jew," by his old adversary, Stark. Stark's charges were as much that Werner was a theoretical physicist as that he defended the abilities of his Jewish colleagues.

The flap had derailed Werner's ascension to Sommerfeld's Physics chair in Munich, and so had kept Heisenberg and Peter in Leipzig. And had kept Peter and Rachel apart.

Worse for Werner, the flap had triggered a secret-police interrogation in Berlin, in the dreaded catacombs beneath 8 Prince Albert Street. Werner said the experience still gave him nightmares, and probably would for the rest of his life. Only the intercession of Heinrich Himmler, the *Reichsführer* of the SS, had cleared Heisenberg. Werner said it was because Werner's mother knew Himmler's mother.

The Horch passed by the highway's northbound entry ramp. Instead, it turned at the southbound ramp, then sped along the deserted, undulating white concrete ribbon.

Peter swallowed. "We're not going to Berlin?"

The policeman on Peter's left shook his head. "No."

Perhaps Peter should have felt relief. But, he was sure, the Nazis had created additional circles of hell in other places.

The Horch entered Munich at dusk, rolled to a stop at the curb. The policeman, against whom Peter had been pressed for the last four hundred kilometers, sprang from the door then held it for him.

Munich.

In that instant it struck him, and a cold pit swelled in his gut. Munich was a common point between Leipzig and the Bergman's country home in the Bavarian Alps. The secret police had brought him here, rather than to Berlin, so he and Rachel could be held in separated cells, but interrogated in tandem. Their stories could be checked one against the other. And threats against one could be used to coerce statements from the other.

If the police didn't already know Rachel was hiding her identity, as a Jewess of child-bearing age, they would discover it soon enough.

What had they been thinking? They could have left Germany

in 1933. Or certainly with Max in 1935. Now they would pay the price for noble indecision.

He stepped out, then stared up at the three-story brownstone building, topped with a scarlet Nazi flag that hung limp on its standard in the evening calm.

Berlin had been Germany's capital since it became a nation in 1871, and Berlin remained the capital of the Nazi's constantly swelling "Third Empire." But the Brown House in Munich, the party offices, remained the National Socialists' philosophical temple.

Hitler's first appearance at a Nazi Party meeting had taken place upstairs in the same Munich beer hall where Peter had first laid eyes on Rachel. In the square to Peter's left, the Nazis had erected a columned mausoleum, the Honor Temple. The temple housed the tombs of the sixteen Nazis shot down in Munich's streets during the Beer Hall Putsch in 1923. In one tomb lay the uncle whom Peter had barely known.

As Peter watched, pedestrians, and even bicyclists, passing by the tomb on the street, raised their right arms in the Nazi salute. Not from emotion, but because the Nazis had made saluting the law. Jut-jawed, helmeted guards atop the temple steps disciplined any disobedient passersby.

Peter had never been inside the Brown House, but the Nazis had obviously been as industrious and self-congratulatory within it as elsewhere. A high-ceilinged vestibule gave way to hushed corridors. Red swastika banners hung on every wall that wasn't decorated with a newly minted hero's bust mounted on a pedestal. It was a bizarre site for interrogations. But the Nazis had made the bizarre commonplace.

A frowning sergeant, in SS black, strutted to the policemen and dismissed them both, while Peter stood silent. The three Nazis traded hails of Hitler.

The SS man led Peter down the corridor.

"Your journey was long, Doctor?"

"Shorter on the new motorway, but yes."

"Perhaps your fatigue kept you from raising your right arm, just now?"

"Ah. Yes."

They stopped at tall, closed, lacquered double doors. The SS man paused before knocking. "I suggest that you overcome your fatigue when you greet the *Reichsführer*. He has just returned from the front lines in Poland for this meeting. He carries the weight of the war on his shoulders and is, I am sure, wearier than you are. And so perhaps less tolerant of fatigue in the right arms of others. Do you take my meaning, Doctor?"

"I do. Thank you."

Peter felt hair rise on the back of his neck. *Reichsführer?* Heinrich Himmler, *Reichsführer* of the SS, had built Hitler's small personal bodyguard detachment into a racially elite private army. The SS now numbered in the hundreds of thousands, and grew daily. Himmler additionally commanded all the conventional cops in Germany. He had also finessed command of the Secret State Police, like the pair of gangsters who had brought Peter to this place, from their creator, who was Himmler's rival, Goering.

Himmler was the second most powerful man in Germany, able not only to make a person disappear on a whim, but also to spare a person with a pen stroke, as he had spared Werner Heisenberg.

Peter doubted that Himmler, if he indeed waited behind these doors, either supervised or conducted interrogations about telephone indiscretions, or about failure to salute.

Peter should have felt relief. But instead his dry mouth went drier. His life, and Rachel's, hung on every word he was about to speak.

Nineteen

THE SS SERGEANT KNOCKED, THEN PUSHED OPEN THE DOUBLE doors.

The drapes were drawn across the windows of the office beyond. Dimly lit by a crystal chandelier suspended from the high ceiling, a web of shadows crisscrossed the room.

The man behind the desk beneath the chandelier wore a German army officer's gray-green uniform jacket, oak wreaths on its lapels, over a white shirt and black tie, rather than the SS doorkeeper's intimidating black.

Himmler stood, strode around his dark, massive desk, and smiled as he extended his right arm. "Hail Hitler!"

The round, black glasses and weak-chinned face below a receding hairline had become inescapable in the newspapers and newsreels.

Peter raised a numb arm. "Hail Hitler."

Himmler, a head shorter than his visitor, clapped Peter on both shoulders, pushed him to arm's length, and looked him up and down.

"Your appearance is just as I imagined, Dr. Winter. I feel the strength, and the purity, of your uncle's blood flowing through you. Have you visited his shrine today?"

"I was brought straight from my flat in Leipzig to you, *Reichsführer.*"

Himmler nodded. "Of course. You must be tired. I have come all the way back from Poland, myself." He waved his palm at his desk chairs. "Shall we both sit?"

The second most powerful man in Germany crossed one leg over the other and laced his fingers across his knee. "Forgive me for coming rather straight to the point. But later tonight I must return to the business of bringing order to half of Poland." Himmler smiled.

Peter suppressed his shudder as he wondered exactly how the head of the SS was bringing order to Poland.

Himmler said, "You are Werner Heisenberg's assistant?"

"I am."

My God! It was about Werner! It had seemed too good to be true that Himmler had cleared Werner because their mothers were chums. Rachel might survive. Peter stifled a shriek of relief.

Himmler said, "But, I am told, you are every bit Heisenberg's intellectual equal."

Peter shook his head. "I am no Werner Heisenberg, *Reichsführer.*"

Himmler smiled again as he removed his glasses, breathed on the lenses, then polished them with his handkerchief. "And that is precisely the point. You're aware of the purpose of Heisenberg's current visit to Berlin?"

Peter nodded. "I believe he's being asked to join a study group, investigating the utility of the radioactive metallic element uranium. Late last year, Hahn and Strassmann in Berlin recognized that the nucleus of the uranium atom can be made to burst when struck by free neutrons. Neutrons freed, in turn, may strike and burst nearby nuclei. Each time the nuclear bonds break, energy is released. Energy can be useful, of course."

"Useful? I'm told it may be possible to create from this metal a weapon. A weapon of supernatural power. An explosive so potent that a single, simple munition could level a city. True?"

Himmler, they said, was fascinated with Germany's supernatural predestiny. In Westphalia he was renovating a castle at Wewelsburg as an Aryan Camelot, and he was sending expeditions all over the world in search of artifacts that linked the Germans to the gods.

None of which changed physics.

Peter said, "Is such an explosive possible? In my opinion, yes. Simple? No. I believe anyone knowledgeable about the physical sciences would conclude that Professor Heisenberg and his colleagues are as fine a team as any in the world to attack such a complex problem."

"And again, that is precisely the point the *Reichsführer* just made."

Peter stiffened and looked around. The voice that purred from the office's shadows was not Himmler's.

Himmler smiled at his little joke as he opened his palm toward the figure who had sat silent and unnoticed in a side chair. "Dr. Winter, may I present Admiral Wilhelm Canaris?"

Canaris stood, silently dragged his chair into the light alongside Peter and Himmler, then sat. It struck Peter that Canaris used his right hand, which finessed the otherwise obligatory Nazi salute. It was very much the entrance to be expected of Canaris, the peculiar enigma who headed German military intelligence.

Under Canaris' command since 1933, German military intelligence had, people said, expanded a thousandfold. Under his guidance it had, before the Austrian reunification, frightened Austrians into believing a nonexistent German invasion force lurked on their borders. Earlier in 1939 it had lured the British to commit an army to defend a nonexistent "imminent" invasion of the Netherlands.

Tall, with side-cut gray hair, icy eyes that seemed to shift between blue and gray, and the wind-tanned face of the decorated U-boat commander he had been during the Great War, Canaris scarcely looked the swashbuckler tonight. He wore a dark, civilian double-breasted suit, and carried a felt hat. The better, Peter realized, to slip unnoticed into and out of the Brown House.

Canaris stroked his chin. "Dr. Winter, if you see this uranium weapon's possibility, do others? I mean others outside Germany?"

Himmler said, "Last year the Jewess, Meitner, Hahn's assistant at the Kaiser Wilhelm, stole the results of Hahn's research, snuck out of Germany with them, and sold them to Germany's enemies."

Peter pressed his lips together as he tried to discern whether Himmler was a hyperbolic liar, an imbecile, or merely misinformed.

In fact, Lise Meitner and Otto Hahn had jointly conducted the experiment, he the renowned chemist, she the brilliant, less-celebrated physicist. They sought to synthesize in the laboratory new, heavier-than-uranium, "Transuranium" elements by bombarding uranium with neutrons, in the hope that some would stick to the uranium nuclei.

After the Austrian unification, it became clear that Austrian-born Jews in Germany, like Meitner, would henceforth be treated as badly as native German Jews. So Lise had fled. When Lise entered the Netherlands, she was carrying Otto's mother's diamond ring, which he gave Lise to bribe the border guards.

After she escaped Germany their experiments bore unexpected fruit. Otto wrote to her about the serendipitous success, before it was officially published by him and Fritz Strassmann.

It was ridiculous for the Nazis first to exclude Jews from their lives' work, then complain when they went abroad to continue it.

Peter cleared his throat. "I believe the results were published openly by Professor Hahn and Dr. Strassmann a few months after Professor Meitner left Germany, *Reichsführer.*"

Canaris waved a hand. "The point is that scientists by nature, like children, share confidences without thought to consequences. And at the moment a number of prominent scientists in this suddenly relevant field have moved abroad. Not just Meitner. Fermi never returned to Italy from Stockholm after he received his Nobel. We understand Fermi is in America now. He and Heisenberg are great friends."

Peter nodded. "Dr. Heisenberg is great friends with Bohr, in Denmark. Also, with Sommerfeld, in England. Almost all of the small number of exceptional scientists who share Professor Heisenberg's gift, and his interests, are friends. Or at least acquainted."

Aha. They wanted to know whether Werner could be trusted. Or they wanted Peter to spy on his boss if Werner could *not* be trusted.

Peter shifted in his chair. "Professor Heisenberg is no traitor."

Himmler waved his hand. "He is also no Aryan. Or at least he is not Aryan enough to forge this sword. Peter, this uranium weapon was revealed first to the Fatherland because the gods know that we alone deserve to wield it. It can only be honed to its cutting edge by a champion through whose veins flows the blood of martyrs."

Himmler sat back in his chair and stared at Peter.

Peter wrinkled his forehead. "Yes?"

"It is evident to me that the gods have delivered us that champion. And that you are he."

Peter sat back in his own chair as though Himmler had slapped him across the face with a glove.

This was no interrogation. This was a job interview.

No, a job interview resulted in an offer, tendered for acceptance or rejection. No matter how bloviated by talk of swords and champions, Peter had just been drafted. There was no refusing.

Canaris said, "Let me explain the operation as the heart of which you will function. The *Reichsführer* believes, and so do I, that Professor Heisenberg and his Uranium Club will fail to create this weapon. They will fail because they are academic dreamers. Or they will fail because they are naive pacifists. Or they will fail because they are lazy, at best, and traitorous at worst. But they will fail."

Himmler leaned forward. "We will therefore allow them to fail. Meanwhile, you will head a separate project that will create this weapon."

Canaris said, "If the Uranium Club's lack of progress is communicated to our enemies and discourages them from contesting this race, so much the better. If information about our enemies' efforts flows back to us through the Uranium Club's perfidious contacts with their friends abroad, better still."

Peter said, "The Uranium Club will be unwitting actors in this?"

Canaris nodded. "The most convincing actors are those who don't believe they're acting."

"You're asking *me* to conceive and implement an enterprise that creates a uranium bomb? The ink is scarcely dry on my teaching outlines."

Himmler punched the air with his fist. "An enterprise with a true German at its head cannot fail. An enterprise without one cannot succeed. The world said Adolf Hitler lacked the experience and education to restore a fallen nation's greatness. The last six years have demonstrated the world's stupidity. Your success will demonstrate it again."

Peter said, "I see obstacles."

"Of course. The true champion sees the future, and the obstacles, that the weak do not. If great things were easy, the weak would do great things. Please, Dr. Winter, be frank about the obstacles you see," Himmler said.

"An enterprise as big as this could not be concealed. No matter how effective Admiral Canaris' misdirection proves to be."

Himmler smiled. "Ask the French and the British whether our air force and our battleships and our tank divisions have surprised them. I assure you they will be even more surprised by events soon to come. We have concealed great enterprises before. We will easily conceal this one."

"The labor and materiel requirements? I can't begin to imagine how Germany could afford them."

Himmler said, "Peter, our enemies may already be in a race with us, thanks to traitors like Meitner. Our lead may already be in jeopardy. What can't be imagined is that we may lose this race. You will tell me what you need. I will see that it is provided. The fuehrer fully supports me in this. Is that clear?"

"The limit—"

"For your planning purposes, assume the resources available to you have no limit. Our resources grow with each kilometer, and with each able-bodied laborer, by which the empire grows."

The gulf between where Peter had stood when he entered this room and where he now sat was wider than the gulf between the Earth and the Moon. He couldn't say no. But he needed time to decide what he could say. Or do.

He said, "What may I tell Professor Heisenberg?"

"You will have no further contact with him after you leave this office. He will be told that you have been enlisted elsewhere in the war effort."

Peter said, "This is quite a lot to absorb. May I think this through, then present a more detailed plan?"

Himmler smiled. "You've anticipated my first order. That's a sign in itself. Prepare a plan tonight. I will arrange office facilities and overnight accommodations here in the Brown House. My staff will deliver your plan to me."

Peter needed time. More than that he needed to escape this place, and warn Rachel.

He said, "As we discussed, I was brought directly here. Is it possible I visit my uncle alone, first? After that I'll walk, to clear my head, then find my own way, and have the plan delivered here tomorrow."

Himmler blinked back a tear, leaned across his desk, and patted Peter's shoulder. "Of course. I understand completely. The true champion often walks his path alone, and in darkness. But guided by the wisdom of his ancestors."

Himmler sat again, then removed a single typewritten sheet from an envelope that lay on the desk's blotter.

His eyes darted across the sheet's printed words, then he signed it, blotted his signature, and handed sheet and envelope to Peter. "However, even the true champion sometimes requires assistance. Should you require any before we confer again, this should help."

The letter, on the thick bond engraved stationary of the *Reichsführer* of the SS and over Himmler's signature, read:

> To whom it may concern,
>
> With friendly greetings, hail Hitler!
>
> The bearer of this instrument, Dr. Peter Winter, is engaged in work of the utmost importance to Germany's war effort.
>
> Render him any and all assistance without delay, and in strictest confidence.
>
> Any questions regarding this instruction should be directed to me, personally and immediately.
>
> Heinrich Himmler
> Reichsführer, SS

Himmler leaned back in his chair. "You're sure my driver can't drop you somewhere?"

"Quite sure, *Reichsführer*. I don't wish to impose further."

Himmler stood, clicked his heels and raised his arm, smiling. "Then, with my best wishes and great expectations, hail Hitler!"

He rang, and as the SS sergeant entered, then escorted Peter from the room, Peter realized that Canaris had disappeared.

The evening was cool and still as Peter walked free, away from the Brown House, and into the street. He wanted to dance to the tune of automobile horns' mundane hoots and distant streetcars' rumble.

Instead he carried his bag the meters across the pavement to the Honor Temple, as he had told Himmler he intended. He paused every few meters in the darkness and adjusted his bag or his clothing, turning and trying to spot any policeman who might be following.

On the face of it, he had just ascended to an elite plane. No policeman would dare follow a man to whom Himmler himself had just handed a blank check, and Himmler was said to be a manager who delegated authority to trusted subordinates. On the other hand, wasn't the man with the blank check exactly the man the Nazis would watch most closely?

Peter climbed the steps of the Honor Temple, between torches that the Nazis intended would burn for a thousand years. He made the obligatory salutes to the guards, then walked the rows of the sixteen dead Nazis until he found the ceremonial coffin of a man he had barely met.

He laid his palm on the coffin lid, knelt there on the stone, and wept.

The guards thought he wept in grief and remembrance. But in fact, he wept with relief at his freedom. And also in fear of what he had gotten himself—and Rachel—into.

Twenty

PETER STEPPED INTO THE FOYER OF THE BERGMAN'S COUNTRY house two hours after he had left the Honor Temple, and had walked to the railway station where Rudolph waited.

Rachel, dark eyes sparkling, and as lovely a blonde as she had been when brunette, leapt into his arms.

Her hair smelled of roses and lemons and he clung to her until she said, "Rudolph, would you put Dr. Winter's bag in my bedroom? And set out a bottle of port, please. From the case of Fonseca Max sent yesterday, I think."

Rudolph made a small, silent bow, then withdrew.

Peter smiled. "Outside the Bergman house, we're at war. And you're an unmarried, Catholic, practical nurse from Alsace. In here, it's still 1929."

"Not entirely." She nodded at a cheap, framed print, depicting winged Valkyries on horseback, hung on the silk-papered far wall, where the Rubens had hung. "The gentleman whom Uncle Max uses to 'import' his port for us also was able to 'export' the Rubens to a safe-deposit vault in Lisbon. Before the Nazis thought up a reason to steal it. It won't be long before they steal this house itself."

"Why would they bother?"

"Hitler started renting a summer place over at the Obersalzberg when he was a nobody, back in the twenties. Now this whole area's crawling with Nazis. They built him that mansion that's in all the newsreels, the Berghof up on Eagle's Nest Mountain, for his fiftieth birthday. They're requisitioning land for everything.

Summer homes for bigwigs. Barracks for SS bodyguards. It's only a matter of time until some Nazi figures out this house is here, and that the name on the deed sounds Jewish."

Rachel sighed. "Also, Rudolph and Traudl just gave their notice. Their son-in-law enlisted, and was killed in Poland. Their daughter can't run the farm alone, so they're moving back north."

Peter frowned and shook his head. "God. To listen to Himmler, you wouldn't know we lost a single soldier."

"Himmler? Was he on the radio, tonight?"

Peter changed the subject. "How will you replace Rudolf and Traudl?"

"Since it's only me and father, there's not much to keeping the place up. All I'll miss is the company. And until you leave, I won't even miss that."

Peter stepped back, held Rachel at arm's length. Her dress was pink silk. Seeing and holding her, after the day's shocks, made him blink back tears.

She said, "You're early. I know the Nazis have made the trains run on time. Have they made them fly, too?"

"I didn't take the train."

She wrinkled her nose. "What does that mean?"

Peter put his arm around Rachel and walked her to the staircase. "We'll talk in the bedroom."

She nudged him with her hip as they climbed. "Eventually."

Two hours later, they sat on her bedroom's floor, nested in the bed's pillows and its duvet, in front of the fireplace, sipping port. Rachel's dress was a rumpled silk mound on the hearth, and the firelight softened the naked pink of her skin, as she stared into the flames with one arm wrapped around her knees.

She said, "We could make a run for it. The Rubens isn't the only asset Max has hidden abroad for the family. Plenty of the other academics that you know got out."

Peter shook his head. "Hans Bethe had already spent years abroad when he left in 1933. Edward Teller was Hungarian, which made it easier for him. And it was 1934. By 1938 Lise Meitner crossed the Dutch border by the skin of her teeth. Now we're at war. The borders are closed."

"Lise didn't have a blank check from Himmler in her pocket. No border guard in Germany would have the balls to stop us."

"Perhaps not. But the Swiss would throw us back like undersized trout."

"No. Uncle Max has plenty of unredeemed Bergman favors to cash in Zurich."

"Rachel, Edward's Hungarian. Lise is Austrian. We're Germans. We knew Germany's house was on fire when we came back here to fight it in 1933. Jacob knew it too, when he went to work at Leica, instead of running away to Portugal. Your father loves this country as much as anybody I know. His mental stability is tied more and more to this familiar place. He won't leave. You won't leave without him. And I won't leave without either of you. If I run away now, knowing what I know, we won't be safe anywhere. And don't discount reprisals. Jacob, your father, maybe even Werner—anyone we left behind—would be at risk."

She sat silent through his soliloquy, then blinked. "I know. Running was wishful thinking. It's not an option."

Rachel turned her glass, and the crystal's facets split the fire's light into slivers, like puzzle pieces. "But are they tricking you? Himmler gives carte blanche to some novice scientist he's never met? Who has no executive or military experience? Simply because your blood is pure?"

"I've just been face to face with Himmler. I believe he accepts the canon, bag and baggage. After all, he invented some of it. As for Canaris, he lives up to his public Machiavellian reputation. And why would either of them bother tricking me?"

She shrugged. "I don't know. But a magic bomb from the gods? It's such perfectly Nazi bullshit."

"The rhetoric is bullshit. The science is real, Rachel. Such a bomb can be built. In a world driven by war, it *will* be built. The question is by whom."

"Can't you just do what they're afraid Werner and the others will do? Smile and salute Hitler, while you crap it up? You're smarter than the Nazis are. They'd never know the difference. When I watch you and Werner talk physics at the chalkboard, it looks like hieroglyphics." She narrowed her eyes. "Peter, the person who invents this bomb will be as big as Werner. As big as *Einstein*. One of the most famous scientists in history. These last years, history has cheated you. Does part of you want to build this machine to catch up with your destiny?"

Peter frowned as he nodded. "I can't say I don't want to see whether it can be done. Whether *I* can do it. But Rachel, this bomb's creation will be one of the most inglorious events in human history. Its creator will also be one of the most reviled scientists in history. I'm not in it for glory."

"We're kicking the crap out of Poland. If the Nazis keep winning, then, glorious or inglorious, you can't be party to giving them this weapon."

"Practical utilization of uranium isn't even in its infancy, yet. It's barely embryonic. This project will go on for years. Possibly this war will, too. Like you said, I'm smarter than the Nazis are. As long as I'm running the project, I can always crap it up and slow it down." Peter frowned. "But in the meantime, I'll have to play it straight and do the best I know how. There's every reason to worry that Canaris has Werner's group looking over my shoulder as much as he's looking over theirs."

Rachel blinked back tears. "There's no way out. Anything we do will be wrong."

"Some ways are wronger than others. And the wrongest of all would be to do nothing. Or to run away, and cede the field to the Nazis."

She sat silent, then nodded. "Even if we die in the attempt. Yes. But it's so unfair." She found her robe, slipped it on, and knotted it at the waist. Then she paced, barefoot, in front of the fire. "God, what have we got ourselves into?"

"Rachel, aren't you the one who taught me not to worry about what we've got ourselves into? But to concentrate on finding a way out?" He slipped his trousers back on and tugged the suspenders up over his bare shoulders. Then he removed a writing tablet and pencils from his bag, laid them on the corner table that stood between two chairs, and switched on the floor lamp behind the table.

He stepped to the closet, returned with Rachel's suitcase, and laid it open on the bed.

Rachel stared as he returned to the table and sat, then said, "What are you doing?"

"Preparing the plan Himmler demanded by tomorrow. In the meantime, you pack that bag, and keep it packed. The instant Max can get you across into Switzerland, you go. Then you prepare the way for your father and Jacob to join you. We both know Max will salvage every penny for the family that he can. And as long as I'm using my blank check to build Himmler his bomb, nobody will question what favors I do for my former banker's family. When the situation with the bomb and the war clarify, one way or the other, I'll join you all."

Rachel stepped to the bed and slammed her suitcase shut. "No."

"What?"

"No. We said when we came back to Germany in 1933 that we were in this together."

"And we are. Well, we will be. Rachel, you're a *Jew*, living on forged papers. In an area that's crawling with Nazis, now. It's too dangerous for you. But not for me. I can handle this end."

She stood next to him, touched his cheek, then shook her head slowly. "Maybe you fooled Himmler tonight. But you'll never fool me." She pointed toward Switzerland. "If I cross that border, I'll never see you again."

Peter felt a lump form in his throat. He swallowed it away. "That's ridiculous. You have to go."

"Peter, no means no. Together means together. Besides, I'm a better liar than you are. And this is going to take a lot of lying."

"But—"

She raised her right hand and set her jaw. "Peter Winter, your bravery is admirable. Your protective instinct is noble. I will love you with all my heart until I die. But if you make me say 'no' one more time, I will slap you silly."

"Oh."

She pulled the empty chair alongside his, sat and picked up one of his pencils. "Now, then. I suppose the first thing one needs for a uranium bomb is uranium. What in hell is uranium?"

"Well. It's the heaviest element in nature. It's a metal. It emits radiation. Radiation is what makes watch dials glow in the dark, and lets doctors X-ray broken bones. But too much radiation will sicken and kill you.

"By dumb luck, Germany since 1938 happens to be sitting on literal mountains of uranium. It occurs in pitchblende. That's a kind of rock left over during silver mining. They've been digging pitchblende out of mines in the Sudetenland for centuries."

"It's that simple?"

Peter shook his head. "Hardly. We know some uranium nuclei can be split. But can the split-off neutrons in turn split successive nuclei? In a self-sustaining chain of reactions? *That* hasn't been proven by experiment."

"So, the first step will be to perform this experiment?"

Peter shrugged. "Yes, if I were an old-fashioned experimental physicist, like Lenard and Stark. Yes, if I were as cautious as Werner's age, and his brush with the Nazis, has made him. Yes, if I were a committee of competing intellects, like Werner's Uranium Club. Yes, if this were an academic exercise."

She cocked her head. "You're skipping the experiment?"

He smiled. "If the experimental result confirms the hypothesis, it will have been nothing but a time-consuming, expensive measurement. If we simply build a bomb that doesn't work, we've confirmed something different. I'm *not* an old-fashioned physicist. I'm *not* Werner's older, wiser self. I'm *not* a committee. And this *isn't* academics. It's a tightrope walk to save our lives and avoid helping the Nazis by seeming to help them."

Rachel sat back, frowning. "A tightrope walker has to be confident. Are you?"

"I'm confident about the physics. I don't know enough about the business of building things to know how I feel about the rest. Only a fraction of pitchblende is uranium. Less than one percent of uranium is, I think, going to be unstable enough to be bomb material. But both fractions are so similar that isolating the useful material will require some technique that hasn't even been invented yet."

"But assuming you invent one?"

"Assuming I invent one, whatever it is, thousands of metric tons of pitchblende will have to be processed. It will require a huge factory. Vast amounts of energy. Electricity would be the most practical energy. The labor force would be gigantic. All of that will be hard to hide. And harder to defend against attack if it's discovered."

Rachel drummed her fingers on her chair's arm, then tore a sheet off Peter's tablet and smoothed it out on the tabletop. "Let's say the edges of this sheet are the external borders of the union of Germany, Austria, and Czechoslovakia. The borders of our country, now. Yes?"

Peter nodded. "All right."

She drew an oval, just above the page's center, and within the oval wrote "Sudetenland—Pitchblende." To the left center of the page she drew another oval and wrote "Lake Walchen—Electric Power." Then she scribbled a dot in the page's center, connected the dot with lines to the electric power and pitchblende ovals, then wrote beneath the dot "Factory."

Peter tapped the dot. "Where is this?"

"Here."

Peter laughed as he pointed to the window. "Rachel, you can't build a secret factory from scratch in the middle of this wilderness. It would cost too much. It would take too long. So much work would be too visible."

She shook her own head. "Not in the *middle* of this wilderness. *Under* it. Your factory is already built. Peter, some of the salt mines around here have been expanding for five centuries. There are hundreds of kilometers of tunnels already dug. There are rooms bigger than cathedrals in them, already. To enlarge rooms the miners just pump in water, dissolve salt, and pump the water out."

Peter stared into space. "An invisible, pre-built, bombproof factory. As far on all sides from our enemies as can be. With ready access to raw materials, and with the hydroelectric plant at Lake Walchen only one hundred fifty kilometers away."

"And right in the middle of so many Nazis pouring concrete and hailing Hitler that no one will notice or breathe a word about the activity."

Peter shook his head slowly. "My God. It's brilliant. You're brilliant. I could kiss you."

"You could do more than that. A man in charge of such a project will need an appropriately grand place to live. I happen to know of a mansion that you can requisition before the other Nazis do. The resident nurse comes with the deal and the word is she's easy."

He said, "You're mad."

"No, the world is mad. I just adapt to it. Like you said, nobody will argue with a man who has a blank check from Himmler. Or make a pass at his live-in nurse." She raised her index finger. "One more thing."

"More? My God. Now what?"

"If the war turns bad, and our enemies arrive at the German borders," she pressed her extended index finger to her temple like a pistol, "it won't do any good to use this bomb like putting a gun to our head when we say, 'Stop! Or we'll shoot!'"

Peter nodded, made a note. "You're right. Himmler will expect some sort of delivery system. If this war turns bad for Germany, it will be because the Russians and the Americans come in, like they did in the Great War. A bomb on the east bank of the Rhine won't deter Roosevelt on the north bank of the Potomac. Or Stalin on the east bank of the Moskva. We won't need just a bomb. We'll also need an airplane capable of dropping it. As far away as the United States."

She stood again, stepped behind him and kneaded his taut shoulder muscles. "My darling, you have mountains of magic rock. You have as much electricity as there is lightning in the sky, a wizard's cave as big as you want, and a blank check from the most feared man in Europe. How are you going to use it all to save us, and Germany, from the Nazis? To say nothing of the British, and the Russians, and the Americans?"

He took her hand from his shoulder, clung tight to her fingers and kissed them as he stared into the dying fire. "I have no idea."

Twenty-one

SEATED IN THE SUNLIGHT, ON GORE CREEK'S BANK, CASS WATCHED Wilmot Hoffman dig through his cooler, then shake cold water off three more beers. He handed one to her, one to Frank, then sank back in the grass.

Wilmot said, "You know, Cass, Frank's hypothesis isn't crazy. It's really just vintage World War II espionage. Before D-Day the Allies faked an army for Patton, that was supposed to cross the channel at Calais. When they really invaded at Normandy, the Germans held back reserves for months waiting for Patton. A phony nuclear program headed by Heisenberg makes equal sense."

"No, Wilmot. Faking that army made sense. Because it hid a *real* invasion. Faking an A-bomb program wouldn't make sense. Because we *know* there was no real A-bomb program to hide."

Wilmot said, "You say that because you know the Manhattan Project was huge?"

"Exactly! The Manhattan Project cost the world's largest economy two billion dollars. Back when even *one* billion dollars was real money. Germany couldn't have fought the whole world, and simultaneously have matched the Manhattan Project."

"That's my point. Cass, to build a serviceable A-bomb, Germany didn't need to come close to matching the Manhattan Project."

"You're saying that, hypothetically, an economy as small as Germany's could have supported both the war we know about *and* a nuclear weapons program that we don't know about?"

"Not 'hypothetically.' India, Pakistan, South Africa, Israel,

173

and North Korea had shallower pockets than Nazi Germany did, relatively. Yet they all built nuclear weapons. On the cheap, and on the sly. If a nation wants to punch above its weight in a hurry, the blueprint's simple."

"Simple?"

"The simplest way is just—and it *is* a big just—get hold of a couple thousand tons of uranium ore. Then take away the fraction of the ore that's just rock. Remove the ninety-nine percent of the remaining uranium that's nonfissionable U-238. When what's left is a hundred forty pounds of uranium, enriched to eighty-percent or more fissionable U-235, you're in business."

"It can't be that simple."

Wilmot said, "It isn't. You need a pinch of polonium to get the party started, and a beryllium jacket to bounce back the neutrons. But the basic uranium fission bomb mechanism isn't much more than a ten-foot-long, one-shot cannon that weighs five tons. It could pass for a delivery truck transmission and drive shaft. Hypothetically.

"The cannon uses conventional artillery explosives that fire a uranium bullet into a uranium target. Just fast enough to bring the hundred forty pounds of eighty percent U-235 together to form a critical mass. At collision, a couple pounds of the critical mass is converted into energy. That's enough energy to incinerate central Washington, D.C. That's the Little Boy—the Hiroshima bomb.

"HEU—Highly Enriched Uranium—bombs are the first bombs some of those shoestring nuclear powers built. Because HEU bombs are relatively easy, and relatively cheap."

Cass asked, "Then what was the rest of the Manhattan Project?"

"The rest of it was redundant uranium enrichment facilities. Plus controlled chain reaction nuclear plants built to synthesize plutonium. It also consisted of the design and construction of the precision implosion mechanism that a plutonium bomb requires."

Frank said, "Then why did we waste our time on the rest of it?"

Wilmot said, "Mostly because we were scared the Nazis would beat us to it. We didn't know what would work. So we chose 'All of the Above.'

"A cynic would say we only tried them all because we had too many cooks in the kitchen. Physicists have egos, and most of the Manhattan Project's geniuses wanted to do it their way. A cynic would also say that the plutonium alternative promised a new mass-production nuclear industry, that would do for physicists what the Model T Ford had done for mechanical engineers."

Cass said, "And that industry, and those physicists, built enough bombs to eradicate civilized life on Earth. A thousand times over."

Wilmot said, "Don't misunderstand my position, Cass. However abominable post-atomic policy has been, stopping the Nazis was worth both the hypocrisy and the inefficiency."

Frank said, "How inefficient are we talking, Wilmot?"

"Ninety percent of the Manhattan Project's expenditures went for low-tech brick-and-mortar infrastructure. To create space within which to do science, and to house the people who would do it.

"The project didn't adapt existing industrial space near pre-existing labor pools. It built whole towns from scratch in remote locations, from Los Alamos, New Mexico, to Oak Ridge, Tennessee, to Hanford, Washington. The facilities were deliberately disconnected puzzle pieces, that not even the workers themselves could put together. All the Oak Ridge Calutron gals knew about the machines they operated was that if they got too close, the magnetism pulled the bobby pins out of their hair.

"At Oak Ridge, the project built the biggest building that had been built on Earth 'til then. But the K-25 building was built just to *demonstrate* gaseous diffusion uranium enrichment. It ended up having nothing to do with the bombs that ended the war. The graphite reactor at Oak Ridge, and *all* of the nuclear reactor complex in Hanford, Washington, were built only to produce plutonium."

Frank said, "It was all dead weight?"

Wilmot shook his head. "No. Like Cass said, the plutonium reactors were the template for the postwar nuclear industry. Modern nuclear arsenals are overwhelmingly plutonium-based. But the only effect plutonium had on the Hiroshima bomb was that plutonium turned out to be unworkable in a gun-design weapon.

"The Hiroshima bomb was simple compared to the plutonium implosion Nagasaki bomb. The Hiroshima bomb was designed and built by a team headed by a navy artillery captain. The Nagasaki plutonium implosion bomb was designed and built by a faculty of geniuses."

Cass frowned as she nodded. "We spent a lot just keeping the project secret in a free society. Secret-keeping was cheap in a nation that could hide the Holocaust until the war ended. So, Germany could have afforded a 'Manhattan Project Lite'? And kept it secret from the world during the war?"

"Exactly." Wilmot frowned back. "But at the end of the war the world sure as hell found out about the extermination camps. If this hypothetical project existed, how could it have vanished?"

Cass's phone rang, and she pressed it to her ear.

Merk said, "How goes the culture war with Frank Luck, today?"

"We're having a beer in the sunshine with Dr. Hoffman right now."

"Great. My news is less great. I did phone that veteran. The one who didn't want to hear about the Horten brothers. I explained what you were looking into."

"And?"

"He was still evasive."

"Well, can I go talk to *him*?"

"He's retired in Tampa. You stay on task for now. I told him where you were, and texted you his contact information. I suggested that if he changed his mind he contact you, or that he get in touch with you through Luck or Hoffman. What's new there?"

"I think it's more plausible than we thought that the plane existed."

"How so?"

"Because it's more plausible than *anybody* thought that the Germans actually did try to build an A-bomb."

"Wow. Well, what's next?"

While she talked, Frank tugged off his boots, rolled up his jeans, and waded back into the creek with Wilmot in tow. There Frank began adjusting Wilmot's elbows and knees and his grip on his fishing rod.

"Next? I watch a couple old men fish. Maybe for quite awhile."

Cass re-pocketed her phone while she watched Frank Luck, the failed cowboy who turned out to be the most sought-after fishing guide in central Colorado.

Apparently, cowboys didn't lie. They just didn't volunteer more truth than they had to. She wondered whether the whole truth about how Frank had come by the map case would turn out to be equally surprising.

Twenty-two

FIVE DAYS AFTER FRANK LUCK HAD, BY SKILL OR GOOD FORTUNE, eluded the Asp in Avon Colorado, the Asp peered out of the Expedition's side window, at the Mississippi River. It flowed underneath him as the big SUV crossed the interstate highway bridge at Baton Rouge, Louisiana.

Slow and brown as it bore North America's silt to the Gulf of Mexico, the Mississippi could have been the Nile, as it bore Africa's silt to the Mediterranean.

The SUV whumped across bridge expansion joints, its suspension compressed by the Asp's recent, weighty acquisitions. They had been dictated by his initial reconnaissance of Upper Pika Lake. Houston was a shorter drive, but shopping there again established a more discoverable pattern. The commercial vendor in Broussard, Louisiana, had found his purchases routine.

The Asp's next acquisition would most intentionally *not* be from a commercial vendor.

After the highway crossed the Mississippi, it angled south and east, roughly parallel to the meandering river's north bank. He exited the highway in the New Orleans suburb of Metairie, then turned off the broad, tree-canopied boulevard of Esplanade Avenue, into a residential neighborhood. The brick home in front of which he parked was as large as his family's home in Cairo had been. But this home was fronted by four white-painted columns, and shaded by gnarled deciduous trees, as well as by palms.

He stepped from the Expedition into warm air thick with humidity, and redolent of the river. The Mississippi flowed past

Metairie on the south. One hundred yards to the north, invisible beyond the trees, lapped Lake Pontchartrain.

He closed his eyes, inhaled, and was again a child at play with his brother on the lawns of the house in Zamalek. Like this neighborhood, Zamalek, on Gezira Island in the middle of the Nile, seemed to the Asp a well-to-do oasis, insulated from the crowded grit of the impoverished city that surrounded it.

Police sirens screamed in the distance and he opened his eyes. The sirens faded as they moved away. He found himself still in this hostile place, with its challenges and uncertainties.

The most frustrating challenge and uncertainty right now was the whereabouts of Frank Luck and the steel case that, almost certainly, he possessed.

It was a challenge the Asp could have, and should have, easily avoided.

The Sheik had properly kept from the Asp the sources and methods by which the old woman's handwritten message had reached him. The original envelope bore only an address in Berlin. The document inside the envelope had revealed not only her place of residence in Colorado, but her physical infirmity.

He should have played the odds. He should have assumed she would be neither willing, nor able, to reveal anything that anyone of importance would believe. He should have left her alone.

Frank Luck had been an unforeseeable, drunken wild card. But the Asp's misjudgment had exposed him to the unforeseeable. He had compounded his error when he failed to silence the old man, before he sounded the alarm.

Luck had then disappeared from his home before the Asp arrived to correct his error. How or why remained unfathomable. The Asp had entered, and searched, Luck's home. But he had found no clue to the steel case's whereabouts, or to Luck's.

Before he had left Luck's place, the Asp had improvised a precaution to remedy that.

The Asp had also studied the online local newspapers of Avon, and of Eagle County. He had found no story about his encounter, except a routine obituary for Eleanor Love, with no kin or funeral arrangements noted. He put those matters, about which he could do no more at this moment, out of his mind.

He walked past the "For Sale" sign on the home's lawn, then rang the bell.

The silver-haired woman who answered was stooped with age, dressed in black, and wore an outsized diamond ring on the third finger of her left hand.

She squinted up at him. "You're the gentleman who called about the advertisement?"

"Yes, ma'am."

Her diamond flashed as she waved him through the door. "Please. Come in."

The home's marble-floored foyer rose two stories. A balustrade of carved white spindles topped with a polished, dark wood rail, edged the foyer's curving staircase. The foyer's crystal chandelier was studded with a half-dozen winged, white-porcelain Christian angels, and gilt-framed etchings hung on the pale green walls.

She said, "May I offer you sweet tea? Or sherry?"

He said, "Thank you, no. You have a lovely home."

"Well, aren't you kind to say so? You can't *believe* what the realtor says it's worth! We built it after my husband made partner. He was a lawyer, you know."

"I didn't. And my sincere condolences for your loss."

"Admiralty Law. That was his field. Mostly for the oil companies. He said if your business involves oil and water you need to be in Houston or New Orleans."

"Yes. I've done business in Houston."

"So, I suppose you would like to get down to business *here*." She stepped through an open archway off the foyer and motioned him to follow. "I'm sure you're anxious to see it. I've set it out in the dining room, on the table."

He laid his hands atop the black, molded plastic case as he turned to her. "May I?"

She nodded. "It's unlocked. Of course, the case is included."

The pistol was, as advertised, a U.S. military M1911A1 .45 ACP automatic. He lifted it from the box, worked the slide to clear it, then hefted it in his hand. There was some grip wear, minor scratching, but overall its condition was excellent.

He said, "You aren't the original owner?"

"Me? Heavens no! My husband bought it secondhand after we moved here. He said New Orleans was a den of cutthroats and thieves. Even in those days. Today it's worse, all over America."

"I believe it." The Asp believed it so strongly, in fact, that he had decided to avoid purchasing a gun illegally, through the violent

American underworld. After his encounter with the coyote, he was less concerned with his ability to deal with North American thieves and cutthroats. But he was even *more* concerned with encountering the police who might be watching them.

She hugged herself with thin arms and shivered. "Crime. That's why I'm selling this place. I'm moving out closer to our daughter."

"Did your husband fire it often?"

"I don't believe he *ever* fired it. He kept it cleaned and oiled. He said the Navy taught him to maintain his equipment. But for all the big talk he was never much for guns. The Navy taught him to shoot a .45, too. So that was the kind of gun he bought." She blinked as she steadied herself with a hand on one of the chairs arrayed around the dining table.

She seemed a gentle soul, and oblivious to the truth of the world in which she lived, in the way that the Asp's mother had been gentle and oblivious.

The old woman said, "He always admitted he could never hit shit with a .45. But he said that if a .45 ever did hit a burglar it would knock the living shit out of the son of a bitch. You're sure you wouldn't care for a sherry, dear?"

"Quite sure, thank you. Yes, the .45 is known for stopping power."

In a gunfight, he preferred the Glock 17's larger magazine to the eight rounds plus one of this .45. But he hadn't seen a used Glock advertised at an address along his route, and he wasn't equipping himself for a gunfight, anyway. And, he had once used a .45 to successfully conduct actual business. He had shot the target through the lower abdomen, and had, indeed, literally knocked the shit out of the man.

The Asp said, "You're asking nine hundred dollars?"

"My husband's partner at the firm said at that price it'll move faster than crap through a goose. He thinks I should hold out for twice that. Naturally. He's a Jew. But I just want to get it the hell out of my house. So, don't try to Jew down an old widow."

"Believe me, I am the last person to Jew down someone. I'll take it, at every penny of your price."

"Done." She raised one finger. "Like I said on the phone, cash on the nail. And, not that a young man like yourself would do it, if one of your amigos gets hold of this *pistola* and knocks over some liquor store with it, you and I never met. *Comprend-ay?*"

"I assure you, no friend of mine would ever set foot in a liquor store."

She shrugged. "If you say so. My husband's partner says here in Louisiana there's no background check required on a private party sale."

"That's my understanding also."

Unlike Colorado, where, even if he were purchasing this gun from this woman, the law would have obliged her to have his identity documents checked through a national system. The Asp was confident that a background check of his identification documents would yield nothing problematic. But buying a gun in Colorado would have injected his identity into a system that, presently, was unaware that he existed. Therefore, he had added a pistol to his Louisiana shopping list.

He had hoped for a seller like her, who desired anonymity. That, and the fact that she reminded him of his mother, had just saved her life. It had also saved him the risk and inconvenience of another body.

He counted out the money.

The old woman pointed at a framed, faded color photograph, that stood on the dining room's sideboard. The stern young man in the photo was shorn of facial hair, and wore a high-collared white uniform jacket, with gold buttons and dark blue epaulets.

"That's my husband. A real Yankee Doodle Dandy. Actually born on the Fourth of July. If he'd made it a couple weeks longer, he would have been seventy-four. He was a lieutenant. On a boomer. That's a nuclear missile submarine. During the Cold War."

The Asp repacked the pistol in its gun safe. "Did he find such a responsible job stressful?"

"You bet your boots. He was always scared they'd shoot a missile off by mistake. If just one nuke went off somewhere then bingo, the other side would shoot back. Then boom, boom, boom. Pretty soon us *and* the commies would be down the tubes. And the meek would inherit the Earth. Or what was left of it. Wouldn't *that* have been the shits?"

"Yes. But less so for the meek."

As she walked him to the door she pointed at the case he held beneath his arm. "Remember, I don't guarantee that thing will go off when you pull the trigger. It's older than I am. But it was made in America by Americans, not in some commie sweat shop. I would bet my bottom dollar on a weapon made by somebody who thinks like I do, no matter how old it is. How about you?"

"I am prepared to bet the Earth on such a weapon."

Twenty-three

IN THEIR BEDROOM AT THE BERGMAN COUNTRY HOUSE IN THE
Bavarian Alps, Peter Winter stood, chin up, while Rachel adjusted
his tie.

Peter watched as she stood back, slitting her big brown eyes
while she admired her handiwork. Then she patted his suit's lapel.
"There. You look as perfect for your visitor as I can manage. I
need to take your suits in again."

The stress and long hours of Peter's work had eaten away
twelve kilos from his frame.

Rachel rested her palm on his unadorned lapel while she
frowned up at him. "Perhaps not perfect. If Himmler is grumpy
this morning, he may make you join the Party. And start wearing a lapel pin."

Peter flicked his eyes over the front page of the *People's
Observer* for October 2, 1941, that lay on the bed beside them.
"He shouldn't be grumpy with these headlines. The Second and
Third Panzer armies are encircling Moscow. Rommel's still run-
ning circles around the British in North Africa."

Rachel sniffed as she slapped at the Nazi propaganda sheet
that had become Germany's most influential newspaper. "You
believe Goebbels' daily fairy tale?"

Peter shrugged. "I believe Swiss radio news. It's reporting
the same. And why would you think the Russians would be a
worthier opponent for the Axis than Poland, Denmark, Norway,
Luxembourg, the Netherlands, Belgium, France, Yugoslavia, Greece,
Latvia, Lithuania, and Estonia?"

In the twenty-five months since Peter's meeting with Himmler and Canaris, the Nazis had conquered an empire that now stretched across Europe, Africa, and Asia, from the Arctic Circle to the Sahara, and from the English Channel's beaches to Moscow's gates.

With Russia back on its heels, Germany's sole remaining serious opponent, Great Britain, hunkered down across the Channel, besieged by U-boats, its beaten armies thrown out of Europe at Dunkirk, and its cities battered by German bombing. The Americans remained kibitzing bystanders an ocean away.

Peter shook his head. "No. Himmler won't make me join the Party. When he looks at me, he already sees the Party pin, even though it isn't there. The director of the Bavarian Mine Renovation Authority shouldn't look like an important Nazi, anyway. He should look like the world's least important file clerk, building the world's biggest file room. To preserve the boring records of an empire that's supposed to last a thousand years."

Rachel said, "You're building a bomb factory. And you're the handsomest file clerk I've ever seen. But if Himmler thinks people will buy that fairy tale about the Salzreich Project, he may buy the rest of what you've proposed."

Peter pressed his lips together and shook his head. "I know this meeting is supposed to be about what I proposed. But I doubt we'll get away with it. I think he's coming to shut the project down. It's been ridiculously expensive already, and it's not even half done. And the war is nearly over. The thing that makes *sense* is to shut down the Salzreich Project. Not just from Himmler's viewpoint. The longer the *world* goes without this weapon, the better."

"Peter, the thing that made sense two years ago was not starting a war in the first place. If the last two years have taught us anything about the Nazis, it's that two years from now the world will have changed in ways we can't imagine today."

"My imagination regarding the future doesn't extend beyond getting through today with no slip-ups."

"The only thing I'm imagining about today is you home before midnight for a change."

"Rachel, I don't have a 'banker's hours' job. I'm managing a project that's ramping up to employ twenty thousand people. I'm doing it without the aid of the usual pyramid of German bureaucrats, so it's kept quiet. I can't clock out like the day shift. I'll be home when I've sold Himmler." He clenched his teeth as he reached for his hat and briefcase. "Or, if he sees through me I won't be home at all."

She took his face in her hands and kissed him hard on the lips, then said, "Rubbish. He thinks you're a genius. So do I. Peter, this is the opportunity that we stayed in Germany to find! A way to make a difference! Like the way Jacob's found, working at Leica. I'll wait up."

Fifteen minutes after he kissed Rachel goodbye, Peter drove his car into a gravel-paved meadow, bounded by pine forest. He parked alongside ranks of empty motor buses. They brought thousands of laborers from Munich to the Salzreich Mine, then transported them home after seven-day shifts.

He walked through the chill October morning, past the tent city that housed the labor force, as late risers scurried past him, heads down to avoid the boss.

The Salzreich was just one of the labyrinthian mines that had extracted salt from beneath the southeastern Bavarian Alps, and from western Austria, for five hundred years. But the Salzreich had become the least efficient, and had failed during the Depression.

The mine's offices, like the mine itself, were dug into the side of an alp. Constructed of limestone block, hewn from the mountain itself, the office facades, and the block-framed mine entrance arch, showed the weather wear of centuries. But above the entry arch a crisp, swastika-emblazoned red and black banner rippled, and proclaimed the Salzreich Project's dull virtue.

Alongside the tram tracks that disappeared into the horizontal entry tunnel workers queued, then clocked in, under the stern gazes of armed, helmeted guards.

This morning's shift change was being repeated across Europe as factories, from Škoda, in annexed Czechoslovakia, to Citroën, in occupied France, poured materiel into the already vast stream of German war production.

Himmler's arrival time was deliberately unscheduled. His closed Mercedes rolled up and stopped at the mine entrance, followed by an open car packed with SS bodyguards carrying submachine guns. In 1934, on the Night of the Long Knives, Himmler and his SS had purged a thousand "undesirable" Nazis, and murdered two hundred more. Himmler took the possibility of assassination seriously. Perhaps because he knew how easy it was.

Peter led Himmler to an open electric tram. Today the *Reichsführer* was decked out in SS black, complete with jodhpurs, jackboots, and a peaked cap with death's-head insignia. He and Peter sat side by side, in the first car behind the tram's engineer. Himmler's entourage packed in to the following cars.

The tram sped them on rails down a horizontal, round-roofed tunnel, lit by strung, naked electric bulbs and hewn through gray limestone and pale white salt. Along the way they passed long files of walking laborers, lunch pails in hand. Only a few, wide eyed, recognized Himmler.

Himmler leaned close to be heard as the tram clattered deeper beneath the mountain, and said, "Have you found a way to mine the explosive metal here, then?"

"No, *Reichsführer*. This mine's advantage is that it provides pre-constructed industrial space. This tunnel is the only way in or out, so it's easily secured. It's invulnerable to attack, and the salt itself is easily removed. So we can enlarge space as needed. The uranium comes from the mines in the Sudetenland. To reduce shipping volume, we concentrate it there."

"How?"

"By mundane techniques used to separate other metals from their ores. Crushing, sifting, application of chemical reagents and heat." Peter tugged a stoppered glass vial of clumped yellow powder from his trouser pocket. "Only this—concentrated uranium—is trucked here."

Himmler frowned. "It looks like chicken feed." The former poultry farmer rotated the vial in his hand. "This powder is explosive?"

Peter shook his head. "No. But it *is toxic*. If I fed it to chickens, or exposed them to it for extended periods, it would kill them. If I intended to carry even that small amount for longer than it takes to show it to you, I would secure it in a lead flask. In that way concentrated uranium is even less useful than chicken feed. Less than one percent of the concentrate in this vial is the type of uranium that can be made to cause an explosion."

The tunnel opened out into a cavern, its high ceiling hidden in darkness, and its flat floor as large as a football pitch. The tram stopped alongside a humming steel structure eighty meters long by twenty meters wide. Elevated on a girder framework in the cavern's center, it was tended by a half-dozen technicians wearing gray, button-fronted coveralls. Each sat on a stool, monitoring specific units' gauges.

Streams of other laborers changing shifts flowed past the tram and the machine. The human streams flowed to and from tunnels that branched left and right from the cavern.

Himmler stepped down from the tram onto the cavern's floor, then peered up, hands on hips. He wrinkled his brow, while he pointed at the humming structure. "What do you call this thing?"

Peter said, "The workers, of course, have no idea what it does. They just call it 'the sausage rack.' But I think they realize that it's the heart of this project. More accurately, it's the prototype for scores of identical hearts. Those will be built if and when this one is perfected. I wanted you to see it. And to see the scale and progress of the operation. But the rest of the agenda I sent you is best covered in my office, back at the mine entrance."

He led Himmler to a flight of steel stairs that led three meters up to a catwalk suspended above the great machine. More accurately, above two rows of twenty individual, identical machines. The paired couplets of C-shaped steel boxes, each box as tall and as wide as a telephone booth, did indeed resemble sausages hung on a rack.

A step away from the stairs, Peter stopped and pointed at Himmler's steel-rimmed glasses, then at a nearby table. "*Reichsführer*, I suggest you remove those and leave them on the table. Also, your wrist watch."

Himmler frowned. "What?"

Peter removed a paper clip from his trousers pocket, laid it on his palm and extended his arm towards the machine. The steel clip twitched. Then it shot one meter through the air, struck the nearest steel box with a metallic ping, and stuck there.

Peter smiled and pointed at the workers tending the gauges. "We learned the hard way to replace their coveralls' metal buttons with wooden disks." He nodded at Himmler's uniform jacket. "You may feel tugs at your buttons, if they contain steel."

Himmler left his glasses and watch, then Peter led him up onto the catwalk, and pointed down at the C-shaped steel boxes. "Each of these housings encloses an electromagnet. In fact, as you just saw, an electromagnet as powerful as any in Europe.

Alongside the magnet, within each housing, is a vacuum chamber. The individual machines are mounted together so they can easily be connected to electric cables. The cables bring power from the hydroelectric plant at Lake Walchen."

Peter paused and pointed. "At each 'C's' lower tip, concentrated uranium is loaded into a heating compartment," he pointed again, "then vaporized. The vapor rises into the vacuum chamber, here. As the vapor moves through the chamber, the electromagnet's field deflects the path of the differentially charged particles. Useless uranium is deflected further than the slightly different particles of fissionable uranium. At the 'C's' top tip, the useful particles are collected in a compartment. The rest pass into a separate compartment, to be discarded. The yield from each individual machine will be miniscule. Even when the complex is fully operational, accumulation will be slow."

As they reboarded the tram, Himmler hooked his steel-rimmed glasses back over his ears, then replaced his peaked cap. As they sped back to the mine offices at the entrance, Himmler frowned. "How does this design of yours compare to other machines of its type?"

"There are no other machines of this type, *Reichsführer*. In principle, it operates like a laboratory process for identifying materials, called mass spectroscopy. But it's only a first step. When we reach my office, the two of us have much to discuss."

Himmler sat back as he refastened his watch around his wrist. "The three of us."

Twenty-four

IN PETER'S OFFICE, ADMIRAL WILHELM CANARIS WAITED FOR them. He stood alongside Peter's conference table, reading a copy of the meeting agenda, which he had presumably been provided by Himmler, his boss. The last time Peter had seen the intelligence chief, the admiral wore a business suit. This morning he wore a coarse work shirt and trousers, and alongside him on the tabletop lay a flat, wool, worker's cap.

Peter's supervising day secretary poured coffee as the three men sat. Himmler watched her backside until she closed the door and left them alone. Per Himmler's orders, no meeting notes would be kept.

The *Reichsführer* eyed the room's centuries-old plaster walls, adorned only with a framed photograph of himself, and a larger one of Hitler. "You know, Peter, war may be hell, but a leader's comfort increases his productivity."

"Everyone works differently, *Reichsführer*. I work best keeping long hours in un-distracting surroundings, and taking no work home with me."

Himmler raised his palm. "Don't misunderstand. Your uncle would be proud of what your hard work has accomplished here, already. You have affirmed my faith in the importance of your bloodline. But even the strong tire. Are your local accommodations as spartan as your office?"

Peter shook his head. "I've moved into a country house, originally built by a Jewish banking family. It's quiet, isolated, and the terms were quite reasonable."

Himmler winked. "And I'm sure the Jews will have no further need for it."

Canaris said nothing, nor did Himmler acknowledge his presence.

Himmler adjusted his glasses, opened his agenda copy and eyed the first page. "Gentlemen, the purpose of this meeting is to assess the Salzreich Project's progress, and to set course for its future."

Peter opened his own copy and tapped the pages. "As you've seen, *Reichsführer*, a working machine that concentrates uranium 235 is already producing tiny quantities. When the design and procedures are optimized, we are poised to add up to two dozen more machines. We've also begun design, and prepared space for production of, the weapon itself. And for production of an aircraft capable of delivering it."

Himmler nodded. "My concern is less with details than with the probability of the ultimate result."

"Of course, *Reichsführer*."

Himmler continued, "Twenty-nine months ago this process of breaking atoms was unknown. You are wagering enormous sums based on your abstract prediction that this breaking can be made to occur over and over within a fraction of a second. To be frank, it sounds like Jewish physics."

Peter shook his head. "A prediction made with mathematical certainty is *theoretical* physics, *Reichsführer*. But to a theoretical physicist it is no less certain for the lack of a physical demonstration. Demonstrating a sustained chain reaction before proceeding would be reassuring. Such a demonstration would also point the way toward large scale synthesis of even more powerful fissionable elements, that don't even exist in nature. Such elements could produce not only more destructive bombs, but as a side effect produce limitless, cheap electric power." Peter shrugged.

"But?"

"But I am certain that we can make a working bomb much faster, and much cheaper, if we forego the delay and cost of those other paths."

Canaris said, "Heisenberg's group seems to disagree. They are focused on confirming, by experiment, this predicted repeating reaction, before moving ahead. To perform this experiment they insist they need a supply of a unique, obscure substance. And they say it's only available to Germany from occupied Norway. Are they stalling?"

Peter shook his head. "No, they aren't stalling. If they want to demonstrate a continuing chain of fission reactions, they need to control the reactions' speed. Excess neutrons that split off from atomic nuclei must be soaked up, to damp and slow the reaction, or freed to accelerate it. This damping could be done by introducing or withdrawing a substance that soaks up excess neutrons. One such substance, possibly the best one, is deuterium. It's an isotope of simple water, but with a greater atomic weight. It's referred to as 'heavy water.'"

Canaris nodded. "Heavy water. That's what they've asked for."

Peter said, "To my knowledge, heavy water is only produced in quantity as a byproduct of one process for fertilizer manufacture. The only facility in Europe I know of that uses that process is, in fact, a plant in Norway."

Himmler narrowed his eyes. "You don't think Heisenberg's group is deliberately sabotaging the war effort?"

Peter's heart, already racing, skipped.

If Himmler and Canaris disbelieved him, many of the best physicists left in Germany, some his friends and acquaintances, would be on the next train to Dachau.

Peter widened his eyes and shook his head. "No, *Reichsführer*! Sustaining a chain reaction is the logical approach, given unlimited resources and time. But, if I may move directly to the point, today's headlines suggest that the war will be won soon, without a German bomb. So before I consume more of your valuable time discussing next steps, may I ask whether you have already decided that Germany would best be served by suspending this operation?"

Himmler turned to Canaris. "Well?"

The intelligence chief shifted in his chair, then said to Peter, "How would you answer your own question if the British, and the Americans, were also working toward a bomb?"

Peter cocked his head. "Britain has the talent. But today she's barely capable of discouraging invasion. America has both the talent and the industrial base. But she's not about to be dragged into a lost war an ocean away. And, I think, not about to undertake an effort like we're making here while she is at peace. And still recovering from the Depression."

Canaris stretched a smile. "A succinct and accurate assessment. But you didn't answer my question."

Himmler raised his palm. "Admiral, Germany is trusting Dr. Winter with this project. It can trust him with the same intelligence you shared with me earlier today. Tell him everything you told me."

The intelligence chief inhaled, then said, "Dr. Winter, the intelligence service as of this morning has concluded, with high confidence, that in fact both Britain and the United States are pursuing atom weapons. In a practical, not merely theoretical way."

Peter raised his eyebrows. "High confidence? You're saying we have highly placed spies in Britain and America?"

Canaris shook his head. "In fact we don't. Ideology often motivates traitors. These days, National Socialism is an unpopular ideology in Britain, and in America. Communism, however, is tolerated in Britain and America. In fact, it is passionately embraced by some of their citizens."

Peter frowned. "I don't understand."

Canaris said, "Unlike Germany, the Russians have successfully cultivated numerous intelligence sources in Britain and America. Particularly among academics. Those sources see the Soviets as their friends, and their own countries as their enemies."

Canaris continued, "But similarly, Stalin's butchery has made him many enemies at home. German intelligence *has* cultivated sources among Stalin's enemies, for years. We have successfully made those enemies of our enemy into our friends."

Canaris drained his coffee cup. "Those friends have told us about reports received by the Russians, within the last month. Those reports come from handlers of well-placed British and American sources. The reports are of such credibility that they have been presented to Comrade Stalin, himself. The reports conclude that work toward a uranium weapon has been approved at high levels in Britain. And may soon be approved in America, as well."

Himmler said, "So Peter, we now *know* that Germany is in a race for this bomb. And we must win it. As you say, Russia will fall by Christmas. But the British are already bombing our civilians. There is no doubt that if they develop this bomb they will slaughter innocent Germans with it. Unless we are equipped to retaliate in kind."

"Winning this race will be even more critical if Russia *doesn't* fall," said Canaris.

Himmler drew back, and said to Canaris, "Admiral, defeatist speculations have no place in this meeting. Russia will fall. Our armies stand this morning before the gates of Moscow."

Canaris said, "So did Napoleon's."

Himmler glared at him through his glasses.

Peter stood and peered into everyone's empty coffee cups. "I'll return with the pot."

He left Himmler and Canaris alone to hash out their differences, but left his office door ajar as he departed.

When he returned, he heard elevated voices, and paused outside the room, coffee pot in hand.

Himmler was speaking. "—nothing improper about detaining and disciplining saboteurs and agitators in an occupied country. We've had this discussion before."

Canaris said, "Apparently without result. In Poland two years ago I didn't see saboteurs detained. I saw roving bands of SS herd civilians into mass graves and murder them. By the thousands. Our sources say Stalin's enraged at the reports *he* has been getting. That similar conduct has become exponentially worse, in the German rear areas in occupied Russia."

"You believe what the Bolsheviks are telling Stalin? Over what I'm telling you? Besides, Stalin himself kills more Russians every month than the Third Panzer Army has killed in the whole war!"

Canaris said, "If you won't have these exterminations stopped as a matter of decency, have them stopped as a matter of enlightened self-interest. You're absolutely right about the Bolsheviks. If the fortunes of war reverse, Stalin will repay Germany ten-fold for these atrocities."

"Decency? You are a career military man. You of all people understand that a soldier must have the courage to kill in the line of duty, and can do so without losing his fundamental decency."

"Gratuitous murder is never in the line of duty."

Peter heard chairs scrape the floor, jumped back from the door, and busied himself at a file cabinet.

Himmler said, "You are dismissed from this meeting, Admiral. Go back to spying on our enemies. Instead of on the SS. Hail Hitler!"

A heartbeat later Canaris, red faced, grim, his worker's cap clutched in one trembling hand, threw open Peter's office door, and stalked out.

As he passed Peter he said, "Dr. Winter, build this bomb of

yours. Build it before the Allies build theirs. Because, if we lose
this war, God will have no mercy on Germany. And even the
devil won't want what's left of it."

As the daylight outside Peter's office window faded, Himmler
sat across the conference table from him, turned the page of his
own folder, then said, "Last item. Personnel."

Peter breathed deep as his heart rate increased.

Himmler tugged his lip. "You want to replace the current
workforce? With detainees?"

"Gradually. As the tent city is replaced by fenced, guarded
barracks. Transporting the shifts to and from the Munich area,
even on the current weekly basis, wastes time, and wastes fuel
that Germany needs elsewhere. The workers will have no difficulty finding other employment. To date, they know only that
we're enlarging and improving a hole in the ground, and laying
in structural steel and other materials for future work.

"But, as the project's true objective takes shape, inadvertent or
deliberate disclosure of secret information becomes unacceptably
likely. A confined labor force eliminates that risk."

Himmler turned the page, ran his finger down a list, then
frowned. "You have already interviewed inmates at Dachau?"

"In the most nonspecific way only. And only for upper level
positions. Commandant Piorkowski was more than helpful as
soon as I showed him your letter."

Himmler tapped his finger on the page. "Saul Hersh. Jew.
Complained stridently when he was lawfully dismissed from his
teaching position. Why him?"

"Professor Hersh is an experimental physicist. I know his work.
He's not an innovator, but his lab and computational habits are
flawless. We can't afford process or math errors."

Himmler sniffed. "Hyman Wolf. Also Jew. The physicist I can
understand. But this one owned a jewelry store."

"In fact, he designed and fabricated precious metal jewelry
from scratch. He holds a degree in metallurgical engineering.
Uranium 235 will be far more precious than gold. Even at full
production, the entire plant's output for an entire week may be
little more than the dregs in a teacup. The metal will have to
be formed and fitted without a milligram of waste, and more
precisely than the mechanism of the finest watch."

Himmler sighed as he flipped the pages. "All of these have similarly indispensable skills? Even the queers?"

"*Reichsführer*, this may be the most complex undertaking in human history. The alternative is to draw skilled Germans away from more immediately vital war work, or even from military service."

"The jeweler has seven children. *Most* of these on your list have large families. And you want to bring the families along?"

Peter's heart pounded. "The cost of maintaining family members in one facility is no different than the cost of maintaining them in another."

Himmler blinked. "Of course. Of course, we're maintaining them."

Peter said, "The commandant at Dachau explained to me that when reluctant workers must be physically motivated, the consequences may impair performance. In his case, the damaged unskilled laborer is easily replaced with another. But the jeweler is irreplaceable. If his wrist is broken by a truncheon blow, he becomes useless to me. Threatening discipline against his children, however, should motivate him even more effectively. While preserving his productivity."

Himmler sat back, eyebrows raised, and steepled his fingers. "I hadn't thought of it that way. Very well." Himmler drew his pen, and initialed the meeting outline. "I trust my subordinates to exercise initiative. So long as progress remains satisfactory."

A knock sounded at the door.

Peter's lead secretary stood, eyes wide, as she stared at Himmler. "Dr. Winter, please forgive the interruption. The day girls were wondering whether you needed them to stay along with the night staff this evening?" She smiled. "With the *Reichsführer* here and all."

Peter smiled, then shook his head. "We're just finishing up, Gretel. The day staff can go. And I won't be needing the night staff this evening, either. You all go on. I'll lock up."

She beamed, said "Hail Hitler!" turned, and left.

Himmler closed his file, stood, and stretched as he replaced it in his briefcase. "Peter, I reviewed your personal file myself before I came. The records show you're unmarried. For a handsome fellow like you I find that incredible."

An invisible hand tightened around Peter's throat.

He stretched a smile. "But I am, *Reichsführer*. To my work."

Himmler laughed and clapped Peter's shoulder.

Then, as Peter walked Himmler to the main doors, where his bodyguards snapped to attention at his approach, the *Reichsführer* leaned close. "That blonde secretary is a superb specimen."

"She's a bright, effective supervisor. Her staff would walk across hot coals for her."

"And for you, I suspect. Peter, your work ethic sets a superb example in a challenging assignment. But you seem tense, tonight. Exhausted. One perquisite of a man's stressful service to the Fatherland is screwing the help. I suggest you try it."

Peter lay, spent and naked, on the carpet in the bedroom. Alongside him on the fainting couch she lay facedown and panting.

She turned her face toward him and said, "You're sure *Reichsführer* Himmler directed us to do this?"

"I swear. That is a direct quote. It shocked me."

Rachel said, "That he wants a pure-blood Aryan to make more Aryans? It shouldn't have shocked you. If you left your bomb cave more often, you'd hear what I hear from other women, when I shop in town."

"About what?"

"About the Fount of Life Association."

"Those Nazi homes for unwed mothers?"

"For blonde, blue-eyed, un-Jewish unwed mothers. There aren't enough new Nazis to replace the expanding empire's undesirables. So, the homes have expanded. Into the occupied countries, like Norway, too. The homes include cabarets, now. Racially qualified single girls go there, meet SS officers, single or otherwise, and bear their blond, blue-eyed babies."

"Whore houses? Himmler's running whore houses?"

Rachel shook her head. "More like naive girls enlisting, to serve as fetal machine guns." Rachel smiled and flicked her eyebrows. "Nonetheless, if Pimp-in-Chief Himmler precipitated this evening, I may reconsider my low opinion of him."

"Don't. Rachel, I overheard him arguing with Canaris today. Canaris confronted him about mass executions by the SS, of civilians in the east."

Rachel rolled her eyes as she tugged at her remaining stocking. "Do you doubt it? Look what they're doing to Germans here in Germany."

Peter sat up and rested his cheek against her bare thigh. "I'm not talking about prison camps, and broken shop windows, and lost jobs, and stolen businesses, and forbidden relationships. Canaris said he'd seen wholesale, organized slaughter of civilians in Poland. By the thousands. And that he'd heard of even worse going on now, in Russia."

"Himmler admitted it?"

"He denied it. And you would think something that massive would be too big to hide."

"But if it's true, it's what we were afraid of. That the Nazis would prove not merely awful, but so awful that you couldn't give Germany this bomb. So you're going to apply the brakes?"

Peter shook his head. "Not yet. If I apply them too forcefully, Himmler might suspect me. He already suspects Canaris, who is an old school German hero."

"Oh."

"But there's another reason to go forward. Himmler brought Canaris to the meeting to deliver the news that the British are working on a bomb of their own."

"Do you believe him about *that*?"

"If I were the British, after the Blitz, I'd be building a million bombs to drop on Germany. Canaris also said the Americans are seriously interested."

"Why? They're not even in the war."

"I didn't say they were as serious as we are. There's no reason to think they will *get* that serious, as long as they can sit back, and offer Churchill and Stalin bullets and moral support from an ocean away."

Rachel's bare shoulders shook as she shuddered. "If Canaris turned out to be right on all counts, and if the Americans did come in, which enemy would be our enemy?"

"I'm too tired to debate impossible choices based on improbable facts."

"Well, then, speaking of the ocean and the Americans, what did Himmler say about the transatlantic airplane?"

"For now, I'm enlarging one of the existing mine galleries to house airplane construction, and ordering machine tools. As for the plane, Himmler's set a meeting in a couple of months. After drawings have been prepared by a couple of aircraft designers nobody's ever heard of."

"What's wrong with Messerschmitt? Or Junkers?"

"In the first place, we don't need many planes. In the second place, building lots of planes is expensive, and attracts attention. But mostly, I think it's Nazi politics. Goering and Himmler are jockeying for position. To succeed Hitler, someday. Airplanes are Goering's preserve, and Himmler can't get caught poaching. These designers are in the air force. But I think Himmler's chosen them because they're young, unknown, smart as hell, and they're dyed-in-the-wool Nazis, which may make them as loyal to Himmler as to Goering."

Rachel slithered down to the floor next to him. "Hmmm. Young, unknown, smart, with impeccable Nazi connections. Just Himmler's type." She bit his earlobe. "Mine too."

"I think Himmler's type is starstruck blonde secretaries with long legs."

Rachel drew back and widened her eyes in mock surprise. "But the *People's Observer* says our *Reichsführer* is a devoted family man."

Peter said, "I'm not sure that in wartime the two are mutually exclusive."

"They are in *this* family." Rachel reached for her pencil and calendar book on the table alongside the fainting couch. "Alright." She sighed. "When is this meeting?"

"Sunday—"

Rachel pouted. "Why Sunday?"

"Ask Himmler." Peter yawned. "Maybe because nothing important ever happens on Sunday."

"Oh really? Have you forgotten that Sunday morning is the one morning of the week when you stay home and screw the help?"

Peter closed his eyes and exhaled. "Rachel, please. I've just spent a very long day lying for our lives to a paranoid mass murderer. And for the lives of every one of the so-called undesirables who we can transfer from those camps to work on this project."

His head felt heavy. He let it slump against her shoulder while he murmured, "I'm too tired to argue. Just mark down the meeting date. Sunday, December 7, 1941."

Twenty-five

THE DESCENDING JUNKERS JU 52 BROKE THROUGH THE MORNING clouds that overhung the central German plain. Peter pressed his nose against the window alongside his seat, and swallowed to clear his ears.

It was his first airplane flight, and the noise and vibration inside the trimotor's corrugated aluminum fuselage surprised him as much as did the snow-dusted fields below.

But the vibration troubled him far less than the snow did. 1941–1942's winter had arrived wetter, and earlier, than expected. The weather had proven to be a Russian ally without a treaty. Germany's Panzers had bogged down in the cold mud, short of Moscow. If winter stayed on Russia's side, the war could drag on at least into spring, 1942.

Seated across from Peter, Himmler concentrated on paperwork he had spread out on the table between them. Himmler was, in both propaganda and fact, tireless in his efforts, and in his travel in the performance of his duty as he saw it. And he saw it as "bringing order" to the far-flung lands and disparate peoples "fortunate" enough to have become part of the New and Greater Germany.

The Junkers' cabin was heated against the sunlit cold above the clouds. But Canaris' bleak prediction, two months earlier, about Hitler's Russian adventure, combined with Canaris' grim condemnation of Himmler's SS tactics in the occupied lands, chilled Peter's gut.

The Junkers banked right, then circled above a solitary,

oversized shed, alongside an elongate green rectangle. The aircraft settled, bounced along the grass runway, then taxied to the shed. Peter craned his neck, but all he saw was a cow pasture.

Himmler climbed down to the grass first, and biting wind out of the north greeted him, as did two young men. The trio were bundled against the cold, in double-breasted military overcoats. Himmler's was stylishly cut, with a fluffy wool collar.

So confident had Hitler been that his armies would winter in the warm apartments of conquered Moscow that such overcoats were in desperately short supply at the Eastern Front. Radio pleas were stimulating donations from thousands of ordinary Germans. Some women gave cloth coats, others gave furs. Some men gave corduroy, others gave cashmere.

Peter had turned in his wool overcoat two weeks before. He walked the fifty meters to the building with his hands thrust into his suit jacket's pockets. By the time he closed the door behind them all, his teeth chattered.

He had expected a bustling aircraft factory. What he saw before him was a bare, high-ceilinged work space, deserted on a Sunday morning. It looked, for all the world, like an artisan's woodworking shop. The cold air smelled of oil and sawdust and something sharp. He supposed the sharp odor was wood glue, because the projects mounted on waist-high jigs above the work-shop's floor resembled curved, wooden pterodactyl skeletons.

The older of the two men greeted Himmler and they traded "Hail Hitlers."

The younger of the two men smiled, then handed Peter a mug of coffee, as he raised his free right hand, and said "Hail Hitler."

Before Peter responded, his host extended his right hand. "Reimar Horten, Dr. Winter. Welcome to Special Air Command Three."

Fresh faced and grinning, Reimar Horten looked even younger than Peter, and was.

Reimar Horten's brother, Walter, according to what Himmler had told Peter during the flight, was no older than Peter. But his creased face showed war's wear.

Like most postwar German aviation enthusiasts, the Hortens had been relegated by the Treaty of Versailles to building and flying gliders. Like so many other boys, and like Peter himself could have been, the Hortens had been swept into the Hitler

Youth. They had graduated to the Nazi party, then later joined Goering's rejuvenated air force.

Walter had flown fighters as wingman of Adolf Galland, this war's version of the Great War's Red Baron. Walter had himself shot down seven planes. Reimar's job had been designing and building gliders to be used during the now cancelled invasion of Britain. A third Horten brother had died in action over Dunkirk. The two survivors now continued this vestigial backwater glider shop, which they grandiosely called "Special Air Command Three."

Peter and Reimar followed Himmler and Walter as the older Horten showed Himmler around the vacant shop.

Peter said, "I'm surprised your staff doesn't work Sundays. Most facilities these days run three shifts." Certainly, his operations at the Salzreich did.

Walter Horten smiled back at Peter as they walked. "A shortfall of funds, not of patriotism. The air force concentrates on powered aircraft, not gliders. Only, shall we say, creative accounting keeps Special Air Command Three ahead of *Reichsmarschall* Goering's auditors."

Himmler, walking with hands clasped behind his back, said to Walter, "If your design meets Dr. Winter's needs, I assure you that your funding shortfall will vanish. However, your need to creatively account for expenditures will become even more critical. I cannot overstate Germany's need to keep all details of this project secret."

Peter hid a smile behind a cough.

Himmler was at least as concerned with hiding the Hortens' work for him from Goering as with hiding it from Churchill.

In a partitioned-off office suite at the shop's rear, the Hortens had laid out on a conference table a stack of charts and drawings to accompany their presentation.

The top item was a meter-wide colored rendering of an aircraft in flight. Or at least part of an aircraft.

The aircraft was just a chevron-shaped wing. It lacked fuselage or rudder, but a cockpit's canopy bulged at the thick center of the wing's forward edge. Judging by the size of the helmeted pilot and copilot, seated side by side beneath the canopy, the craft's wingspan dwarfed the span of the trimotor Ju 52 airliner parked outside.

The craft's shape was odd. Its apparent lack of a propulsion mechanism was odder.

Large bombers and transports were driven by propellers, spun by engines housed within pods, which protruded from their wings' forward edges. In *this* wing's forward edge yawned forward-facing portholes, three on each side of the cockpit, where the propellers should have been.

The drawing's lower right-hand corner was labelled:

Horten Ho XVIIIA

Himmler's eyebrows rose, and he snorted.

The two brothers turned the page, as rapidly as chambermaids turning down a bed.

The second sheet was blank, but in its center rested a business-letter-sized photograph of what looked like a smaller Horten XVIIIA, without portholes or propellers, in a grassy field. The craft was tilted, resting on its belly and on one tapered wing tip. A smiling blonde wearing pilot's garb, who looked familiar, rested a small hand on the airplane's wing, while spectators looked on.

Walter Horten said, "Our proposal is obviously unconventional. But it's field tested, not some Buck Rogers nonsense. We have been building and flying gliders that employ this all-wing design for years, *Reichsführer*, as you see here. Flight Captain Reitsch, herself, has spoken highly of our designs."

It was Peter's turn to raise surprised eyebrows.

Hanna Reitsch was a photogenic civilian aviatrix. A personal favorite of Hitler himself, she had been showered with titles, medals, and celebrity as an example of blonde, superior, Germanic womanhood. But she had nonetheless also been a champion glider flyer, and she now served as an intrepid civilian test pilot of advanced military aircraft.

The next page was a three-view engineering drawing of the larger plane.

Reimar Horten leaned across the table and tapped the aircraft's profile view. "The Junkers that brought you flies because air forced across its wings generates lift. Your Junkers' design, like all conventional designs, is inherently inefficient. Its fuselage adds weight and drag, but contributes no lift."

Himmler said, "My Junkers has a rudder. A ship has a rudder. This plane has no rudder. How can it turn?"

Walter Horten smiled. "Birds have no rudder. They turn by

varying their wings' shapes. Our all-wing gliders use similar mechanisms and maneuver quite as well as their conventional competitors."

Himmler scowled. "You can't glide across the Atlantic. Where are the propellers?"

"We intend to power the aircraft with a new system."

Himmler frowned. "*Another* novelty?"

Reimar Horten turned to another page, a diagram of a tube. He pointed at it. "Propellers pull your Junkers' wing forward, to generate lift. This system expels gas rearward, which thrusts the wing forward to generate lift."

Himmler said, "What is this novelty's advantage?"

Reimar Horten said, "Again, *Reichsführer*, this is no novelty. Messerschmitt first flew a fighter-bomber prototype powered by two of these Junkers turbojets seven months ago. *Reichsmarschall* Goering himself is quite keen on the project."

Himmler narrowed his eyes. "Will Goering's new baby finally be able to keep up with a Spitfire?"

Walter Horten smiled. "That is exactly the jet engine's advantage. Jet powered aircraft will generally and routinely sustain speeds of nine hundred kilometers per hour. The Spitfire might manage six hundred. And this aircraft's efficiency should allow it to cruise easily at altitudes that piston-engine interceptors would struggle to reach. As you see, we've designed in no defensive gun positions. They would add weight, and drag, to a plane that nothing the Allies have can come close to."

"This Junkers engine will work in your design?"

Walter Horten shook his head. "We expect the air force will move heaven and Earth to produce as many of the new Messerschmitts as possible. Junkers engines will be scarce. We've designed the airframe around a similar engine that Bavarian Motor Works is developing. As of now we think BMW's design will be ready sooner."

Himmler jerked a thumb toward the woodworking shop. "You propose to construct *this* airplane from *wood*?"

The brothers looked at one another and their mouths hung open in small O's.

Walter Horten stammered. "*Reichsführer*, we don't propose to construct this design, at all. This aircraft is beyond our facilities' scope."

Peter said, "That's understood. Your role will be as design consultants. I believe the *Reichsführer* is asking whether so advanced an aircraft can be made from wood at all."

Walter Horten said, "Of course it *can*. The British Mosquito is made from wood, and it's brilliant. *Reichsmarschall* Goering has wished publicly for a plane as good."

Peter hid his smile at Himmler's frown.

The older Horten may have been a devout Nazi, a heroic pilot, and an innovative airplane designer. But favorable references both to Germany's most stubborn external enemy and to Himmler's most challenging internal enemy, in the middle of a sales pitch, demonstrated that Walter Horten was a poor politician.

Reimar Horten said, "This aircraft will extend the limits of aircraft construction and performance, as it is. In addition to the range, speed, and payload requirements we were given, it would be helpful to understand any specific, unusual mission parameters the aircraft is expected to fulfill."

Himmler just stared at him. What the Horten brothers didn't know about the uranium bomb, they couldn't tell, to the enemy, or to Goering.

Reimar cleared his throat. "To answer the question, *Reichsführer*. Yes, a steel frame and aluminum skin would be preferable. But the amount of aluminum that would be required to build a fleet of these would be immense."

Himmler nodded. "Assume in your work that enough aluminum will be available to build as many of these planes as Germany needs. Very well, gentlemen." He glanced at his wristwatch. "I'm due in Munich this evening."

Walter Horten wrinkled his forehead. "*Reichsführer*, if I may ask, what do you expect us to do next?"

Himmler nodded at Peter. "I expect you to do whatever Dr. Winter, here, asks of you. And I expect you to do it quietly. And without disturbing whatever it is that you're doing here in any noticeable way. Is that clear?"

"Yes, *Reichsführer*. Hail Hitler."

As the Junkers bumped through the dark sky toward Munich, Himmler dozed in the seat across from Peter.

The copilot walked back to his passengers, staggering from handhold to handhold, then bent and whispered to Peter, "Sir, we've just heard on the radio that Japanese planes bombed an American naval base in the Hawaiian Islands. It's morning in the Pacific, and the attack is reportedly ongoing. Do you think I should wake the *Reichsführer*?"

Peter snapped upright in his seat. "Why *wouldn't* you wake him?"

The copilot said, "Well, because the report must be wrong. What country would be stupid enough to get into a war with America, if it didn't have to?"

Peter peered out his window into the suddenly darker night. He could only think of one.

Twenty-six

BEFORE SUNRISE ON MAY 31, 1942, SIX MONTHS AFTER HITLER had responded to America's declaration of war on Japan by declaring war on America, Peter drove down the road that connected the Salzreich Mine, now generally known as the Salzreich Records Repository Project, to the public road. The surrounding forest's edge had been cut back, so that the two-lane entry now merely defined the centerline of a flat grass field thirty-eight hundred meters long.

The road paralleled one side of a double three-meter-tall wire fence, punctuated every fifty meters by guard towers, that enclosed the new workers' quarters.

Inside the fence, the workers' tent city and motor bus parking area had been replaced by bleak rows of dark, wooden laborers' barracks. Already they housed eight thousand people, counting the laborers and their families.

At the road's end, Peter cranked down his car's window. The guard, Mauser cross-slung atop his threadbare civilian overcoat, limped out from the guard box. In front of the red-striped barrier gate he raised his palm.

Peter stopped the car.

The guard, barely twenty, bent and peered in the side window's opening, his two-fingered hand resting on the window's sill. He had lost the fingers to Russian shrapnel, and also toes and cheek tissue to frostbite, during the 1941–1942 winter retreat from Moscow. His wounds relegated him to guarding this obscure government facility.

The boy raised the dark glasses that he wore onto his forehead. "Early morning, even for you, Doctor." So slurred was his speech that his Swabian farmer's accent was barely recognizable.

"Lothar, I've had to move up the morning staff meeting. Just so you know, I'm expecting a high-level visitor today."

"Might I inquire when and who, sir?"

"You might. But all I know is someone, and sometime this morning. As soon as you see the car, please phone Gretel."

The boy flexed his right cheek into half of a smile. "You know I always keep my eyes peeled, Doc."

It was a macabre joke, and a lump swelled in Peter's throat.

Frostbite had also caused the boy's eyelids to shrivel and drop off. Ghastly as the disfigurement of his bulging stare looked, the worst of it remained to come for him, and for thousands of survivors of the Winter Campaign who had suffered the same injury. Unable to blink, they would in time go blind, as their un-moistenable eyeballs ulcerated.

Maimed veterans were but one of many thunderclaps that had echoed across Germany, during the first half of 1942.

Even Goebbels' propaganda couldn't hide the casualties, and the defeats the army had suffered. German dead were estimated to exceed one hundred thousand. Others, captured by the Russians, were assumed dead.

The army was only too happy to reassign mutilated veterans to isolated locations. Out here, Lothar didn't remind civilians of the price of folly.

Peter was only too happy to accept veterans like Lothar. The crazy brave, and the psychotics, were either dead or had returned to the fight. Survivors like Lothar had returned disabused of war's glory, cynical about the politicians who sent them to fight it, and disinclined to inflict suffering, like their own, on the fellow human beings they guarded.

Lothar craned his neck toward the dark sky. "Goebbels' Nose said that the Tommies bombed Cologne bad last night. Don't you think we ought to get us some flak guns around here, Doc?"

"Goebbels' Nose" was what people called the government-subsidized bargain radios that intruded into ordinary Germans' kitchens and parlors. "People's Receivers" picked up little except nearby stations. Nearby stations rebroadcast only what Berlin sent them. What Berlin sent them was rank propaganda wrapped in music and comedy. The radios' owners knew it. But they could neither afford, nor legally buy or listen to, receivers that picked up foreign broadcasts.

However, the sensitive receiver in the Bergman's expensive console phonograph, with its roof-mounted antenna, often picked up the BBC. Even more credibly, it picked up news from nearby, neutral, Switzerland.

Swiss radio had reported British claims that a thousand planes had dropped over three million kilograms of bombs on Cologne last night.

Since work had begun at the Salzreich on the Horten brothers' "New York Plane," Peter had educated himself about airplanes, and about the business that aerial bombardment had become.

Peter believed the Cologne reports. He also believed that the thousand-plane raid was just the beginning. Roosevelt had challenged Americans to remake their economy and build *fifty* thousand war planes *per year*. The American economy had been churning out over three *million* motor vehicles per year. Roosevelt's challenge was no empty exhortation.

In September 1940, Hitler had expanded an accidental night bombing of London into the nightly London Blitz. Its goal, breaking Britain's will, had merely redirected Britain's will to revenge.

Rachel, who listened to the BBC in English, said that Harris, the British air marshal, vowed publicly that Germany had "sown the wind, and would reap the whirlwind." The British now referred to him not as "Sir Arthur," but as "Bomber" Harris.

Despite Peter's fear, he shook his head as he answered the gate guard. "Lothar, Cologne's on the west bank of the Rhine. Allied bombers don't have anywhere near enough range to reach us here."

"The Russians didn't have anywhere near enough troops to push us back from Moscow, either, Doc. But here I am."

"Well, even if the Allies could bomb us, they wouldn't. Before an air force wastes bombs and planes on a target, it flies over and photographs the place. From the air, we look like what we are. A prison camp that the Allies' enemy uses to imprison *its* enemies. Flak towers would tip off the Allies that this place isn't their friend."

Lothar raised the gate with his undamaged hand, as he said, "Friends? Enemies? All the corpses in Russia smelled the same."

✧   ✧   ✧

When Peter stepped into his office, to prepare for his staff meeting, he found the lights already on. A lone figure, wearing a laborer's uniform smock, sat in a side chair at the conference table. Flanked by the framed photographs of Hitler and Himmler hanging on the wall behind him, he bent close to his work, copying numbers with a pencil, transferring them from loose note paper into a ledger.

Bespectacled, his frizzy, graying hair topped by a yarmulke, Hyman Wolf looked up from his work only when the office door latch clacked as Peter closed it behind himself.

Peter made a show of frowning at the metallurgist. "Hyman, how did you get outside the wire before shift change?"

Plant personnel entered and exited the camp only in guarded shift groups, not individually.

The jewelry maker stretched his back, removed his spectacles, and pinched his nose between thumb and fingers. "I didn't. I stayed here in the lab last night. Cluster three went online yesterday. I wanted to assay the first production."

Peter deepened his frown. "Those assay results aren't time-critical. You know you violated the camp rules. I might have you and your family disciplined."

"They aren't. I did. You might." The man winked. "But you won't. That's the real reason I stayed. So I could express myself to you, alone. Before the others arrived for the meeting."

"I have no patience with squabbles and tattling."

"It's you I am tattling on."

"What?"

"For your own good. And for the good of all of us who live inside the wire. Not all Nazis are stupid. Not even most of them are."

"Hyman, if you weren't already behind the wire, talk like that would land you there."

"No. Talk like that would get me shipped east. To be murdered. Don't think Jews are stupid. We know what they're doing to us now."

Peter bit his lip.

The Nazis' grand plans to "purify" Occupied Europe by resettling Jews, and other "Undesirables," to places like Madagascar had always seemed nonsense. But the Nazis, and the world, wanted to believe them. After all, the world said, the British themselves had been advocating for European Jews to leave, and resettle Israel as the Jewish homeland, since the Balfour Declaration in 1930.

However, something had changed early in 1942. Himmler inquired about Peter's progress less often. It was as though other matters consumed his attention. Goebbels' Nose rarely spoke about the "Jewish Problem" now. The changes could simply reflect the deteriorating military situation's changed priorities. Or they could reflect darker changes, in already evil policies. Changes that were too evil either to believe or to admit.

Peter said, "You're accusing me of complicity in some conspiracy?"

"Just the reverse. I'm warning you. You're running your own conspiracy here. To save all of us behind the wire."

"That's absurd."

"The Nazis are fooling most of the people most of the time because people don't want to believe the truth about what they're doing. And you're fooling all of the Nazis all of the time, because right now they've got their hands full fighting the whole world. But if the Nazis figure out what you're up to, you will only be the first of us who dies, Dr. Winter."

Hair rose on Peter's neck.

Hyman was right, but the only way to keep fooling the Nazis was to maintain the fiction that Peter Winter was one of them, and that he was bringing in Jew labor because it was efficient. Himmler trusted Peter's bloodline. He trusted even more the progress Peter was making. He trusted both so thoroughly that Peter had been allowed to operate without the State Secret Police, or the SS, looking over his shoulder.

Peter forced himself to smile. "Hyman, you're delusional. You're not here in order to save you from some imaginary horror. You're here because you have skills I need."

"Ah. And what such skills do my five-year-old twins have?" He shook his head. "I understand this role you're playing. And why you play it. A few of us inside the wire have figured it out, even if the Nazis haven't. If any outsider asks, I will say, and say until they cut out my tongue, that you are a slave-driving ogre."

Peter folded his arms, leaned against his office's wall, and forced a smirk. "Slave-driving ogre? Hyman, with a friend like you I need no enemies."

"My family and I pray for you, and against your enemies,

every night, Doctor. Not just because you're a human being. But because without you, the Nazis will kill us all."

Gretel stepped through the door, saw them, and gasped, eyes wide. "I'm sorry. I should have knocked. I thought the lights had been left burning overnight."

Wolf stiffened.

Peter said, "I asked Mr. Wolf to stay at the lab last night. To compute figures for the morning meeting. We're just reviewing them. I neglected to mention it to the camp personnel. Please phone them, Gretel. So there's no confusion at head count."

A twitch of doubt flickered across her face, then she nodded slowly as she backed out. "Of course, Doctor. I'll bring the coffee when it's ready."

After Gretel left the metallurgist said, "You saw the uncertainty in her face? You didn't 'neglect to mention.' You never neglect anything, and she knows it." Before Peter could answer the old man raised his hand. "Don't bother to deny what you're doing. We'll do our jobs. You do yours. And perhaps, just perhaps, we will all live to see the end of this."

Peter peered around his conference table at four of his five department heads.

A "records repository" could easily request personnel records by the box full. And Rachel digested written material, and grasped its essence, as fast and as intuitively as Werner Heisenberg digested and grasped the universe's essence.

Not only were Peter's "guest laborers" handpicked, so were all of the Salzreich Records Repository Project's key personnel.

Unsmiling, Peter said, "Reports?"

At his immediate left, Saul Hersh, the bulb-nosed experimental physicist who directed the magnetic separation complex, cleared his throat. "The magnetic separation units in cluster three came on line yesterday. They're the first ones using the silver wire-wound magnets, instead of copper. The silver sparks less then copper. So we got twenty-four uninterrupted hours of operation. That means we drew more electricity from Lake Walchen than usual."

Peter jotted a note.

Rising electric consumption would soon require circulation of a story out in the civilian economy, about increased power shortages, to mask the drain.

At Peter's right, Hyman Wolf read from the ledger into which he had copied his assay notes. "I've already analyzed yesterday's output. Cluster three's uranium 235 concentration was fifty-five percent."

Hersh smiled. "Up six percent, compared to cluster one and cluster two's averages."

Wolf snorted. "Dr. Winter's minimum requirement is eighty percent concentration. If you give me fifty-five percent, I might as well be making sausage. I suggest you change back to male separator operators."

Hersh snorted back. "You ignorant Jew! Don't tell me how to utilize my people. The girls concentrate on their jobs. The men daydreamed about girls and football every two minutes."

"Me? I only see one ignorant Jew at this table, and it's you!"

Peter raised his palm. "Enough! Gentlemen, we are on the same side here."

Both men sat back, silent.

Hersh glared across the table at his fellow Jew, as Peter said, "Saul, I compliment you and your staff on the concentration improvement."

Peter turned to Wolf. "And Hyman, I compliment you on your quick analysis. And on your focus on our goals."

Peter turned again to the physicist. "Saul, Hyman is correct, at least about the ultimately required result. We need eighty percent concentrated U-235. I'm afraid we're going to have to shut down production and reexamine the process."

From the table's opposite side, Becker, the dueling-scarred Prussian artillery officer in charge of designing and building the weapon mechanism itself, leaned forward and coughed into his handkerchief. "I'm a cannoneer, not a scientist. But what if we took the high-grade output from clusters one and two? Then ran it again through cluster three? Then rerun the improved output again?"

Becker, who everyone simply called "the Prussian," came from a military family, but had been disqualified from combat by tuberculosis. He had escaped medical retirement only because of family connections. Like many German military men, he was a patriot and a professional. He saw the Nazis as brutes and amateurs. But amateurs who were Germany's duly-elected sovereigns. Prussians' professionalism obliged them to obey their sovereigns without question.

The trouble with Becker the Prussian, Peter had found, was that his allegiance to sovereign authority did not keep him from thinking straight, and from thinking out loud.

Hersh was a careful plodder. It might have taken him months to think of recycling the separators' output to increase concentration.

Wolf the Jeweler shook his head. "A day's concentrate output is less than a pinch of snuff. We'd have to collect a week's worth of concentrate just to charge one of Saul's units. And we don't know how the concentrate would respond to reheating. A week's output could be lost in one flash incident, for nothing."

Hersh, who was an unimaginative but precise physicist, was smart enough to recognize a good idea when it smacked him on his bulbous nose.

Hersh said, "But if it works, we could rerun the new concentrate accumulations over and over. Eventually, the product would reach eighty percent."

The Jeweler frowned. "It's a gamble. I don't like gambling."

Peter stared at his fourth director, who sat, unsmiling with arms crossed, at the table's foot.

Mueller's official title was "Director of Personnel." In reality, he was a prison camp commandant, and everyone called him "the Jailer."

Rachel had searched long, and hard, for a résumé like the Jailer's. Early in his career, during Weimar's civil liberties heyday, Mueller had earned a reputation, in the German civilian prison system, as a soft touch. After the Nazis took over, the Jailer had joined the National Socialist Party. Most career bureaucrats who wanted to keep their jobs had held their noses and done the same. The Jailer's soft reputation had gotten him demoted anyway. Mueller was a Nazi in name only. But he wouldn't risk or tolerate treason. And, like the Prussian, he wasn't stupid.

Wolf the Jeweler's warning came back to Peter. Peter was walking a tightrope. If he fell off, he would be only the first to die. The brakes had to be applied subtly. Peter knew improving concentration by rerunning the output was a good idea. He knew because he had worked it out himself, weeks earlier. Rejecting good ideas could arouse suspicion.

Peter drew a breath, then said, "Hyman, it *is* a gamble. But you're right. If we don't try something to increase U-235 concentration, you may as well be making sausage."

He turned again to Hersh, the bulb-nosed physicist. "Saul, the Sausage Factory is your domain. Choose the operator mix you think will give the best results. I don't give a damn whether they're male, female, or Martian."

Peter flipped his agenda's page and looked up at the Prussian.

The scar-faced artillery officer shuffled his notes and prepared to report on his weapon development unit's progress.

A knock on the conference room door turned all heads, then Peter's secretary, Gretel, tiptoed in and whispered to him. "Sorry to interrupt, Doctor. Your visitor may be trying to arrive."

"Trying? Tell Lothar if their papers are in order he should let the car pass."

"Not a car, Doctor." She pointed at the ceiling. "An airplane is circling the camp."

Peter stood.

The Prussian stood too. "A bomber?"

Gretel shook her head as she held up her thumb and index finger, five centimeters apart. "It's a tiny one. It buzzes like a dragonfly. And it has iron crosses on its wings."

Peter smiled. "Gretel, we have no airstrip. He's probably just trying to get his bearings."

Peter wrinkled his brow. Allied photo reconnaissance aircraft were mostly powerful, stripped-down speedsters. Spitfires and Mosquitos, they flew high and fast. And they were marked in their own country's livery. But perhaps...

Gretel shook her head again. "He just threw a streamer out his window. Lothar doesn't think he's lost. Lothar said in Russia he saw generals' planes at the front throw streamers. To test the wind at ground level, before they landed."

As Peter walked out the door he said over his shoulder, "We'll pick this up later, gentlemen. We're adjourned."

Twenty-seven

OUTSIDE, PETER VISORED HIS HAND OVER HIS EYES AS HE JOGGED toward the guard box, pushed along by a breeze at his back.

Silhouetted against the low clouds, and buzzing like a distant bee, a high-winged, single-engine monoplane banked, then straightened. The plane lined up to approach the narrow entrance road, then floated to Earth like a drifting feather.

Peter reached the guard box as Lothar unslung his Mauser, worked its bolt then raised it to his shoulder.

Peter pushed the rifle's muzzle down.

Lothar said, "Doc, say the word and I can shoot it down. I was the best shot in my regiment."

"No. I think my visitor's aboard."

The olive-painted Fieseler Stork's wheels were fixed to landing-gear struts as gangling as its namesake's legs. The wheels touched the roadway one hundred fifty meters from the guard box. The plane bounced, settled, rolled only seventy meters, then stopped with its engine idling.

Peter had previously seen Storks only in newsreels. They flew low and slow, took off and landed in tiny spaces, and could drift above a battlefield affording unparalleled views to a single passenger, who sat behind the pilot in the narrow fuselage. The press loved the Stork, and loved heroic officers, like Rommel, who were modern and daring enough to fly in it.

The plane taxied into the new-seeded grass alongside the guard box and its engine stopped. There was no passenger aboard.

The helmeted, goggled pilot, covered head to foot in a khaki civilian flying coverall, stepped down and stalked toward Lothar.

The guard raised his rifle again. "Halt!"

The pilot kept walking. "Put that thing down! I'm expected. Where will I find Dr. Peter Winter?"

The sentry lowered his rifle when he heard the voice. He stammered at the blonde hair the pilot shook out as she removed her helmet and goggles.

Peter said, "I'm Peter Winter. I was expecting *someone*. Just not—"

She raised her chin. "A woman?"

"—a pilot. Arriving by air. Alone. You make a dramatic entrance Miss—"

"Jaeger. Ilse Jaeger." She thrust up her right arm. "Hail Hitler!"

As Peter walked Jaeger toward the mine's office, she handed him a flat manila envelope. She had removed it from a flight bag that she carried in her left hand, along with her helmet and goggles.

She said, "My credentials. You didn't demand them. Neither did that mumbling gate guard."

"He mumbled because he lost cheek tissue to frostbite, during the retreat from Moscow. He carried his wounded platoon sergeant across his shoulders for twenty-four hours before someone noticed that the man had died. Lothar did his best then. He does his best now."

She blinked, said nothing, then stared at the camp through its wire fence.

In the assembly yard behind the wire, guards blew whistles. In response workers spilled from the barracks into the assembly yard. They formed up into ragged ranks and marched toward the mine to begin their shifts.

While Jaeger stared, Peter eyed a crisp, typed letter clipped to the envelope.

On Himmler's letterhead it read:

My dear Peter,

In response to your expressed need for a test pilot, this will serve to introduce Miss Ilse Jaeger, whose qualifications have come to my attention. They are detailed in the attached file.

Please orient her to those aspects of your project that she *needs to know*, and make her feel welcome as a member of your organization.

Should you have questions, please contact me personally.

With friendly greetings, Hail Hitler!

The signature Peter recognized as genuine. It matched the one on the letter Himmler had given him two years earlier, which Peter still kept in the office's vault.

Jaeger said, "I could have been an Allied spy. The *Reichsführer* told me I would be astonished at what I found here. And I am. But unfavorably. This place doesn't look like a military aircraft factory. And it certainly isn't run like one."

"We rely on the Allies to share your expectations, Miss Jaeger. And to send their spies, and drop their bombs, elsewhere."

"Clever. I suppose." She narrowed her eyes. "Is whatever you're hiding in this place worth the pasting that Cologne took last night?"

"Decide for yourself." He turned back to the mine entrance, made a small bow as he extended his hand to usher her forward. "After you."

Despite Jaeger's concern, securing the Salzreich Mine was simple. The place was a vast, multi-chambered vessel, encased literally within a mountain. The only way in or out was the elongated bottleneck that connected the chambers to the entrance. Inside the mine's echoing tram turnaround gallery Peter and his visitor paused and waited.

The tram's headlight glowed, then grew, as it emerged from the tunnel's dimness. It pulled around and stopped in front of Peter and Ilse Jaeger.

The pilot stripped off her bulky coverall, tucked it and her goggles and helmet into her flight bag, and raked tangles from her blond curls with a tiny brush. Beneath her coveralls she wore gray civilian trousers and a white silk blouse closed at the throat by a red and black cloisonné Nazi party badge.

The tram operator stared at her, mouth open, as he said, "Usual inspection route this morning, Dr. Winter? The Sausage Factory first, then the Bird Cage?"

The workers had nicknamed the caverns where electromagnetic separators heated and concentrated uranium "The Sausage Factory."

In Himmler's letter Peter detected a hint. A test pilot candidate needed to know about the revolutionary airplane she might be hired to test. She did not, at least initially, "need to know" about the even more revolutionary weapon the airplane was designed to carry.

Peter said, "Direct to the Bird Cage this morning, Zev."

Peter sat alongside Ilse Jaeger, rocking side to side as the tram sped into the mountain. Peter normally didn't notice the tram driver's eyes, visible in the rearview mirror that allowed him to monitor his passengers. Today Zev's eyes flicked to the mirror constantly. Peter wasn't surprised.

Ilse Jaeger was what Himmler would, and probably did, call an Aryan "specimen." As blonde, blue-eyed, and athletic for her genre as Peter was for his, she had a movie star's cheekbones. And, evidently, a movie star's high opinion of herself.

Peter flicked open her folder and read.

Jaeger was the only child of a Berlin couple, her father a surgeon, her mother a violinist. Both had joined the Nazi Party before Hitler's ascendance to the chancellorship in 1933. Both had been acquainted with Himmler, socially, for years.

Jaeger had earned glowing reports from her adult leaders in the Band of German Maidens, the Hitler Youth's female counterpart. Jaeger had moved on to active party membership as soon as legally permitted, on her eighteenth birthday.

She held a university engineering degree, but had spurned job offers so she could fly gliders competitively.

Since 1939, Jaeger had worked for both Focke-Wulf and Fieseler as a civilian test pilot, of both single- and multi-engined aircraft. Her file included a detailed personal recommendation from Hanna Reitsch, the celebrity aviatrix.

The tram's brake squeal echoed as it stopped short of the closed entry doors in the wall that separated a cathedral-sized mine chamber, now known as the Bird Cage, from the rest of the mine.

Lothar the gate guard was supposed to, and did, look and act as though the facility he had been assigned to guard was insignificant.

But the helmeted door guards at the Bird Cage's entrance were sharp, able-bodied infantry, armed with MP 40 submachine guns. Like their counterparts who guarded the Sausage Factory's entrance, they inspected Peter's identification papers as though he were a stranger, as they did every day. They allowed Jaeger entry only because he told them to. He led her through the man hatch set in one of the Bird Cage's massive sliding doors.

On the other side of the wall, beneath the cavern's arched ceiling, a steel girder framework supported overhead hoists that moved on tracks. The frame gave the vast aircraft assembly room its nickname.

But it was the pair of floodlit silver birds that the cage enclosed that made Jaeger's jaw drop and eyes widen.

"My God."

Twenty meters in front of her Horten XVIIIA Prototype One rested, its profile toward them, on its tricycle landing gear atop a flatcar. Behind Prototype One Prototype Two's steel skeleton rested on its own flatcar.

Prototype One was a silver-skinned aluminum crescent that measured only sixteen meters from nose to tapered tail. But its fifty-meter wingspan overhung the flatcar on each end by fifteen meters. The first of Prototype One's engines, a propeller-less thing, which reminded Peter of a drainage culvert, dangled above the plane's fuselage.

The chain hoist's clank echoed through the cavern as workers lowered the cradled engine into the airframe.

After the engine nestled safely on its mountings, the red-headed bear of a man who had supervised the job walked to them, head cocked to one side as he stared at Jaeger.

Fritz Fromm's expertise was aircraft construction. Like Mueller, the Jailer, and Becker, the Prussian, Fromm the Bear was neither a Nazi fanatic nor a Jewish prisoner.

Peter said, "Fritz Fromm, this is Miss Ilse Jaeger."

Fromm smiled as he extended his hand. "I suppose this beast looks familiar."

Jaeger hailed Hitler, before she took Fromm the Bear's big hand. Then she shook her head. "I've never seen anything like it. No one has. Why would you suppose otherwise?"

The Bear said, "Before the war I saw you fly at the gliding meets at Wasserkuppe. These two prototypes are basically expanded and powered Horten gliders."

She pointed at the empty engine sling above the Horten XVIII. "It's a squeeze-prop, then? The first one I've seen."

The Bear smiled and nodded. "Turbo jet."

"The Junkers engine?"

He shook his head. "Those are mostly earmarked for the Messerschmitt 262. This engine is the BMW 003. It's heavier than the Junkers, with a bit less power. That's alright, though. This design has lift to burn."

The Bear led her beneath the plane's wing to its blunt nose, and Peter followed.

Jaeger nodded as she reached up and ran her fingers across the plane's riveted aluminum underbelly, then counted the open ports in the wing's leading edge. "Six engines? It *is* a beast."

"The design top speed is projected at eight hundred eighty kilometers per hour. Nothing in the air will touch it. The all-wing provides so much lift and so little drag, and so much room for fuel, that it will cross the Atlantic and return easily."

She stepped back and stared up at the glazed cockpit in the nose. "How soon can I fly it?"

The Bear shot Peter a look, then said to Jaeger, "You can't."

Jaeger stiffened. "What? Too much airplane for a lady to handle?"

"No. That is, yes, the controls will be heavy, even with the hydraulics. But..." The Bear's voice trailed off.

Peter smiled.

The Nazis embraced the Nordic myths of Aryan supremacy. But they expected Aryan women to contribute to the war effort by making babies and munitions, while the men did the fighting.

Combat pilots were male. They were also increasingly scarce. Therefore, female pilots, like Jaeger's mentor, Hanna Reitsch, filled some test pilot jobs, as civilians. This relationship between Peter's aircraft builder and his new test pilot, handpicked by Himmler, was off to a rocky start. If Peter couldn't smooth things over, Himmler might take more interest in the Salzreich Project than desirable.

Peter said, "What Fritz means is that *nobody* is going to fly either of these prototypes for a while. BMW had a head start over Junkers in building its engine. But these engines are revolutionary, and development problems slowed BMW down. Now that the war's changed, BMW's priority is building interceptors' piston engines. The engine you see is the only complete production unit in existence."

Jaeger said, "Messerschmitt's tooling up to build hundreds of Me 262s. Reallocating a dozen Junkers jet engines from Messerschmitt can't be that big a problem."

The Bear shook his head. "The problem's less allocation than design. The Junkers Jumo 004 is twenty-three centimeters longer, and fifty-four centimeters wider, than this BMW. The Junkers won't fit, unless we redesign and rebuild most of the airframe. If we did that, Walter Horten would piss his pants. The changes would ruin the aircraft's lines, increase drag, and cut range and payload."

Jaeger said, "Then I'll speak to someone about persuading BMW to hand build a few engines."

The "someone" Jaeger was talking about was obviously Himmler. Peter had deliberately *not* asked Himmler to intervene, because BMW's problems were a perfect excuse for delay.

Peter didn't think Himmler had sent Ilse Jaeger to spy on him, or to push him along. The plane needed a test pilot. Himmler had found one who was professionally and ideologically qualified. And who was, because of her gender, available.

But Jaeger was a dedicated Nazi, had the ear of the second-most dangerous man in Europe, and was both skeptical and aggressive. She was, also, suddenly in the middle of Peter's business.

The tightrope he was walking had just grown shakier.

Twenty-eight

ON HER SECOND MORNING IN COLORADO, CASS SAT ON THE BED in Frank Luck's spare room and tugged on a running jersey and tights. She gathered her Nikes and a headband, then followed the aroma of coffee.

Across the cabin's timber-ceilinged main room, alongside a stone fireplace, Wilmot Hoffman sat at a work table. Head bent over a vise clamped to the table's edge, he wore magnifying lenses clipped to his glasses, and fiddled with tweezers, pliers, and bits of colored thread.

Bent behind Wilmot, Frank grunted and pointed as he supervised his fly-tying student.

Cass padded in her socks to the kitchen, poured herself a cup, returned, and stood alongside Wilmot and Frank. "Frank, when can we start looking for the guy you got the map case from?"

"I think one of us already has. How late were you up clicking that laptop?"

"Not as long as you think. I exhausted my online options before 2:00 a.m. And Merken's shy veteran is still shy."

Wilmot said, "If you can't find the airplane, try to find the bomb it was designed for, first. Assume the *Uranverein* was a decoy."

Cass said, "Then what?"

Wilmot cocked his head and sighed. "Then assume parallel problems beget parallel solutions. Look for the Manhattan Project. But with differences."

Cass sat on Frank's sofa and tugged her Nikes on. "Meaning what?"

"Look for the things that the Manhattan Project got right. For starters, look for a project that sounds too mundane to attract attention."

"The Manhattan Engineer District."

"Exactly. Look for it in sparsely populated interior areas, where the enemy couldn't get at it, or get wind of it. The European equivalent of Oak Ridge, Tennessee, or Los Alamos, New Mexico. Preferably near electric power. At full tilt, Oak Ridge consumed twenty percent more electricity than New York City. They built Oak Ridge in the Tennessee River Valley, so they could tap hydroelectricity created by Tennessee Valley authority dams built to make jobs during the Depression."

"What else?"

Wilmot shrugged. "Peculiar materiel allocations. The Manhattan Project consumed so much electricity it couldn't get enough copper to conduct it all. So it substituted silver, which is actually a better conductor."

"Enough silver to notice?"

"Notice? In 1940, total U.S. silver production was seventy million troy ounces. The Manhattan Project borrowed *seven hundred* million troy ounces of bullion from the U.S. Treasury. That's fourteen tons."

"Wow. Okay, what else would the Nazis have needed to add?"

"Not add. Subtract. Forget plutonium entirely. It doesn't even exist in nature. The first pinch of it was lab-synthesized in 1940, in America. Reactors to breed plutonium in quantity didn't exist, either. And plutonium only blows up in an implosion-style device like the Fat Man bomb. The first implosion bomb was so complex they called it 'The Gadget.' They were so unsure it would work that they test-fired it first.

"By comparison, the Hiroshima gun-type uranium bomb was so simple that they didn't test it first. Besides, plutonium's more toxic than uranium. It would have left behind an ineradicable footprint that we would know about. Most of our nuclear waste problems are plutonium-related."

"You seriously think the Germans could have managed a uranium-only bomb project? On the side?"

Wilmot nodded. "If they kept it simple. The only really hard part is separating the one percent of uranium that's fissionable from the other ninety-nine percent."

Cass said, "But they did. How?"

"Lots of ways. The Hiroshima bomb's U-235 was collected mostly by electromagnetic separation. It took almost three years to collect enough U-235 to build one bomb by that process."

Cass said, "How much smaller would the project been without plutonium?"

Wilmot said, "Not just without plutonium. Process experts say that one should always choose the third best technology. The best technology will never be ready. The second-best technology won't be ready in time. The K-25 gaseous diffusion demonstration plant was the largest building built on Earth when it was finished. But it was the second-best technology, and it wasn't ready until after the war."

Cass said, "So, how downsized a project am I looking for?"

"Manhattan Project employment peaked at one hundred thirty thousand. Cut the plutonium and the redundancies, you could cut the project by an order of magnitude." He cocked his head. "If the Nazis housed the facilities in preexisting brick and mortar, instead of creating factories and towns at green field sites, the project is smaller still."

"It will take forever to research this problem that way. Frank, I wish the guy you got this case from would just show up and ask for it back." Cass propped one ankle on a stool, alongside the fly-tying bench.

She inhaled, then held, a deep breath, while she stretched her fingertips toward her upraised ankle.

When she relaxed, Frank said, "Did you just hold your breath?"

She repeated the stretch with her opposite ankle.

Before she inhaled, she nodded. "Voluntary hypoventilation is a trending strategy to improve cardiopulmonary function."

Frank snorted. "More hippie crap."

She stared at him, her hands on her hips. "You have a better strategy?"

"Live in the mountains. Your red cell count will increase. So will your maximal oxygen uptake. You won't breathe any smog, you won't get hit by cars or get mugged when you're out jogging. You won't need burglar bars on your windows, either."

Cass slammed Frank's front door behind her as she left.

The man was insufferable. When she got back from her run, she would call Merken and demand a ticket home.

❖   ❖   ❖

The mountain air smelled of pine, birds chirped, and the sky was impossibly blue. Even in late June, morning chill refreshed her, unlike the sultry D.C. mornings she had left behind. She trotted down the winding gravel path that Frank called a drive-way, past Frank's truck and Wilmot's sedan, parked side by side. The trouble with Frank was that he was probably right about the benefits of mountain living. In fact, annoyingly enough, he was right about a lot of things.

She picked out a thick-trunked ponderosa alongside the drive, pressed both palms on its bark, and leaned in as if she were try-ing to push the tree over.

As she stretched her calves and Achilles tendons, she arched her back and peered up into the pine's branches.

She blinked, stared harder, then stepped back, tugged off her wraparound sunglasses, and squinted up into the shadows.

Whether Frank was right or wrong about hypoventilation, any opportunity to contradict him was too good to bypass. She ran back to the cabin, took the porch steps two at a time, and stepped back inside.

Frank and Wilmot turned and stared.

Frank said, "Too much hypoventilating?"

Cass pointed through the door and down the driveway. "If burglar bars are unnecessary up here, why do you have those?"

Frank walked to the door and peered out. "Trees?"

"Surveillance cameras."

"Surveillance cameras? I don't even lock my shed."

Cass led Frank and Wilmot down the driveway to the tree, then pointed up into the shadows. Clipped to a branch, twelve feet above the ground, dangled a white plastic egg, its lens aimed back toward Frank's cabin.

She said, "You didn't stick that up there?"

Frank shook his head.

He hung his hands on his hips. "Who the *hell* . . . ?" Then he turned and stalked back toward the cabin, gravel crunching beneath his boots.

Cass's jaw dropped. "You're just going to *leave* it there?"

"Yep."

"Why?"

"You hunt deer?"

"What? No. I'm *vegan*, Frank."

"Oh. Well, it's not sporting, but if you put out apples, the deer come to you."

"What the hell does that mean?"

"That you might get your wish."

"What?"

"If we leave that camera in that tree we may not need to go looking for the guy I got the map case from."

Twenty-nine

IN A SUPERMARKET PARKING LOT, OFF THE INTERSTATE HIGHWAY near Avon, the Asp loaded his groceries into the Expedition's vast rear compartment.

Already the rear compartment contained his other purchases. Those included replacement tires for a horse trailer, an air compressor to inflate them, a commercial-grade cordless drill, large-diameter metal-cutting bits, and an assortment of nuts and bolts of similar diameter. At the automotive store where he bought the tires, he had also purchased, and had installed on the Expedition, a high-capacity front-mounted winch.

He hurried back to the big SUV's driver's seat.

He had been on a tight schedule since the moment he had stepped from the home of the elderly widow in Louisiana who had sold him the pistol. In that instant, he had seen the path that God had illuminated for him.

As he sat behind the Expedition's wheel, he thumbed an app on his three-day-old replacement smartphone.

He drummed his fingers on the Expedition's steering wheel while the cheap app slowly loaded.

The surveillance camera to which the app connected the Asp's phone was one of three from the kit that had proven useless as a warning system, due to the lack of internet connectivity at Upper Pika Lake.

From its hiding place in a tree, the system of which the camera was part transmitted a silent color image of the vehicle parking area in front of Luck's cabin. The Asp had opted not to risk emplacing the kit's other cameras inside the cabin, where their discovery might alert Luck. The camera uploaded an image every ten minutes, and the app saved them for the next twenty-four hours.

This outside camera told the Asp what he needed to know. He had checked the app the previous day, while crossing Oklahoma, then reasonably inferred that the old American pickup truck parked at the cabin belonged to Frank Luck.

So, Luck, and almost certainly the map case, were now inside the cabin.

Luck's truck hadn't moved. But parked alongside it today sat a huge, black American sedan, that must have arrived earlier in the morning. The number plate on Luck's truck bore white characters on a jagged green background, topped with white. The design represented the mountains of Colorado, the American state where the vehicle was licensed.

The sedan's number plate, however, bore blue characters on a white background. The characters were separated into two groups by two horizontal red bars, like the "equals" symbol in an equation.

The Asp searched up an internet chart showing the distinctively designed number plates of the American states and territories.

He scrolled the display until his breath caught.

Washington. Not the American state, but the "District of Columbia."

"Washington D.C." was the headquarters of the American national police in charge of counter-terrorism, the FBI. Even more alarming, Washington was the nerve center from which the CIA, and the American military, managed America's worldwide assault on Islam.

True, Washington D.C. was also home to perhaps a half million Americans who were unaffiliated with official Washington. All of them were as free as he was to drive across state borders, and to visit Colorado, and Frank Luck, by pure coincidence.

But in the Asp's line of work, coincidence was suspicious by definition. Sometimes, the prudent response to suspicious circumstances was to ignore them. If he had ignored the dying old crone in Avon, Luck and the missing map case would never have become a loose end.

The prudent course was simply to keep to his recently fixed timetable at Upper Pika Lake. Before anything else could go wrong.

The Asp fastened his seat belt, swiped to his phone's navigation app and set it for the interstate exit that led to Upper Pika Lake. After he started the Expedition's engine, he swiped back to close the camera app, and peered one last time at the sedan in Luck's driveway. Taped inside the sedan's rear window was a hand-lettered paper sign, which he had not noticed at first.

He frowned at the image, then zoomed it.

Over his lifetime, he had learned to read printed English well. But deciphering hand-lettered English, which read left to right, came harder to someone raised reading the Arabic abjad, which read right to left.

Finally, he made out the sign's fragmentary words:

COLO TAG APPLIED FOR

He remembered what the Mexican girl in Texas had warned him about relocating to another state with the Expedition's Texas number plates.

"If you settle in a different state, you're supposed to apply for new plates. But they won't stop you to check. Unless you... put a sign in your window that says, 'Tag Applied For.' Anglos don't much mind getting stopped, and warned, to get local tags."

Five minutes later, the Asp stared at an entry in the *Vail Daily Online*'s "Newcomers" column:

East Vail Newcomers Wilmot and Velma Hoffman: Retired from the Washington, D.C. area. Interior decorator Velma enjoys gardening. Wilmot, a federal civil servant and physics Ph.D., plans to fish.

Another five minutes' research turned up the abstracts of seven papers authored or co-authored by Dr. Wilmot Hoffman. All seven concerned nuclear weapons design and policy. The contents of six of the papers were restricted to authorized government users.

The Asp felt beneath the driver's seat for the .45, checked again that a round was chambered, then replaced the pistol. He reset his phone's navigation app destination to Frank Luck's cabin, then pulled out of the store's lot headed west.

Some coincidences were too suspicious to ignore.

He had gone through too much, preparing for the result that now lay just out of reach. According to the story the Sheik's papers told, the old woman had also gone through too much preparing, many years before today.

Thirty

ON OCTOBER 20, 1944, ILSE JAEGER STOOD ALONGSIDE THE SALZ-reich Project's landing strip, trembling as she watched the single-engine plane land. The Fieseler Stork's very important pilot settled the two-seater onto the grass, with a surgical delicacy that shouldn't jostle the Stork's even more important passenger.

The rest of *Reichsführer* Himmler's welcoming party surrounded Ilse. Peter Winter and his directors, Fromm the Bear, Becker the Prussian, and Mueller the Jailer, stood to her left. To her right stood Himmler's bodyguards, assistant, and photographer. His entourage had arrived earlier, by car, and stood as stiff as the surrounding trees. Winter's two high-level Jews Wolf the Jeweler, and Hersh, the physicist, were, of course, absent.

Himmler and his celebrity pilot, Hanna Reitsch, crossed the grass as the photographer dashed forward, knelt, and took their photo.

Ilse hadn't seen the *Reichsführer* in person since he had interviewed her for this test pilot position, two years and five months earlier.

The sight of him still took her breath away.

On Ilse's tenth birthday, her mother had enrolled her in the Band of German Maidens' Young Girl's League. Afterward, Ilse had asked her mother why so many women proposed marriage to Adolf Hitler. And why he did not accept. Because Ilse thought the fuehrer a most ordinary-looking man.

Her mother had said, "The fuehrer is *not* an ordinary man. He is already married. To the German nation. He could never prefer one woman over it. And that makes his power all the more aphrodisiac."

At the time, Ilse had been forced to look up the word "aphrodisiac." But at Ilse's first Party meeting, Heinrich Himmler had greeted the giggling Band of German Maidens graduates, but had spoken only to *her*. In that instant, as his fingers lightly brushed her shoulder, she had understood the word. And her life had been forever altered.

And when Ilse had been called to his office to interview, the grace with which this ordinary-looking man shouldered his unimaginable responsibility dizzied her.

Today, his face brightened when he saw her. When he stepped past the others, and greeted her, and remembered her name, she felt faint.

He leaned close to her, while Winter and the others walked Hanna around the airplane.

The *Reichsführer* said, "Ilse, after you have completed the demonstration flight, would you be able to spare a moment for me this evening?"

"I would be honored, *Reichsführer*."

He patted her arm. "Please. Call me Heinrich."

Ilse turned in front of the mirror in the women's washroom in the Salzreich Mine's offices. She checked that her flight coverall was both clean, and pressed. That was routine for her. Today, she also checked her hair and makeup.

"Heinrich." A god had invited her to call him "Heinrich!"

Flight Captain Hanna Reitsch came and stood beside Ilse, reapplying her own lipstick. Ilse's mentor was also a civilian, despite her title. She was also Germany's most-decorated woman pilot.

Hanna said, "Does the aircraft's performance match its looks?"

Ilse said, "The controls are heavy, even with hydraulic assistance. And it's prone to Dutch roll. But overall, it's astoundingly responsive, considering its size. And breathtakingly fast." Ilse turned to her mentor. "It is really quite well wrung out by now. But you know, the right-hand seat is empty, today. Your impressions of the aircraft's characteristics would be invaluable."

Hanna shook her head. "Not since the crash, Little One."

Small as a pixie, Hanna Reitsch called Ilse by the ironic nickname she had given her taller protégé, years before.

Today, Hanna was barely a year recovered, after a horrific crash, during her testing of the Comet rocket plane. The accident had broken her back and skull, and severed her nose. Yet, while trapped, broken, and bleeding in the cockpit, she had made notes of the flight characteristics, which she expected might save others' lives, after she died.

For her devotion to duty, the fuehrer had personally presented her the Knight's Cross First Class.

Ilse said, "You don't fly because of ongoing pain, Hanna?"

Hanna laughed, as she shrugged. "Pain I can ignore. The fuehrer no German can ignore. When he presented my Knight's Cross, he forbade me from experimental flight testing. All I do now is fly big shots around."

Hanna traded her grin for a frown. "Although your flight today is hardly an experiment. I know why Himmler called me away from my assigned duties to fly him here. He wants to impress someone who has the fuehrer's ear in aviation matters. Someone who isn't Goering. As you grow, you will learn how the great political mind works."

"Did the *Reichsführer* tell you that on the way down here?"

Hanna Reitsch's frown deepened. "He said very little on the way down here."

Ilse smiled. "Storks *are* too noisy for subtle discourse."

Hanna shook her head. "That wasn't the reason. Before we took off, I stole a private moment with him. I showed him a leaflet. A diplomat friend of mine brought it with him, from the German consulate in Sweden.

"Ilse, the Allies are spreading the most abominable propaganda, to poison public opinion in the neutral countries. They say we're operating extermination factories in the East. That we are slaughtering fancy boys, and Jews, and gypsies, like cattle. Can you imagine? I told him we must not allow such vile libels to go unchallenged."

"What did the *Reichsführer* say?"

"He agreed with me, of course. He said, 'Hanna, that is merely the rope by which they will hang us, in the case of defeat.' But he is such an honorable man. I'm afraid the scale, and viciousness, of the Allies' lies shocked him to silence for the rest of our journey here."

"Extermination factories." Ilse rolled her eyes. "How stupid do the Allies think people are?"

✧　　✧　　✧

Minutes later, Fromm, the red-bearded bear, led Ilse, along with Hanna and Peter Winter, as they walked beneath Prototype One's vast, silver wing. Fromm's great child slept in the sun, waiting to awaken at Ilse's touch.

As they walked, Himmler's photographer's shutter clicked repeatedly.

Hanna asked Fromm, "In this airframe, how many hours do you get from each engine? I'm hearing that the Me 262 engines' service life can be as short as ten hours. The engine temperatures weaken the turbine blades' steel."

Fromm shrugged. "These aren't the Junkers engine, Flight Captain. They're BMW 003s. We have a different problem. So few of these engines have been manufactured, much less flown, that we have too little data to predict their life under operational conditions. But we don't dare wear out the few engines that we have, simply to test their lifespan."

Heinrich, who had commandeered Winter's office to make telephone calls, joined them, as the photographer clicked away.

It was interesting to see how the photos one saw later in the papers and magazines were composed. The photographer most often photographed Heinrich from a low angle, which made him look taller. And the photographer always snapped pictures from an angle that kept the fenced workers' compound out of the background.

For just an instant, Ilse wondered whether Hanna's Allied extermination propaganda brochure simply described reality from a less flattering angle.

Hanna frowned at Fromm. "It will take more than durable engines for this airplane to win the war."

Hanna shooed Fromm away from the plane. She took Himmler's arm, and pointed up at the Prototype, while Ilse and Peter Winter looked on.

Himmler's photographer's shutter clicked again.

Hanna said to Himmler, "This prototype is magnificent. Dr. Winter and Captain Fromm, and of course Miss Jaeger, have shown us the future. But, as I have told the fuehrer, himself, machines such as this one are but embryos. The wonder weapons that could turn the tide for Germany are the grandchildren of these embryos. At this late hour, this airplane, or even a hundred like it, could not turn the tide."

The rebuttal to Hanna's argument, of course, was that the weapon that this plane would carry would give it the strength, not of one hundred, but of one *thousand*, planes, and more.

Ilse glanced at Heinrich.

He shook his head, minutely.

No one else mentioned the bomb to Hanna, either.

And regardless, Hanna was right. For Germany the hour was perhaps too late to reverse the tide, no matter what. In the East, the Russians were rolling across Poland toward Germany almost as fast as the German army had rolled over the Poles in 1939. In the West, the British and the Americans had landed in Italy a year ago, and Italy had affirmed its reputation as a nation of cowards by switching sides. This past June, the Allies had also landed in Normandy, and by August had recaptured Paris, and landed yet again, in the south of France. Meanwhile, Allied bombers and fighters roamed the skies, raining indiscriminate death on innocent German civilians.

That the *Reichsführer* chose to record this moment measured his confidence, and the prescience of his vision. He believed—he *knew*—that, against all odds, this war would be won. Or at least concluded in a manner that preserved the honor, dignity, and territorial integrity of the National Socialist state. And these dark times would be remembered, for a thousand years, as Germany's finest hour.

Hanna asked Fromm, "What is this design named?"

Fromm the Bear said, "I was thinking of 'Barn Owl.'"

Himmler squinted through his spectacles. "'Barn Owl'? You're joking."

Hanna said, "*Reichsführer*, traditionally, we name aircraft for birds. The most warlike birds' names are already taken."

Himmler said, "Birds don't win wars. A weapon gifted to us by the gods deserves a name that honors them. Why not Valkyrie?"

Hanna smiled at Himmler. "I think it's a marvelous choice. The fuehrer would love it."

Fromm shrugged. "Then Valkyrie she is."

As the Valkyrie's engines howled, and the aircraft strained against the brakes that tethered her to the earth, Ilse glanced out through the plane's canopy, toward Heinrich and the others who stood alongside the airstrip.

A quick climb out, reverse course, then back for a low, thundering, high-speed flyby for the photographer, then around again, and land.

Fromm, as always, had been blunt and honest about their ignorance of these engines' service life. Whatever that life was, there was no point wasting it on this flight, when engine replacements were so scarce.

And, if she were honest with herself, the shorter the flight the sooner she would find out what Heinrich wanted to discuss with her.

She advanced the throttles, released the brakes, and the Valkyrie rolled forward. Acceleration pressed her back against the pilot's seat.

As Ilse lifted the great aircraft's nose, she felt the familiar jolt, as the landing-gear struts unloaded.

Then, within the port wing, a tremendous bang exploded.

Something struck her left thigh, as though it had been hacked by a giant butcher's cleaver.

The controls froze.

Rudderless, enormous, prone to Dutch roll, the Valkyrie was a beast, even when she was behaving.

Now, suddenly, she was simply an aluminum meteor, spewing fire as she plunged to Earth.

In that instant Ilse knew. A blade in the inboard-most port engine's whirling turbine had failed. That blade, in turn, had sheared off or damaged others. One or more blades had shot through the cockpit, and through her thigh. Worse, other blades had severed the hydraulic lines. Without hydraulic augmentation, the massive wing's control surfaces could barely be budged by human muscle.

Prototype One, so recently christened Valkyrie, crashed short of the airstrip's end.

Ilse was hurled forward against her seat harness, and her face struck the instruments.

Ilse awoke on a litter, in the secretarial bay outside Peter Winter's office.

She felt little pain, and realized she was heavily sedated. A red-filled transfusion bottle dangled from a metal rod attached to her litter. A tube connected to it was taped to a needle in her left arm.

She saw Fromm, then pushed the medic away from herself with her right hand. She said to the Bear, "How bad is it?"

Fromm leaned close to hear her, then looked at the medic, who said to her, "Your left femur is fractured in multiple places. Your femoral artery was severed. You suffered a severe concussion. Also burns. But fortunately, your face—"

"Not me! The plane!"

Fromm shook his head. "Ilse, the important thing is they say you'll recover. Although you won't be flying for a while. The aircraft is a total loss. There was nothing whatever you could have done to prevent it. We may be able to salvage one engine, and parts for another. But—"

Fromm was pulled back, by a small, black-gloved hand on his massive upper arm.

Then the *Reichsführer*, himself, stood, peering down into her face.

She said, "I'm sorry."

He knelt beside her, and stroked her hair. "You have nothing to be sorry for, my brave Valkyrie. Rest."

Heinrich Himmler removed his black cap, with its silver death's-head insignia, then bent and kissed her forehead.

She closed her eyes and let the drugs take her away.

But she would be back.

Thirty-one

AFTER ILSE JAEGER HAD BEEN BORNE AWAY BY AMBULANCE, AFTER Fromm had issued his gloomy prognosis for the wreck, and after Hanna Reitsch had flown Himmler away in the Stork, Peter Winter unlocked his front door.

He entered the house that he and Rachel had now shared with Peter's father-in-law for five years.

Rachel slumped on the bottom step of the house's foyer staircase. Her house dress, which was always pressed, was rumpled. Her eyes were red, and swollen. A hunting rifle lay across her thighs.

Peter dropped his briefcase, ran, and knelt in front of her, grasping and holding tight to the rifle's stock. "Are you alright? What's happened?"

Rachel opened her fist, and stared at a balled paper in her palm. "A salesman from Wetzlar delivered this note, from his mother, Jacob's landlady. For Father. It says that, two weeks ago, the police came in the middle of the night. And took my brother."

"Why?"

"Who knows? Jacob stopped telling me what he was doing a year ago. Because what I didn't know, I couldn't tell. And couldn't be blamed for."

"I remember. We figured he had joined the Resistance."

She nodded. "Jacob always did the right thing. Especially when it was the stupid thing. Not that whatever he did mattered to the police. Today it's enough simply that he was a Jew."

Peter said, "Alright. Next they'll schedule one of those public shouting events they call a trial. In the meantime, I'll think up something to tell Himmler. So don't say 'was.' We don't know—"

"We do know. They made him kneel on the sidewalk, then woke everyone in the street. Then they shot him in the face. As an example. To whom, or for what, the landlady didn't know. Or wouldn't say." Rachel collapsed against Peter, sobbing.

"Why the gun?" Peter slid the rifle off her lap, then pushed it out of her reach. "You weren't thinking..."

"Of shooting myself? No. I was insane, but in a different way. I got the rifle from Father's gun cabinet, up in the study. I was going to drive over to the Salzreich. Then break in to your meeting with Himmler. And shoot him in his pig face. Like his police shot my brother."

She paused while she swallowed. "But it's not market day. So you had the car. Isn't that a ridiculous reason for an assassin to fail?"

Peter said, "How did your father—?"

"I haven't told him. He's having one of his passive days. Who knows how he would have reacted? But, I think, in his mind he already believes the Nazis have taken Jacob's life away. I may tell Father. It's almost better to know. Compared to these people who are just disappearing to the east. For those whom they leave behind, not knowing is crueler."

She wiped her eyes. "So. How was *your* day? It had to be better than mine."

Peter hesitated, then said, "It was. We'll talk in the morning."

He held her, and rocked her, while she cried herself to sleep in his arms. Then he carried her upstairs, laid her down, and covered her with the duvet.

He sat in a chair alongside her, holding her hand. Two hours later, he drifted off himself.

The next morning, Peter watched as Sheldon Bergman sat at the breakfast table in the conservatory, at the table's head, while Peter and Rachel sat to his left and right. The three of them shared, and read, sections of the previous day's *People's Observer*.

Sheldon chewed day-old bread, which Rachel had toasted on the kitchen's wood stove, while he squinted at the print through his pince-nez spectacles.

Rain rumbled on the roof's glass panes, then wept down

its sides. Rachel served breakfast in the conservatory, despite the rain, because its gloom offered adequate reading light. The alternative was to run the electric generator, for the lights. That would deplete their gasoline stock. Commodities as mundane as bread and gasoline were now scarce luxuries, even for Germans of Peter's status.

Sheldon Bergman slapped his section of the paper. "How long does Goebbels think Germans will believe this manure? If the perfect German war machine is producing so much of everything, why are we eating stale bread, in the dark?"

Rachel's father oscillated between dementia and normalcy. In terms of his condition, at least, today was a good day, so far.

Peter's father-in-law stood. "Therefore, I'm going out to turn the vegetable garden. So we won't starve come spring."

Peter stared up at the rain coursing off the glass roof, and opened his mouth.

Rachel raised her palm and shook her head at Peter.

After Sheldon had left the room, Peter said, "Rachel, it's pouring! You can't let Father—"

"Relax. He'll forget about it before he finds his boots."

"Sometimes you treat him like a child."

"No. With a child, one always has the 'because I said so' alternative."

Peter said, "Yesterday—"

"What's this?" Rachel reached in to Peter's briefcase, open on the table, and withdrew the flat, stainless-steel case she noticed peeking from it.

Peter said, "It's a case to contain the airplane's pilot's checklists, maps, and equipment. Hyman Wolf's people fabricated it."

Rachel pointed at Peter's briefcase. "What's wrong with a leather case, like yours?"

Peter smiled. "Not a thing. But Hyman proposed this, and I approved it. It took four man-weeks to design and build it. The bomb casing is being manufactured from the same material. But—"

"Something changed yesterday. I see it in your eyes. You're stalling."

"Prototype One crashed on takeoff. Ilse Jaeger was the only casualty. And she should recover. But the plane is scrap."

"My God. In front of Himmler? Why haven't you been hung already?"

Peter shook his head. "There were unavoidable reasons for the accident. An engine exploded. The engine manufacturers have had to make do with steels that can't withstand turbojet engines' higher operating temperatures."

"So where does that leave things for us?"

"With a decision to make about completing the bomb."

"No. We already decided. You make things look good, but go just slow enough that the bomb will never be complete. You let Germans be Germans, and let them choose complicated, slow solutions to every problem."

"Letting my subordinates drift in circles may no longer be the best answer. Rachel, the situation is different now than when we charted our course. America is coming up to speed as a military force. In the East the Russians have turned the tide. Germany sits between two giants that will inevitably crush us. The American economy is four times ours. What Russia lacks in factory output it makes up for in determination to revisit on Germany the atrocities Russians suffered when we invaded. We can't win this war now. But we also don't dare lose it. I heard Canaris predict this reversal to Himmler in October of 1941, before the winter retreat from Moscow."

"You're saying the Allies will bludgeon us with a repeat of Versailles?"

Peter shook his head. "A peace only as bad as Versailles was would be a miracle. The victors won't repeat their mistake. The Allies won't stop at our borders this time."

Rachel nodded slowly. "You're right. And the Nazi fanatics won't stop fighting when our borders are breached. They will fight to the last German, if they have to hold guns to the backs of children to make them charge into cannon fire. The Nazis will fight to the last brick in the last house. And to the last blade of grass, in the last pasture. Britain, what's left of France, the United States, and Russia will make sure that this time any Germans left standing will be ankle-deep in rubble, starving, and unable to start another war. Ever again."

"That's not even the worst case. Hitler escaped the army plotters' bomb in East Prussia three months ago. But the war has gone from worse to worst since, and he's surely lost support even among the officers who escaped his revenge purge. The next coup could collapse the German military entirely. Before Pearl

Harbor, the American people didn't like the Nazis, but they were eighty percent opposed to joining this war in Europe. In their view, they went to war against Japan, then got this mess into the bargain. If German resistance collapses, America could easily declare their work in Europe finished, then turn their attention to the country that actually attacked them."

"If the British stood alone their friendly enemy Stalin would bully them all the way back to the Rhine."

Peter nodded. "Then he would take a revenge on Germany worse than Versailles multiplied by one hundred. This bomb could help all the Germans who *aren't* fanatics survive Armageddon."

"How? You can't give the Nazis, of all people, the ability to set off this bomb."

"I don't intend to. Remember, if one keeps trying, there is always a way out to be found."

"What are you saying?"

"To prevent the bomb from detonating prematurely, a plug that allows the electrical circuit to be completed has to be inserted. The plug I've had Wolf the Jeweler design is intricate, in the best German tradition of over-complex solutions to simple problems. He's making only one, and I'll be the only one with access to it."

"Peter, that's you playing god."

"That's me playing the only card in my hand. And only until we can think of a better way out. The crash has bought us time to find a better way out."

"How?"

"Fromm is a miracle worker. But the second prototype won't be ready to replace the wreck until next spring. Even before then the bomb should easily be complete. Which raises another problem."

"What?"

"Facilities construction is already complete. We'll have enough U-235 within a month. If Speer's people realize we have idle laborers, they will reassign them to other, harsher, camps and factories. Or worse, they will be sent on the trains to the east, and murdered. We've faced the underutilization problem all along. We've built and allowed to be built all kinds of make work projects, to stretch out the process since it became apparent that the war was lost."

"But with that Nazi bitch Jaeger gone nobody's looking over your shoulder, now."

Peter said, "Not entirely. Himmler told me he's been noti-
fied by Speer's office to expect auditors. But Himmler told me
to stall them."

Rachel paled. "Auditors? Himmler's onto us?"

"No." Peter shook his head. "If Himmler were onto us, auditors
wouldn't visit, and especially not auditors from Speer. Speer isn't
the rival to Himmler that Goering is, but he's no friend, either.
If Himmler turned on us, an SS detachment would hit us like a
lightning bolt. That's how he purged the Nazi party during the
Night of the Long Knives in 1934."

"But why audit at all? Do they think you skimmed? From all
the silver Himmler sent? The stuff you spun into wire for the
magnets? How typically Nazi. Rob candelabras and flatware by
the ton from Jewish families, then count every dessert spoon as
though it had been Nazi property since the Flood."

"It's not that kind of audit. Since Speer took over as armaments
minister, in 1942, production is up, propaganda notwithstanding.
Despite all the Allied bombing."

"Maybe if the Allies bombed factories, instead of people's
houses, they would get better results."

"Speer is more than the beneficiary of incompetent bombing.
He's an effective manager. But mostly, the ministry fills in gaps
with an unlimited supply of impressed laborers."

"Otherwise known as slaves. Whom they literally work to
death."

"Yes. Which is exactly why you and I have done what we've
done here, since 1941. To keep as many innocents as we could
away from *those* camps."

"Then what's the problem?"

"Part of the audit will focus on problems with the Salzreich
Project's labor force."

"The Salzreich Project's labor force is fine."

"That's the problem."

Thirty-two

ON THE EVENING OF MARCH 9, 1945, AFTER ALMOST FIVE MONTHS of stalling the audit that Himmler had warned about, Peter sat with his hands folded, at his conference table in the Salzreich Project offices.

The senior Armaments and War Production Ministry auditor seated across the table from Peter closed the last ledger that Peter had provided to him and his two junior auditors.

The senior man passed the heavy book to one of the juniors, who piled it atop the stacks at the table's end.

The audit team had arrived the previous morning, by car, before sunrise. Not to surprise Peter. They had driven all night. Germans who had gasoline, and travel authorization, drove by night, to avoid strafing by Allied fighters.

The Allies owned Germany's sky. Within weeks, they would own the rest of Germany. Yesterday, the Americans had crossed the Rhine, because retreating German forces had failed to blow up the last remaining bridge across the river, the Ludendorff Bridge at Remagen.

The senior auditor stared at the table top and drummed his fingers. Then he leaned back, hooked a thumb in his waistcoat pocket, and stroked his broad mustache with his other thumb.

He said, "Dr. Winter, I understand you do most of the book-keeping yourself. I compliment you on your records' thoroughness and accuracy. We find nothing worthy of adverse comment, much less worthy of reprimand."

Peter said, "Thank you. Is there anything else?"

One of the junior auditors had slicked-back hair, and displayed his Party lapel pin prominently.

The Nazi steepled his fingers beneath his chin. "We do have one concern. In evaluating a facility's efficiency, we try to compare it to an analogous facility."

The senior auditor said, "The underground fuel depot project at Kohnstein Mountain, is, in many ways, comparable to the Salzreich Records Repository Project."

Peter nodded. "Ah."

Kohnstein Mountain, near the village of Nordhausen, was a "fuel depot" in the way that the Salzreich was a "file room." The gypsum mine beneath Kohnstein Mountain had been converted to a V-1 and V-2 rocket factory. One advantage of being a phony civilian project was that run-of-the-mill auditors weren't officially supposed to know about the project's real work.

The slick-haired Nazi said, "Minister Speer has recognized the Kohnstein Mountain Project as an industrial achievement equaling, or surpassing, the finest American factories. And, from 1943 to date, no fewer than twenty percent of Nordhausen's guest workers have succumbed to the stresses of their employment. In fact, that number does not even account for a large number of unregistered workers who may also have perished."

The senior man stroked his mustache. "Over the comparable period, fewer than two percent of your workers have succumbed, Dr. Winter. Two percent is roughly equivalent to the survivability of a comparable population in the general economy, during the comparable period. But you have not yet submitted a request for replacements, even for those few."

Peter said, "I see. You're recommending that to narrow the gap I shoot eighteen percent of my healthy, trained workers? So I can waste time training their replacements?"

The senior man smiled. The Nazi did not.

The senior man said, "It's not our purpose to question your methods. *Reichsführer* Himmler's office has made that clear to us. However, Germany needs all of its facilities, including yours, to operate at maximum efficiency. By utilizing available resources fully."

Peter said, "Of course."

The mustached man continued. "In these times, the ministry must alleviate many resources' shortage, by substituting other resources. One resource Germany has to spare is labor. Therefore, Dr. Winter, we will report that we have encouraged you to at least request *replacements* to fill your vacancies. And to determine whether positions held by unregistered, but deceased, workers *also* can be productively filled."

Peter said, "Is it worth requesting replacements, if the Americans will arrive before they do?"

The senior man smiled briefly, while he flicked open his pocket watch. Then he frowned.

His team had only a few hours of darkness left, when they could drive in relative safety.

He said, "Dr. Winter, if you request those replacements tomorrow, new workers will begin arriving at your gate by April 1. In Minister Speer's name, I guarantee this."

As the senior auditors hurried to the door, the slick-haired Nazi stuffed papers into his briefcase.

He said, "Dr. Winter, after we win this war, if you intend to continue your work as a comedian, I suggest you choose your audiences carefully."

Rachel sat across from Peter at the candlelit conservatory dining table.

She said, "Did they actually count heads?"

"No. They're good German bureaucrats. They asked for records. I brought them records, and the numbers added up. Today, auditors don't want to know what really goes on in defense facilities. Frankly, these were principally concerned that they get home before any bridges they had to cross got blown up."

"They told you there were 'unregistered' workers at the V-2 factory, up at Nordhausen? If there's one thing German bureaucrats do, it's register and catalogue things."

"Thousands of 'unregistered' workers have died up there, from what I've heard. That's because bureaucrats don't run Nordhausen. The SS does."

"That's perfect."

"What?"

"The easiest life to take is a life that doesn't exist. A worker never put on the books doesn't have to be accounted for."

"I don't understand."

"Write to the ministry tomorrow. Say, 'by the way, we actually found out we were tougher on our workers than we thought. Two thousand more workers died over the last years. But we didn't have time to register them.'"

"That sounds like confessing to murder. Why would I do that?"

"First, the Nazis will give you a medal for killing undesirables. Second, they'll send you replacements by April 1."

"Where the hell will I put them? Every bed is full, and then some."

"You won't actually put them anywhere. Have Jews you trust, like Wolf, drive out and meet the trucks delivering the replacements, before they get to the Salzreich. When the delivery trucks leave, release the new laborers. If we report two thousand vacancies, then, after two thousand replacements are delivered we have no vacancies, all the numbers add up. It's German bureaucracy at its finest."

"Some of those workers will be caught without papers. They will talk, and expose everything."

"They can't expose what they don't know. That's why they will never see this place."

"That won't work for long."

"It doesn't *have* to work for long. The war may be *over* by April 1. If it isn't, the Americans will be on our doorstep. Already the Nazis have us blowing up our own bridges, and cutting down our own telephone poles to block the roads and slow down the Americans. A month from now, nobody in Germany will know what's happening in the next town, much less be counting refugees. Peter, the local police here spend more time helping old ladies across the street than checking papers. They're hardly SS fanatics."

"Rachel, you're proposing an insanely dangerous gamble."

"No more dangerous than the gamble I proposed in 1935. And here we are, after a decade in darkness, with the sun about to rise."

"If we try this, we may not live to see it rise."

"Would you rather we live with the knowledge that thousands died, because we didn't try? At least my brother tried."

The following morning Rachel awoke Peter with an insistent kiss.

Beneath the duvet, her fingers untied his pajama bottoms' draw string, as she slithered on top of him.

"Rachel, I'll be late for work."

"Today, this is your work."

He rolled the two of them so that he was on top, pinned her arms to the bed, then said, "Wait. Isn't this the wrong time of the month?"

"Not for what I have in mind."

"What? It was your idea in 1935 that we start our family after this mess resolved."

"Well, now it's my idea that ten years is damn long enough. There are grandmothers younger than I am. And the mess is close enough to resolved."

"Hardly. If we do escape the Nazis, then what? We've spent six years making the Salzreich look like a concentration camp, run by me. I'll be tried as a war criminal. Or shot on the spot, if the Russians have a say."

"The Americans are on our doorstep, not the Russians. They will see that the plane was ready. The bomb was ready. But they will see that you avoided using them."

"Maybe. Or maybe they'll just give me a fair trial before they hang me."

"No. First, the Americans are better than that."

"All you know about them is what their novelists write."

"Second, Wolf and the others will tell the Americans what really happened. That you saved their lives.

"Third, the Americans are pragmatic business men. They will already be looking forward to their next war, against the Russians. We'll barter your expertise. We'll go to America, and you'll do physics there."

"You mean I'll build bombs there."

"Well, somebody else will build them if you don't. Better to build them for the Americans than for the Nazis. Or God forbid for Stalin. At worst, we can run for Switzerland, with Father. Until Max can sneak us across to Portugal."

"You think what we get ourselves into doesn't matter. Because you will always find a way out."

"And my record in such matters looks good after all these years. How about me? Do I look good, after all these years?" She wriggled beneath him. "But if you feel that strongly about this, stop anytime."

✧   ✧   ✧

When Rachel sat down at her dressing table, she found, alongside her hairbrush, a folded brown paper, scarcely bigger than a postage stamp.

Peter stepped behind her, bent, and kissed her neck. "I was waiting to give you this. Until the mess was truly and fully resolved. But I think we've agreed to proceed on the assumption that it's close enough to resolved."

Rachel unfolded the paper, then lifted out a woman's ring. It was silver, formed in the shape of two roses, their stems intertwined.

As she turned it in her fingers, she looked up at Peter's reflection in her mirror. "It's the most beautifully made ring I've ever seen. For me?"

"Obviously. We agreed no ring the first time we married. I propose we consider today the second first time."

Rachel turned and hugged him, and when she finally drew back, tears glistened in her eyes. "Where did you get it?"

"Hyman Wolf, the Jeweler, cast it from leftover silver shavings. He said I should hold on to it. Until I met the right woman."

Rachel held out the ring, and extended the third finger of her left hand. "Well? After all these years, are you sure you've met her?"

Peter slipped the ring on her finger.

She held out her hand, turned it. "It fits perfectly."

"You can't wear it, for now. At least not on that finger."

She moved the twin-rose ring onto her opposite ring finger, and said, "Well, one finger or the other, I'm never taking it off again. For as long as we both shall live."

Thirty-three

FRANK LUCK STEPPED OUT ONTO HIS CABIN'S PORCH AND PEERED into the still night's darkness. He laid the Winchester on the porch planking beside his chair, sat down and rocked. Wilmot had gone home.

The door creaked open behind him as Cass stepped out. "So you really think this old 'three blind mice' woman, and the map case, and this guy who knocked you out, and the camera in your tree, are all connected?"

"Yep."

"And you really think he's coming here?"

"Yep." Frank lifted the Winchester, then rested it across his thighs as he rocked.

Cass said, "A gun? You've actually got a *gun*? You're going to try to shoot it out with him?"

"Not unless he tries to shoot it out with me."

"This is ridiculous. I'm calling the cops."

"Don't. I think the cops scared him off once. They'll scare him off again. I already told you twice tonight. Drive the pickup into town. Rent a room. When this sorts out, I'll call you."

"Cops are *supposed* to scare criminals off. It's called deterrence. Deterrence is better than you shooting him. Or him shooting you. Which sounds more likely, if he's this total badass you say he is."

Frank shook his head as he patted the Model 94's stock. "He's a knife man."

"He was a 'knife man' the first time you fought him. What

255

if this time, instead of a knife, he brings a *gun* to a gunfight? And more badasses?"

"If he does, maybe Sam Colt made all men equal." Frank stroked the Model 94's stock as he rocked. "But Oliver Winchester made some of us more equal than others."

"Seriously? I'm in a Clint Eastwood movie?"

Frank sat forward in his rocker as hair rose on his neck.

He stared hard into the darkness, and whispered. "Too late. Get inside. Now. Lock the door behind you. Turn out the lights. Get yourself a butcher knife out of the drawer next to the kitchen sink. Because we're about to find out who's in this movie."

On the road that led to Frank's driveway, a car's headlights flickered through the trees, as it crept forward. Six hundred yards before it reached the cabin turn-in, the car kept rolling, but its lights went black.

Behind Frank, Cass whispered, "Oh fuck."

Frank heard the door bolt clack, as Cass locked the door behind herself. Then the interior lights went out.

The darkened car turned onto Frank's drive, stopped fifty yards from the house, and shut off. Its interior lights flashed on for an instant, then winked out as a man-sized shadow disappeared into the brush along the driveway's right-hand side.

Frank heard only crickets and his own breathing. The visitor could now advance toward the house unseen. And unheard, because he had left the gravel drive.

Frank froze, watching and listening, with the rifle across his thighs. He waited for as long as it would take a man to negotiate the distance to the clearing that surrounded Frank's cabin.

Then Frank knelt behind the cover of the porch's stacked stone roof support, worked the Winchester's lever action, and listened as its metallic click echoed through the night.

Snake Eyes might not recognize a lever action, but he seemed like the sort who knew the sound of a rifle cocking.

Frank called, "Let me see your hands when you come out of that tree line, you trespassing son of a bitch."

Silence.

Frank fired high, into the treetops, then recocked.

"Now!"

A shadow emerged from the trees, hands held shoulder high.

Frank squinted over the rifle's iron sights as accurately as the darkness allowed.

The man dropped one hand and reached across his body.

Frank fired again, this time low, kicking dirt onto the man's shoes. The intruder spun, then ran down the driveway toward his car.

Frank ran forward as he chambered another round. "Stop! Don't make me shoot you in the ass, you bastard!"

The fugitive had made it a third of the way back to his car, and Frank had cut the distance between them in half, when Frank raised his rifle skyward and fired a third shot. The man didn't break stride, but Frank was close enough now that he could hear the man's ragged breathing.

Frank dropped the Winchester, lunged, and drove his shoulder into the small of the intruder's back.

The two of them fell, then writhed in the pine needles, until Frank straddled the man.

"Tonight I'm sober. So now you're not so tough, are you?" Frank drew back his fist, then peered down into his adversary's face.

Frank said, "Who the hell are *you*?"

"None of your business, you goddam lunatic!" The man was a gray scarecrow, old enough to be Frank's father. He held up bony hands, the right one scarred, in front of his face to shield his wire rimmed spectacles.

Cass ran up and bent over the two of them, a flashlight in one hand and a butcher knife in the other.

She panted. "Frank? You okay?"

Frank rolled off the little old man and said, "Fine."

Cass held the light close to the old stranger's face, then said to Frank, "*This* is your badass terrorist?"

The man sat up. "I think you broke my hip." He rolled onto his knees, flexed his left leg, grasped Cass's arm to steady himself, then stood. "Maybe not."

Frank said, "What's your name?"

"Still none of your business."

"You're trespassing on my land. That makes it my business. If you won't talk to me, I'll call the sheriff. You can talk to him."

Cass said, "Don't. I already called."

She stepped around the old man's car, opened its passenger door, poked around, then returned.

She shone her flashlight on papers she held in one hand and read. "According to the rental contract in your glovebox, you're James Enrico Righetti." She paused, looked up from the paper, eyes wide. "From Tampa, Florida? You're the guy Howard Merken talked to?"

"Maybe."

"I'm Cassidy Gooding."

"Why are you out to get me?"

"I'm not. I just wanted to ask you some questions. About your experience during World War II. You could've just emailed and answered them."

"If I wanted to answer them, I would have done it seventy-five years ago."

Frank said, "Why'd you sneak up here, then?"

"I don't trust people I don't know. Especially people who ask questions I don't want to answer. They might turn out to be crazy old fuckers who shoot people."

Cass said, "But why did you come all the way out here from Florida, at all?"

"To make a deal, face-to-face. I tell you my story. You don't take notes. You don't tell anybody 'til I'm dead."

Cass said, "Then what's the point?"

"The point is I get it off my conscience, before I die. The heart guy says I got four months. Tops."

"Oh. Oh. I'm sorry." Cass thumbed her phone. "Okay. I've texted the sheriff's office that there's no problem here."

Frank turned his back and walked away.

Cass said, "Frank? You still think there's a problem, here?"

Frank pointed the Winchester's muzzle toward the cabin's door, and called over his shoulder. "Come inside. Both of you. A man who's got a conscience worth clearing deserves to clear it over a couple of bourbons."

Thirty-four

"SERGEANT RIGHETTI, WHEN YOU GOT OFF THE BOAT FROM THE States, did someone misinform you that you were sent to England to replace General Roosevelt?"

On April 16, 1945, Jimmy Righetti, elbows on the photo-strewn table in front of him, looked up from his stereo viewer.

Major Thomas Kane stood in the doorway of the office that Jimmy shared with another photo intelligence interpreter.

Poker-faced behind his red mustache, Kane twitched a teletype sheet crumpled in his fist.

The twitch meant "join me in the hallway." Kane was, by reputation, a man of few and gentle words. He used hallway conferences to offer fatherly advice, to impart unofficial news of recommendation for promotion or decoration, and to conduct succinct ass-chewings out of earshot of one's peers.

Jimmy swallowed as he stood. Kane's question eliminated fatherly advice, promotion, or decoration.

Jimmy had to sidestep behind the other PI's work table to reach the door. This was because the other PI, a pipe-smoking college man of twenty-two, was a first lieutenant. Rank entitled him to the table next to the window that overlooked the gardens.

Today the window was open a slit, admitting the chirps and aromas of the English countryside in spring.

The "office" was in fact a bedroom, in the servants' wing of some big shot's requisitioned weekend house. The house was in the village of High Wycombe, northwest of London. The servant's bedroom was twice as big as the Brooklyn apartment bedroom

Jimmy had shared, for all his nineteen years of life, with his brother, uncle, and grandfather.

On April 13, 1945, Jimmy Righetti, a nineteen-year-old grass-green graduate of the photo reconnaissance school at Lowry Field in Denver, had reported as a replacement to the U.S. Army Eighth Air Force's 325th Photographic Wing (Reconnaissance).

Also on April 13, the 325th's commanding officer, Brigadier General Elliott Roosevelt, had indeed been replaced.

Jimmy knew this because, like most GIs, he was a student of scuttlebutt. The scuttlebutt had it that FDR's son had got caught swapping his support, for the new reconnaissance plane Howard Hughes was peddling, for a weekend with Hollywood hookers.

When Jimmy joined Kane in the hallway, the major drew a deep breath, then said, "Son, you're aware we are a Forward Interpretation Unit?"

"I am, sir."

Exposed film, unloaded from returned reconnaissance aircraft, went immediately to the lab, was developed, printed, and marked for identification. Then, married to the debriefed pilot's report, the prints were first analyzed by Forward Interpretation Unit Photo Interpreters like Jimmy.

Based on that analysis, the FIU distributed the prints back up the chain to the Central Interpretation Section. Hot stuff, like troops on the move, went up the chain immediately, as Flash messages. Less-hot prints that showed military hardware went to one set of experts, fortifications to another, industrial facilities to yet another.

Eventually, the boiled-down product was called "intelligence." Intelligence was presented to the appropriate brass. The idea being that the brass would then add the intelligence to the Big Picture that only the brass was fully capable of understanding, and win the war.

Jimmy cocked his head at Kane's question. "We may be 'Interpretation.' But major, we aren't 'Forward.' We're west of London. With respect, sir, the King of England's farther forward than we are. Most of what the 325th does these days is report weather over the North Atlantic, and measure bomb craters."

Unlike the 325th, other photo recon units had displaced forward, as the Allies pushed the German army back across Europe. Those forward unit's recon planes flew short missions, so intel about enemy troop movements could be delivered straight to field commanders, like fresh milk on their doorsteps.

Those PIs had slept in tents alongside airstrips in France. Then in Belgium. And now, with the krauts on the run, and the war's end maybe only days away, *those* PIs were deep inside Germany.

By the hour, Jimmy Righetti grew more afraid that when his unborn children asked what he did in the war, all he would have to say was that he sat in an office, counted holes in the ground, and guessed where it would rain.

Kane pressed his lips together, then nodded. "You want to whip the Nazis all by yourself. When I was fresh off the boat, so did I." As Kane spoke, the teletype sheet he held fluttered in his trembling fingers.

The scuttlebutt on Kane was that he damn near *had* whipped the Nazis all by himself. He had piloted B-17s, from the first milk runs over France, through the meat grinder of daylight precision raids into Germany without fighter escorts. Too many units on those precision raids had lost eighty percent of their planes and crews, during single missions.

Before the losses, and the survivor's guilt, broke him, Kane had won four Distinguished Flying Crosses. He had also had flak dug out of his skull, twice. They promoted him to a ground command slot. But he had refused to order crews up, unless he could fly with them.

They couldn't can a hero for *that*. But they couldn't send a pilot with the shakes back up, either. So, they reassigned him outside the chain of command. Kane had become a staff paper pusher, in the 325th. Recon planes carried no guns, or bombs. Staff officers just gave advice to command officers. Then the command officers ordered other people to get themselves shot down, while taking photographs.

Kane uncrumpled the teletype sheet he held. "You sent a Flash news teletype up the line yesterday? On your own authority?"

"Yes, sir." Flash messages reported immediately vital information, like enemy troops or equipment moving to engage friendly forces. A PI didn't send a Flash message on his own. Especially a PI three days off the boat.

"How?"

"I figured it out."

"Why?"

"I guessed I saw something important, sir."

"First rule: PIs don't guess. Ever. And they especially don't send their guesses up the line unvetted, as Flash news. Because the brass don't have the time or the expertise to distinguish fact from a bad guess. If the brass act on a bad guess, people die."

"I'm sorry, sir."

Kane blew out a breath as he reread the teletype. "I hope you don't have reason to be sorry, Righetti. This came back down in response to whatever you sent. Whatever it was, that you thought you saw, got somebody's attention." Kane slapped the teletype with his free hand, "Now, I have to do something I don't want to do. Did you keep a copy of your Flash? And a copy of the prints, and supporting material, that you sent back with it?"

The same sign hung over the door in each of the PIs' offices, including the office the college man and Jimmy shared. The sign read:

ALWAYS KEEP YOUR EYES AND EARS OPEN.
ALWAYS KEEP YOUR MOUTH SHUT.
ALWAYS KEEP A COPY.

"Always, sir."

"Show me."

Back in the office, Kane sent the college man away to get a cup of coffee—or two—while Jimmy laid out the photo strip, and the pilot's report, on which he had based his Flash news message.

He and Kane bent over the documents Jimmy had laid out on his table.

Jimmy ran his finger over the raw pilot's trace, the route and activity record made in flight by the pilot. In this case, by a first lieutenant named Bookman. While in flight the pilot had sketched the trace, on a clipboard strapped to his thigh.

Jimmy pointed to the trace's date. "This mission was flown two days ago. From here in England all the way to Berchtesgaden and back. Although I don't know why a closer unit wasn't tasked."

The last sentence was a white lie. Jimmy told it because he wasn't supposed to *know* why a photo recon unit closer to the front hadn't been tasked. The 325th didn't only fly weather missions. When the brass wanted to know something *now*, and on the Q.T., the 325th flew a long-distance custom job that returned the film back here in England. This eliminated the delay and security-leak risks of a mission flown by a forward-deployed unit.

This overflight of the Berghof, Hitler's Bavarian vacation retreat in the Alps, and of the military installations that had grown up around "The Eagle's Nest" at Berchtesgaden, was ordered from way up the chain of command. Because the chain of command, all the way up to Ike himself, were scared shitless. Or so the scuttlebutt had it.

Scared that Hitler, and a core of SS fanatics, were digging in, to mines and caves in the Bavarian mountains. From there, they would prolong the war for months, or even years.

In the Pacific Theater Americans were already dying, digging every fanatic Jap out of every hole on every island. And those Japs were dying, too. And taking civilian Japs with them. Nobody wanted more of the same in Europe.

Kane eyed the pilot's trace, and the typed interrogating officer's debrief report. "I figured it was about this." He snorted. "'Alpine Redoubt' my ass! Personally, I don't care whether Hitler wants to rot in some cave, as the King of Nothing, until the Red Sox win the pennant. I don't think it's worth one more GI's life to go in there and dig him out."

"I wouldn't know about that, sir." Jimmy tapped a finger on one wiggle in the pilot's trace route. "At this point, on his second pass back over Berchtesgaden at twenty-one thousand feet, this pilot took flak. The flak knocked out his aircraft's oxygen system. He dove to evade, and to reach a lower altitude, where he wouldn't black out."

Jimmy pointed. "He leveled the aircraft here, off the planned mission track, and down to ten thousand feet above sea level, and seven thousand five hundred feet above this mountain valley."

Jimmy ran his finger along a part of the trace, drawn in red. "In the heat of the moment, he mistakenly triggered a photo strip, here. In the apparent middle of nowhere."

Kane turned, then swept his hand above the line of black-and-white paired prints. They depicted a swath of the Alps. "These prints?"

Jimmy nodded as he slid his stereo viewer over a single pair. "Actually, just this one pair matters, Major."

Kane tugged off his glasses as he pulled the photos and viewer across the table toward himself. He was trained as a pilot, not a photo interpreter.

Jimmy rotated the photos. "Orient the pair with the shadows pointing at your belly button, sir. The human brain processes the stereo images better that way."

Kane bent over the viewer, adjusted it, then grunted. "Looks like an airplane wing."

"That was my first thought, sir."

"What do you make of the compound next to it?"

"Single-story barracks. Close packed. Surrounded by double rectangles of wire fence. Twelve feet tall, according to the shadows thrown by the fence posts and the guard towers. Fifty-foot-wide clear-cut field of fire outside the wire. Based on the shadows thrown by the guard boxes, the observation points mostly face inward."

"Agreed. It's a detention facility. POW camp?"

"POWs are men. This camp has separate latrines. It's co-ed."

"One of those concentration hellholes we've started liberating?"

Jimmy shook his head. "Most of those seem to separate males from females. I don't see internal wire dividing the compound. Or anything like gallows, or those factory buildings with the chimneys. I'd say it's a labor camp. Maybe with male and female workers."

"Working at what?"

"It's an airplane factory."

"One wing's no factory, Righetti. That wing could be wreckage."

"No, sir. If it's wreckage, where's the rest of the debris? And why is it unpainted aluminum? The krauts seem short of most things these days, but they seem to have plenty of paint. They camouflage every inch of every vehicle they send into battle."

"Alright, then where's the factory where these laborers made this wing?"

"These traces that lead away from the wing-shaped object are the width of narrow gauge rail tracks. They run right smack up against this mountainside. We know that up in north Germany, to avoid our bombing, the krauts have been using slave labor to build their rockets, and buzz bombs, and their jet Messerschmitts. They've relocated factories into mines under mountains."

Kane tapped a pointer on the boomerang-shaped object, then looked up. "I suppose it could be one of those rocket-propelled interceptors."

"A Messerschmitt Komet, Sir?" Jimmy shook his head. "From

overhead it does present the same basic shape. But a Komet's vertical tail would cast a shadow, and there isn't one. More importantly, a Komet's wingspan is about thirty feet. This black rectangle alongside this wing is a Kübelwagen. A kraut Jeep. Kübelwagens are just over twelve feet long. Wing tip to wing tip this thing measures just over fourteen Kübelwagens. One hundred seventy feet. A B-29's wing-span's only one hundred forty-one feet. The krauts don't operate any aircraft even as big as a B-29."

Kane nodded. "You are one bright replacement, Sergeant."

"Thank you, sir. I graduated number one in my high school class. And number one in my class at Lowry. I enlisted on my eighteenth birthday. And I'm the smartest Wop you ever saw."

"Modest, too." Kane said. "So, if the wingspan's one-seventy, how big do you think the whole plane would be?"

"I think we're looking at the whole plane, sir."

"Come again?"

"It's mostly unpainted, but the right wing tip is marked. Rational aircraft builders don't paint planes as they go along."

"That's just guessing, Righetti."

"Yes, sir. But look at the marking. It's a swastika."

"You expected the Star of David?"

"The krauts mark horizontal surfaces, like wings, with the iron cross, not with the swastika. They reserve the swastika for vertical surfaces, like the rudder, or the fuselage flanks. But if the aircraft *has* no rudder, no fuselage flank, no vertical surface at all, they replace the iron cross on the wing with the swastika."

"Maybe. But planes without rudders don't exist. Because they can't fly. I know. I tried it in a B-17 that had its tail shot away."

Jimmy raised a finger as he opened a 1937 London newspaper, and pointed at a photo of a boomerang-shaped all-wing glider in flight. It had no rudder, and a swastika decorated the little plane's starboard wing tip. "But they *do* exist, sir."

Kane's eyebrows rose as his jaw dropped. "Where did you get this?"

"The library in town, sir. The krauts were flying these when the U.S. was still proud of its canvas biplanes."

"Righetti, are you sure you've only been doing this for three days?"

Jimmy smiled at his boss. "There's more, sir. Look at the ground on both sides of this two-lane road, that the Kübelwagen's parked on. The vegetation, in this strip that extends about fifty feet on each side of the road, and for eleven thousand feet down the road, forms a rectangle. It's darker than the rest of the vegetation on the valley floor."

Kane crossed his arms. "And?"

Jimmy pointed to the rectangle's corner furthest from the silver wing, at a pair of irregular dark shapes, each slightly bigger than the Kübelwagen. "We've started seeing these shapes associated with airfields lately. The krauts are so short of gasoline that they've been using ox teams as field-expedient tugs, to move aircraft around on the ground. Sir, I make these objects oxen hitched to carts. The krauts have loaded 'em up with cut pine boughs, that are turning brown."

"You think—?"

"I think the krauts not only build planes like this inside this mountain, they fly them in and out, and camouflage the grass airstrip, that this road marks the center of, before and after."

Kane sagged, slack-jawed, into Jimmy's chair. "You sold me. So now I understand why you sold people higher up the chain, too. Righetti, you may be the smartest Wop *anybody* ever saw." Kane frowned. "It's good work. But you've made *my* work harder."

Kane's work, at least during the immediate shakeup following Elliott Roosevelt's abrupt replacement, had shifted from staff to command.

Jimmy said, "What do you mean, sir?"

"I mean that at this moment leading elements of our infantry are closer to the place in this photograph than you and I are to London. Americans may capture Berchtesgaden before I get my next haircut. Nonetheless, I've been ordered to put up another mission over this place, and 'with all deliberate speed.' They also want it diced. And they want handheld camera images, in addition to obliques."

Jimmy raised his eyebrows.

"Dicing" was photo reconnaissance conducted not from high altitude, which was dangerous enough, but "on the deck." Dicing aircraft flew so low and so fast that they often returned—if they returned—with bellies scraped down to bare metal by contact with the ground, and with shrubbery wedged into their wings and fuselages.

Opinion was split whether the term "dicing" derived from the aircraft's buffeted, erratic path over the ground, which resembled dice bouncing across a crap table, or because the Brits called any risky business "dicey." Or because the technique was as foolhardy as betting one's life on a dice roll.

The photos Jimmy had just analyzed had been shot from high altitude, by automated cameras mounted aboard an F-5. The F-5 was a P-38 Lightning fighter, stripped of guns and armor for increased speed, ceiling, and range. A single-seater, the F-5's pilot flew the plane, navigated to and from the target, triggered the plane's auto-mated cameras with cockpit switches, and made notes while he flew.

Flying at three hundred fifty miles per hour, at altitudes ranging from zero to fifteen feet, it would be impossible for an F-5's pilot to additionally snap photos, using a bulky, handheld reconnaissance camera.

Therefore, the plane would have to be an F-8. The F-8 was the American photo reconnaissance version of the British Mosquito fighter-bomber. Mosquitos famously could fly low and fast. Stripped of crew-protecting armor, and of guns, the F-8 flew even faster than other Mosquitos, and probably just as low. Most importantly, the F-8 carried a camera operator in addition to its pilot.

Jimmy said, "I'll take it, sir."

Kane wrinkled his brow. "Take what?"

"Check my file, sir. My last two weeks at Lowry, I qualified as an aerial photographer specialist. I been up there, sir. So, you've got half your aircrew."

Kane shook his head. "Two weeks training 'up there' is zero weeks combat experience, Sergeant."

"It's barely even combat, sir. The flak the pilot caught was over Hitler's house. There's not a gun or a flak tower in sight at this target. I can't fly a plane, but I don't need to. The reason they sent me to Lowry in the first place is the Righetti Family Studios photograph half the Italian weddings in Brooklyn. I've been a professional photographer since I was nine. Experience? The experience this job needs is in my blood. Besides, who knows what to look for at this target better than I do?"

Kane shook his head again. "Righetti—Jimmy, is it? Jimmy, I understand that you want to do your part. I understand that you're running out of war to do it in. But the only sorrier soul than the last man who dies in a war is the soul who sends him to die needlessly. Then has to live with the guilt the rest of his life."

"Which is why I've got to be your man, Major. If I hadn't screwed up and sent that Flash, *nobody* would have to fly back to Berchtesgaden.

"Now, if you don't send me, you have to send somebody else. But if you do send somebody else, it'll be me who might have to live with the guilt the rest of my life."

Thirty-five

THE NEXT MORNING, JIMMY RIGHETTI SAT ALONGSIDE A DRIVER, in a canvas-topped Jeep as it rattled and swerved down narrow lanes through the English countryside.

As Jimmy rocked in his seat, he struggled into his hastily issued sheepskin flight jacket, suspendered trousers, and enormous, fleece-lined boots. They were twins to the ones that he had barely been taught to put on at Lowry.

Ten minutes later, the Jeep's brakes squealed, pitching Jimmy forward, as the driver said, "End of the line, Mac."

Jimmy hoisted the aerial camera in its fat case from the Jeep's rear seat, gathered his flight helmet and yellow Mae West flotation vest, then stepped out into the airfield's grass.

The Jeep rolled away, as Jimmy clumped across the dewy grass, like an Eskimo wearing a parka and snowshoes.

Ahead loomed the F-8 Mosquito that would carry him, and the K-20 camera, into battle.

It was the first Mossie he had actually seen. Crouched tail-down in the grass, wearing pale, "Photo Reconnaissance Unit Blue" high-altitude camouflage, it looked even sleeker and more glamorous than its photographs.

So did its pilot.

He walked around the aircraft, running his fingers over its wooden skin and kicking tires, like his life depended on it. Which it did.

The Jeep driver had told Jimmy the pilot was a first looie, a grizzled veteran at age twenty-four, and a wavy-haired California college man. Like Jimmy's short-term office mate photo interpreter.

The pilot wore a brown-leather flight jacket, hand painted on its back with a cartoon Hitler overlain by crosshairs, and a visored crusher cap, soft-crowned so it could be worn in flight, under earphones. Those trademarks spelled "Flyboy" to British girls. As if Yanks' teeth, accents, and access to rationed luxuries weren't attraction enough.

Without returning Jimmy's salute, the pilot smiled and shook his hand. "Cal Bookman. You're Jimmy Righetti?"

"Yes, sir. Lieutenant Bookman? You're the same pilot who overflew this target three days ago? In a Lightning?"

Bookman's grin sparkled, and he clapped Jimmy's shoulder. "Relax, Spaghetti. I fly Mossies, too. I'm the best pilot you ever saw."

"But why—?"

"Because I've just been there and back, so I know the way. Besides—"

"You're the best pilot I ever saw."

Bookman winked. "You catch on fast."

The pilot slipped into his own sheepskins, and even wearing them moved like Fred Astaire.

Jimmy waddled behind him, then climbed the handspan-wide ladder that led up through the Mosquito's belly hatch. Inside, Jimmy wormed back into his seat, which was staggered to the right of, and behind, the pilot's.

The Mosquito succeeded because it was fast, and it was fast because it was all teeth and no tail. Left out of its design were armor plate and guns. Also left out were the crew they would have protected, including a copilot, and a copilot's redundant controls.

Left in were two monstrous Rolls-Royce Merlin engines, and the capacity to carry four thousand pounds of bombs. Or enough high-octane aviation gasoline to fly from England to the Bavarian Alps and back.

The Mosquito's bombload nearly equaled that carried by a B-17 Flying Fortress. But the B-17 was twice as big, had four engines, required a ten-man crew, carried thirteen machine guns, and was armor plated to protect it all.

Bookman helped Jimmy fasten his parachute and flight harnesses, then strapped in himself.

Jimmy's hands trembled as he adjusted his harnesses. "Do I have a job on the way to the target?"

Bookman raised one finger. "Just one. And don't screw it up. You know Morse code?"

Jimmy frowned. "Only a little."

"Every five minutes we're in the air, you rap out a message on the fuselage with your knuckle."

Jimmy tapped the plywood next to his hip. "Like this?"

"Perfect."

"What message?"

"Tell the termites to keep holding hands."

Bookman turned back to the controls, then fired up the Merlins.

He said over the intercom, "Hear that music? Nothing purrs like a Merlin."

To Jimmy, it sounded like thunder that wouldn't end.

The Mossie bounced down the grass strip, lifted off, and climbed before Jimmy had time to think up an answer back.

After a minute airborne, Bookman said, "Hold on."

A heartbeat later the Mosquito's nose dipped, and the plane dove toward a river. Bookman pulled up, feet above the water, and an eyeblink later a railroad bridge loomed ahead. A locomotive, pulling flatcars and spewing black smoke, inched across the trestle. Instead of pulling up, Bookman dropped lower. Before Jimmy's heart beat again, they had shot *under* the bridge.

Bookman thundered on, hugging the water and skating the plane side-to-side. He dipped each wing, until its tip kissed water, and spray erupted. Ahead, in midstream, a barge pushed by a tug came at them. Bookman pulled the Mosquito's nose up, then kept climbing.

Jimmy said. "Are you *crazy*, Bookman?"

Bookman laughed. "No. There are crazy pilots and there are live pilots. There are no crazy live pilots. Mosquitos are modified to do different jobs. The F-8 is optimized to fly high altitude recon. I needed to be sure I could still fly her low. Or we'd go home and call this off."

"I almost peed my pants."

"Relax, Spaghetti. You have a relief tube back there. Use it."

"Or the termites drown?"

Bookman laughed harder. "You *do* catch on fast."

Without further aerobatics they sped east. Green England below changed to the English Channel's regal gray.

Then James Enrico Righetti, who before he enlisted had never been to New Jersey, was over France, his second foreign country in a month. The Merlins' purr *did* sound musical. All things considered, Jimmy's war was off to a magnificent start.

He had even earned a nom de guerre, already. Although he wouldn't have chosen "Spaghetti."

He leaned back in his seat and smiled behind his oxygen mask, as the Mosquito climbed above ten thousand feet.

Two hours later, Jimmy's war had turned less magnificent. Bookman was cruising through the Allied-controlled skies over France at the Mosquito's most efficient speed and altitude. Those were two hundred miles per hour, and sixteen thousand feet.

At sixteen thousand feet, the outside temperature was two degrees Fahrenheit. The Mosquito's cabin was, theoretically, heated. But neither Jimmy's sheepskins nor bladder could handle the actual temperature inside.

When he removed his mittens to use the relief tube, his fingers stiffened so that he wouldn't have been able to operate the camera, and could barely operate his wang. The second time he tried to use the tube, the first time's urine had frozen in it. Pee overflowed onto his hands, his sheepskin trousers, and the Mosquito's interior. He didn't tell Bookman.

An eternity later, Jimmy Righetti, human Popsicle, had passed from shivering to numb.

Bookman finally spoke. "Ten minutes to the Bavarian border. Somewhere after that we'll overfly our farthest-forward elements. So look alive. The krauts probably don't have the gas or the inclination to intercept a single plane. But sound off if you spot a silhouette that looks like a twin-engine shark, or like a flying bat. We can outrun anything the krauts have except their jet, and that damn little rocket plane."

"What about flak?"

"If we stay below fifty feet, and on the throttles, we're past it before they know we're there. But fifty feet will scare the shit out of you."

"It's warm below fifty feet?"

"Like the beach at Malibu."

"Scare me."

✧   ✧   ✧

Jimmy had crawled forward from his seat, and had knelt in the Mossie's transparent Perspex nose, cradling the Fairchild, for ten minutes when Bookman said in his ear, "Five minutes 'til we turn up the valley. Ready in the fishbowl?"

The Fairchild K-20 infinity-focused handheld was more beast than Kodak Brownie. But compared to the even larger, remote-triggered oblique cameras that peered out from the Mosquito's rear flanks, the K-20 was small. The K-20 shot fifty five-by-four-inch negatives, one frame at a time when manually triggered, rather than the obliques' rapid-fire strips of bigger nine by nines.

Jimmy checked the camera's settings again, flipped up the K-20's rectangular viewfinder, and peered ahead at the speed-blurred landscape.

A stone barnyard fence loomed, its chest-high top at the level of Jimmy's knees.

Jimmy gritted his teeth, slitted his eyes, and braced for impact.

At three hundred fifty miles per hour, Bookman hopped the fence in half a blink, then something banged the tailwheel as Bookman hopped the farmhouse's roof, too.

"Jesus, Bookman!" Jimmy's fingers trembled on the big camera's handles, and his voice quavered as he said, "Ready up here."

When Bookman banked the Mossie left, up the valley in which the target lay, it was a relief after the hedge-hopping.

Forested slopes rose on both sides of a spring-melt swollen stream. The stream was just wider than the Mossie's wingspan, but compared to the farm scape Bookman had bounced above, the water was mostly flat. Bookman hugged the wave tops as the Mossie tracked the stream's twists, thundering feet above whitewater.

Ahead a fish leapt, and Jimmy swore he felt it thump the wooden fuselage beneath his knees.

"Dinner!" sang Bookman.

The stream and the valley slopes narrowed, forcing Bookman above the treetops.

Then they were barreling five feet above the mystery target's runway. It *was* a runway, and at the moment was uncamouflaged. Oxen grazed alongside it, oblivious to the intruder.

The all-wing plane sat there, big as life. Jimmy braced the Fairchild's back against his chest, while he thumbed the shutter repeatedly, as fast as he could.

Then they were past. Bookman pulled up at the valley's end and banked around so hard that Jimmy could barely breathe.

Bookman said, "Is *that* thing what the flap's about? Did you get pictures?"

"Think so."

Bookman lined the Mossie up to cross the valley at right angles to his first pass. "First pass they don't even know what happened. Second pass they run and hide, because they think you're strafing."

On this pass Jimmy shot frames of the tunnel mouth, into which the tracks led. From this low angle, he saw that the plane rested on its tricycle landing gear, atop a railroad flat car. He realized that it could be towed sideways into and out of the narrow portal that opened out from the mountainside. Trackways, stacked aboard the flat car, would be used to roll the plane from the flatcar to the ground.

Below the Mosquito, small figures dashed from the barracks, pointing up. And so close that Jimmy saw their wide eyes.

Bookman shouted, "Kids! They got *kids* in there!"

As Bookman banked the plane, to come around again, he asked, "You got more film to expose?"

"Yeah. But what happens on the third pass?"

"By the third pass, they shoot." He paused. "But there's no flak here. Right?"

Again Bookman barreled up the valley, five feet off the deck. Again he lined up on the road that formed the runway's center line.

Now, to Bookman's left, the kids in the compound lined the wire fence. Their kerchief-headed mothers dashed toward some of the kids, tugging them back from the fence, then pushed them flat. Other children jumped up and down, punching the air with their fists. The port-side obliques would record that. If those were ever de-classified, they would make the cover of *Life*.

Ahead, Jimmy noticed for the first time a lowered, striped gate that blocked the road, and a striped guard box to the gate's left.

A helmeted, uniformed guard stood in front of the guard box. As the Mosquito bore down on him, he threw himself flat.

Bookman laughed. "Low bridge, Fritz!"

In the instant that Jimmy realized the guard had thrown himself prone not in terror, but to aim and fire his rifle, its muzzle flashed.

The Mossie nosed up and circled back down the valley once more. But this time, as it climbed, it wobbled.

Jimmy called, "Bookman?"

No answer.

"Bookman!"

In Jimmy's ear, Bookman rasped, "Christ! What a mess."

Jimmy scuttled back to the cockpit and found wind howling in through the bullet-shattered hinged window left of the windscreen. Bookman, pale, gasping, with eyes wide behind the goggles he had lowered over them, gripped the control stick. Blood gushed from his neck, and had already soaked his jacket's sheepskin collar. The cabin's interior, the window panels, even Bookman's goggles were spattered red, too.

Jimmy snatched his mitten from alongside his seat, turned it inside out, and pressed its fleece against the gaping, spurting wound in the pilot's left carotid artery.

"Cal?"

Through gritted teeth Bookman said, "We need to cross back over our lines before I set this thing down. The film—"

"Screw the film. We need to get *you* down, and to a field hospital. Even if it's a kraut hospital. Cal, I can't stop the bleeding."

"No. Film comes first, Jimmy. And the krauts don't take kindly to the people who've been bombing the shit out of them. A farmer will stab you with his pitchfork as fast as an SS butcher will bayonet you."

It seemed only seconds later that Bookman's eyelids drooped. His head sagged slowly left, and the left wing tip dipped along with it.

"Cal! Set us down! Now!"

Bookman's head snapped back up, and he nodded. He lifted just his index finger, and pointed toward the instrument panel. "Lower the gear. When we're down, you get clear pronto. We still got half our gas aboard."

"You'll get us down. You're the best pilot I ever saw. Remember?"

Bookman slowed the Mosquito, and it drifted down toward an open field alongside a road.

He croaked, "Gear down! Now!"

Jimmy scanned the cockpit, bewildered by his choices. "Cal, where—?"

Bookman slumped forward, limp, against the control column. The plane's nose dropped.

The Mosquito plunged, and burrowed, nose-first into the earth. Jimmy rocketed forward.

His head struck the windscreen as the plane flipped, tail over nose.

Gasoline odor pricked Jimmy awake.

He lay flat on his back, in tall grass, beneath the inverted Mosquito's left engine nacelle. Twenty feet away, Bookman lay, twisted alongside the shattered Perspex nose. Alongside Bookman lay a crackle-finish black box. The K-20 handheld!

Jimmy crawled toward them.

He was ten feet from Bookman and the camera when he heard liquid trickling.

Then he saw and heard the first whoosh.

Then orange flame exploded.

Then there was nothing.

Jimmy's hand was on fire. Not literally. It just hurt like that. He now lay on his stomach, and saw only blackness. Not the plane, not Bookman, not the camera, not even the ground on which he lay. Black smoke that stunk of what he realized must be burned fuel, burned wood, burned tire rubber, and his own seared flesh, roiled around him.

A silhouette burst through the smoke, carrying something the length of a rifle—or a pitchfork—in one hand.

Jimmy stretched both arms forward as he lay still and called, "I am unarmed."

The figure knelt alongside him, and said, "Don't worry, buddy. I'm armed enough for both of us."

The GI screamed, "Medic! Medic!" as he dragged Jimmy feet-first out of the smoke and into daylight.

Jimmy turned his head as he lay, blinking and coughing, in weedy mud. "Pilot?"

The GI shook his head. "I'm sorry, fella. Your friend . . . he don't need no medic."

Jimmy turned his head away, then swallowed as tears blurred his vision. "Film?"

The GI said, "Film? This was a recon plane? I really am sorry to tell you this. There's nothing left of your plane but charcoal."

A second GI, helmet marked with red-cross white roundels, dashed up and knelt beside Jimmy.

After ten minutes' examination the medic said, "You've got third degree burns on your right hand and forearm, cuts and contusions on your face and forehead. Your right shoulder, I think, may be mildly separated. No obvious broken bones or evidence of internal bleeding. Considering what's left of your plane, you're the luckiest man in the European Theater today. In the long run, I expect you'll be fine."

He cut Jimmy's left sleeve away with scissors, then stuck a needle in Jimmy's forearm. Warmth oozed up through, and numbed, Jimmy's arm as the medic said, "In fact, with this, in the short run you'll be better than fine."

Thirty-six

"RIGHETTI? JIMMY?"

The voice wasn't the medic's. It was familiar. Jimmy hurt all over, especially his right hand, and shoulder, which he saw were swaddled in a white cloth sling. With his left hand he touched something above his right eyebrow, and realized it was a plump gauze bandage.

Major Kane said, "Sorry. I let you sleep as long as I could. I hope you feel better than you look."

"I doubt I do, sir. I feel like shit." His voice croaked, he coughed, and the cough made his throat hurt worse than everything else already did.

Kane unscrewed a canteen's cap, then folded Jimmy's fingers around the canteen's body. "Water. Just sip."

Jimmy coughed his first sip out and it dribbled down his chin. The second sip helped.

He looked around, and realized that his arm rested on a bed pillow, and that he sat alongside Kane in a staff car's back seat as the car moved through darkness.

"You came to Germany to see me, sir?"

Kane shook his head. "No, you were flown here."

"Here?"

"London. What happened, Jimmy?"

"The film, sir?"

"The film didn't make it. Neither did Bookman. I understand you already know that. What went wrong?"

"Kraut rifleman. Lucky shot on our third pass over the target. Cal caught a bullet in his throat."

"So, you did see the target before you were shot down?"

Jimmy nodded. "It was all there, sir. The plane, the runway, the factory set in the mountain, the camp. Exactly like we expected."

"Like *you* expected, Jimmy. That's why you got this express ticket."

The car pulled to the curb, and a white-helmeted MP who had been riding in the front passenger's seat sprang out, opened the car's rear door for them, and snapped off a salute that Kane returned.

As Jimmy stepped from the car, he looked down at himself and realized that somewhere between Bavaria and this place somebody had not only treated his wounds, they had dressed him. Not in hospital pajamas, but in khakis. Just shirt, tie, and trousers, no jacket or cap. The uniform bagged on him, a size too big, but it was clean and pressed.

"Can you walk, Jimmy?"

"Yes, sir. To where?"

They stood on the sidewalk in a narrow, darkened street somewhere in the city, lined on both sides by a solid wall of tidy brick apartment buildings, each four stories high. It resembled the neighborhood where he grew up, except these buildings weren't brick boxes hung with fire escapes. They exhibited what Jimmy's father called "historic photogenic patina," which meant they had probably been built when Brooklyn was a forest where Indians hunted deer.

But a hundred feet down the sidewalk there was no building. There was only a pile of bricks. From the pile twisted plumbing pipes sprouted like weeds. A broken baby carriage, and people's mattresses lay among the bricks.

Jimmy stared.

Kane said, "First bomb damage you've seen from this angle?"

Jimmy wrinkled his forehead until the skin tugged at the bandage over his eye. "Bomb damage? Sir, the krauts haven't been close enough to England to bomb it for months. Families *lived* in that building. But nobody's lifted a finger to rebuild it."

"Nobody's done much to rebuild a lot of the rest of London. Or every bit of Cologne, and Hamburg, and Dresden. Jimmy, the belligerents are still too busy knocking things down to build things up. Which is why you're *here*, instead of in a hospital, where you belong."

"Sir?"

"Apparently somebody thinks you may be able to help end this war sooner. I hope to God they're right." Kane stood aside and extended his palm. "After you, Sergeant."

The MP led them past a shoulder-high sandbag revetment that surrounded an open stairwell, that led below street level.

At the stairs' base, the MP handed Kane and Jimmy off to a silent pair wearing civilian suits, who led them down a dim corridor that ended at a metal door, flanked by two uniformed Limeys armed with Thompson subs.

A striped-pants civilian with slicked-back gray hair sat behind a desk that blocked the doorway. He peered at an open ledger on the desk, checked a line, then stood, smiled, and extended his hand to Kane. "Thank you so much for accommodating us on such short notice, Major. It will only be a moment."

The civilian turned to Jimmy, stared at Jimmy's bandaged brow, and wrinkled his forehead. "Sir, may we offer you something to make you more comfortable while you wait?"

Jimmy licked dry lips. "Water?"

The doors opened, a U.S. Army Air Force full bird colonel stuck his head out, then said to the civilian, "They're ready for Sergeant Righetti now."

Kane stepped around the desk with Jimmy, but the full bird raised his palm. "This is as far as you go, Tom."

The full bird carried a manila file as he led Jimmy through the door and down another corridor.

The colonel said, "How you feeling?"

"Lousy, sir."

"Hang in there a few minutes longer, Sergeant."

Fifteen yards further on the full bird stopped outside a set of double doors. These were dark wood.

He knocked on the left door, then said to Jimmy, "Speak when spoken to. Answer any question asked frankly. And with absolute honesty. Be polite. Be succinct. It's already an hour and a half before midnight, and they haven't gotten through half their agenda."

Someone on the other side of the doors opened the right one.

Jimmy turned to the full bird. "Sir, who—?"

"Don't salute. But don't sit unless he invites you to sit. Address him as 'Sir.' Or as 'Prime Minister.'"

The full bird followed Jimmy through the door and closed it behind them.

The windowless room in which they stood had a cellar's low ceiling and whitewashed brick walls, and its bright overhead lighting was diffused by an evening's tobacco smoke haze.

Fifteen men sat in upholstered chairs around a long mahogany conference table, arranged broadside to, and centered on, the doorway through which Jimmy and the full bird had entered.

Behind the table stood an easel, its board concealed by a white cloth drape.

Those men with their backs to the door turned, while those who faced the door looked up at Jimmy.

A couple were coat-and-tie civilians. Most were military, some Brit, some American, all at least field grade. A light colonel at Jimmy's side looked to be the lowest ranking commissioned officer in the room, and Jimmy was young enough to be grandson to any of them.

Most, regardless of dress, had heads full of hair. Most had mustaches.

One had neither. The civilian at the table's center wore a dark suit and bow tie. He was clean shaven, balding, jowly, and peered at Jimmy over spectacles that had slid down his nose.

Jimmy's father had taught him that the camera added fifteen pounds, and indeed Winston Churchill looked slimmer than the newsreels and his photos showed him.

A brigadier general in Brit Air Force blue read from a paper and announced, "Item twelve. Prime Minister, this is Sergeant James Righetti, the U.S. Army Air Force Photo Interpreter who produced the Flash news analysis that prompted the overflight of which we spoke earlier in this meeting."

Churchill looked Jimmy up and down, eyeing the bandage and sling. Then he looked left and right. "Have I been misled about the hazards of photo interpretation?"

The full bird cleared his throat. "Sir, Sergeant Righetti was also the aerial photographer, and the only surviving crew member, aboard the aircraft that was lost. The film was also lost when it crashed. Sergeant Righetti's impressions, such as they may be, are currently the only new information we have. Weather permitting, we're preparing to fly the mission again, as soon as another crew and another aircraft can—"

Churchill cut the full bird off with an upraised palm, then pointed at the empty chair across the table from himself. "Sergeant, please be seated."

As Jimmy sat, Churchill frowned and again looked left and right. "For God's sake, will someone fetch this man a brandy?" He flicked his elbow at an empty snifter beside it. "And fetch me another, also."

As his jowly frown faded Churchill leaned across the table. "Righetti. You are Italian, Sergeant?"

Jimmy shook his head. "One hundred percent American. Fifty percent Italian. My mother's a Mick—Irish. I was born in Brooklyn, sir."

Churchill smiled. "My mother was born in Brooklyn, too. So I count myself fifty percent American and one hundred percent English. And neither of us count well enough to advance beyond fourth-form mathematics."

"Yes, sir."

"What is the extent of your injuries, Sergeant?"

"I'm fine, sir."

Churchill frowned. "Indeed?"

"Just sorry we lost the film. Sorrier the pilot didn't make it."

"How did it happen?"

"A kraut—sorry, sir, a German—"

Churchill waved a hand and shook his head. "Sergeant, no description of the German nation, under its present management, is too pejorative. I personally prefer 'Hun.'"

"Yes, sir. A rifle bullet fired from the ground hit my pilot. He managed to get us down among American advance elements, or I wouldn't be here."

A Brit at the table's end exhaled. "In view of the hour, and of the sergeant's evident discomfort, perhaps we should move ahead to a presentation about recent related developments, Prime Minister?"

Churchill nodded.

An Army Air Force one-star, seated at the table's end, stood, walked to the easel holding a long wooden pointer and flipped back the cloth to reveal the board beneath.

Only then Jimmy realized that empty chairs lined the walls in the room's shadows. In less highly classified situations the chairs would have been filled with enlisted flunkies, one of whom would have pointed at things, while the one-star talked.

The board's left side was a map of Germany. To its right was a blown-up black-and-white photo that showed grinning American infantry. They knelt, rifles in hand, alongside the nose wheel of an airplane that looked, for all the world, like a smaller version of the one he had just seen on the runway in Bavaria.

Jimmy felt his face flush and his uninjured hand trembled. Bookman had bled to death to get a picture of a plane we had already captured?

The one-star said, "Prime Minister, we learned earlier today that two days ago, as Sergeant Righetti prepared to fly to Bavaria, U.S. Third Army elements overran the Gotha aircraft facilities at Friedrichroda." With his pointer, he slapped a dot on the map located in north central Germany. "Here."

The one-star held the pointer in both hands and continued, "In an outbuilding they discovered, and captured, three aircraft, including this one, at various construction stages." He pointed at the blown-up photo. "Note these aircraft are tailless, with a wingspan of approximately fifty-five feet. The openings on each side of their cockpits are air intakes for turbojet engines, of the Junkers type that power the Messerschmitt 262.

"This discovery corroborates Sergeant Righetti's independent analysis that German aircraft development has progressed far beyond our previous intelligence projections. Frankly, the krauts have had us fooled six ways to Sunday."

Churchill glowered. "General, in how many other ways to Sunday might the krauts have us fooled, even now?"

The general shrugged. "My expertise is limited to aircraft, Prime Minister. And I need to point out that these aircraft are obviously just prototypes. In great numbers, they could have changed the war. As is, well, even a few hundred Messerschmitt 262s in actual operation have been too little too late."

Churchill turned to Jimmy. "Do *you* think this factory you saw is turning out these aeroplanes of tomorrow in great numbers?"

A two-star Brit, his nose in the air, said, "Prime Minister, I hardly think this enlisted man, however valiant, is qualified to assess—"

Churchill raised his hand. "General, in due course I will hear you out fully. I will afford your assessment the weight to which I deem it entitled. But in this moment, the only man in this room who possesses novel information is Sergeant Righetti. I, for one, would like to learn it. Therefore—"

The Brit said, "Nevertheless—"

Churchill glared down the table. "General, will you *cease* interrupting me, while I am interrupting you?"

The Brit clammed up.

Churchill said, "Well, Sergeant?"

Jimmy shook his head. "No, sir."

"No sir what?"

"No, sir, these krauts in Bavaria aren't cranking out a lot of planes."

"What makes you so sure?"

Jimmy looked around. "Does anybody here have a copy of the first photo pair? And a viewer?"

The full bird leapt up, laid the stereo pair and a viewer in front of Churchill, then stepped back.

Jimmy said, "Do you see the pair of marks on the flat tail surface?"

Churchill removed his glasses, bent over the viewer, then grunted.

Jimmy said, "In that photo, it's hard to make them out. But I just saw them fifty feet below me. They're the letter 'P,' followed by the roman numeral 'II.' And with that in mind, it's now clear to me that the same markings are on the plane in that photo. It's the *same plane*, sir. And if it were one plane from an operational unit, the unit would be identified by a couple letters plus an Arabic numeral. There would be a chevron and bar pattern to identify the individual plane, and the pilot's rank within the unit."

"Then what is 'P II'?"

"Prototype number two, Sir. In my opinion. The aircraft has moved around since this photo was taken. And when I saw it the runway was cleared, and the flatcar they move it in and out on was visible. They wheel this plane out of the mountain, clear the runway, test fly it, land it, wheel it back inside, then re-cover the runway."

A different Brit two-star steepled his fingers and smiled. "A horde of these could devastate London. But one or two? A tragic nuisance, perhaps. But no more than that."

An American said to Jimmy, "It's big. I suppose it has the range to be a nuisance over New York or Washington, too?"

"I'm no engineer, but in my opinion, yes, sir. Why build a plane with six engines, and more wing than a couple of B-29s, except to cross the Atlantic?"

One of the striped-tie Brit civilians pursed his lips. "Worryingly, with what cargo might it cross the Atlantic?"

Churchill flicked his eyebrows up. "Ah. Whatever may be a scoundrel's last refuge, he needs a means to get to it? You're suggesting this may be Herr Hitler's 'getaway car' to South America?"

The striped-tie civilian nodded. "It is a continent rife with Fascist sympathizing Germans, Prime Minister. And for what other purpose would the Huns continue diverting such vast resources to so obviously lost a cause? This labor camp is obviously larger than required simply to hand-build one or two airplanes."

Someone said, "Here, here."

Someone set a snifter of brandy in front of Churchill, and another in front of Jimmy.

Churchill looked around the table. "Gentlemen, before we move to the next agenda item, I propose a ten-minute recess."

Chair legs squealed and the others in the room, except Churchill, stood.

Jimmy pushed his own chair back, but Churchill waved, palm down, for him to remain seated. "If I may impose further, Sergeant, a private word before you go? As one son of Brooklyn to another."

Thirty-seven

CHURCHILL WAITED UNTIL THE ROOM CLEARED, THEN RAISED his snifter. "I raise a glass to the fallen. To your comrade, in particular. And to you, Sergeant."

Jimmy sipped, then coughed. "Thank you, sir. Is there anything else? I think my boss is waiting outside."

"I think your boss will not forsake you." Churchill stood, walked to one of the windowless room's whitewashed walls, then ran the fingers of one hand across the rough brick while he sipped brandy from the snifter in the other. "Do you know how many long nights like this one I have spent, sequestered in these war rooms, or in other equally stifling rooms, since His Majesty called upon me to form a government in 1940?"

"No, sir."

"Nor do I. But I know that those dark, early days have now given way to an impending sunrise. And during that journey from darkness to light, I have often been forced to choose the least vile among alternatives."

"Yes, sir. I think history will understand that. And it will be kind."

Churchill turned and smiled. "Of course history will be kind. For I intend to write it." He again sat across from Jimmy. "Nonetheless, there will be critics. Sergeant, do you recall what your countryman, Theodore Roosevelt, said about critics?"

"I'm sure I don't, Sir."

"He said, 'It is not the critic who counts; not the man who points out where the doer of deeds could have done them better.

The credit belongs to the man who is actually in the arena, whose face is marred by dust and sweat and blood; who strives valiantly, but who does actually strive to do the deeds.'"

"Yes, sir."

"Then I ask you, as the man who has actually striven in the arena, in this moment what would you do about this facility, and about this airplane, that you have seen with your own eyes?"

Jimmy shifted in his chair, then sipped brandy. "Well, I suppose we should capture the plane. And we want to release all those prisoners. And in a week or two we will."

Jimmy pointed at the plane, in the photo blowup on the easel, "Like the colonel said, these planes could teach us a lot. And if we don't capture the one I saw, and Hitler uses it to go hide in some cave in South America, I'd hate that. But a good man just bled to death on me, for no reason except to take pictures nobody will ever see. I hate that more. If Hitler got away, we'd catch him eventually. I wouldn't spend one more drop of one more soldier's blood to catch him sooner."

"Ah."

"And it wouldn't just be soldier's blood. Sir, I assess bomb damage every day. We count a crater a hit if it's within a thousand feet of the aiming point. And still only one bomb in five is a hit. If we bomb that place, then unless we miss it altogether, we'll flatten everything. So if what you're asking is whether we should bomb it, I'd say 'hell no.' Because there are mothers and kids in that camp. I saw hundreds. There are probably thousands more people in that camp."

"What if, as you just heard, those thousands were engaged in more than building a few prototypes?"

"You mean if there were a thousand of those planes? But sir, there aren't."

"Then what if today, or tomorrow, or the day after, that one plane could wreak the havoc that a thousand planes like it could?"

"You mean like Hamburg? Like Cologne? Like Dresden? Burn a whole city in one night? Sir, everybody knows one plane can't do that."

"But if it could? If that one single plane could tomorrow destroy *this* city, beneath which we sit at this moment? Or New York?"

"*My* New York?" Jimmy drew a breath, then closed his eyes.

"Sir, my mother, and my brother, and my sisters, and my friends are in New York. That's an unfair question."

"Sergeant, war poses unfair questions. But it demands that we answer them anyway. So, I ask you again. Would you annihilate perhaps twenty thousand suffering innocents, who stood to walk free from their prison within days, rather than risk annihilating ten times, or twenty times, or even thirty times, their number, of equally blameless human beings? On the very eve of victory?"

"It's not a math problem."

"Yet it is precisely that."

Jimmy ached everywhere that he did not burn. He was weary beyond sleep. He was desperately thirsty, and Churchill's brandy had gone down like vinegar, and only made that worse. He searched the room's dark corners, and its bright spaces, but found no way out.

Jimmy said, "I couldn't take the chance. I'd bomb that place to charcoal. To be sure that plane never left the ground."

"And then what?"

"And then I would shut my mouth. I'm a good Catholic. But I wouldn't even whisper it to the priest in the confessional, as long as I lived."

"You would lie?"

"Not to God. That's impossible. He would know what I did. In the end, he'd tell me whether I did right or wrong. In the meantime, I would take responsibility for the decision I made onto myself. Not blab about it, to spread the blame around to all the people involved, who didn't know what they were doing."

"As Jesus on the cross implored his father? To forgive those who knew not what they did?"

"Sir, I wouldn't know. I'm a good Catholic, not an analytical one. And it's just a hypothetical."

Thirty-eight

FRANK WATCHED AS JIMMY RIGHETTI LEANED FORWARD FROM his seat across the table from Frank and Cass. The old man's hand, red with puckered scar tissue, trembled as he set down his empty bourbon glass.

Jimmy said, "On April 25, 1945, twelve days before the war ended in Europe, and seven days after I met Churchill, the Allies bombed Hitler's house. The house Bookman photographed that started the whole mess. Six hundred planes. They plastered the Berghof, and targets all around it.

"It was payback, not strategic bombing. The Brits let Polack crews fly some of the Brit planes, so the Poles could get even with the Nazis. Some of the crews were Aussies and Kiwis, flying to celebrate Anzac Day. Everybody just wanted to bury that sonuvabitch Hitler alive in his own bomb shelter. Or burn him alive in his own bed. But it turned out he was in his bunker in Berlin that day. Five days later, on April 30, he shot himself, up there in Berlin. Then his own people burned his body."

Frank glanced at Cass, his head cocked.

She nodded. "That's all true, Frank."

Jimmy said, "Me, I was in my *own* bed, feeling sorry for myself, in hospital in London the whole time. Just waiting to get shipped home and discharged.

"On May 8, 1945, the war in Europe ended. I snuck out of the hospital, and talked my way into a berth on a troopship home. By rotation order, those berths should've gone to GIs who had fought their way across Europe. But there were GIs who missed a train, or who were still alive only on paper, who didn't show up. So the paper pushers filled out forms for me, rather than let a berth go home empty. I promised myself that I'd never think about anything I did during that war again."

Cass said, "But you did."

Jimmy said, "As soon as I walked down that gangplank in New York, I called my girl from a pay phone on the dock. She proposed to *me* over the phone, right there, on the spot. At our wedding everybody said we'd hit the Daily Double. Because we got married August 7, 1945. The day after the big one dropped on Hiroshima. So, everybody knew then the Japs were finished, too. The war was really over. For everybody." His voice caught.

He blew his nose, then said, "But on our wedding night, I cried. Because that's when I figured it out. We didn't just bomb Hitler's house. We bombed that camp and that factory, too. We buried, or we burned alive, twenty thousand innocent prisoners, who were twelve days away from surviving the war. For what? To keep the krauts from dropping a bomb that Churchill was afraid they had. But they never did have. Then we covered it up." Jimmy's voice cracked, and he wiped away tears. "Because of what I told Churchill."

Cass reached out and touched Jimmy's heaving shoulder. "Jimmy, that's not fair. It wasn't you. Your boss, Major Kane, would tell you that."

"I never saw Tom Kane again. I heard he stayed in the Air Force, and died in a plane crash in Korea in 1950. When they pulled in that gangplank in Southampton, I swore I'd never get into an airplane again, either. But, in 1958, I flew back to Germany. Because I had to know."

Cass leaned forward. "And?"

"Before I left, I went to the library, and found a place that sounded right. A big salt mine, that closed during the Depression. It was called the Salzreich."

Cass said, "That means 'Salt Kingdom.' Like Salzburg, across the Bavarian border in Austria, means 'Salt Fortress.' They started digging salt in the Bavarian Lake District about the same time Columbus found the Bahamas."

"This place might as well have been the Bahamas. There was nothing there but overgrown, crumbled foundations. And birds singing in the trees. And overgrown rubble where the tunnel entrance had been. No plaques. No graves. No bones. Nothing. I even walked that whole valley with a metal detector. What was left of the railroad tracks were there, rusting away underneath the weeds. That just proved there had been a salt mine there."

Cass said, "Nothing else at *all*? A metal detector responds worse to aluminum than steel tracks. But it responds if there's enough aluminum."

Jimmy shook his head. "I found a ring. Not a Cracker Jack prize, but not expensive jewelry. Just two roses, with their stems wound together. A jeweler gave me thirty bucks for it. The silver wasn't worth half that, but he liked the workmanship. No airplane parts of any kind. If the Berchtesgaden raid blew up that plane, I should've found *some* kind of debris. I didn't. As far as the world was concerned, the all-wing bomber, the camp, how Bookman died, the whole megillah, never happened."

"And you never told anyone?"

"What part of that story would *you* brag about? A desk jockey, who couldn't even find a landing-gear switch, talked his way into an airplane. Then got his pilot killed? Then jumped the queue, and got home before soldiers who had done real fighting? Or mothers and children, buried alive for nothing?" Jimmy stood, hiked up his pants, then said to Frank, "If I hit the road tonight, I can return the car at the airport in the morning. That saves a day's rental, and I can make my next doctor's appointment. Has this place got indoor plumbing?"

Frank pointed. "Down that hall, on the right."

After Jimmy disappeared down the hall, Frank raised his eyebrows. "Well, that's some yarn."

"You *can't* think that man is lying."

"Didn't say that. Folks like Jimmy and me are too old, and too tired, to bother lying. We just remember stuff that isn't true."

"Frank, every detail Jimmy remembered is *precisely* true. Elliott Roosevelt *did* get replaced as commander of the 325th recon wing on April 13, 1945. Over a procurement scandal. The Allies *were* scared shitless that the hardcore Nazis planned to dig in and hold out in the Bavarian Alps. Unescorted daylight bombing *was* a bloodbath that broke flyers like Jimmy's boss. Today we call it PTSD. During World War II, they just called it 'losing your nerve.' Swastikas *were* mostly painted on tails and fuselages, not on wings. Late in the war, some Luftwaffe aircraft *were* towed by ox teams. And Jimmy didn't misremember that scar tissue on his hand."

"But the Churchill business?"

"Churchill's mother *was* born in Brooklyn. And he bragged about it to Americans every chance he got.

"Exotic weapons fascinated him. And he *did* inspect aerial photos first hand, when the subject fascinated him. In 1943 he talked the Allied air forces into diverting from strategic bombing to blowing the hell out of Peenemünde, after he saw overhead images of the V-1 and V-2 facilities there.

"Some of the planes on that Berchtesgaden raid carried Tallboy penetrator bombs. Tallboys were armored, time-delayed, five-ton bunker busters. They could hit the ground traveling faster than the speed of sound, and burrow sixty feet underground before they exploded. Tallboys would have been just the thing to collapse that underground factory.

"And it wouldn't have been the first time, or the last time that civilians used a military target as a bomb shelter, and died. That would explain the lack of bodies."

"But thousands of people were in those planes. Thousands more people saw them come and go. Somebody would have talked by now."

"Only if they knew what they bombed. Frank, even the lead bombardier in the lead plane in the lead squadron on those big raids didn't really know what was under the roof he aimed at. And once the first wave blew things up, the later waves were dropping bombs into smoke. And there was no GPS then. Whole formations took wrong turns and bombed the wrong city, more than once. People *thought* they had bombed what they were *told* they had bombed.

"The Berchtesgaden raid used multinational crews to bomb multiple targets. It was complicated enough that a target could have been hidden in the shuffle. The mountains confused some of the formations' direction-finding equipment. It was daylight, but in some of the mountain valleys the targets were obscured by clouds."

"The *Germans* would've talked."

Cass snorted. "Even less likely. The German pilot in our photo, Hanna Reitsch, said that after the war you couldn't find a single person in Germany who had even voted for Hitler."

"So you think the man who was in the arena's right? And history's wrong?"

"Frank, for the first thirty years history is crap because the people who lived it write history to hide their mistakes. After that, history is crap because the people who write history write it to push their agendas."

Frank smiled. "Seems the more time you and I spend together, the smarter you get."

She sighed. "Anyway, Churchill *did* say history would be kind to him because he intended to write it. And he did write it. Six volumes. And I've read them all. And nothing remotely like this is mentioned. Most of what other people wrote was also kind to him, and to the Allies, too. And the British hide embarrassing official secrets even longer than the U.S. does. We're still waiting to read documents about the Duke of Windsor's relations with the Nazis."

"But would Churchill really have done that?"

"He was the only person in that room—one of the few people in the *world*—who knew, in April 1945, that an A-bomb, and a plane that could carry it, were only months away. And he knew that Germany had started the A-bomb race way ahead of us.

"By late 1944, the Allies had captured documents that *did* suggest Heisenberg's Uranium Club had flopped. But contradictions, and examples of intelligence failures, kept cropping up. In March 1945, the Allies dropped seventeen *hundred tons* of bombs on a suspected uranium processing factory in Orianenburg.

"From Churchill's viewpoint, it would have been no time to gamble."

Frank said, "So, that's it? That plane, and whatever it was part of, are gone. Lost forever. This trail that you and I were following just dead-ended?"

"Looks that way. Dammit." Cass's shoulders sagged. "Maybe I can hitch a ride down to the airport with Jimmy."

Frank raised his palm, shushed her with a finger to his lips, then stood. He picked up the Winchester, then listened.

A second footfall thumped the front porch.

Cass mouthed, "Snake Eyes?"

Frank waved Cass to the kitchen as he aimed, chest high, at his front door.

Someone knocked, a metallic thump against the door's wood.

Frank sighted down the Winchester's barrel, drew a breath then began releasing it, slowly.

"Frank? It's Cody Gates. You okay?"

Frank inhaled. He laid down the rifle, stepped to his door, then yanked it open.

Cody, the sheriff's deputy, stood there, long black flashlight in hand.

"What the hell, Cody? Sneaking up like that, I could've shot you."

"I wasn't sneaking. I was hiking. There's a rental Chevy blocking your driveway."

"Oh. Well why'd you come?"

"Dispatch reported a trouble call from here that got cancelled. But after the cancellation, one of your neighbors called in shots fired. When I heard, I was sorting out a wreck that closed the interstate. But when my rounds got me down this way, I thought I'd drop by. Because you seem to be turning up in the middle of too many things, lately."

Cass, who was, tattoos and face hardware notwithstanding, one pretty young girl, came and stood alongside Frank.

The deputy's eyes widened.

Frank said. "House guest."

Cass extended her hand and smiled. "Cassidy Gooding. Nice hat, by the way."

Cody didn't shake her hand, just smiled broadly and touched his Stetson's brim. "Ma'am." He jerked a thumb toward the driveway. "That your car, then, Ms. Gooding?"

Jimmy Righetti elbowed past Frank. "It's mine. I was just leaving."

Frank said, "'Nother guest. This one's just passing through."

"Really. Well, Frank. Aren't you just *full* of surprises tonight?" The deputy pointed back and forth across the three of them. "The three of you were doing a little target shooting this evening, were you?"

Frank shook his head. "Black bear. Sniffing for garbage. Shot high and ran her off."

Cody cocked an eyebrow. "Three times?"

"Maybe she was deaf. Cody, there's no law against discharging a firearm in Eagle County, outside city limits."

"True. You're bullshitting me, but true." The deputy stared at the three of them.

Finally, he sighed. "Well, whatever story you told me, no reasonably prudent law enforcement professional would believe it anyway." He tipped his hat to Cass again. "You all have a pleasant evening."

As Cody turned away Frank said to him, "By the way, how'd that business with the lady who passed away over at Bristlecone Apartments ever turn out?"

The deputy shrugged. "You're in the clear, Frank. The attending physician signed off on natural causes when he examined the body the next morning. The coroner never even took a look. Normally, that would have been the end of county involvement."

Frank said, "Normally?"

"The county had to make disposition of the remains. The family's not legally *obligated* to claim the body. And the county had nothing to go on but her last name. And the first name of her son."

Cass and Frank both said, "Son?"

Thirty-nine

THE ASP, PROTECTED FROM UPPER PIKA LAKE'S COLD BY HIS wetsuit, paused to decompress fifteen feet beneath the lake's surface.

Two nights earlier, he had watched, and listened, concealed in the pines, one hundred yards from Frank Luck's cabin, while rifle shots had been fired. Later, a local policeman had arrived.

Anonymity remained the Asp's most valuable asset, and he now operated on a schedule that was counting down. There was too little time to do anything but withdraw without contact.

He peered up through the clear water at the flotation bags, then at the object that hung beneath them.

It was of a size, shape, and weight similar to various items of oil drilling equipment, but was heavier than most automobiles. He, as part of a team, had often raised such objects, from both greater and lesser depths, from the North Sea's bottom, and from the Netherlands' canals.

Using the equipment he had purchased from the commercial diving supplier in Louisiana, the lift process was uncomplicated, but delicate.

First, panels and clamps that obstructed the object's upward movement were cut away. Deflated flotation bags, of suitable size and design for the job, were secured to the object to be lifted, using slings and cables. Then air was introduced, in tiny increments, into the bags, through a hose attached to a scuba tank. When the lift object achieved neutral buoyancy, the lift object inched upward.

Care was critical. Any margin for error was erased by the fact that he worked alone.

Too much air, or too little, or an ill-chosen attachment point, or any equipment failure, would have spelled disaster. If the object fell back to the bottom, and either buried itself in silt, or was damaged, all was lost.

The Asp dragged himself out onto the ice, then ran back to the old woman's horse trailer, its rotted tires now replaced.

He had backed the trailer, with its open end in the lake, so that its load floor was beneath the water's surface.

The cable he had affixed to the object ran beneath the surface, under and along the open-water channel. A rusted, steel-wheeled ore cart, which the old woman had modified into a cradle, rolled on scavenged steel rails. These he had laid, segment by segment, on the lake bed.

The Expedition was parked nose to nose with the trailer, and the cable passed above the cradle, then through the horse trailer, then was wound onto the cable spool of the Expedition's front winch.

By the time the Asp reached the winch controls, he breathed heavily, and his heart hammered in his chest.

It was not merely overexertion, though the days of virtually sleepless labor had left him exhausted.

If he pulled too fast, if the cable failed, if the winch malfunctioned, if the path from the lake to the cart, then into the trailer, was misaligned, there would be no recovering.

Yet God was on his side.

The Asp shivered in his wetsuit, recited a final prayer, then engaged the winch.

The machine whined, then took up slack. When the cable came taut, the whine's pitch rose.

The winch motor was, however, minimally stressed. The old woman, like most people, had failed to appreciate the degree to which water reduced the effective mass even of nonbuoyant objects.

The Asp reeled in his prize, inch by inch.

An hour later, it floated above the modified ore cart, which rested on the rusted, salvaged, mine tracks.

The Asp waded back into the water, deflated the bags gradually, and guided the object onto its rusty cradle.

He returned to the winch, breathing normally. The time of greatest risk, at least insofar as exhuming the object, was past.

After a further two hours, the object had been drawn into, then secured in, the trailer. The Expedition had towed the heavily laden trailer back to the old woman's workshop, then inside. As summer darkness fell across the mountains, the Asp started the old woman's gasoline-powered electric generator outside the workshop, then closed the workshop's doors.

The place was a malodorous, high-ceilinged barn, really, and piled with junk the woman had accumulated in pursuit of her dream. A dream that tonight the enemy of her enemy had brought closer to reality than it had been in seventy-five years.

He changed out of the wetsuit, ate, and drank. Then he prayed with particularly reverent thanks to God for the blessings of this day, and for those soon to come.

He laid out the original checklists and explanations that he had taken from the case. He also laid out the photocopies, with his handwritten translation notes from German. Much remained to be done.

He began by removing a hopelessly corroded battery, and refitting the object to accommodate the new battery he had purchased. He estimated the remaining work, then the time required thereafter to reach his goal, then set the alarm on his phone.

As he lay down on the workshop floor, his elation almost denied him sleep.

But, only months earlier, the goal had been in sight for his brother, yet something had gone wrong.

And seventy-five years earlier, something else had also gone wrong.

Forty

ON THE PRAIRIE BETWEEN DENVER AND BOULDER, IT WAS 10:00 a.m., and was three days after Jimmy Righetti had left Frank's place, headed back to his home. Also three days after the Eagle County sheriff's deputy had told Frank that the dead woman, Eleanor Love, had a son.

While Frank parked his truck in the long driveway of a board-sided farmhouse, gray for lack of paint, Cass stared through the pickup's window at the place.

With nothing to go on but the son's first name, Cass had eliminated fifty-three "Elliott Loves," who were too old, too young, too distant, or too dead.

Fifty yards behind the gray farmhouse a corrugated metal barn stood. Alongside the barn an orange pennant dangled limp atop a flagpole. It didn't look like a working farm, and according to Zillow, the twenty-acre parcel had been bought in 1983.

The property backed up to the Rocky Mountains' red rock foothills, and was on a two-lane highway that connected Denver to Boulder.

Frank nodded toward the other pickup parked alongside them. "Somebody's home. You think this 'Elliott' might be the one?"

Cass nodded. "Now that I see this place, I think he might."

Frank said, "Oh?"

"The mother of the Elliott Love we're looking for was a pilot." Cass pointed at the flagpole beside the barn. "That orange thing hanging from that pole is a windsock."

✧　　✧　　✧

303

As Cass and Frank walked to the house's front door a man slid aside the barn's rolling door, stepped through it, then closed it behind himself.

He wore a faded, blue, front-zip coverall. As he walked, he wiped his hands with a rag, and called, "Can I help you?"

No taller than Cass was, herself, he looked as old as Frank did. He had less hair, just a salt-and-pepper fringe of dark hair above his ears. Behind his thick glasses, his dark eyes were bloodshot. He squinted into the morning sunshine.

A patch, sewn above his coverall's right breast pocket, read "Elliott," in embroidered script.

Cass said, "We're looking for Elliott Love."

His eyes darted from hers, to Frank's, then back. "Why?"

"Mr. Love, this is Frank Luck. I'm Cassidy Gooding. I curate aircraft at the National Air and Space Museum."

"Oh! Come in. I'll make tea." He grinned, then led them to the house's front door.

Cass sat alongside Frank on the sofa in Elliott Love's neat, unadorned living room. Love returned from his kitchen, after putting on his kettle.

He sat across from them. As he spoke, he rocked backward, then forward, and he blinked often. "How did the Museum find out about me? I don't have an 'internet presence.' I have a résumé, and a brochure. In my office, out back."

Cass said, "You're an aircraft mechanic?"

"Oh." Love frowned. "Restorer, more precisely. But my FAA certifications are current. You didn't know?"

Cass shook her head. "No. Mr. Love, I'm sorry. We didn't come here to hire you. I didn't even know what you did for a living."

"Oh." Love sat back, frowning. "Then what do you want with me?"

"We're looking into something that came up in connection with your mother's death."

The old man stiffened.

Finally, he said, "My mother and I haven't spoken since I was sixteen. I'm sure nothing I might recall would help you with whatever you're looking into."

Cass reached into her bag, then passed across a copy of the

photograph from Frank's map case. "Have you seen this photo of your mother before?"

Elliott Love held the copy in both hands and stared at it.

After thirty seconds, he nodded. "Well, now this makes sense." He laid the photo on the coffee table that separated him from his guests, and his hand trembled.

He stood, looked at his wristwatch, then walked to his kitchen.

He said, "It will take my tea kettle three minutes longer to boil. If you two are still here when I come back, I'm calling a lawyer." He pointed to his front door. "Please take your photo graph, and let yourselves out."

He closed the kitchen door behind him.

Frank said, "Odd duck. With no soft spot for Momma."

Cass said, "Or for Dad. That may not be surprising, because she and the blonde hottie may not have been married. The Nazis had a program called 'Lebensborn.' It hooked up racially pure single women with racially pure Nazis, particularly SS officers, to breed more Nazis. Usually outside of marriage. It's logical that the blond guy came with her to the U.S. But he may not have stuck around."

"Elliott's dad died in 1945."

"Frank, the blond hottie wasn't even wearing a uniform. You can't be sure he died in 1945."

"Didn't say he did. I said Elliott's father died in 1945. Breeding livestock taught me enough genetics to know the odds of two blue-eyed blonds producing a dark-eyed, dark-haired offspring like Mr. Love are worse than the odds of filling an inside straight."

Cass's jaw dropped.

She whispered, "Himmler? Holy crap! *Himmler* was the blonde pilot's 'beloved'?" Then she nodded. "Of course. Himmler fathered at least two illegitimate children during the war. Apparently, he fathered at least one more."

Cass tapped a finger on her lip. "No wonder this guy doesn't have a website. Super villains' bastard sons don't advertise."

Frank nodded. "There's a reason Elliott said he was going to call a lawyer. Most people would have said they'd call the cops."

Cass stood and stepped toward the front door.

Frank touched her elbow and shook his head.

Cass whispered, "Cops or lawyers, when a man whose father murdered two thirds of the 'undesirables' in Europe, and who seems slightly odd, orders you to leave his house, you leave. After we get clear of here, we'll text the FBI."

"Why? Choosing the wrong parents isn't a crime."

"Murdering people who find out about it is!" Cass pointed at the closed kitchen door. "He may be in there sharpening an axe."

"He isn't. Simmer down." Frank patted the couch alongside himself. "Take a seat."

She sat, then rolled her eyes. "This is another cowpoke life lesson, isn't it?"

"Jimmy Righetti was hungry to confess. And to have somebody tell him it wasn't his fault, before he died. Elliott's hungry to talk, too. And he's finally got somebody who he figures has already guessed the worst part." Frank sat back. "He'll come to us when he's hungry enough. Like trout."

"*That's* your life lesson? 'Life is like fishing'?"

Frank shook his head. "No. Life's more like farming."

"Really. Why?"

"Elliott's not a bad seed, just because he came out of the wrong bag. Let's wait. We'll see what sprouted."

Frank crossed his arms while he sat and stared at the kitchen door.

A minute later he said, "Elliott's squirrely. But he seems smart enough. *Most* Germans I've met seem smart. Smarter than trout, anyway. Never understood why the Germans took the Nazis' bait in the first place."

"Because life is like farming, Frank."

Frank narrowed his eyes at Cass.

"No. I'm not messing with you. You're actually kind of right. After World War I, Germany suffered one disaster after another. Like farmers and ranchers have droughts, then floods, then go bankrupt. The Allied blockade that ended World War I starved seven hundred thousand German civilians.

"Then, two hundred thousand more died in the 1918 Spanish Flu epidemic.

"A revolution forced the Kaiser out, but the Weimar Republic that replaced the monarchy inherited two million men dead, two and a half million disabled veterans, a million war orphans, and a half million war widows. Plus reparations the Allies demanded in the Treaty of Versailles."

Frank shrugged. "Dealer gets to choose the next game."

"Whatever. The reparations were absurd. Thirty-three billion dollars, when the U.S. Treasury's 1918 total receipts were only thirty-*five* billion dollars.

"Weimar hyperinflated its currency to pay. Hyperinflation wiped out average Germans' life savings. So, there were at least three more revolutions. Then the Depression piled on."

"No drawing a winner from a deck that's out of aces."

"If that means Germany had no good options left, yes. Even so, Germans didn't really take the bait. Hitler only got a third of the votes when he became chancellor, in 1933."

"And he made a mess."

"Not at first. The Nazis cut unemployment by two-thirds. They built the autobahns. They set up programs, so regular Germans could own radios, and eventually VW Beetles. They hosted, televised, and won the Berlin Olympics. They built subsidized cruise liners, and resorts on the Baltic. So ordinary workers could afford to vacation alongside their bosses."

"They also started a World War."

"In 1939 the war seemed crazy. But by 1942, the Nazis had stuck it to the countries that stuck it to Germany at Versailles. They won an empire that stretched from the Arctic Circle to North Africa. And from the English Channel to Moscow. In the meantime, the western democracies could barely deal with the Depression. The Nazis appalled most smart people in the rest of the world. But even the smart people had to wonder whether the Nazis were smarter than they were, after all."

"When the rain dance works, maybe the medicine man's *not* a fraud."

"Not the way I'd put it. But yes."

Ten minutes later, Elliott Love peeked back through the kitchen door, and said, "I'm glad you stayed. If you two would care to listen, I've been waiting a long time to talk."

Thirty minutes later Cass and Frank sat at Elliott Love's kitchen table with him, drinking organic tea.

Elliott stared into his cup. "I had never seen that photo of my mother with Himmler. Or any photo of her, for that matter. As you can imagine, she was camera shy."

Cass said, "But you knew she knew airplanes. Your profession can't be coincidental."

Elliott nodded. "Every moment she could spare she taught me about aircraft. But she never worked in aviation. As far as anyone in America was concerned, she was born in America to German immigrants, and raised on a farm. But, under her supervision, I rebuilt a Fieseler Storch's engine, before I turned twelve."

"Where did she get a Storch engine?"

"It came with the Storch."

Cass's jaw dropped. "You're messing with me."

"Not at all. She bought a ratty one, that was imported thirdhand to the U.S. during the fifties, then converted for crop dusting.

"It sat in a Kansas barn, with its wings folded, after the engine seized. You'd be surprised how many idiots think oil changes are optional. But then, you understand all that."

Elliott leaned back in his chair while he stared past his guests. "My mother taught me to fly in that Storch. Not an ideal trainer, with the instructor seated behind the student. There was lots of yelling. Lots more near-disasters. But those are my best memories of her. Like Hanna Reitsch, the other woman in your photo, the sky was her kingdom."

Cass wrinkled her forehead. "Importing a German aircraft after the war was one thing. Importing a German *test pilot* was another thing, altogether. How did that happen?"

Elliott said, "After the war in Europe ended, Heinrich Himmler bit a cyanide capsule, while in British custody. Eight months later, my mother gave birth to me here in Colorado. With just a midwife's help. I'm named for Franklin Roosevelt's son. And my mother took Roosevelt's widow's first name. I suppose she thought they, plus the surname 'Love,' were very American."

"Ah." Cass nodded. "Operation Paperclip?"

Frank said, "What?"

Cass said, "After World War II, the Allies put on trial, then hung, the most visible surviving Nazis. But *some* of our enemies' enemies became our friends. The U.S. recruited Nazis, if they could help us win the *new* war against the Soviet Union.

"Wernher von Braun got a ticket to Huntsville, Alabama. Then he got us to the Moon ahead of the Russians.

"We laundered Nazi spies, because, for decades, Germany had a broad, deep spy network among the communists. Where we had squat. Your mother tested advanced aircraft. She would have been a prime Paperclip candidate."

"I know about Paperclip." Love shook his head as he smiled. "But no government entity in the U.S. was ever aware my mother existed. Except in the rudimentary 'did she pay her taxes and obey the law' way."

Cass said, "Wait."

Elliott shook his head. "I'm quite serious. There were no credit card receipts, no digitized phone records, no surveillance videos, no DNA tests. It was easy to be who you said you were in America."

Cass raised her hand. "That's not why I said 'wait.' Before that, you said we already understood. And before that, that our showing up here made sense. Did you mean we understood about oil changes?"

Elliott shook his head. "No. I meant you must have already seen my mother's Fieseler Storch. When you went to her place."

"Her place?"

"After I learned she had died, I went up there myself. To see whether the Storch was still there. It was, and I spent a couple days up at the lake, making it airworthy again."

"Lake? Elliott, your mother died in a senior citizen apartment in the middle of Avon, Colorado."

"The Storch is stored at a weekend place my mother owned since the 1950s. Just below Upper Pika Lake."

Frank cocked his head. "Upper Pika's in the Eagles Nest Wilderness."

"It wasn't when she bought the place. It's an inholding."

Cass raised her hand. "Whatever. Elliott, why would you think we've *been* there?"

"Well, *somebody* certainly has been there recently. Then suddenly, here you are, asking about my mother."

Frank looked at Cass, then back at Elliott. "Wasn't us."

Elliott said, "My mother hadn't been healthy enough to go there in years. But when I got there, I had to leave my truck at the gate, climb over, then hike to the shed where the Storch was stored. Because somebody had replaced the gate lock. With a brand new one."

Cass said, "Elliott, if your mother wasn't Paperclipped, how did she get to the United States?"

Elliott stood, then turned to his stove. "That story's going to require another pot of tea."

Forty-one

ILSE JAEGER BRAKED HER CAR, THEN TURNED IT ONTO THE ROAD that led to the Salzreich facility.

She sighed, relieved that she had survived her drive from Munich. In late April 1945, Allied fighters, unimpeded by the impotent German Air Force, hunted for anything that moved within the small bits of Germany that Allied armies hadn't yet overrun.

Ilse had returned from hospital to the Salzreich two months earlier. What she found there so dismayed her that she had begged time off, claiming fatigue from her injuries. And the action she had taken was about to bear fruit.

Ahead of her, the cripple who guarded the Salzreich Project's modest entrance stepped from his guard cabin, stood in front of his lowered gate, then waved her to stop.

Peter Winter, hands in his sport jacket's pockets to defeat the overcast April morning's chill, followed the guard, and conversed with him as they stood there.

She nodded to herself.

Winter's presence outside the mine would simplify the next few minutes.

Ilse stepped from her car, and walked to Winter and the guard.

The cripple was speaking, and the subject was evidently the most recent reconnaissance overflight.

"It was a Tommie Mosquito, but with American markings. It was painted blue, as pale as the sky. But he never fired a shot."

Winter said, "He had no guns to fire with, Lothar. The blue

paint is a high-altitude camouflage the Allies apply to photo reconnaissance aircraft. The guns are removed to save weight."

"High altitude? Two meters isn't high, Doc."

Winter turned at Ilse's approach and smiled. "Welcome back. You look well. The additional convalescence appears to have agreed with you."

She said to the guard, "I was told last night that you saw another plane two days earlier. But you failed to report that one to Air Defense."

"Didn't need to. I only was looking for it because I heard flak around the Berghof. Air Defense had already shot at it."

Ilse said, "And when you looked, what did you see?"

"It was flying real fast. It was gone before I could count to six. I estimate its altitude was at least three thousand meters above us, here. And it was American."

"You made out American markings under those circumstances?"

"No, miss, I made out that it was a silver plane. So I applied the new, simplified aircraft identification test that *Reichsmarschall* Goering issued last month."

"I'm unaware of any such test."

"Yes, miss. If you see a silver plane, it's American. If you see a black plane, it's British. If you see no plane it's German."

Winter snorted behind his hand, then said, "Lothar, would you return to the guard box? Miss Jaeger and I have things to discuss."

The guard walked away as Ilse pointed at his receding back, and told Winter, "That man should be disciplined. If not for dereliction of duty, then for his insubordinate attitude toward me."

Winter shook his head. "'Dereliction of duty'? Ilse, 'that man' was the only person in this facility who lifted a finger to defend it against that plane. And he can't technically be insubordinate to a civilian."

"You find his treasonous defeatism funny?"

"I find a wounded veteran's repetition of gallows humor excusable. And it's barely a joke. The air force is so beaten that the Americans have stopped painting their planes, because silver is more visible. To lure our remaining planes into the air, so their fighters can pick them off."

"But we agree the first plane was high-altitude reconnaissance? And then the Mosquito was sent for a closer look?"

"Yes. And, unfortunately, the Valkyrie was out there for the looking both times. But did you know Lothar got off a shot? A shot that he insists hit the plane. In fact, hit the pilot. Any photographs it took may never have been seen."

"We need to prepare for the worst. Not hope for the best, based on a half-blind marksman's delusion."

"Or we do both."

At that moment, guard whistles sounded inside the camp, then echoed across the runway.

Ilse turned, and saw men, women, and children pouring from the camp barracks. They assembled in the central quadrangles that the barracks surrounded. The guards meandered around the assemblages' fringes, like sheep dogs carrying Mausers.

She said, "What's going on?"

"I'm hoping for the best but preparing for the worst. We're temporarily moving the camp population into the mine. As a precaution. And of course the Valkyrie, and the bomb, will remain safely in there for the next few weeks."

"A bomb shelter? Well, as long as their presence doesn't interfere with necessary work." As she spoke, Ilse turned and peered up the pine-bough-covered runway, toward the main road.

The road remained empty. Where the devil were they?

She said, "With the bomb and plane complete, the only organizations involved going forward will be the Bear's, for the plane, and the Prussian's, for the weapon itself. What do they think about this Jew exodus?"

"They don't know about it. The Bear's family lives in Silesia. The Prussian's lives north of Berlin. The Russians will overrun those areas in a matter of days or weeks. By all accounts from areas further east, Russian occupation is a bloodbath. Both the Bear and the Prussian volunteered to train and lead home guard units, the week after you left. Their subordinates can handle their duties going forward, easily. Fromm, himself, flight-tested Prototype Two while you were hospitalized."

"They're both soldiers. Soldiers can't choose their duty."

Winter continued, "They didn't choose. They asked. They were detached and assigned to me, so I had authority to approve their requests. And I did. The Bear and the Prussian have earned the privilege of defending their homes and families. As you say, they're both trained military men. God knows the old men, and boys, in the home guard units need all the help they can get to do their jobs."

"Well, it's unfortunate. It's almost like you don't want Valkyrie to do *her* job."

The camp gate guards swung open the gates. They opened not just the man-sized doors through which shift-change groups entered and exited single-file, but the three-meters tall, wide gates in which those smaller doors were set. Those gates normally opened only for trucks.

The camp's population flooded out, orderly, yet disorganized, in the way that spectators exited a great city's athletic stadium, or workers emerged from the exits of a city's subway network.

This flood, massive as it was, totaled no more than a small town's population.

Ilse imagined ten times that number, twenty, even thirty times. Bustling through the streets of London, or New York, or Moscow. All peering curiously skyward as a single, tiny silver wing floated high above them, harmless in a cloudless sky.

Then a flash. Then, for every one of them, nothing. For every one of them, the searing horror that had incinerated the innocents of Cologne, of Hamburg, of Dresden. And most importantly, of Berlin.

While Ilse had lain in her hospital bed, powerless to save them, her parents had been incinerated in *their* bed, by Allied bombs.

If the door was closing on National Socialism, she would assure that it closed with a bang that would shake the world.

"Ilse? Ilse!" Winter touched her elbow.

She blinked, then said, "As I was saying, Valkyrie should be readied to do her job. With or without the Bear and the Prussian. We need to execute Case Yellow, immediately."

"Case Yellow? Case Yellow is arming and fueling the Valkyrie for combat."

"Of course. Finally the plane is ready. Finally the bomb is ready. We may need to use them or lose them."

Winter shook his head. "Only *Reichsführer* Himmler, or the fuehrer himself, has authority to order Case Yellow."

She said, "Risk capture of Valkyrie, sitting inside the factory, as harmless as a hen on her nest? And the bomb as well? Absurd! Also, at the first sign of threat, Valkyrie should execute Case Green."

Winter shook his head again. "Dropping the weapon on an Allied target? That's beyond even Himmler's authority. You think the Russians are vengeful, *now*? Allied reprisals for such an attack would jeopardize the continued existence of the German state. Implementing Case Green not only exceeds my authority, it's beyond the bounds of rational human behavior."

"Then you formally acknowledge that you refuse to execute either Case?"

"Stop the barrack room lawyering, Ilse. It's pointless."

From the main road, Ilse finally heard an automobile's roar. A Mercedes' brakes squealed as it turned in, then rolled slowly down the runway road toward her, and toward Peter Winter.

Ilse sighed, relieved.

Winter frowned. "Now, who the hell is this? Another auditor? Is Speer still checking cabin assignments as the ship of state sinks?"

It struck her that today Winter displayed an open cynicism she hadn't seen in the past. It was as though he looked forward to National Socialism's defeat. Which, she had come to believe, he had all along.

Ilse raised her chin. "I disagree with your assessment about Case Yellow and Case Green. In fact, I believe *you* already have jeopardized the continued existence of the German state."

"What are you talking about?"

"Your pattern of calculated delay. Your management has been incompetent, at best. And deliberately treasonous at worst."

"That's ridiculous."

"I should have seen it earlier. But only while I laid in bed, with no distraction but pain, it became clear. Valkyrie could have struck her blow for Germany months ago. Perhaps years ago. But you dragged your feet, in pursuit of perfection. If not in a deliberate act of sabotage."

"Ilse, have you lost your mind?"

"Why in God's name build a bomb casing from stainless steel that will last a century? When the bomb is designed to be blown into atoms within weeks of its completion? Why waste effort making a waterproof case for the actuator and instruction manuals? When they will be used kilometers above sea level? It's ludicrous."

"Hardly. If one discourages innovation and attention to detail, one gets shoddy results. It's simply a question of management style."

"Perhaps. But how many months did 'management style' set the project back?"

"Style had nothing to do with the BMW engine bottleneck."

"But all you had to do was ask the *Reichsführer*, and BMW would have quietly delivered hand-built engines on a plate. *I* asked him, and they did."

"There was no point having the plane ready, then waiting months for the bomb that was its reason for being."

"Rubbish! My list goes on. I've assembled quite a dossier, Dr. Winter."

"You know how few grams of U-235 we produced. Even in the best of weeks. Do you quarrel with my physics, too?"

"I don't even know whether your Jew physics are real. But I do quarrel with your Jew physicists. And all the other criminal undesirables you coddle here. While our troops in the field, and now even our loyal civilians, freeze, and starve, and die, in rubble."

"'Coddle'? No. I keep my work force just healthy enough, and motivated enough, that I don't have to replace them every month, with untrained workers who make mistakes. *You're* the one who bets her life that the Valkyrie is constructed and maintained perfectly. You should be glad the Salzreich Project emphasizes perfection over haste."

"Taking risks is my job."

"Not *foolish* risks. Arrogating the decision to deploy the weapon is a foolish risk. It jeopardizes the very existence of the German nation."

Winter paused and breathed deeply. "Ilse, we both know this is Germany's dark hour. We've all contributed so much of ourselves to this project. And we're all under stress."

"Some of us respond to stress with growth and courage. Others cheat. And betray."

Winter glanced at the approaching car and frowned. "Ilse, come to my office. We'll discuss your concerns. If, after that, you're still dissatisfied with aspects of my performance, I promise we will jointly present your concerns to the *Reichsführer*."

"No need. I already have."

The Mercedes drew alongside them, then stopped.

A jackbooted SS major climbed from the passenger's seat, then marched toward them, carrying a manila envelope in his left hand. Kluge was a skeleton in black, with sunken cheeks and dead eyes.

When Ilse had met him at last night's planning meeting, she had thought he resembled the assassinated martyr, Reinhard Heydrich. And, indeed, Kluge had served under Heydrich in Poland, and in Hungary.

The Skeleton stopped in front of Ilse and Winter and snapped his right arm up. "Hail Hitler!"

Winter threw up a tepid palm. "Hail Hitler. I'm Peter Winter. Director of this facility. How may we assist you, Major?"

"Dr. Winter, Allied Forces are temporarily in close proximity to this facility. It may be necessary to assure this facility's defense and security. Or to evacuate its personnel and assets to a more secure location. Until the Allies have been repulsed."

"I understand. I frankly expected something like this sooner. As you see, evacuation would be cumbersome. And fortunately, to date, this facility's security has been perfect."

"I fear you may be misinformed. And not merely about your facility's security record."

Winter blinked, before he said, "Oh?"

"Effective immediately, this facility is under military jurisdiction. I am assuming primary control."

Winter stiffened. "By what authority?"

The major handed over his envelope to Winter.

As the scientist read, the soldier said, "You will note that these are signed by *Reichsführer* Himmler, himself. That copy is yours."

Winter flipped to the last page. "I recognize the signature. I have an even broader authorization signed by the *Reichsführer* in my office vault. We'll need to establish the limits of our respective authorities."

"We won't. At least you won't. Dr. Winter, paragraph twelve of the document you're holding specifically revokes your authority. It also appoints Miss Jaeger to replace you as senior civilian authority. Until the current threat from Allied forces is repelled."

"*Current* threat? *Repelled*? You're joking."

"SS officers are men of honor, Dr. Winter. We neither joke about serious matters nor lie about them. And we expect reciprocal candor from men of honor with whom we interact."

"What are you implying?"

"Perhaps you should direct that question to Miss Jaeger."

At that moment a half dozen canvas-topped troop trucks turned in off the main road, then rumbled toward the three of them. The trucks pulled up, stopped, and helmeted, armed SS troops spilled over the trucks' tailgates.

The major spun around, then stalked away, to oversee the arrival. His troops formed up in ranks, as their sergeants barked commands.

Meanwhile, the Jews continued their exodus into the mine.

Peter Winter, hands clenched into fists, and voice quavering, hissed, "Ilse, what have you done?"

"Set in motion the salvation of the German nation and race. More precisely, the *Reichsführer* has set it in motion. I am a mere instrument in his strong hands."

"What the *hell* are you talking about?"

"The *Reichsführer* met with the fuehrer on April 20, in Berlin. On the occasion of the fuehrer's birthday. The fuehrer has decided to remain in Berlin. And to die there, if necessary. His ultimate sacrifice will inspire the German people. They will rise up, avenge him, and hurl the Allies back. To the Rhine and to the Polish border."

"The first part of that I don't doubt. The second part is fantasy."

"Possibly. Therefore, the *Reichsführer* has assumed effective leadership, due to the fuehrer's impaired ability to communicate with Germany's armies, and with the German people."

"Goering may disagree. To say nothing of Hitler, himself."

Ilse sneered. "Goering? I've met Goering. He's a drug-addled shell of his former self. The *Reichsführer* has opened negotiations, through Sweden, to make peace with the Western Allies. So that Germany may turn its efforts against Russia, the common enemy."

Winter's eyes widened. "Churchill? Accept us as friends? Because we're the enemy of his future enemy? Is Himmler—are you—that divorced from reality? Churchill would sooner sleep with the devil."

"Then how do you explain that at this moment the *Reichsführer* is at the Swedish consulate in Lübeck. Negotiating, as provisional leader of Germany, with Count Bernadotte, the head of the Swedish Red Cross."

"Negotiating? Eisenhower has Germany in his grasp. Except for the part of Germany that Stalin has under his boot. Himmler has no negotiating leverage."

Ilse smiled. "Really? At the appropriate moment, the *Reichsführer* will reveal Valkyrie and the bomb, and use them as a carrot. Or as a stick, as he feels will be most effective."

"Carrot?"

"The obliteration of Moscow. Or the stick of the obliteration of London."

Winter snorted. "Bernadotte will throw him out on his ear, before he says a word about carrots and sticks." Winter stood rigid, his jaw slack. "But you're serious."

Kluge the Skeleton returned.

Winter said to him, "I can't allow the deployment of this weapon. Neither can you, Major."

Kluge said, "What can't be allowed is that you fall into Allied hands, Dr. Winter. You know too much." He twitched his head, and four SS troops with submachine guns at the ready stepped around Winter. "These gentlemen will act as bodyguards. To safeguard you inside the facility."

"You're arresting me?"

"Nothing of the sort. The *Reichsführer* is mindful of your service. And of your heritage. He has insisted that these gentlemen assure your comfort, and grant reasonable requests. But your assistance in an official capacity is no longer required."

As Winter was marched away, the Skeleton said to Ilse, "The Americans remain days away, so we have time to establish liaison. With the personnel who will actually do the work if you have to fly the thing."

Ilse shook her head. "No, we don't have time. Since we spoke last night, I've become more concerned that the Allies may bomb this facility at any time. Rather than wait for their ground troops to overrun it."

"Then what do you propose?"

"The leaders of the units that prepare and maintain the aircraft and the munition are new. They should give you no trouble. First, you'll need to have them move the aircraft into the open. Then fuel it. Then install the munition in the bomb bay. You get started on that. I'll begin pulling together the necessary materials to get the plane to whatever target the *Reichsführer* directs."

Ilse walked into the secretarial bay outside Winter's office. The long benches were divided into work stations for fifty typists, but only fifteen stations were occupied. Some vacancies resulted from the end of construction activity.

If word of their boss's firing had circulated already, they gave no sign.

Winter had probably also released some of the farm girls, to return home. There, they could help their parents run up white flags, and collaborate, at the first sign of an American.

Ilse crossed the big room, to the vault set in its opposite wall.

From her pocket she plucked the paper on which the vault's combination had been typed. Only Winter, Becker the Prussian artilleryman, Fromm the Bear, and herself had the combination. Ilse rotated the dial, first left then right, then tugged the handle. The door didn't budge.

She rotated the dial again, more carefully lining up each number.

Again nothing happened.

Gretel, Winter's lead secretary, had just come on shift. She left her typewriter, walked over and smiled. "Miss Jaeger! You're back again, and looking well. How may I help you?"

"I can't get this vault open."

"Of course not, Miss. Dr. Winter had the combination changed after you left. Only he has it, now. I'm sure if you ask him, he can help."

"Of course. In the meantime, find Major Kluge. Bring him with you to Dr. Winter's office. By the way, it's now my office."

Forty-two

ILSE WATCHED AS GRETEL, WINTER'S SECRETARIAL SUPERVISOR, sat in a straight-backed chair set in the empty floor space between Winter's desk and his conference table.

Kluge had pulled the chair away from the table. In this way, the table did not offer the interview subject a protective barrier between the subject and the questioner. The girl was made to feel more vulnerable.

But Kluge scarcely needed additional leverage to intimidate this subject.

He paced in front of the girl, hands clasped behind his back.

The girl's hands, clasped in her lap, trembled, and she stared at the floor. Ilse hardly blamed her. Kluge scared even Ilse, herself.

He said, "Was anyone else given the new combination?"

"Dr. Winter always arrives earlier than the rest of us. I'm sure he's around the facility somewhere. Really, the simplest thing would just be to ask him to open the vault."

"If necessary we certainly will. But now I am asking you."

"I can't think of anyone, Major."

Kluge said to the girl, "Miss, be in no doubt of the seriousness of your position. Think harder. Does *anyone* other than Dr. Winter know the new combination?"

Staring down into her hands, she whispered, "Dr. Winter's handwriting isn't the best. So he dictated it to me, and I typed it onto a slip of paper for him. I try not to retain in my memory sensitive material I type for him. But perhaps I could recall it."

Kluge smiled. "How fortunate for both of us." He snatched

a pencil and paper from Winter's desk and handed them to the girl. "Shall we test your powers of recall?"

Ilse flicked on the open vault's electric light, then peered inside. Stacked banknote packets filled the petty cash shelves. Boxed personnel records and classified documents, and valuable and easily pilfered supplies, occupied most of the space.

On the floor stood leftover spools of silver wire, which had been used to wrap the uranium concentration machines' electromagnets. The wire had been spun from flatware, candlesticks, jewelry, and coins, recovered for the state from the sideboards, dressing tables, and vaults of Jews. Lead flasks, which had stored the enriched uranium now gathered into the bomb, sat empty alongside the spools.

From a shoulder-high shelf, Ilse snatched the only item that concerned her, the flat stainless-steel map case that contained the actuator plug. She closed the vault behind her, then stalked to the office that Fromm had occupied, where maps and navigation charts remained filed.

She selected the necessary charts for London, and for Moscow. Then she thought about the raid on Berlin that had murdered her parents. They had been incinerated in their bed, shortly after sunrise. The British and Americans divided their joint butchery, the British by night, the Americans by day. She plucked out charts for the American East Coast, also.

She opened the flat case, flipped through the preflight checklists, and bomb-arming diagrams and procedures already inside. Then she folded the charts, preparatory to tucking them into the case.

She wrinkled her brow. Something looked amiss.

The actuator. It wasn't in its clip. Had she just removed it without thinking? She lifted the map stack, then glanced underneath. Nothing.

Frowning, she hurried back to the vault, then searched it, top to bottom, finally on hands and knees.

At last she stood, slammed the vault door, and swore.

Then she dragged Gretel the supervisor away from her typewriter, and again sought Major Kluge.

In the conference room again, Kluge asked Gretel the typing supervisor, "Has there ever been anyone who had access to the vault, when it was unattended? Even if *you* don't think they had the combination?"

The girl's voice quavered. "I remember sometimes Mr. Wolf used to work all night. And he worked with the powder in the lead bottles, when Captain Becker took the bottles to him. But I don't know that Mr. Wolf ever had the combination."

Kluge furrowed his brow, the skin wrinkling like parchment stretched over bone, as he looked a question at Ilse.

Ilse said to the SS man, "Wolf's a metallurgist. Proficient with metalworking tools. As would a safecracker be. And one of Winter's favorite Jews."

Kluge called in one of his sergeants. "Find the Jew called Wolf. Have him brought to the camp's disciplinary facility."

The sergeant said, "Sir, I've just returned from the camp. The place doesn't even *have* a disciplinary facility. Where you would expect one to be, they do have a shed. But they use it as a school for the little kikes. I don't know what the hell kind of resort they were running, out there."

"Then bring this bigger kike *here*. After that, find out if he has children. And bring one of them, too."

After Kluge had dismissed the whimpering secretary, he asked Ilse, "What is this missing object? And why is it so important?"

"This bomb should produce maximum damage if detonated three hundred meters above ground level at the target. A barometric altimeter switch mounted in the bomb's tail trips at the altitude the bombardier sets. When the switch closes, an electric circuit through a battery is completed. That detonates a conventional explosive charge, also in the bomb's tail. That detonation, in turn, drives a projectile forward, into a target."

"There is a cannon inside the bomb?"

"Essentially, yes. The projectile's impact on the target will unleash an explosion of a ferocity never before seen on Earth."

"And this missing part?"

"It completes the electrical circuit that fires the cannon. To prevent the conventional explosive's detonation, either by inadvertent tripping of the switch, or by the aircraft crashing during takeoff, or landing, a wooden plug is inserted between the switch and the detonator. Once the plane is airborne, the bombardier goes back to the bomb bay, sets the detonation altitude, then replaces the nonconductive wooden plug with the actuator. Electric current can then flow, and the bomb is live. The actuator is fitted like a key, so the bomb can't be made live by inserting a screwdriver, or a similar bit of metal."

"How many of these actuators are there?"

"Only one. There's only one bomb to activate. I assure you, one bomb is plenty. But if we don't find the actuator before we're tasked to drop the bomb, or before bombs drop on us, the bomb is useless. And without the bomb, the plane is equally useless. We need to question Winter. Immediately and vigorously."

Kluge shook his head. "Your evident disdain for Dr. Winter isn't shared by *Reichsführer* Himmler. Winter is the legacy of a martyr. My instructions are to detain him respectfully, in the absence of evidence of deliberate malfeasance. Besides, first presuming a Jew guilty is simple common sense."

Hyman Wolf, the frizzy-haired jeweler, had replaced Gretel, Winter's secretarial supervisor, in Kluge's straight-backed chair. But Wolf's hands were bound behind his back.

The man's breath came in gasps, even though Kluge hadn't laid a finger on him.

The Jew sobbed, "I tell you again! I don't *know* how to get into the vault. I've never even *seen* the inside of the vault. I swear on my eldest son's life."

Kluge stepped to the door and called out.

A moment later the SS sergeant, whom Kluge had tasked to fetch Wolf, and another SS man, wrestled in a boy perhaps twelve years of age. His dark hair was curly, his dark eyes and complexion were the essence of the Jew, and his eyes were open wide.

Kluge drew his pistol, then fired it into the ceiling.

Wolf and the boy screamed, and Wolf rocked so far that the chair tipped, and he fell back and struck his head.

Kluge motioned to the sergeant, who stepped across the room and righted Wolf in his chair.

Kluge said, "Where is that actuator?"

"I don't *know*! If I knew I would tell you! I'll tell you anything. I swear I will. Just don't hurt my son."

Kluge said, "All you have to do is tell me. I don't have time to discuss the matter further."

The sergeant held the boy's left arm, while the other SS man held his right.

Kluge stepped behind the boy, and pressed the pistol's muzzle against the base of the boy's skull, while he stared at Wolf. "Where. Is. That. Actuator?"

Wolf thrashed in his chair as he shook his head back and forth. "I don't—"

Blam!

In the confined office space the shot reverberated like thunder. But, loud as it was, Wolf's scream pierced Ilse's ears more painfully.

The boy's head hung, lopsided and bloody, as his body slumped. Blood and bits of tissue had spattered the wall behind Wolf, and covered his face and clothing.

Eyes shut tight, the Jew wailed, over and over, "Why? Why? I don't *know.*"

Ilse stumbled backward, her hand to her forehead and mouth agape.

She turned away, bent, and vomited into the waste paper basket in the room's corner.

She wiped spittle from her lips with her fingers, then turned back around.

Kluge stepped over the boy's body, which the SS men had allowed to fall to the floor.

When Kluge came within arm's length of Wolf, he swung his still-smoking pistol up again, and shot Wolf through the forehead.

The impact rocked Wolf back, and Kluge pushed the chair over backward with a booted foot.

Ilse felt as though her eyes would pop from her head as she stared.

She said to Kluge, "Why?"

"He didn't know."

"But, then, *why?*"

"I put him out of his misery."

Ilse steadied herself against Winter's desk. "My God. What have you done?"

Kluge holstered his pistol, then spread his palms. "You said yourself we don't have time. The boy was only a *Jew*, for God's sake. Wolf was not only a Jew, he was a Jew who didn't know anything."

Ilse closed her eyes, to get the SS major out of her sight, at least until her rage passed.

She said, "He may not have known where the actuator was. But he knew how to make a *replacement* actuator. You *idiot!*"

The SS sergeant looked down at the two bodies, so he could pretend he hadn't heard her call his major an idiot.

The sergeant said, "Well, the way they keep score around here, no one will notice two more missing Jews."

Ilse frowned. "What do you mean?"

Kluge said, "He means that we were delayed arriving here this morning because some of the local police flagged us down en route. They reported what *they* considered a problem. It seems that they've recently detained a disproportionate number of non-residents who lacked appropriate documentation."

Ilse said, "I've lived in this place since 1942. I can tell you the local police are incompetent. And idiots if they don't realize that perfectly loyal German civilians, who flee the distant thunder of American artillery, will forget to pack their identity documents."

"Of course. But some of these undocumented wanderers volunteered that they were Jews, and other undesirables, in the process of custody transfer, from other camps to this facility. At the place where they were transferred from the long-haul trucks, they were left unattended, until they simply walked away."

Ilse snorted. "If the locals procure 'voluntary' admissions like you do, somebody among these Jews probably confessed to the Reichstag Fire."

Kluge's lips curled in a thin smile as he said, "Yes. It requires patience, and practice, to separate confessed truth from expedient lies. The difference is found in the details. The *details* reported in some of these cases are compelling. After the first few were picked up, your local 'incompetents' had the genuinely bright idea to let the next few go, then follow them."

"And?"

"Several made their way to an estate, over in the next valley. The housekeeper there was observed providing them food, and clothing. And in one instance permitting them to shelter from rain in the property's stables."

"How is that detail compelling? Is it a violation of some sort? Certainly. But these are difficult times, and true Germans are charitable by nature."

"The estate turned out to be the house occupied by Dr. Winter."

Ilse paused, then frowned. "Whatever Winter's other short-comings, I've been around here long enough to say he is the hardest worker I've ever known. He spends so little time away from this facility that he very well might be unaware of what his housekeeper does when he's gone."

"Perhaps I should have the good doctor's minders bring him here, right now. We'll determine soon enough how aware he is of his housekeeper's activity."

Ilse said, "If Winter and his housekeeper *are* running a halfway house for escaped Jews, queers, and gypsies, why do you think he will confess it to you?"

"They *always* confess it to me. Sometimes even when there's nothing to confess." Kluge turned to his sergeant. "After you clean up this mess, round up a dozen more Jew children before you bring Winter in here."

Ilse narrowed her eyes. "Wait. Did the local police bumpkins say anything else? About this housekeeper?"

The SS sergeant said, "That she was a woman. Known in the area to be a German. But born and raised in Alsace, so with French papers. And quite a knockout."

"Oh really? Well. Those *are* compelling details." She turned to Kluge. "You may not need to round up any children, after all."

Forty-three

AS SOON AS RACHEL HEARD THE TWO MUFFLED SHOTS, SHE DUCK-waddled, bent beneath the electric generator cellar's low rock ceiling, as fast as she could. She moved away from the darkness, toward the light at the stairwell that led back up into the house.

She screamed, "Father? Father! What was that noise?"

Sheldon Bergman shouted down the cellar stairs, "People were trampling my garden!"

She shouted back. "*Relax*! Those people are *fine*! I'm on my way."

Her hands stunk of gasoline, and were wet with it, after she had refilled the generator's tank. Her fingers slipped, as she grasped the creaking stairs' bannister.

She dragged herself back up to the big house's ground floor, without enthusiasm.

The laundry remained to be done. The vegetable garden remained to be tilled. Despite her father's ownership claim to the garden, the tilling job would fall to her. So would the job of emptying his chamber pot, and of splitting fire wood.

Managing this house alone hadn't become less exhausting since she had hired herself to do the job in 1935, to dodge the Nurembergs.

But now it was nearly May 1945. After ten years, a new beginning was in sight, for her and for Peter. And the end was in sight to the Nazis, and to their disastrous war.

She reached the light at the stairs' top. There, Sheldon Bergman, mustachioed, regal, and bewildered, waited. He stood in the pantry closet, from which the stairs led down, amid the shelves now sparsely stocked with canned goods, flour, and generator-fuel tins. Her father held one of his shotguns, and smoke trickled from both its barrels.

She snatched the weapon from him. "What did you *do*?"

"Just scared them off."

Rachel clutched her forehead with her trembling free hand. "I *told* you we would be getting unannounced visitors. For handouts and such."

"No you didn't."

"Not today, no."

She clenched her teeth, as she added "change gun cabinet lock" to her mental chore list.

She said, "We had this conversation *yesterday*. Again. And at least *five* times before that. When they show up, let me handle it. Then you forget they were ever here."

That last part, at least, would be no problem.

At times her father was active, lucid, aware of the current world with all its problems, and of his place in it.

But a change as simple as stepping from one room into another could turn a mental page in his mind. Then he would revert to a prior reality, or withdraw into a passive shell.

He pulled her close, patted her back, and kissed her forehead. "What's wrong, little one? Did school go badly today?"

On the days when her father was active and lucid, being with him was a joy. On other days it was like raising a small child, but without the endgame parental option of sending him to his room.

Therefore, on days like today, the prospect of motherhood loomed more than it beckoned.

She drew away from her father, felt dizzy, and leaned a shoulder on the pantry wall.

She was late, and in a way that she had never been late before. She was certain she knew why. She didn't know whether the exhaustion and dizziness were related, but she dreaded the prospect of coming months of morning sickness.

Peter was an only child, so he thought two children would be plenty. She thought at least three. Jacob's loss left her without a sibling, and she assumed the empty feeling of being alone would never fade. It was a possible pain she wouldn't inflict on her children.

"They're still out there." Her father had wandered out of the pantry, and now spoke to her from the foyer. He stood beside the front doors, peeking out around the drape, which covered the narrow window beside them.

Rachel said, "Get away from the window. Let me handle it."

"Now they have rifles. Mausers, I believe."

"Rifles?" Rachel pushed her father aside, then peeked out, too. The sickness in her gut grew.

Beyond the vegetable garden that she had made in the forecourt, out on the road, a gray army staff car, and two canvas-topped troop trucks, were parked, nose-to-tail.

Soldiers sheltered behind the vehicles, their helmeted heads peeking above the vehicles' hoods. Their rifles were trained on the house.

In the forest alongside the vehicles, additional troops peeked around trees. Still others lay prone beneath the trucks, sighting down the barrels of even more rifles.

A human skeleton of a man, dressed in SS officer's black, strutted from behind the staff car, followed by a young blonde, wearing a gray jacket and trousers.

The pair stood exposed, ten yards closer to the house than the cowering troops.

Rachel realized that the pair's exposure was less daring than it first appeared. They remained well beyond shotgun range. Her father's warning shots had been fired from his shotgun.

She realized that her father had turned what had probably begun as an unwelcome interrogation visit into an armed standoff.

The thin officer in black raised a rowing coxswain's small megaphone to his lips, then shouted, "You in there! I am SS Major Rutger Kluge, Commanding Temporary Operational Group Salzreich. Your building is surrounded. Throw your weapons out. Onto the ground, where they can be seen. Then come through the front doors with your hands raised."

He paused, then said, "If you do that, you have my word as an officer of the SS that you will not be harmed. You have three minutes!"

Rachel sniffed the air, then turned, frowning.

The pantry door that led to the generator cellar stood open. Her father knelt on the foyer's Persian carpet, soaking it with gasoline, which he poured from a twenty-liter tin that he took from the pantry.

She ran to him and snatched the tin away. "What are you *doing*?"

"The bastards took my bank. They took my son. They won't take my house and my daughter."

She set down the tin, then raised her palms. "Stop! Stay put! I'll talk us out of this."

Outside, someone shouted orders, and Rachel heard footsteps on the road.

Rachel crept to the front doors, unlatched them, then stood to the side.

She stretched out her hand, pushed the left door open a handspan, then shouted through the opening. "There is no one here but me. And an old man whom I care for. I am a nurse. I was born a loyal German, in Alsace. I am a French citizen with fully appropriate work authorizations. The old man suffers from dementia. He mistakenly discharged a fowling piece. Please! His error was inadvertent, and harmless. We will pay for any damage."

The SS major shouted back, "Then you have nothing to fear. Come out. You now have two minutes."

Rachel hadn't expected a much different response. It was the way the Nazis had operated for years when they stumbled onto Germans assisting Jews.

She wondered whether, when Jacob was taken, it had been like this.

She should have done as Peter told her. It had been risky enough turning detainees loose, without lending them a helping hand.

In that instant, she realized that the situation was infinitely worse. The SS major had announced himself as commanding "Temporary Operational Group *Salzreich*." The tall, athletic blonde woman! She had to be the fanatic, suspicious test pilot Peter had worried about, since the day she had arrived at the Salzreich.

Rachel tugged the front door shut. As she turned away, the crisis's enormity nauseated her, and she bent, clutching her belly.

The Nazis had discovered the game that she and Peter had played, although they had played it so perfectly for nearly three years. Peter was already in custody, if not dead.

She looked up, and her father was gone. So was the gasoline tin. It, and another like it, lay on their sides on the stairway landing, halfway to the upper floor. From the stairs gasoline dripped and drizzled down onto the foyer floor.

She raced up the stairs, two at a time. Her shoes splashed gasoline from the stairs' soaked carpet. She kicked the tins aside, and realized they were empty. Then she followed a trail, of even more gasoline, to her father's study.

The study's two windows looked out across the forecourt to the road, and their drapes were open.

Through the left-hand window, she saw the trucks and troops, the blonde pilot, and the SS major with his megaphone.

The right-hand window's sash had been raised, leaving a handspan-wide opening between sash and window sill.

But even with the ventilation that the opening provided, gasoline fumes so saturated the air now that they dizzied her.

Beneath the window's sill, hidden from those on the road, her father crouched with his back toward her. Alongside him stood a third gasoline tin. As he crouched, he extended the stiff leg that he had injured, which had kept him out of Germany's last war.

The SS major's shout echoed, from beyond the open window.

"You have thirty seconds remaining. As a duly-empowered representative of the fuehrer Adolf Hitler, and of the German people whom he personifies, I order—"

In a blink, Sheldon Bergman sprang to a kneeling position, swung up one of the deer rifles from the gun cabinet that stood open on the study's far wall, aimed through the window opening, then fired.

The range was perhaps seventy meters, and her father routinely hit deer from farther.

The SS major's head snapped back. Something exploded from the back of the major's head, and his black cap fluttered into the air, lopsided, like a wounded crow.

Even before the man's body fell, Rachel dropped to her knees, scrambled to her father, and dragged him away from the windows.

He said, "Finally, I've defeated an enemy of Germany."

"You shot a German Army officer!"

"Those black-suited SS monkeys will never represent Germany. Any more than that lunatic Hitler will personify us."

She muttered, "God!"

Her father had picked the worst possible time to experience a lucid episode.

Suddenly, fifty rifles' roar answered her father's single shot.

Rachel crouched, and covered her ears.

The study's windows disintegrated in a storm of shattered glass. The drapes flapped like flags in a gale. Bullets chewed the books on the study's shelves into a paper blizzard.

Then stillness filled the void.

Her father said, "Bastards!"

An object twirled through the jagged hole that had been the study's left-hand window. The object resembled a tin can, attached at the end of a wooden stick. It landed on the carpet and spun there, amid the broken glass, for what seemed like seconds.

Rachel's father leapt away from her, then curled his body around the grenade, as though he were returning to the womb.

His body so thoroughly muffled the explosion that, for an instant, she thought the grenade had malfunctioned.

Whether it had malfunctioned or not, it set the study's gasoline-soaked carpet ablaze. The flames ignited the book pages that littered the floor, spread in seconds to the drapes, then reached the gasoline tin by the window.

The tin exploded with a chuff, and the explosion's force blew across her skin like a searing wind.

Deafened by the rifle fusillade, she dragged her father toward the study's door.

As she reached the door, fumes and flammables in the stair-well flashed into a fireball. The heat forced her into the study, and she slammed its door closed.

She flattened herself on the floor, so she could breathe, beneath the expanding smoke that filled the room.

Her father lay alongside her, still, and she knew instinctively, dead. Peter was dead, or soon would be. The war would now engulf and consume those thousands at the Salzreich who Peter, and she, had risked and lost everything to save.

She couldn't cross the flames to reach the study's windows. And if, somehow, she did escape through a window, and survived the fall, the SS who surrounded the house would finish her more painfully than if she burned alive.

She felt behind her for the closed door, then snatched her hand back. The heat she felt confirmed that an impassable inferno lay beyond.

The ammunition in the gun cabinet began popping, and steel and wood fragments whizzed around her. The pops quickened, into staccato thunder, and the fragments stung, cut, and burned her.

Now, the floor beneath her grew so hot that it burned her exposed skin. The air itself grew so hot that breathing felt like swallowing molten lead.

There were no escape options. She realized that she had finally gotten herself into something that she couldn't get out of.

Two minutes later, the fire-weakened floor on which she lay creaked, then trembled beneath her.

An instant later the floor collapsed.

Rachel Bergman Winter, along with her father's body, and with his grandchild in her, who she now realized would never be born, plunged down toward hell.

Forty-four

ILSE JAEGER SAT IN THE STAFF CAR'S REAR SEAT AS IT LED ONE of the two troop trucks back along the road that wound down one valley, then up another, and would return her to the Salzreich Mine. Kluge's body was in the truck, along with half of the SS detachment.

She again examined her face in her compact's mirror. The speckles of Kluge's blood she had wiped away with a handkerchief. But her blouse and suit were unsalvageable. She needed a shower, and a change, and soon. But the shower wouldn't wash away what she had seen.

The detachment's other troops, and one of the trucks, remained at Winter's house, and would remain there until the fire burned itself out.

While they waited, they would search the surrounding forests for escapees, like the ones which had led the local police to the house in the first place.

The SS captain who was next-senior to Kluge rode in the car's front seat.

She leaned forward and said, "Captain, what are you going to do after the fire burns out? About recovering the bodies."

"I'd say that's a waste of time, miss. That fire was accelerated. I've seen enough of these to estimate there won't be enough recognizable remains to hang."

"Hang?"

"Alongside the area's main roads. We get better results with random executions than with hung corpses. But how we teach the lesson to the locals is really up to you."

"Me?"

With Kluge dead, and his troops entirely new to the Salzreich situation, Ilse was now effectively, but not officially, in charge of the SS detachment.

Heinrich had told her, in the intimate moments after they had made love, how it was possible to take human lives, yet retain one's decency. She had thought at the time that it was just another example of the quiet strength that had drawn her to him in the first place. But her experiences over the last few hours enlightened her about the truth in what he had said.

Heinrich had also explained to her how he counseled his personnel to avoid being identified with "civil pacification." She could scrub Kluge's blood off her face, but she couldn't afford to have too many others' blood overtly on her hands.

She said to the SS captain, "We need your troops more back at the facility. Captain, the 'locals' here are the very German citizens whom you are sworn to defend, not Poles, or Hungarians. Let the traitors' corpses rot and stink among the ashes until rats gnaw their bones. The word will get around."

"As you wish, Miss Jaeger." He sounded disappointed.

The staff car turned up the valley toward the Salzreich, and she watched the pines roll by.

She was desperate to know how Heinrich's negotiations with the Swedish Red Cross go-between, Bernadotte, were going in Lübeck. Heinrich had explained to her the nuances of carrot and stick.

There would be initial maneuvering. The neutral Swede cared only about the release of Scandinavian detainees. But to disguise his selfishness, Bernadotte would seek the release of others.

At this stage of the war, Heinrich didn't care a fig about a few thousand Jews, one way or the other. He would allow himself to be persuaded. He had already released busloads of detainees, to show good faith, during earlier meetings. He would dangle that carrot again. That would entice Bernadotte to secure a direct line of communication between Heinrich and Eisenhower.

America, as a nation, was beyond salvage, polluted by Jew and Negro blood. But Eisenhower's German Protestant blood remained undiluted. He was undoubtedly a man who could be reasoned with. He was also a professional soldier, and so could be tempted by the promise of personal glory.

The carrot of immediate "victory" for Eisenhower's armies would tempt him. The offer of Valkyrie's destruction of Moscow, and so victory over America's next enemy, would be irresistible.

Heinrich's bold, lucid vision, and the control it gave him over his adversaries, awed Ilse.

However, without the missing actuator plug, that simple bit of silver coated metal, Heinrich's vision could not be realized. And she was more certain than ever that Winter had stolen it.

Ilse had intended to use the housekeeper, Winter's obvious concubine, as the carrot and stick that would motivate him. But that plan had literally burned up before her eyes.

An hour after she had arrived back at the facility, then showered in the staff women's locker room, and changed, Ilse paced Winter's recently cleaned office with her arms crossed over her breasts.

The room reeked of disinfectant. But it was the imagined stench of blood, and death, that caused her to breathe through her mouth.

She turned when she heard a knock at the door.

She had expected Winter, in the custody of his so-called bodyguards. But instead, it was the SS sergeant who had held the boy, while Kluge had blown the child's brains out.

Now the sergeant held a double armload of loose objects.

"What do you want, Sergeant?"

"These are Major Kluge's personal effects, miss. I don't know where to put them."

"What are they?"

The sergeant looked down at his double armful. "Identity papers, billfold, cigarette case and lighter. Wedding ring, wristwatch. And his pistol belt. The pistol's not technically personal, but his SS dagger on the belt was presented by *Reichsführer* Himmler himself. Every SS man's dagger is intensely personal."

Ilse waved her hand. "If you must leave them somewhere, place them on the desk, there, for now."

As the sergeant was leaving, she asked, "Did you serve with the major long?"

"Since Poland in 1939. He was a brave and honorable soldier and man. I will miss him."

"What combat experiences did you share with him, during those six years?"

"Combat? None, miss."

"Then what did you do together?"

"Killed Jews, gypsies, and queers."

Ilse sat at the conference table that had been Winter's, and now was hers. To her right sat the SS captain who had succeeded Major Kluge.

Across the table from them sat the SS corporal who, along with three privates, had escorted Winter into the mine earlier.

The corporal continued, "Yes, miss. The doctor did stop at the vault in the secretarial bay. He unlocked it, then removed several dozen personnel files. He needed them so he could work on them in the vacant office we were escorting him to."

Ilse asked, "Nothing else? Other than files?"

"Not that any of us noticed." The smooth-cheeked corporal shifted in the chair, then said, "To be honest, the bay was deserted when we got there, but a few of the early shift secretaries arrived while he was gathering the files. So some of us may have been distracted. Just for a moment."

Ilse nodded again. "And after that?"

"He was never out of sight of any of us. He was in the office working, except when he went to the washroom. I personally watched him piss twice. All he left behind in there was urine, miss. I swear on my dagger."

Winter arrived in his old office with one of the three privates assigned to "protect" him, leading, and the other two trailing.

Their smooth-cheeked corporal, who had searched the office where Winter had been held, as well as the washroom where Winter had urinated, and places in between, entered behind them all. He caught Ilse's eye, and shook his head.

Either the actuator plug was on Winter's person, or the SS guards were incompetent, or Winter was wholly innocent. She doubted the last two possibilities.

Winter sniffed the disinfectant-laden air, glanced at Kluge's personal effects piled on Winter's desk, then frowned.

He said, "These gentlemen, and the rest of Major Kluge's SS cadre seem disturbed. Are the Americans closer than I think?"

The SS captain said, "Please sit, Dr. Winter."

Ilse stared at Peter across the desk. There was no flicker of emotion or doubt. He displayed precisely as much annoyance as someone should, whose workday had been needlessly interrupted.

She said, "The weapon's actuator plug is missing from its case. Do you have any idea where it may be?"

Peter wrinkled his forehead. "Are you *sure*?"

The SS captain said, "Then your answer is no, you don't have any idea?"

"Obviously."

The captain said, "To answer your earlier question, Major Kluge's troops are upset because he was killed today."

"What? How?"

"Shot from ambush without warning by a German traitor. Just like his mentor, Senior Group Leader Heydrich, was assassinated in Prague."

"Are you sure it was a *German*? I would never put it past the Americans to infiltrate assassins behind our lines."

"Well, fortunately, the assassin didn't survive the attack. Unfortunately, we were unable to examine the body, or the body of an accomplice. They set the house, from which the shot came, on fire. Then perished when it burned to the ground."

Finally Winter paled, almost imperceptibly. Still, all he said was, "That is unfortunate."

Ilse said, "Particularly unfortunate. Because the house was *yours*."

Winter sat rigid as the color drained from his face.

Ilse admired his calm audacity. The Jews called it chutzpah.

She said, "What made you do it, Peter? You were one of the *Reichsführer*'s absolute favorites."

He stared, neither flinching nor blinking.

The SS captain motioned to two of the SS privates. "See if he's got it on him."

One private stepped back a pace, drew his pistol, motioned with it for Peter to stand, then trained it on Winter's head, while two others knelt, and searched him, from his shoes, up.

The actuator was tucked into his right sock.

Ilse smiled. "Aren't you even going to say you have no idea how it got there?"

The private who found the actuator plug laid it in her hand. She realized that through all the training, it was the first time she had touched it.

Preparing the bomb during flight was the bombardier's job. The Valkyrie was designed for a crew of three, but it could be flown by one.

Of course, no operational crew had been assigned or trained. That failing further proved Winter's perfidy.

The actuator itself was exquisitely formed, a sinuous, machined-steel helix. Its conductive contact surfaces were cast silver, which imparted to the object a divine heaviness.

It was, in fact, a work of art. It suddenly struck her that it was now a more precious work of art, because Wolf, the artist who created it, was dead. Shot, while sitting in the chair in which Peter Winter now sat.

Ilse walked to the desk, and laid the actuator alongside Kluge's belongings. The legacies of two men who had been in life as opposite as humans could be.

She crossed her arms as she leaned back against the desk, and stared at Winter, the traitor.

He was a beautiful man.

From the first moment she had seen him, it puzzled and displeased her that, unlike most men, he seemed immune to her. Now she understood. The "housekeeper" must have been extraordinary.

Ilse said to Winter, "Who was she, Peter? An Allied spy? A femme fatale, dropped in by parachute? To play you like a violin?"

Winter blinked, then looked up at her. "What?"

Ilse smiled. "No? A Jewess in disguise, then? Who bewitched you, and drew you into her orbit?"

Ilse watched Winter's eyes. There was no light in them, no spark of hatred at her insults.

The SS captain stepped alongside Ilse, and said, "Miss, I recommend he be shot immediately, and in front of the workers. They outnumber us, and alive he might inspire resistance."

Ilse shook her head. "No."

The captain said, "But miss, he's a traitor. He's earned a bullet."

Ilse said, "I don't mean that he should live. I mean that he's harmless. He truly loved the woman. The only reason one carries on, after a great love is taken away, is revenge against the takers. Look into his eyes. Dr. Winter, here, has too little thirst for revenge to inspire a rebellion."

Twenty minutes later, the laborers were herded into the vast, but now idle, gallery called "The Sausage Factory." In it the uranium that Wolf the dead jeweler had formed into the bomb's core had been refined.

While Ilse and the SS captain stood by and watched, a four-person detachment marched Winter, hands bound in front of him at the wrists, up onto the catwalk suspended above one of the mammoth machines he had invented.

His white shirt open at the neck, Winter stood quietly, chin high, and eyes straight ahead, as two soldiers unbound his hands, then each held him by one arm, and extended them.

The sergeant in charge peered out across the assembled laborers and pointed at Winter. "This man is a traitor. He is a coward, and an enemy of our beloved fuehrer. Let his fate guide your conduct in the future."

The fourth SS man, who stood behind Winter, drew his pistol, then pressed its muzzle against the back of Winter's head.

Ilse squeezed her eyes shut.

The shot's report reverberated through the vast space. When Ilse opened her eyes, the SS men were lifting Winter's lifeless body. They threw it over the catwalk, and it thudded onto the cavern floor.

A vast wail erupted from the crowd, then devolved into weeping.

The SS sergeant climbed down from the catwalk, marched to his captain, saluted, and said, "I admit, he died with more dignity than most of them do. But these Jews are wailing like he was their savior, not their jailer."

The captain shrugged. "I wouldn't worry about it. They reacted the same way the last time the King of the Jews was killed, and two thousand years later look where it's got them."

The following morning, April 25, Ilse sat reading correspondence that would normally have been routed to Fromm the Bear, or Becker the Prussian, or through Winter, himself. One priority message, addressed to Winter, reported that both Fromm and Becker, and their families, had perished resisting Russian troops.

Ilse didn't doubt that they were dead, but wondered whether

they had really gone down fighting. Hanna Reitsch, whose family had already fled Silesia ahead of the advancing Russians, had feared that her father would kill her mother and sister, then himself, rather than risk their rape, torture, and murder. Already, civilian victims of Russian troops' atrocities numbered in the hundreds of thousands, and suicides to escape the atrocities numbered in the tens of thousands.

She crumpled the report and hurled it across the room, then closed her eyes, and prayed aloud. "Dear Heinrich, assign me a target soon." She paused, then whispered, "And let it be Moscow."

A heavyset radio telephone operator, his headphones pushed up above his ears, with their cord dangling, entered after knocking.

He said, "You sent for me, miss?"

Ilse said, "Have you located *Reichsführer* Himmler, yet?"

"No, miss. We did inquire with the Swedish Consulate in Lübeck, as you instructed. No one would admit it outright, but it does appear that the *Reichsführer was* there on the twenty-third. He met with someone there at ten hundred that morning. But the meeting only lasted thirty minutes. The *Reichsführer* is presumably in transit somewhere. But with Allied planes strafing anything that moves, his itinerary is held very close."

Ilse said, "Keep trying to locate him. That takes priority over all else."

The radio telephone operator hesitated, then said, "Yes, miss. But, just before you sent for me, we got word from Air Defense. Large Allied bomber formations have been reported by the spotters we still have inside Allied-controlled airspace. The formations are headed east, for Bavaria. But whether the target is Munich, or the Berghof, or something else, they can't say yet."

Ilse said, "I can say. The target for at least some of those planes will be right here. Keep searching for the *Reichsführer*. But also keep me updated as more information arrives about the incoming air raid. Notify me immediately of developments regarding either matter. No matter where I am."

"Yes, miss. Where should I look for you first?"

"Out on the runway. With the Valkyrie."

Forty-five

ILSE SAT ALONE IN THE VALKYRIE'S COCKPIT, WHILE THE GROUND
crew made the great silver plane ready. She tucked the actuator
case, with the bomb's actuator plug once again clipped into its
recess, alongside the pilot's seat. Then she took the photograph
of Heinrich, Winter, Hanna, and herself, wrote on it, then tucked
it into the case, for luck.

She draped her pilot's helmet, and goggles, over the control
yoke, ran her fingers over each of the six engines' individual
throttles, then reached forward and touched the landing-gear lever.

She switched on the aircraft's hydraulics, then listened, as the
muffled electrics whined evenly.

As she depressed the left, then right, rudder pedals, she
peered over her left, then right, shoulders. Each wing's outboard
control surfaces responded precisely. In flight, their deformation
would produce the differential airflow control provided by a
conventional-tailed aircraft's rudder.

It had been months since she had flown the aircraft, but each
control responded to her input, in the way that a childhood bicycle
responded to inputs that an adult's body duplicated years later.

Ilse wriggled, feet first, back to Valkyrie's belly hatch, then
swung down through it, without touching the crew ladder. The
strength and agility that she would need had returned to her
since the crash.

Outside the aircraft's sealed crew compartment, the kerosene
fumes of turbojet engine fuel hung in the cool morning air.

When the great wing's last tank was topped off, the ground

crew disconnected the tanker truck's fuel hose, then the truck rumbled away.

The ground-crew chief stepped alongside Ilse. Then they walked side by side to the bomb, itself.

It rested in the great wing's shadow, on the wheeled tow dolly that the ground crew had maneuvered into place, beneath the open-doored bomb bay.

The polished steel cylinder was shorter, from blunt nose to finned tail, than two corpses laid head to feet. Its girth was no wider than a coffin.

Ilse ran her fingers over the barometric sensor that bulged from the bomb's tapered tail. She opened the sensor's hinged clamshell lid. The dial inside was set to its default detonation altitude, for an airburst three hundred meters above sea level. Three of Valkyrie's likely targets, London, New York, and Washington, were close to sea level. Moscow was one hundred fifty meters above sea level. If Moscow proved to be her target, the dial would have to be rotated. For the other targets, it would only be necessary to remove the dummy plug, then replace it with the actuator.

She closed her eyes, then walked her fingers from the barometric sensor, until she felt the wood texture of the dummy plug that protected the slot into which she would have to fit the actuator.

With no bombardier, she would have to engage Valkyrie's autopilot, then crawl back into the bomb bay and arm the bomb herself.

She repeated the actions, over and over. Finally, she was certain that she could arm the bomb, even in total darkness, if necessary.

She stepped back, then nodded to her ground-crew chief.

A ground crewman switched on the dolly's motors. They groaned, the dolly shuddered, then the four-thousand-kilogram bomb inched upward. The clang of Valkyrie's internal clamps echoed from the bomb bay as the bomb was locked in place.

A crewman operated the bomb-bay door switch, and the doors whined closed.

Ilse said to her ground-crew chief, "She's ready to go?"

He nodded. "As ready as we can make her, miss. If she goes, may I ask where she will be headed?"

"I don't know, yet."

Ilse heard, high above, the distant purr of a single aircraft's Merlin engines.

She and the crew chief shaded their eyes, and she spotted the tiny silhouette of a lone British Mosquito.

She shuddered, as she realized the worst.

This Mosquito was not another reconnaissance plane, but a pathfinder. Pathfinders either circled high above the target, guiding in the heavies that followed them, or dropped incendiaries in advance that marked the target for the heavies.

This pathfinder dropped incendiaries. The waves of lumbering four-engined bombers that would follow, whether British Lancasters, American Liberators, or Flying Fortresses, would simply target the resulting fires.

The Mosquito's markers struck several buildings in the deserted camp, exploded, then set the wooden barracks aflame.

It measured the Allies' viciousness toward this target that, even in daylight, they marked with incendiaries.

The crew chief, breathing rapidly, said, "Miss, it's too late to move the aircraft back into the mine."

"I know, Chief." She placed her left hand on his shoulder. "Get out of here with your crew. Ride this out, safe in the mine."

He spun away, and ran so fast that he didn't return her "Hail Hitler."

Woodsmoke odor, and haze, drifted from the burning barracks, across the runway. Sparks from already burning barracks ignited adjacent barracks.

Ilse glimpsed a figure running from, not toward, the mine's entrance. She recognized the chunky radio telephone operator, then sprinted toward him. Even on aching legs, she outraced the ground crew.

She and the radio telephone operator met, breathless, halfway between the mine entrance and the Valkyrie.

She panted, "You've located the *Reichsführer*?"

He puffed, hands on knees, as he shook his head. "No, miss. Not a word. But Air Defense now reports with high confidence that we're one of today's targets." He glanced at the burning barracks, while he cursed under his breath. "I'll thank them for the timely warning."

She shook her head. "No. Thank *you*. Get back inside."

She reversed course. As she ran back toward the Valkyrie, her mind raced ahead faster than her legs could carry her.

She couldn't allow the Valkyrie, and the bomb, to be destroyed on the ground, or allow them to be captured. If she got airborne, and clear, and high enough that the fighter wolfpacks couldn't climb fast enough to intercept her, she could risk radio transmissions.

But it was fantasy to think that her transmissions would be heard, much less be responded to with instructions from Heinrich. Any German airfield where she might land wouldn't remain German for long. Then she would have delivered the Valkyrie to the Allies on a silver plate. That somehow seemed even more actively treasonous than allowing the plane and the bomb to be captured here.

The entire camp was ablaze, now, and smoke from the fires blanketed the runway.

She was fifty meters from the Valkyrie's belly-hatch ladder when a silhouette loomed in the smoke, blocking her path.

The crippled gate guard stood before her, with his rifle aimed at her chest. What the hell was his name?

She slowed, then stopped. Arms wide, she said, "Lothar, it's me. Let me pass."

"My orders are the plane doesn't leave the ground, Miss Jaeger."

"Whose orders?"

"Dr. Winter's. Just before you arrived the other day."

"I have relieved Dr. Winter. His orders are countermanded."

She heard inbound bombers' distant rumble.

Lothar said, "I can't take your word for that, miss."

"Don't play stupid. You know the SS is running this place now. If you don't let me pass, Captain Metz will have you shot."

"I stopped taking orders from the SS when I saw what they were doing to civilians in the East."

The bombers' drone grew.

Ilse stepped forward. "Lothar, I need to get that plane off the ground, to save it."

He shook his head. "I'm just following orders. That's what the SS in Russia told us when we asked them why they were herding civilians into trenches, then machine-gunning them."

Ilse took another step forward in the smoke.

The guard poked his rifle's barrel forward. "Don't, miss."

"You would shoot an unarmed woman?"

"I watched the SS shoot plenty of them."

She ducked as she rushed him.

In the same instant that she heard his rifle fire, the ground kicked up beneath her feet, as though the earth had quaked.

She, and the guard, were hurled through the air.

Her right thigh seemed to explode with pain.

Then she, and the guard, lay on the ground.

Her ears rang from the bomb's concussion.

She realized that she owed her life to an Allied bomb. Its concussion had displaced the guard, and his aiming point, from her heart to her thigh.

The guard's rifle had been torn from him, and lay on the ground between him and Ilse.

As she dragged herself toward his rifle, he stirred.

He had gotten to his knees when she reached the rifle, got to her own knees, worked the rifle's bolt, then shot him through his chest.

The effort dizzied her, and she sprawled on her back, looking toward the Salzreich's entrance. The mountain's shape above the mine entrance seemed different, somehow.

An object flashed through the smoke, a streak of bright-painted green, above the mine. The streak disappeared into the ground.

Her heart beat once.

Then, again, the earth rose beneath her, hurled her into the sky, then slammed her down again.

She realized the earthquake-like explosions were caused by bombs the British painted bright green, and called "Tallboys."

Tallboys were as long as a Lancaster's bomb bay, longer even than Valkyrie's uranium bomb. They weighed forty-five hundred kilograms each, even more than the uranium bomb. Tallboys were so heavy that a British Lancaster could carry only one.

Streamlined, Tallboys spun like rifle bullets as they fell, then struck the ground faster than the speed of sound. They burrowed deep into their target before they detonated.

Hits by just two British Tallboys, and concussions from others that missed, had capsized the *Tirpitz*, the world's mightiest battleship, in under fifteen minutes.

A third Tallboy struck the mountain above the mine entrance. Then it seemed that the mountain collapsed on itself. And on everyone inside. The SS, the prisoners, and, fittingly, on the body of the traitor, Winter.

Thirty meters from Ilse, Valkyrie sat, apparently undamaged.

As Ilse crawled past the guard's dead body, she wondered again what it was about Winter, who had been a spineless traitor, that sparked such loyalty, first among the Jews when he was executed, then in the crippled guard who had blocked her path. She supposed it had to do with their latent inferiority.

Using the dead soldier's rifle as a crutch, Ilse limped toward the plane.

Two more Tallboys' concussions hurled her to the ground. She thought that the British had outsmarted themselves. Using a pathfinder's incendiaries to visually mark the target, in daylight, had ended up obscuring it.

Yet these Tallboys had found their marks. Lately, the British had taken to claiming that they aimed their bombs with radar, when the target required accuracy. She had dismissed their claims as propaganda, to divert attention from their actual tactics throughout the war, which were to sneak over cities by night, then firebomb civilians indiscriminately. But it appeared the British really did have the tools to hit what they were aiming at, when they chose.

At last, she sank to the ground beneath Valkyrie, at the crew-ladder's base.

Her flight coverall's right leg was slick and crimson. She lay there while she fashioned a tourniquet from the rifle's sling. She applied it above her wound, then discarded the rifle.

Hand over hand, she dragged herself up the ladder, through the crew passage, and into the pilot's seat.

Unlike the Messerschmitt 262's Junkers engines, Fromm had rigged Valkyrie's six BMW engines to start without piston-engine starter motors. What had seemed another delaying complexity now seemed genius.

Even so it seemed a lifetime before all six engines whined. As their turbines spun up, the great wing trembled, like a predator eager to spring.

Operating the right rudder pedal felt like setting her right leg on fire. But she repeated the movement, with teeth gritted, and realized she could manage.

She peered down the runway, expecting at any moment to see a conventional bomb, dropped by a later bombing wave, to crater it.

She released the Valkyrie's brakes. The turbojets thrust the big wing forward, into the smoke.

The first conventional bomb struck the runway, but behind her.

Fully laden, the Valkyrie accelerated slowly. The airspeed indicator needle seemed to swing by imperceptible increments, as in a nightmare. Finally, the needle passed minimum takeoff speed.

She drew the control yoke back against her belly. The Valkyrie's nose lifted, and Ilse glimpsed a startled ox, meters below her, as the Valkyrie rose through the darkness.

Ilse retracted the flaps as she climbed straight, but blind. The valley's slopes remained invisible beyond the smoke, to her left, and right.

The Valkyrie burst into sunlight, above the smoke.

Ilse craned her neck, but saw no fighters.

In the distance, a forest of smoke plumes roiled above the Berghof. The bulk of the Allied bombers had also been busy.

The Valkyrie attained her cruising altitude, which at her cruising speed placed her out of practical reach of Allied fighters. Fromm's insistence that the cabin be heated, and pressurized, no longer seemed treasonably luxurious.

For one hour she flew an irregular pattern, high above those portions of Germany most likely to remain in German hands. As she repeated her pattern, she broadcast on several frequencies. No help or guidance was forthcoming.

In Norse mythology, the Valkyrie were Odin's winged handmaidens. They flew above the battlefield, selecting, from among the slain, those who would join Odin in Valhalla.

Now, Ilse flew above the battlefield. But with no orders, it fell to her not to choose the slain, but to choose those who would be slain.

If Heinrich's strategy had played out as expected, her target was Moscow. But it didn't appear that Heinrich's strategy had succeeded.

And the Russians hadn't killed her parents. The Americans, and the British, had. They had rained ruin from the air upon Germany for four long years. The Russians had not. Moscow had not. Moscow was also distant. So was Washington. So was New York.

Ilse thumbed through the maps at her side, then plotted a course toward London.

With luck, both Churchill and King George were at home. As the Allies had no doubt hoped the fuehrer had been.

She turned to that course, then set the autopilot to hold speed and distance.

Drowsy from blood loss, and punished by the throbbing in her leg, she scanned Valkyrie's instruments.

There was no way to know whether the Tallboys' concussions, or shrapnel from the bomb that had fallen behind her during takeoff, had damaged the plane. If such damage revealed itself later, she would deal with it. But at the moment, the damage that most threatened Ilse's aircraft was the damage to its pilot.

Ilse loosened the tourniquet that encircled her right thigh, then adjusted it to a compromise, between constriction and comfort.

Even at Valkyrie's cruising speed, London was hours distant. Ilse leaned back, then closed her eyes.

For just a moment.

Forty-six

MILD, CLEAR-AIR TURBULENCE STARTLED ILSE AWAKE.

She peered down, and saw not the green and brown checkerboard of rural Europe, but silver-sprinkled water.

She stiffened in her seat.

God! She had slept so long that she was already crossing the English Channel.

Ilse glanced at the instrument panel's chronometer, frowned, then tapped it with her finger.

Then, she tugged her coverall sleeve up, eyed her wristwatch, and felt sick in her belly.

She had been out for five hours. The sun remained in front of her. So the Valkyrie had continued its travel west. The water below wasn't the English Channel. It had to be the North Atlantic.

With no history of wind speed and direction aloft, she had little idea how far the Valkyrie might have been pushed, pulled, and diverted from its set course.

No landmarks were visible. Nor were stars, by which she might fix her position using the sextant that was tucked beside her seat. All she could be sure of was that she was roughly equidistant from both North America and Europe.

The great silver wing flew with a migratory bird's efficiency. Therefore, fuel was adequate to reach any target she chose.

She could turn back. But finding London, inland, and inbound from the east, presented an unfamiliar perspective. Besides, she would be flying into the teeth of the Allied air forces, and air defenses, that dominated European air space.

On the other hand, North America was too large a destination to miss. Insulated by an ocean from the war it fought in Europe, America would be a fat, unsuspecting target.

Regardless of her precise position over the North Atlantic, Washington was more distant from her than New York. And she couldn't kill Roosevelt, because he was already dead.

She replotted, then reset, a course, that should keep Valkyrie seaward of the Canadian and American East Coasts, and so invisible to land-based observers, as the Valkyrie flew the Great Circle route from Europe to North America.

Ilse laid out maps of America's eastern seaboard, against which she could match the coastline, when she finally turned due west.

Then she sat back again, while the Valkyrie raced the sun.

At what North Americans called five o'clock p.m. Eastern Standard Time, Ilse sighted land. The weather along America's eastern seaboard was clear, and she quickly matched the coastline to her charts. Her position was north of Atlantic City, in the state of New Jersey.

Ilse turned north, then revised the autopilot's settings. Valkyrie would remain unseen over the ocean, as it approached New York from the south.

She took the last of the Valkyrie's first aid kit's painkillers, then redressed her leg wound. It appeared the bullet had exited from her thigh without breaking bone.

Ilse had fashioned a pressure bandage that had stopped the bleeding from both the entry and exit wounds. But for loss of blood, and the weakness it created, her injury was more survivable than she had at first thought.

Carrying the actuator plug, clipped in place in the map case, she crawled on her belly back toward the bomb bay, to arm the bomb. She pulled herself forward using her elbows, and dragged her injured leg, to avoid reopening her wounds.

She was halfway between the cockpit and the bomb bay when she heard the bangs, in rapid succession.

The Valkyrie banked sharp left as Ilse felt its nose dip.

She inched backward, to the cockpit, and realized what had happened as she adjusted the aircraft's trim.

Heart pounding, she peered out at the port wing. Torn

aluminum skin had peeled back above Engine One, the farthest outboard port-side engine.

Fromm had salvaged Engine One from Valkyrie One after her crash in October 1944. The engine had operated for more hours than the other five engines. The unavoidable weak link, one or more of the salvaged engine's metal-fatigued steel turbine blades had now failed. This time blade fragments had apparently wrecked adjacent Engine Two, as well.

Fromm the Bear, in his wisdom, had mounted the salvaged engine outboard. There it could inflict the least damage. Had the engine that just failed been inboard, Ilse had no doubt this Valkyrie would have crashed, like its sibling had crashed in 1944.

The Valkyrie could fly on four engines. But it had lost altitude, as well as airspeed.

Ilse manipulated the controls, one by one. The plane's hydraulics remained intact, for the moment. But altitude was down to two thousand meters above the Atlantic.

Finally, she looked up from the controls and instruments, and her eyes widened.

The Valkyrie was no longer above the Atlantic. It was above what the maps called "Upper New York Bay."

Below, and to Ilse's left, the weathered-copper green Statue of Liberty rose from a tiny island.

Ahead, Manhattan Island's skyscraper forest loomed in the afternoon sun, as the Valkyrie approached it from the southeast. The island itself seemed to rush at her, its southern tip like a ship's prow, flanked by the Hudson River, left of the island, and the East River, on its right.

Dead ahead, she recognized her aiming point, the Empire State Building's needle spire.

Her heart beat faster, as her goal neared. It seemed so real, and so close, that she felt as though she could reach out through the windscreen and touch it.

But the actuator plug remained at her side, not in the bomb.

Before she reached Manhattan Island, Ilse turned the Valkyrie east and south, back and out over the sea. There she would remain unnoticed as she climbed again. Then she would again return to the bomb bay, and install the actuator plug.

✧   ✧   ✧

At bombing-run altitude, above the Atlantic, east of New York, Ilse turned Valkyrie west. Ilse again set the autopilot, then unbuckled her harness, preparatory to crawling back again to arm the bomb.

As she rose, she felt light-headed, and collapsed back into the pilot's seat.

She looked down at her injured leg.

Her panicked return to the cockpit, after Engine One's disintegration, had dislodged the pressure dressing from her wounds, and they had reopened.

Already weak, she had lost even more blood. She adjusted the pressure dressing, but felt her eyelids droop.

Was there no end to the obstacles the gods hurled into her path?

She screamed her frustration, and realized her voice was scarcely a squeak.

She punched at the canopy with a gloved fist, but could not even reach the Plexiglas.

She had had New York dead in her sights! But her will could not triumph over her weakness, and over circumstances.

She had failed! Failed Heinrich, failed Germany, failed herself.

Almost ten kilometers above Manhattan Island, the Valkyrie would appear from the ground as no more than a silent, west-racing silver speck, glimpsed through broken clouds. Unable to alter the course either of history or of the aircraft that confined her, Ilse let consciousness slip away.

Forty-seven

THIS TIME, ILSE WAS AWAKENED NOT BY TURBULENCE, BUT BY pain. So weak that she could barely adjust her blood-soaked pressure bandage, she peered out into the late afternoon.

This time, calculating by the Valkyrie's current airspeed, and because it was still late afternoon at her current location, Ilse concluded that the Valkyrie had reached a longitude more than half the distance across the North American continent.

Mountains stretched away beneath her, in all directions. They weren't the Alps' craggy gray, but red brown, and snow-covered. She was flying above the North American Rocky Mountains.

The Valkyrie's altimeter showed its altitude was seven thousand meters above sea level. But these mountains were far closer to her than they should have been, had she been flying at a similar altitude above the Alps. The peaks seemed to rise above four thousand meters, and stretched away in all directions, with no visible hint of human habitation.

As the Valkyrie flew above this deserted, alien landscape, Ilse realized that the fuel gauges read far nearer empty than her calculations suggested they should be.

The turbine blades' shrapnel had spared the hydraulic lines, but apparently had not spared all of Valkyrie's fuel lines and tanks.

There was no time to agonize over her failure again. Simply living to fight another day would require every scintilla of concentration she could summon. In this unforgiving terrain, any flat spot was a good spot.

She banked above a teardrop-shaped, ice-covered lake, then

circled the peak that shaded it. She came around again, lined up the Valkyrie, and eased off the throttles as she drifted lower, on final approach.

The landing gear failed to respond when Ilse tried to lower it. But with fuel nearly spent, she dared not go around again.

Fifty meters above the lake's surface, and one hundred meters short of its shoreline, Valkyrie's remaining engines died, one after another.

The silver wing touched its belly down on the lake's snow-covered ice. The plane screamed ahead, shrouded in the blizzard it created.

Blind in a fog of snow and ice, Ilse struggled to hold the plane straight. But the Valkyrie hurtled forward, seemingly without scraping off any speed whatsoever.

At last, the aircraft slowed, screaming and groaning. It tilted to port as it slid, then slewed left as the port wing tip dragged across the ice.

The plane stopped.

In the sudden silence, the snow shroud dropped away.

The plane rested perhaps one hundred meters from the shore, at the teardrop lake's wide end.

Ilse sat back, her hands trembling on the control yoke, and breathed.

Two breaths later, something groaned beneath her. The Valkyrie listed further to port, as the lake ice cracked beneath the great plane's weight.

Ilse unbuckled her seat harness, then was hurled aside.

The port wing tip had broken through the ice. The aircraft tipped up, capsized, then sank.

Disoriented as the plane turned bottom-up, Ilse struggled to reach the belly hatch.

The Valkyrie plummeted, from light down into frigid darkness.

The cockpit and crew passage flooded. The water's cold shocked her like electricity.

At last, she found the belly-hatch release, pushed out of the aircraft, then swam toward the light of the open water created when Valkyrie broke through the ice.

Ilse lay on her back on the ice, gasping, alongside the open water. Beneath her the Valkyrie, and the bomb, now rested.

The sun set. The air turned even colder. She shivered there, too weak and numb to move.

She waited to pass again into unconsciousness, then, painlessly, into death.

She had failed. She had failed the fuehrer, who was now, or would soon be, dead. She had failed her beloved Heinrich. Now, without the Valkyrie's leverage and power, he would fail Germany, and would join his fuehrer in death.

In that moment of realization, Ilse understood the hopelessness that the traitor, Peter Winter, had felt in the moments after he had learned that the woman he loved was dead. Like Winter, Ilse now had no reason to fight on. No reason to live.

Her half formed dreams, of ruling at Heinrich's side over a National Socialist empire that would endure for a thousand years, lay drowned and crushed beneath her. Crushed as surely and as irretrievably as Peter Winter and the Jews he had so treacherously protected.

She rolled onto her belly, then vomited out across the translucent ice.

And she realized that her sickness, and weakness, were morning sickness. She carried her beloved Heinrich's child within her belly, in the same way that the Valkyrie carried within its belly a weapon.

The gods had gifted her a child, and a weapon, with which to avenge the losses, and the humiliations, that were closing the door on National Socialism. So she would survive no matter the pain, no matter the obstacles, no matter the years that passed. And she would train her child to take up the struggle, when she no longer could, if necessary. And then, in the gods' own good time, National Socialism would leave the world stage, but it would slam the door so hard that the universe would shake.

Unlike Peter Winter, Ilse Jaeger still had something to live for.

Forty-eight

ELLIOTT LOVE SAT IN HIS KITCHEN, HIS BACK TO HIS HOUSE'S rear door. He looked up from his empty teacup, across his kitchen table at Cass and Frank, then shrugged.

He said, "That's her story. The only proofs I ever had, that it was true, were that she knew things that were consistent with the story being true.

"She knew German. I always resisted her attempt to teach me the language. Kids want to be like other kids, not different. She knew the Fieseler Storch, inside out. She knew how to fly. Extraordinarily well, I now realize. And, frankly, I look more like Himmler than I care to admit. When I checked the historical record even the minutest details that she mentioned about Himmler proved true."

Cass said, "What split you and your mother up?"

"It's hard to be a Nazi in America. It's harder to try and raise your American-born child to become one. When I was sixteen, and in what I thought was true love, with a girl, I told her the truth. Whether she thought I was crazy or terrifying, the truth ended that relationship. The loss broke my heart and it was the beginning of the end of my relationship with my mother.

"A week later my mother told me, for the thousandth time, that my father had died a martyr and a hero. I pushed back. I suppose most teenagers do, at some point."

Cass said, "You had more to push back about than most teenagers, Elliott."

"I said my father was a murderer, a coward, and a villain. I

361

told her she was delusional, at best, and a complicit villainess at worst. I said that if there were heroes and martyrs in her story, they were the physicist, Winter, and his wife, because they had tried to do the right thing.

"The argument escalated to the point that, frail as she had become, she pummeled me with her fists. I retreated, afraid that if I retaliated I would kill her. I stormed out, a sixteen year old with no plan, no means, and no family. I never returned."

Cass said, "Never? Did you ever feel guilty?"

"About leaving my mother, yes. I sent her money every month. But guilty about what the Nazis did? Why would *I* feel guilty about that? I didn't do those things. And I certainly couldn't undo them. As for the rest, I believed that she had been a Nazi, a test pilot, and had slept with Himmler. But her story about the aircraft and the bomb were upside down to history. As a sixteen year old, I chalked it up to her delusions."

Cass tugged the steel map case from her messenger bag, then passed it to Elliott. "You've never seen this, then? The case she's holding, in the photo I showed you?"

Elliott turned it in his hands as he frowned. "No. She didn't own much stuff. What she had, I knew pretty well. After I left home, like I said, I still sent her cash, every month. But not enough to shop for antiques like this."

Cass turned to Frank. "You said that on the night Elliott's mother died, she kept reciting 'three blind mice.' Could she have been saying, 'zee blybd im eyes'?"

Frank cocked his head. "Now that I hear you say it, yes."

Cass said, "She wasn't saying 'three blind mice.' She had lapsed into German. 'Sie bleibt im eis' means 'She remains in the ice.' She wasn't delirious, Frank."

Elliott said, "Are you saying my mother died because someone was stealing this map case from her?"

Cass said, "No. You said she never *had* this case. You said she barely got out of the airplane wearing her own skin."

"Correct. She didn't return to her mythical airplane beneath the lake before I left her, of that I'm certain. The repeated injuries to her left leg had crippled her. She walked more by willpower than muscle power, even when I was young. By the time I left her, she wasn't healthy enough to engage in activity like diving. As she began to realize that I wasn't buying in to her plans, she began writing to anti-Semitic groups. But her story was too far-fetched, and they ignored her."

Frank pointed at the steel case, as he said to Cass, "You're saying Snake Eyes didn't come to steal this case from her. He'd already gotten it out of the lake. He brought it *with* him."

Cass nodded. "His group, whatever it is, have begun salvaging things from the wreckage. Elliott, your mother was excited when she saw this case. Because she realized someone had finally taken her seriously."

Elliott shook his head. "No. No. If that's true, this whole thing isn't over yet. Hasn't she twisted my life enough, already?"

Cass drew her phone while she raised her free palm. "Let me make a call, Elliott." She walked from Elliott Love's kitchen back to his living room.

Cass paced Elliott's living room as she thumbed her phone's keypad.

Wilmot Hoffman answered. "Cass? What's new?"

"Wilmot, we found the airplane in the photograph. Or at least the story behind it."

"How did that happen?"

"Long story. Wilmot, if the Hiroshima bomb was still around today, could it explode?"

"Are you suggesting there might have *been* an actual bomb?"

"I'm asking a question."

"Well, U-235's half-life is seven hundred four million years. So the fissionable material would remain 'fresh.' But after seventy-five years, the bomb's peripherals wouldn't remain viable."

"Wilmot, fifteen percent of the bombs dropped during World War II didn't explode. Two thousand tons of leftover conventional explosives have been found in Europe every year since the war. Most of *their* seventy-five-year-old 'peripherals' are viable enough that they have to be defused."

"A worm-eaten, rusty bomb is still dangerous, of course. And if the propellant charge were still attached to a hundred-forty-one-pound gob of highly enriched uranium, the splatter would make a small, although very dirty bomb, but—"

"What if it weren't 'rusty'? What if the bomb had been packed in a casing, as perfect as that rustproof map case you saw? And kept motionless, in a meat locker, for those seventy-five years?"

"Well, the Little Boy's peripherals were electrical. At a minimum, the battery would be shot. Why these hypotheticals? What's going on, Cass?"

"Nothing. At least nothing a 9-1-1 operator would believe."

"Alright. But what do you *believe* is going on?"

"Worst case? I believe it's like you said. The Germans built a simple A-bomb, like the Hiroshima bomb. And it's still around. And radicals have it now. Coming from me, that sounds ridiculous. Coming from you, less ridiculous. Right?"

Wilmot was silent for so long that Cass said, "Wilmot? You there?"

Wilmot said, "Alright. There are still people in the security community who will talk to me. They can certainly pass the information along. The Europeans *do* deal with unexploded ordnance all the time. They'll take it seriously."

"Wilmot, if it exists, it's not in Europe. It's here."

"Here? In the U.S.?"

"Here, in Colorado."

More silence.

Wilmot said, "How could that be?"

"I didn't say it could be. I am saying *if* it could be, the risk is too great to ignore."

"I'll make some calls."

"We'll call you back, when we know more. Or you call us if you know something sooner." Cass tucked her phone away.

A door slam sounded, on the other side of the door that connected Elliott's living room to his kitchen.

Cass ran back to the kitchen. It was empty.

She ran to the kitchen window, and saw Elliott Love stalking toward his barn, with Frank in pursuit.

"Shit." She sprinted after them.

By the time Cass caught up to Elliott and Frank, Elliott had covered half the distance to his barn, and Frank strode alongside him.

Frank said, "Where you headed, there, Elliott?"

"Upper Pika Lake." Elliott kept walking west.

Frank pointed at the foothills that rose behind the barn. "Long walk. Want a lift?"

"I'm not walking." Elliott pointed at his barn. "There's a helicopter in there. If something's been going on up at my mother's place, I want to know about it. Now."

Frank said, "Fair enough. Care for a traveling companion?"

"I've never found much use for traveling companions."

Frank said, "Oh."

Cass said, "God, I love the way this conversation's going."

Frank said, "If you find what I think you might find up there, Elliott, you might need some backup." He turned away, and walked toward his truck.

Elliott said to Cass, "What's he talking about?"

"Elliott, Frank got that map case outside your mother's room the night she died. Frank got into a fight with a guy who dropped it. The photo we showed you was in the case."

Elliott said, "Who was this guy?"

"Frank believes he's an Islamic terrorist."

"Is he?"

"Well, the case came from *somewhere*. Your mother died at the same time the fight happened. But according to the experts, she died of natural causes. And Frank's the only one who's ever seen this guy. Frank keeps thinking this guy is stalking him. But he's never shown up."

"You think Frank's old and crazy. Like me?"

"I did, at first. Now I think Frank's right more often than he's wrong. I think I just don't understand him, sometimes. Elliott, I think I don't understand you, either."

"You understand why I don't advertise my family tree."

"I do."

"You expect me to either be a neo-Nazi, or to be wracked with guilt. But I'm not a Nazi. And I can't undo what the Nazis did, either. So I don't feel guilty about that."

"Then why are you rolling out a helicopter?"

"If there's the slightest possibility that what was done isn't finished, and that I made it worse by walking away from my mother and her ideas, I can't just do nothing."

Frank returned, carrying his rifle.

Cass said, "I'm going, too."

Frank said, "Nope. I shouldn't have let you hang around my house the other night."

"Frank, nothing happened then. Nothing's going to happen now."

Elliott shrugged, "I can violate FAA regulations as easily with two passengers as I can with one."

Elliott unlatched the barn's rolling door, then put his shoulder to it, and rolled it aside.

Cass blinked at the gray-primer painted object that squatted in the barn's shadows.

Frank said, "That's not a helicopter. That's a toaster."

Cass smiled.

The Kaman H-43A Huskie did, indeed, look like a toaster. It was a mid-1950s design, with a wide, boxy fuselage. Two masts, topped by side-by-side intermeshing rotors, jutted from the fuselage's top like toast slices. Nicknamed "Pedro," because the drooping rotor pair resembled a sombrero, the H-43A squatted like a cockroach, on four tiny landing wheels, set in skids that resembled snowshoes.

Cass said to Elliott, "A Pedro?"

Elliott nodded. "A Navy pilot, who ditched off Vietnam, made a fortune in later life. A life he owed to the Pedro that fished him out of the Gulf of Tonkin. I'm restoring this example for him."

Cass walked around it, running her fingers over its square-tailed empennage. "The museum's example is a static display. This will be flyable?"

Elliott nodded.

Cass said, "Why restore a piston engine version? Parts must be impossible."

Elliott said, "You know your aircraft. This is one of eighteen piston engine examples built for the Air Force. The parts *are* scarcer. But Pedro rotor blades are scarcer still, and the set on this example was perfect. My experience with piston engines is why I got the work."

"How far along are you?"

"It needs modern avionics, radios. Paint, obviously. The right seat harness hardware's balky, and needs replacing. The magneto switch is a workaround. But as of last week she's flyable. According to me, not according to the FAA. I was going to sneak it into the air today, anyway." He stepped to the fuselage's rear then said, "If the two of you will help me push?"

Frank said, "Did you just say flying this thing breaks the law?"

Elliott grunted, as he put his shoulder to the fuselage. "About a dozen FAA regulations that I can think of, offhand."

Frank said, "I like the sound of that."

✧　　✧　　✧

Thirty minutes later, Elliott closed and locked his barn, then the three of them walked to the chunky aircraft as it squatted in the grass.

The Pedro had room for four, but only the pilot and copilot rode up front. Crew, passengers, and other payload were relegated to a bay behind a partition.

Cass pointed to the helicopter's rear compartment. "Frank, you ride in back."

Frank frowned. "Seems to me the person with the gun rides next to the driver. That's why they call it 'shotgun.'"

"No, the person with a private rotorcraft license and twenty-three solo hours in her logbook rides next to the driver, in case he becomes incapacitated."

Frank said, "You told me you were a professional historian."

"Frank, flying's not a profession. Flying is a way of life."

When they were settled in, in, Cass twisted in her seat, and dangled an intercom set of earpieces and mic, twin to the one she wore, in front of Frank.

He pushed the headset back toward her. "I don't need hearing aids yet."

"Plug that in and wear it or you *will*! Frank, even *modern* helos are insanely noisy. Everybody wears a headset."

Frank snorted.

Cass chucked the headset into his lap. "Think of your headset like your knife. It's better to have and not want than want and not have."

She turned forward, then rested her palms lightly on the Pedro's right-hand set of duplicate cyclic and collective controls, and tapped her feet on her duplicate set of pedals.

Elliott rested his pre-flight check list on his thigh, then reached to the instrument panel and inserted a brass key into a rotary switch.

Cass said, "Helicopters don't have keys."

Elliott smiled. "New ones don't. Lots of the old piston engine models' magneto switches were keyed. This switch is a workaround part from a scrapped Bell H-47. Welcome to 1953."

Although the Pedro's basic controls resembled the basics of the sleek modern helicopter she had learned in, the Pedro was not just older than she was, it was older than her mother.

The old airframe shook and thundered as Elliott started the engine.

As Cass rocked in her seat, she peered up through the Pedro's Plexiglas fishbowl canopy. The intermeshing rotors above her whooshed past each other in opposite directions, an accident waiting to happen from second to second. But they allowed the Pedro to fly without a tail rotor to counteract main rotor torque, so it could hover with extraordinary stability.

Cass pulled her feet off the pedals, removed her hands from the cyclic and collective, and frowned.

Elliott shouted into his mic, and his voice rasped in her ears. "What's wrong?"

"I learned in a Robinson. The Pedro's a little disturbing."

Elliott said, "A lot about Operation Paperclip was a little disturbing."

Cass smiled at the bitter inside joke.

The Pedro's designer, Anton Flettner, had designed helicopters for the Nazis. After the war, Flettner was Paperclipped, came to the United States, and designed helicopters like the Pedro for his old enemy, to use against his other old enemy, the Soviet Union.

But before that, during World War II, the Nazis had shipped Flettner's wife, who as a Jew was their enemy, to safety in Switzerland, so Flettner could keep designing helicopters for them.

The frequency with which World War II had made the enemy of one's enemy one's friend *was* a little disturbing.

Cass looked over her shoulder. Frank had put on his headset, and his shoulders rocked as the Pedro shook.

She shouted into her own headset's mic. "Frank, can you hear me okay?"

"If okay is you sounding like a dog barking through an electric fan."

"Do you like your first helicopter ride?"

"Does a rock like riding in a washing machine?"

Elliott flew the Pedro west, toward the Continental Divide, above the Rockies' vast mountain scape.

Cass sat back in her seat and enjoyed the ride.

Forty minutes later, the Pedro drifted above the mountain retreat where Elliott Love's mother had taught him to fly.

They hovered, pointed into a slight breeze out of the southwest. Beneath them a tiny log cabin stood in a seventy-yard-wide clearing, amid the pine forest that blanketed the mountainside below tree line.

No vehicles or activity were apparent.

Elliott said into his mic, "This cabin was the only structure here when she bought the property during the early 1950s. It's remote today, but back then it was so inaccessible that it was dirt cheap."

He pointed down, at a narrow, rocky trail, visible beside the cabin. The trail disappeared into the woods, both upslope and down. "This trail was here, too. It leads upslope, to the lake. Also downslope. A mile downslope from here this trail passes through a gap in an escarpment. The previous owner gated the gap. That's where I got stopped by the new lock, when I came up here and serviced the Storch."

Cass said, "Where's the Storch now?"

Elliott pointed at a ridge to their front. "In a shed on the other side of that ridge. The shed's in an alpine meadow, about a hundred yards long. That's plenty of run for a good pilot to take off or land a Storch. And my mother was a very good pilot. We cleared a trail over to the meadow, then built the shed. The plane's stored over there. Near as I could tell when I worked on the Storch, whoever changed the lock did nothing over there."

Elliott banked the Pedro, then flew upslope three hundred yards, toward the mountain's rocky peak, then hovered again.

At tree line, the forest gave way to gnarled, stunted pines, then to bare rock. A barn-like building stood alongside the trail.

Elliott said, "This is the second building my mother added. She called it the workshop."

Frank leaned forward, then pointed. "Those tire tracks would've been washed away if they'd been made very long ago."

Elliott nodded. "I walked in. Those aren't mine. So somebody was here. But nothing's obviously disturbed. And nothing seems to be going on at the moment."

Frank pointed again. "The tire ruts don't stop at this barn. They head on up, toward the lake."

Elliott nodded, then swung the Pedro past his mother's workshop, and followed the trail across the rocky slope toward the peak.

Elliott hovered the Pedro again when it reached an altitude

a few hundred feet higher than the mountain tarn's surface, and above its south shore line.

The mountain peak rose to Cass's right, and the lake filled the rockbound, bowl-shaped depression beneath the peak. On this summer afternoon, the peak's north face was in shadow, but the lake's surface reflected the afternoon sun.

The lake's surface was, however, ice. At least most of it.

Elliott said, "Dammit. *Something's* been going on."

A path of open water, perhaps eight feet wide, and edged with broken ice, stretched from a point a hundred yards or so offshore, to the shore immediately beneath them.

A pair of rusty lines emerged from the open water, then continued up onto the shore for perhaps thirty yards.

Cass said, "Those look like railroad tracks."

Elliott said, "They're rails for an ore car. You're close enough."

Cass said, "What does that mean?"

Elliott said, "I'm not sure. But now I know where we need to look next."

Forty-nine

THE ASP RAN, HIDDEN IN THE TREES THAT BORDERED THE TRAIL
that led past the old woman's cabin. He turned, then began to
climb the ridge opposite the cabin.

As he scrambled up the rocky slope, he tugged the field
glasses he carried from their case. He dropped the case, watched
it bounce down the rocky slope, but kept climbing.

He continued upslope, scrambling for handholds, and dislodg-
ing rocks. The Expedition, and the bomb in the horse trailer that
the big SUV towed, were now a half mile behind him.

He arrived at a rocky knob above the trail, then rested, hands
on knees, and gasping. The knob overlooked the cabin. From the
knob he could also see the old woman's workshop, where he had
prepared and loaded the bomb. Beyond the workshop the trail,
which led both up to the lake, and down to the gate, was also visible.

When he had first heard the distant, approaching helicopter
rotor whop, he had pulled the SUV and trailer as far beneath
dense tree cover as possible.

He had feared that the Americans had found him out, and
had surrounded the property.

But his brief glimpse of the helicopter, as it flashed above,
confirmed his initial impression. The helicopter lacked the turbojet whistle of, and did not resemble, modern military or civilian
helicopters.

He trained his glasses on the helicopter, which now hovered
above the lake. Why it hovered, above the open water and apparatus that he had left behind, was obvious.

Why the helicopter and its occupants were here at all was not obvious.

He had watched and listened as the helicopter hovered, first over the cabin, then over the workshop, and now above the lake.

The machine itself resembled nothing he had seen, with two ungainly rotors mounted atop a squat, beetle-shaped fuselage.

What he saw relieved him. If the Americans suspected what he was doing, a flotilla of military helicopters would now blacken the skies.

This lone antique was clearly something else.

However, those aboard were seeing what they saw. And they were reporting it. If not now, then eventually. He could not prevent that.

It was a terrible turn of events. He offered a prayer for guidance, and for assistance.

In that moment, the helicopter rotated slowly, drifted down from the lake, then settled in the clearing in front of the workshop. Its engine shut off, then three people climbed out.

The Asp inspected each through his field glasses.

Immediately, he recognized Luck. The old cowboy carried a repeating rifle.

The second man was Luck's age, shorter, and apparently unarmed. He wore coveralls, had exited through the door in the helicopter's left side, and was obviously the pilot.

The third person was a young woman. She wore blue jeans, and her arms and short, red hair were uncovered.

Luck turned his head, periodically, observing his surroundings. But none of them moved with obvious urgency.

If they carried cell phones, they knew, or would soon discover, that they were useless here. Therefore, so long as they remained away from the helicopter, and from its radio, they could not compromise his situation more than they already might have.

Simply running from this place was not an option. The Expedition could only tow its heavily laden trailer slowly. The main highway was hours away, and the country through which he had to pass was largely exposed. He could easily deliver the bomb anywhere in America that he chose. But only as long as no one was looking for him.

If the three visitors had reported what they had seen, help

for them was already closing in on this place. In that case, running was futile.

The Asp considered his immediate options.

The cowboy carried a longer-range weapon than the Asp's. The Asp couldn't be certain that the other two didn't carry handguns. Regardless, he could easily defeat them all, even one-against-three, in a fair fight. But a prudent warrior made every fight as unfair for his enemy as possible.

While the Asp watched, the second man opened the workshop's door, and the other two followed him inside. The Asp's enemies had now confined and concentrated themselves, and limited their awareness of their surroundings.

Napoleon had counseled that one should never interrupt one's enemy while he was making a mistake.

So the Asp moved downslope, then crossed the open clearing to the helicopter.

His original plan, developed as he moved, had been to disable the helicopter, or to use its gasoline to set fire to it, and to the workshop building. But, when he peered into the helicopter through its bulbous canopy, he saw dangling wiring where the antique helicopter's radio should have been.

The federal police who patrolled these lands principally concerned themselves with preserving them. A fire's smoke, in these dry forests, would attract police more quickly than any report of suspicious activity his adversaries might make.

And whatever activity these three visitors *might* report, they had not reported it yet.

Therefore, the Asp withdrew to the tree line that bordered the clearing, then reassessed. He located a fallen log that provided cover, concealment, and a vantage from which he could observe both the workshop and the helicopter.

He checked both his knife and his pistol. Then he settled back behind the log, and awaited his enemies' next mistake.

Fifty

IN THE WORKSHOP BUILDING'S GLOOM CASS STOOD SILENT, WHILE her eyes adjusted from the afternoon sun she had just left.

She drew her phone from her pocket, to use its flashlight, and realized that she had no service.

Elliott saw the light that shone on her face, then said, "There's no cellular service for at least twenty miles in every direction."

The high-ceilinged space smelled of old wood, and the older, colder stone that formed its floor. Cass shivered in the place's chill dimness, the way she had shivered in the cathedral at Cologne, when she had backpacked across Europe, before graduate school.

There was history here, in the way there had been history there. She began to understand why Merken had pushed her into this quest.

Elliott removed lanterns from hooks on the wall inside the door, pumped them up, lit them, then handed one to Frank, and one to Cass.

Elliott held his own lantern high, as he said, "My mother built this place over three summers. There's a generator for the lights. But we won't need it to look around."

Beyond their lanterns' light, shadowed ranks of shelves, all overflowing with indistinct objects, surrounded a rectangular central space.

Elliott said, "This place looks like a dump, but she acquired all this stuff purposefully. Her process bogged down somewhere between acquiring and purpose."

Cass said, "What was her purpose, exactly, Elliott?"

"Her purpose was *not* to entertain her preteen son, of that I'm sure. I spent more time exploring every goat trail and bear den on this property than paying attention to what she did in here."

Frank knelt in the floor's center, while he held his lantern above it. He ran his fingertips across the shed's floor. "Somebody moved something out of here recently. These tire tracks are a few weeks old, tops, Elliott."

Elliott said, "Decades ago, my mother bought a used horse trailer. It used to be parked in that spot. Although she didn't use it to haul horses."

Frank pinched tufts of something off the floor, examined it by his lantern's light, then sniffed, and tasted it.

He said, "Well, somebody hauled horse *feed* in it. And not long ago. June's a hay-cutting month. I'd say this hay wasn't baled more than a week ago."

Cass said, "Are you sure?"

"Pretty sure. I baled my share."

Elliott said, "The trailer could've hauled it, that's for sure. The suspension had been reinforced. It could have hauled an elephant."

Cass said, "An elephant weighs about as much as the Hiroshima bomb weighed."

Cass walked to a work bench along the shed's far wall, then peered at old, brittle papers she found there. "Look at this!"

Frank and Elliott joined her, and looked over her shoulder.

Cass held a booklet close to her light, then said, "Elliott, have you ever seen these?"

Frank said, "What are they?"

Cass ran her finger across typed text, in German, and translated as she read aloud. "'Parking brake set...Fuel flow off...Flaps up.'"

Elliott said, "It's a preflight checklist."

Cass nodded. "And not for your mother's Fieseler Storch. Unless she switched out its engine for six BMW 003 turbojets."

Cass lifted a second sheaf of papers, then flicked through its pages. Her fingers shook, as she whispered, "'*Vorbereitende Schritte zur Bombenbekämpfung*'—'Preparatory steps for bomb arming.' Holy crap."

Frank said, "So Snake Eyes took these instruction books out of the map case."

Cass nodded. "I don't think these lists are *all* he took out of the case, Frank." She laid the second list on the bench, open to a cutaway diagram of a blunt-nosed, finned, aerial bomb. She tapped her finger on the illustration of a corkscrew-shaped piece, near the bomb's tail.

She said, "This piece is what was missing from the clip in the case. The clip we thought held a flashlight."

Frank squinted. "What is it?"

"It's a metal plug. When it replaced an inert wood plug, it completed the electric circuit from this battery, here, to the primer that fired the explosive, here. Then, when the device was triggered, the explosive shot the uranium bullet into the uranium target."

"You sure?"

Cass nodded. "Pretty sure. Like Wilmot said, great minds think alike. The Little Boy bomb had safety plugs like this. If the plane crashed on takeoff, the safety plugs prevented the firing circuit from detonating the conventional explosives that triggered the bomb. After takeoff the crew manually replaced the inert plugs with live electricity conducting plugs. The museum actually has a green-red plug set from one of the later Little Boy bombs."

Frank said, "Without the plug, the bomb's dead?"

Cass said, "Not quite. The crash impact, itself, or more likely any resulting fire, could have detonated the bomb anyway. But with the live plugs in place, detonation on purpose is easy, and detonation by accident is not that hard."

Frank said, "So Snake Eyes took the bomb, and the plug? And he's loaded them into the trailer that used to be here?"

Cass shrugged. "From what we saw up at the lake, he tried. But like I said, a bomb like the one this arming checklist describes would weigh as much as an elephant." Cass lifted her lantern, then circled the shed's interior. "We need to know more."

"Dammit!" She had stubbed her toe in the dark, against a metal cylinder lying on the floor.

Frank said, "You okay?"

"Yeah." Cass knelt, then inspected a scuba tank, and flippers, on the stone floor.

She said, "Elliott, did your mother scuba dive?"

Elliott said, "I never even saw her swim."

Cass lifted a neoprene wetsuit and a face mask off a shelf next to the tank. "This stuff is brand new. Whoever was working up at the lake brought it here. But they couldn't have brought *all* that stuff we saw up at the lake."

Elliott said, "They didn't. My mother acquired it over the years, as part of the grand plan. Failed gold mines are all over the Rockies. Rusty ore carts and rails are abandoned in place for the taking, or can be bought for a song. My mother scavenged junk for years, then hauled it up here in her trailer.

"When I was a kid, I assumed *she* was prospecting for gold. When she decided I was old enough to be a Nazi, she told me she planned to lay rails into the water, recover an A-bomb that she had flown to the United States, then haul it ashore on a trolley. It sounded crazy then. It still does."

Cass said, "There's one way to find out how crazy it is." She held the wetsuit up against her chest. "What do you think? My size?"

Frank and Elliott frowned at her.

Cass said, "I'll walk up to the lake. I'll hold my breath, then swim down. Then we'll know what's there."

Elliott said, "Or we could just fly back down the mountain. Then we can phone someone. Whose *job* it is to investigate these kinds of things."

"And tell them what? This has been Frank's and my problem all along, Elliott. You didn't believe your own *mother* about this. What makes you think anybody we try to tell will? We need more than old papers."

Elliott jerked a thumb toward the workshop's door. "Maybe the proof we need is down at my mother's cabin. Or over the ridge, at the Storch shed. You and Frank go see what's in the lake. I'll take a look at the other places."

Frank and Cass watched from the workshop's doorway, as Elliott walked down the trail, in the direction of the cabin they had seen from the air.

Cass squeezed the sleeve of the neoprene wetsuit she held between her fingers and said, "This thing is, like, three times as thick as a triathlon wetsuit."

"Alpine lake water's cold. You'll be glad it's thick."

"How deep do you think that lake is, Frank?"

"Most tarns in the Rockies are deeper than twenty feet. Shallower than a hundred."

Cass returned to the workshop and rummaged through the gear until she found a web belt, strung with lead weights. "That suit's buoyant. So am I. If I have to go down very far, I'm going to need to wear extra weight."

Frank walked back inside and pointed at the scuba tank. "You know how to use the rest of this stuff, too?"

"Like I can fly a helicopter. I know how to do a lot of shit. I don't know how to do it well enough to bet my life on it. Scuba diving at altitude's complex. You can get the bends. And I don't know how to fill up that tank, anyway."

"Then how—?"

Cass carried the suit behind a row of shelves. As she changed, she said, "Remember hypoventilation? That you called crap? If I free dive, I finish with the air I start with. Decompression's not a problem."

While Cass searched for dive booties and gloves, she said, "Frank, if I find out there really is a plane, and if the bomb is gone, what do you think Elliott will do?"

Frank shrugged. "You mean will he blame himself, now? For leaving his mother?"

"Wouldn't you? He seemed a little unbalanced when we met him. Do you think he might—?"

Crack!

Cass's heart skipped.

She said, "Was that—?"

Frank nodded. "A gunshot."

Fifty-one

FRANK GRABBED HIS RIFLE. "I'LL HAVE A LOOK. YOU STAY PUT."

"You don't think Elliott just shot himself."

"Hell no I don't. Elliott's got common sense. A man with common sense only feels guilty about what he could have changed. I know."

"Life lesson? *Now?*"

"The second worst day of my life was the day the bank foreclosed on my ranch. But I knew that was the weather and beef prices. Not my fault. The day I got my final divorce papers, I finally admitted to myself the problem was ninety percent me being an asshole, and ten percent Peg finally quit on making me a better man. That *was* my fault, and the *worst* day of my life. But I haven't shot myself over either one." Frank turned away, and stared out the open door through which Elliott had left.

"Oh." She swallowed. "Which one of those do you think applies to Elliott?"

Frank stepped into the sunlight. "Maybe neither."

Cass said, "Because you think it's Snake Eyes. And you think it's dangerous for me so I should stay behind because I'm a girl. Which is a bullshit reason."

Frank marched down the trail, toward the bend around which Elliott had disappeared.

He called back, "No. I think that shot might have just been some idiot up here poaching mountain goats. And if it wasn't, somebody needs to stay behind and make sure Snake Eyes doesn't steal the helicopter."

"Me?" Cass pressed her palm to her chest. "Do I look like SEAL Team Six to you?"

Frank shouted back to her, "Didn't say you should fight him. When we got out of the helicopter, Elliott left the key in it. Take the key, then go hide in the woods with it, until I get back."

"Hide in the *woods*? Can't I just go ahead and–"

"What you can go ahead and do is what the Cowboy who brung you tells you to!"

"No wonder she gave up on you!"

Frank stopped in his tracks for a heartbeat. Then he walked on, and disappeared around the bend.

As Cass walked back to the helicopter, she spoke out loud. "Probably shouldn't have said that."

With the helicopter's key tucked inside her bra, Cass stood alongside the open water channel that extended one hundred yards from Upper Pika Lake's shore.

She tugged the wetsuit's hood down over her head, then ran the suit's zipper up beneath her chin. Then she tested the ice with one dive-bootied foot, and shuffled out toward the channel's end.

Triathlon swimming wasn't free diving. But free diving wasn't much more than snorkeling, with no snorkel. Sitting still, she could hold her breath for three minutes. In water, her body reacted to cold, and she could hold for four minutes if she didn't exercise. Unlike scuba diving, she finished with the air she started with, so she could come up for air, then dive, again and again, until she had thoroughly explored whatever she found beneath the ice.

The lead-weighted belt would help her descend. She didn't know how deep the lake was, but surely deeper than she had ever snorkeled. In an emergency, she could discard the belt, and the combined buoyancy of her body and the suit would carry her to the surface.

At the corridor's end, she sat on the ice, her lower legs extended into the icy water. She pulled the mask down over her nose and mouth, then gulped air.

Whatever she found beneath the ice, Merken would no longer be able to accuse her of being a library rat.

She slid into the water, gasped at the cold, then gulped more air. The wetsuit was less protective than she had expected, and her exposed hands and cheeks already felt numb.

She hung, limp in the clear water, and let the weights pull her down.

She was probably twenty feet above the lake bed when it first appeared out of the dimness like a gray ghost.

A moment later, she touched down, feet first, and stood on the lost bomber's wing tip. She estimated that she had been under one minute.

Enough light penetrated the still, clear water that she could discern both shapes and muted colors.

She knelt on the great wing, as though she had come upon a mummified dragon. Her feet were planted in the center of the red wing tip's white swastika roundel. Unwilling to believe what her eyes saw, she touched her fingers to the seventy-five-year-old aluminum.

She had been down two minutes.

She looked away, toward the vast wing's root, and realized that the aircraft lay belly-up, but with its landing gear still retracted. The wing tip opposite the one on which she knelt had snapped off, but the airframe otherwise looked intact, under a film of silt.

She swam toward the plane's centerline, and saw that its belly had been hacked open. Both bomb bay doors had been cut away at their hinges, and lay on the lake bed.

Within the open bay, crescent-shaped clamps had also been cut, so they clamped nothing.

The bomb had been clamped in the plane. Snake Eyes' people had cut it free. They weren't *preparing to* recover an A-bomb. They already had it.

By now, they could be anywhere.

Her lungs were bursting.

She swam up, feared that she had stayed down too long, unclasped the weight belt, and shot upward toward the open water, exhaling as she rose.

She emerged into the air, so buoyantly that she popped up out of the water like a cork.

She sank back, gasping, and realized that, without the belt, she would be unable to return to the bottom.

She muttered, "Crap."

In the open water, she paddled herself around. Through her fogged faceplate she saw a figure standing on the ice, twenty feet from her. She tugged her mask up onto her forehead to determine whether it was Frank or Elliott, and as she wiped her eyes she coughed.

At the sound, he turned.

He was dark, smaller than Frank, and his eyes glistened. They were expressionless, and as black as a snake's eyes.

He raised his right hand, then the pistol he held roared.

Cass ducked back beneath the surface. A bullet sizzled through the water, inches from her face.

She kicked away, to shelter beneath the ice, as two more bullets whooshed past her.

Her heart pounded. She had barely inhaled, and her body had built up carbon dioxide she hadn't gotten rid of. Within a minute, or two, she would have to surface again.

Half blind, she replaced her mask, cleared it, then swam down, as far as she could, then back up. She butted the ice with her shoulder, and got nothing in return but a sore shoulder.

She pressed her cheek to the ice's undersurface, but found no air pocket there.

She swam, parallel to the open water, to distance herself from the man who was trying to kill her.

She saw his silhouette, dark against the ice's brightness, then broke the surface with only her face, exhaled, and gulped air.

He had his back to her, but her exhalation gave her away.

He whirled, fired, but she escaped again, beneath the ice.

A minute later, she surfaced.

Once more, he fired.

Once more, she survived.

With each repetition, the breaths she drew shortened, and the carbon dioxide in her blood increased. The length of time she was able to remain down shrank, proportionately.

This whack-a-mole game could ultimately end just one way. Unless she changed its rules.

This time, she located the silhouette above, on the ice. She swam to it, not away from it.

She would surface, explosively, then lunge for his legs. If she could drag him into the water, the fight would be fairer.

She reached a point beneath him, then gathered herself.

One way or another, it would be over within seconds.

She kicked up, burst from the water, caught his leg, and threw her weight backward.

He slipped, but caught his balance.

"Dammit!"

Cass shook water off her mask's faceplate. "Frank?"

He knelt, then tugged her, gasping, out onto the ice.

She said, "What the hell?"

"I was already on the way up here. I heard shots."

"What happened to Snake Eyes?"

"He brought a pistol to a rifle fight. At a hundred yards, I might hit him, but he couldn't hit me. Two rounds ran him off."

"You let him get away?"

"You're welcome."

"What about Elliott?"

"Don't know. Maybe dead. Maybe hiding. Meantime, I expect Snake Eyes has decided to take the bomb somewhere. Where it will do the least good."

"What do we do now?"

"I'd say that depends on what we think Snake Eyes is going to do."

Fifty-two

BEHIND THE EXPEDITION'S WHEEL, THE ASP DROVE THROUGH THE open gate, away from Upper Pika Lake for the last time. The sun hung low above the mountain peaks to his west. Most of his slow journey back to the interstate highway would be negotiated under the cover of darkness.

He accelerated, cautiously. Time, now more than ever, was both his friend, and his enemy.

When the helicopter pilot had emerged from the workshop building, and walked downhill, toward the cabin, the Asp had followed him.

The Asp's enemies had voluntarily divided their forces. That should have allowed him to engage, then defeat, them one by one. He had drawn his knife, then trailed silently after the pilot, gaining ground gradually.

The man had moved with economy and ease, as though this terrain were home. Like most people at home, he had noticed a small something out of place. He had knelt alongside the trail, then straightened holding an object. The Asp realized it was the field glasses' case that he had dropped in haste when he had heard the helicopter approach.

The pilot had turned, scanned the forest all around him. Then he had begun running, down the trail, and past the old woman's cabin.

When the pilot rounded the trail's second bend, he had to have seen the Expedition, and the trailer it towed.

The Asp then abandoned stealth, and sprinted forward, knife in hand.

Fifty yards separated them when the old man turned, and glimpsed his pursuer.

The man veered off the trail, into the woods, at the dead run.

It was a clever tactic. The Asp was younger and faster, but the old man obviously knew these woods.

The gap between them grew. Suddenly, the old man turned, at right angles to his direction of flight.

He dashed along an escarpment's lip. Beyond, the ridgeline dropped away fifty feet.

As the Asp chased his quarry along the escarpment, the old man leapt from rock to rock, with a nimbleness born from familiarity. Meanwhile the Asp slowed, to avoid a misstep that would plunge him over the cliff. The old man had made the terrain, which should have been his enemy, into his friend.

The gap between them grew. Finally, the Asp drew his pistol, knelt, sighted, then fired a single shot.

The old man tumbled over the escarpment.

Panting, the Asp stopped at the place where the old man had fallen then peered over the edge. No body lay below.

The old man had been hit, or had feigned it. But without doubt the shot, the fall, or both, had wounded him.

He had become less a threat than his two companions were and the shot had probably alerted them.

The Asp had reversed course and had run back to deal with the two greater remaining threats.

When he had reached the workshop, he found it empty. Then he had glimpsed the girl, en route to the lake on foot, wearing the wetsuit he had left behind.

He had pursued.

Luck's intervention had been either a deliberate trap, or, more likely, simple misfortune.

Regardless, the Asp had elected to disengage from all these nettlesome enemies. He didn't have time to hunt them all down. More importantly, he did not need to.

The old pilot was dead, or wounded, and isolated. Luck, and probably the girl, were alive, but surely neither could fly the helicopter. On foot, by the time any of the three could raise the alarm, the Asp, and the atom bomb he possessed, would have disappeared into America, like a fish disappeared into the sea.

The Americans didn't know where, or when, the Asp would strike, but he did.

The blow that had been struck against America on the eleventh of September 2001 had been frail, yet it had so angered America that it embarked on a crusade against Islam that bled both sides to this day. The blow that the Asp would now strike with the fist with which God had gifted him would be vastly stronger. It would enrage America to lash out far more destructively, and in turn to bring destruction upon itself, and upon the godless nations who were both its enemies and the enemies of true Islam. Islam's greatest enemy would become its unwitting friend.

Then, as the old woman who sold him the pistol had prophesized, the meek would inherit the earth.

Fifty-three

TWO HOURS AFTER FRANK HAD RESCUED CASS, THEY GAVE UP the search for Elliott Love, and arrived back at the workshop.

The Pedro sat, like a gray ghost, in the risen moon's light.

Cass said, "Do you think Elliott's alive?"

Frank said, "Don't know. Don't know how to get to the place where his mother kept her airplane, either. I do know Snake Eyes is alive. And the farther away from here he gets before anybody starts looking for him, the harder he'll be to find."

"So we have to do something."

"Nearest summer rental cabin has to be at least four hours walk, if we knew where we were walking. By the time we walk down in the dark to someplace where we have cell service again, he'll be long gone."

Cass pointed at the Pedro. "If I fly that thing south toward the interstate, I'll fly into a cell tower's bubble in ten minutes. And if I take these German checklists along, there will be *some* tangible evidence, at least, that corroborates what I saw and the story we're telling."

Cass gathered the papers, her phone, and the helicopter's key, then walked across the clearing to the Pedro.

She settled into the pilot's left hand seat, felt her way across the instruments until she found Elliott's improvised magneto switch, then inserted the key.

Frank climbed in alongside her, through the copilot's door.

She said, "Frank, you stay here. Walk down."

He sat and shook his head while he felt for his harness straps. "Cowboys don't have much use for walking."

Cass gripped the Pedro's cyclic with her right hand as she turned and peered into Frank's eyes. "Frank, you think I'm a smug know-it-all. I get that. But right now what I know is that I'm scared to death. A novice pilot trying to fly a completely unfamiliar aircraft in the dark is reckless and stupid. I may die trying to do it. I don't want you to die trying too."

Frank stared back at her. "And you think I'm a stubborn, old know-it-all. But what I know is I tried to ranch right but got it wrong. I tried to be a husband right but got that wrong too. I'm going to die soon enough anyway. Might as well die trying to do one last thing right."

"But there's no *reason* for you to die trying too."

Frank wrestled the right hand seat's balky old harness clasp until it finally clicked and locked him in. "Sure there is. It's easier for people to be scared to death together than alone."

Fifty-four

ELLIOTT LOVE LEANED AGAINST THE FUSELAGE OF HIS MOTHER'S Fieseler Storch, sucking his breath in through clenched teeth. He and the delicate airplane rested in the moonlight, in the open mountain meadow from which, so many times and so many years before, he had taken off, and in which he had landed.

Light and fragile as the Storch was, dragging it tail-first from its shed had been heavy lifting, for one old man with a newly sprained shoulder.

The Storch's crop-duster-white paint wanted touching up, and the design looked like a praying mantis had been mated to a refrigerator carton. But a Storch had rescued Mussolini from a mountaintop prison. Another had survived Russian antiaircraft fire and delivered Hanna Reitsch to Hitler's Bunker during World War II's last days.

This Storch had one last, historic job for its kind to do.

Elliott had spent an additional half hour swinging out, then locking in place, the plane's wings.

Again he had rested.

He knew precisely what his mother would do if presented with the same options that the gunman, in this place and time, had available.

Elliott also knew what his own options were, in response.

He hand-rotated the old prop until the engine's cylinders were primed, then climbed into the cockpit.

He hand-cranked the plane's flaps and slats into takeoff

position, using the plane's eccentric and archaic system of vertical bicycle chains.

Then he pressed the starter, listened to the old engine chug, then growl, while he pulled on his flight helmet.

The Storch was "a helicopter before there were helicopters." It had been created to fly into places where other airplanes were too heavy, too clumsy, or too fast to go.

It was uniquely suited to do the job for which it had been created.

So, Elliott Love thought, was he.

He advanced the throttle, the Storch rolled across the meadow, and was airborne within three hundred feet.

As he climbed, he saw movement. It was the Pedro. It rose, wobbling, above the ridgeline, headed south.

He smiled. He had assumed that the gunman who had pursued him had killed Cassidy and Frank. But the gunman, and his henchmen, if any, had no reason to bother with the Pedro. Therefore, happily, it appeared Cassidy and Frank were alive. And so far it appeared that Cass was handling the unfamiliar aircraft capably.

Elliott watched the Pedro, moonlight glinting off its rotors, shrink as it drifted south. He had no idea what they intended to do. And, like the Pedro, the Storch had no working radio, so he couldn't ask them.

But he knew precisely what he was going to do.

The Pedro continued south. Elliott flew east.

Fifty-five

THE PEDRO'S NOSE DRIFTED RIGHT IN THE MOONLIT DARKNESS, and Cass pressed its left rudder pedal with her left foot to bring it back. She overcorrected, and the nose dropped. With her left hand she lifted the collective alongside her left hip and overcorrected again. The aircraft swung beneath its rotors like a pendulum. Heart pounding, she nudged the cyclic until the Pedro stabilized.

She said into her mic, "Sorry. These controls and my muscle memory don't match yet."

Frank said, "Feels smooth as a slow float down the Arkansas to me."

"Liar."

Cass and Frank had been airborne for five minutes when her phone's ringer sounded, in the Bluetooth earpiece she wore under the helicopter's intercom headset.

She answered.

Wilmot said, "Cass? I've been trying to reach you and Frank for hours."

"We've been busy. And beyond cellphone coverage until just now."

Wilmot said, "Well, I think I can set your mind at ease. The people who will still talk to me say, unofficially, that, at this moment, the external terrorist threat level is lower than it's been since the beginning of this century."

"Well, they're wrong." She nudged the nose right.

"You don't understand, Cass. And I can't be specific. But a

year ago the world got very lucky. By all the intelligence esti-
mates and bellwethers available to us, it's mighty quiet out there
at the moment."

"Wilmot, five hours ago, I was standing on the perfectly preserved wreck of a German jet bomber. It crashed here in 1945.
It crashed here carrying a gun-type uranium bomb. I know that,
because I have the original bomb-arming documents tucked in
to the seat alongside me. A guy tried to shoot me. And he may
have shot somebody else."

"My God. Frank?"

"Frank's riding shotgun with me. And he's hearing my half
of our conversation."

Wilmot said, "What are you talking about? And why are you
screaming."

"I'm flying a helicopter. North of Vail. Badly. So I'm not talking much. Use your contacts. Get somebody off their asses, and
find this guy, and this bomb, okay?"

"What do they look for? And where?"

"The bomb is probably in a horse trailer. Most likely it's being
towed somewhere now. But it could have been removed days, or
weeks, ago. Wilmot, they need to put everything available on
this. Right now."

"They don't have much available, right now."

"You said things were quiet."

"I said there weren't any known threats. I didn't say we weren't
spread thin, preparing for them, anyway. Cass, this is Fourth of
July weekend. That's as target-rich an environment as America
offers. There are forty-five Major League Baseball games. There
are parades, fireworks displays, concerts, auto races—"

"This is a frigging A-bomb, Wilmot! And nobody says he has
to set it off this weekend. He could just hide, and wait."

Wilmot paused.

Then he said, "No. The reason my contacts aren't hearing
any chatter is that this group, or just this one guy, is operating
autonomously. Precisely so there is no chatter. And nobody's
hiding. The plan is to detonate the device on the Fourth of July.
In Washington, D.C."

Cass said, "How can you be sure of *that*?"

"Because I've seen this picture before."

Cass asked Frank, "If Snake Eyes absolutely has to be in

Washington D.C., on the Fourth of July, what route would he take?"

"Towing a heavy trailer? If he expects to get to Washington on the fourth, back roads add too many miles. He needs to drive the same route I did, when I came to see you. A straight shot on I-70 east, all the way to the coast."

Cass said to Wilmot, "Can you get them to intercept him? On I-70 east?"

"If I knew what they're supposed to intercept. And if I get their attention. Which won't happen immediately. Cass, interception could result in a nuclear detonation. It's not a knee-jerk solution."

"According to the diagrams and checklists, this bomb has an actuator plug, Wilmot. Like the Hiroshima bomb, to prevent premature detonation. Logically, he wouldn't plug it in, and activate the bomb, until he gets near Washington."

Wilmot said, "The bomb is already armed."

"What?"

"Great minds may think alike, but one thing that makes them great is not repeating someone else's mistakes. Like I said, I've seen this picture before. These terrorists may have seen it too. That bomb is *armed*. A nuclear detonation in a suboptimal location is more useful for their purposes than no nuclear detonation at all."

"Okay." Cass peered down through the bubble beneath her feet, at the interstate highway now beneath the Pedro.

Then she checked the Pedro's fuel gauge.

She said, "Frank and I have a little gas left. We'll scout the interstate. Maybe we can at least tell you what they're supposed to intercept."

Wilmot shouted, "Don't try to stop that vehicle!"

"I know. We could get ourselves blown up."

Wilmot said, "Cass, that's the least of it. If you cause a nuclear detonation within the continental United States, you could start World War III."

Ten minutes later, Cass flew the Pedro east above I-70, the highway's dual ribbons white in the moonlight. To her right, Lake Dillon shone silver alongside the highway.

Traffic in both directions was sparse, because of the night closure west of Avon.

Ahead, a lone SUV, towing a closed trailer, crept east.

Cass said, "You think that's him?"

Frank said, "That's a horse trailer, alright. It's moving slow. That makes sense, if he's towing an extra nine thousand pounds in that trailer. From here at Lake Dillon the grade climbs all the way up to the tunnel."

Cass said, "I think I'll follow a little while, before we land."

"To get a better description?"

"To burn fuel and lighten the ship before landing, and to get more familiar with the controls. Even in a helicopter I'm familiar with, my landings need work."

Cass inched the Pedro forward, pacing the SUV as it climbed east, toward the Continental Divide, at perhaps forty-five miles per hour.

Ahead of, and below them, the SUV and trailer lumbered on. Three miles further up the highway, the eastbound lanes entered their side of the Eisenhower Tunnel.

Cass said, "Frank, if we climb over the mountain, then pick him up on the other side, I'm not sure we'll have enough gas to find a landing spot. I'm turning back west, back down into the valley, to find a flat spot."

Frank pointed ahead, to eleven o'clock, and higher than their altitude. "What do you suppose that's about?"

Cass looked where Frank pointed. A high-winged, single-engined plane's navigation lights flickered, above the Continental Divide, while the aircraft carved slow figure eights, back and forth above the highway.

The plane crossed the moon. When Cass saw its spindly silhouette, she hovered the Pedro while gooseflesh rose on her arms.

She said, "Frank, that's a Fieseler Storch."

"Elliott?"

"Who else?"

The Storch stopped circling, climbed east, then over the ridge, and disappeared beyond the mountain's east side.

Frank said, "What do you think—?"

Cass rotated the Pedro until it pointed west, then accelerated.

She said, "What I think is that we need to get the hell away from here."

Fifty-six

ELLIOTT LOVE WATCHED AS THE LONE VEHICLE, TRAILED BY THE
Pedro above and behind, climbed toward the Eisenhower Tunnel
in the moonlight.

He turned away from the peculiar two-vehicle convoy, then
advanced the Storch's throttle. He wrung out every one of the
little plane's two hundred forty horsepower as he climbed.

The tunnel's elevation was eleven thousand feet, but the
mountain that the tunnel penetrated rose to twelve thousand six
hundred feet. The Storch cleared the Continental Divide's rocky
crest with one hundred feet to spare.

Elliott banked the Storch as he descended the eastern slope.
Below the tree line, ski runs, and lift towers, gashed the pine forest
that carpeted the Divide's east side. In summer, hikers and bicyclists
ruled Loveland Ski Area, but tonight the mountain was deserted.

Elliott Love was alone.

As he had been most of his life. At sixteen, there had been
a girl. He could no longer remember her name, only that after
he told her his story she had rejected him. And so he had never
told his story again, and had done his best to ignore it.

Until today. And now his story had changed. He couldn't change
what his family had been. But he remained part of his family.
And he could change what his story and his family *would* be.

He pressed the button on his watch, and by its light noted
the seconds ticking away.

Timing was everything.

Fifty-seven

THE ASP INCHED THE BELLOWING EXPEDITION UP THE GRADE TO the Eisenhower Tunnel. There was no traffic, either to impede his progress or provide him cover.

Therefore, he maintained a steady speed, to conserve both the engine and the vehicle's other mechanical systems. The engine's stress, evident from its roar, would end once he passed through the tunnel. The long descent down to Denver would shift the burden to the brakes, and to the transmission as it downshifted. Once the road flattened, the way east to Washington was largely flat, and straight.

At legal speeds, and allowing for refueling stops, he would deliver his precious cargo into Washington, D.C. before noon on America's most self-congratulatory day, the Fourth of July.

Despite the Fist of God's age, its reliability worried him less than his vehicle's reliability did. The aerial bomb's altitude-triggered barometric detonating mechanism, which he regarded as a foolishly unreliable mechanism in any event, was now irrelevant. He had removed the barometric sensor from the firing circuit, and replaced it with a cell phone, connected through its vibrating ring circuit. Then he had replaced the inert plug with the live actuator plug.

Islam's soldiers had relied, across theaters of war and for decades, upon the simple and dependable cell phone expedient, which turned their enemies' old munitions into remotely triggered Improvised Explosive Devices. Now, by placing a call to the phone embedded in the bomb, the Asp could turn Washington into a fireball.

Tempting as it would have been to simply park the trailer, then watch the joyous fireball from a distance, he would remain with the bomb. If the Americans jammed, or disabled, cell phone communications, he could simply manually detonate the bomb. Or, at worst, he could set fire to the hay bales he had purchased, then piled atop the bomb, to hide it from a casual glance into the trailer. As a last fail safe, the flames would likely set off the conventional explosives and detonate the bomb.

However this ended, he would, within thirty hours, be reunited in Paradise with his brother, his parents, and with so many of his fellow holy warriors.

This plan, at first so improbable, and now revealed as so elegant, demonstrated God's hand at work. The most difficult obstacles to striking a nuclear blow against True Islam's deadliest enemy had always been, first, obtaining a bomb, and second, getting it into the United States. As the sheik had noted so long ago, those obstacles had been overcome without the Asp's involvement, by the long dead enemies of Islam's enemy.

An electronic message board mounted above the eastbound lanes' tunnel entrance became legible as he drove closer. He was advancing so slowly that he actually had time to read its inane American advisories.

Scrolling orange letters cautioned him to refrain from texting while driving. They thanked him for his patience, regarding roadwork that would make Colorado a better place, and they reminded him that vehicles carrying hazardous materials were prohibited in the tunnel.

He lunged forward in the driver's seat, as though his effort would carry the big SUV to the tunnel mouth without blowing its engine. During the final yards' approach to the tunnel, the road flattened. The engine's roar relaxed, and yet another hurdle was cleared.

The irony of the "hazardous materials" warning made him smile.

Fifty-eight

EVEN THOUGH ELLIOTT LOVE HAD PULLED THE STORCH OUT OF a shallow, banking dive, its airspeed was only one hundred ten miles per hour, so it floated, like the "helicopter before there were helicopters" that it was. It skimmed due west, ten feet above Interstate 70's two eastbound lanes. The Storch's controls were as heavy as the plane itself was light. Keeping the aircraft centered on the tunnel's yellow-lit exit portal required greater strength than he remembered. Or age had weakened him.

The Storch's wing span was nearly forty-seven feet, and the tunnel's traffic lanes were twenty-six feet wide, plus the width of the pedestrian walkway.

Elliott braced for the jolt, then both wings' leading edges clipped the tunnel portal's unyielding concrete.

The impact threw him forward against his seat harness, then both wings sheared at their hinge points.

The Storch thumped down on its undercarriage, and its engine's growl reverberated in the tunnel's confines.

The aircraft's momentum, and its still-churning prop, propelled the fuselage west at one hundred miles per hour.

The flimsy wings, still attached by cables and struts, dangled alongside the fuselage. They screeched, and showered sparks, as the Storch dragged them with it.

Aviation gasoline spewed from the Storch's ruptured wing-root fuel tank, and aviation gasoline's aroma filled his nostrils.

Ahead, a single pair of headlights approached.

Elliott estimated the vehicles' closing speed was one hundred fifty miles per hour.

Fifty-nine

THE EXPEDITION, UNBURDENED AT LAST FROM CLIMBING, ENTERED the flatter tunnel, and accelerated to fifty miles per hour.

The Asp relaxed his hands on the wheel, closed his eyes, and rolled his head and shoulders to relieve combined tension and monotony.

When he opened them, in the tunnel's dim yellow light, he blinked.

The distance between the Expedition and a slow-moving vehicle ahead, which had no taillights, shrank rapidly.

The vehicle showered sparks, and he realized that it was narrow, perhaps a motorcycle crashed and sliding. By the time he realized that he was closing the gap to the vehicle too rapidly, he was approaching the tunnel's midpoint.

The reason he seemed to be closing the gap was that the other vehicle was careening *toward* him.

It trailed not only sparks, but flame.

Reflexively, he braked hard. Then he felt, and remembered, the immense and unstable weight in the trailer he pulled. He eased off the brake pedal.

When the other vehicle came within his headlights' range, its gangling shape and whirling propeller could not have astonished him more if it had been a charging tiger.

Again he stabbed the brakes, so forcefully that his entire body stiffened. His elbows locked as he clutched the steering wheel with his arms straight.

The single-engined airplane and the Expedition collided.

The plane's fuselage overrode the Expedition's hood, as the Asp pitched forward, and his forehead struck the steering wheel.

The Asp awoke to heat, flames, and gasoline's pungent odor. The Expedition's front end had collapsed, so that he was pinned in place by the dash and steering wheel. The driver's side window was shattered, and missing, and the SUV's left side was, in turn, pinned against the chest-high white tile of the tunnel's wall, below the pedestrian catwalk. The passenger seat had been rammed backward. Where it had been, the airplane's nose intruded. It appeared as though a steel-and-aluminum shark had leapt into a boat.

Through the opening where the windshield had been, the Asp stared up at a bald, old white man, who stared back at him through the airplane's missing side window.

The man's face was bloody, his eyes vacant. Like the Asp, he appeared unable to move.

The Asp turned his head, and realized that the trailer had jackknifed, but remained upright alongside the SUV.

Like the airplane, it was burning.

The Asp groped with his free hand for his phone. Whether he would be able to trigger the bomb, or whether the flames would set off the explosives that would trigger the uranium explosion, soon enough, the Asp would know whether an atom bomb would explode seventy-five years after it had been built.

The Asp shouted to the old man, through the broken windshield, "Who are you? Why have you done this?"

Only then he realized that the crash had so deafened him that he couldn't hear his *own* voice, and so the old man did not hear it either.

Clearly, the man was not his friend. Neither was he obviously the Asp's enemy.

The Asp assumed that who the man was, and all such questions, would be answered when he entered Paradise.

Sixty

CASS REDUCED THE PEDRO'S ALTITUDE EVEN AS SHE PUT AS MUCH distance between the tunnel and the Pedro as possible. The Pedro's ground speed was only eighty-five miles per hour, and their retreat from the tunnel seemed just a crawl.

Frank said, "What's your hurry?"

Cass said, "Frank, Elliott knows where Snake Eyes is taking that bomb as well as Wilmot does. His mother probably had a wall poster with crosshairs drawn on the White House.

"Elliott figured out that the safest place to stop that bomb is inside the Eisenhower Tunnel. He probably saw the van and the tow vehicle, so he knew what he was looking for. All he had to do was loiter at the tunnel."

"You think he plans to block the tunnel exit, on the east side of the Divide?"

"I think he plans to ram that SUV head on, *in* the tunnel. At best, Snake Eyes will be stuck. At worst, an underground nuclear test is better than a shoot-out in Downtown Denver that ends with a nuclear explosion."

A flash behind them lit the landscape like daylight.

In the instant after it faded, Cass flicked her eyes back. She expected more, until she realized that only a sliver of light and heat the size of the tunnel mouth had escaped.

Even so, a dark wave seemed to roll across the ground, toward them.

She realized it was a great, hot, surface wind. It bent the pines' tops as it raced toward them.

Frank pointed down. "Flat beach below us. Beside the lake."

The blast's wind and thunder struck the Pedro. She knew Pedros didn't like tailwinds. But this was less a wind than like being punched by a giant's fist.

The Pedro swung violently beneath its rotors.

The little helicopter spiraled down, and no input she might try would stop it.

Frank said, "Beach!"

Cass looked down at the water beneath them and shook her head. "Can't get there. We're gonna be in the Hudson. Hang on."

The Pedro's belly struck Lake Dillon's surface and the fuselage lurched right.

The right rotor's whirling tip touched the water and shattered. Blade fragments exploded in all directions.

In an eye blink the fuselage rolled further onto its right side. The left rotor's blades also exploded. The shrapnel that the blade became shattered the canopy.

The fuselage lurched again, Cass's chin struck her chest, and dazed her.

The engine had quit.

The only sounds were of hissing steam, released as the cold lake water contacted the engine's hot metal, and of roaring water.

The Pedro, now fully on its right side, admitted water so rapidly through the wide rear compartment doors and the ruptured canopy that, in the time it took to glance at Frank, and see that he was unconscious, Cass was completely submerged in freezing water. She punched out of her harness, then leaned toward Frank, shook him, and screamed into the water, "Frank!" No response. She punched his harness release, but it didn't budge.

As the fuselage sank, she pulled herself across the cabin, unlatched the pilot's door, slid it open, pushed out, then kicked to the surface.

She gulped a breath, dove, and reentered the cabin. Half blind in the dark, she tore at Frank's harness again. Nothing gave.

The helicopter's right flank struck bottom. She surfaced again.

The Pedro rested in water so shallow that its left side was barely a foot beneath the surface, and one rotor blade's jagged root poked into the air.

She pounded the water and screamed.

The shore was eighty feet away. Frank was less than ten feet beneath the surface. But without a knife to cut him loose, he may as well have been at the bottom of the North Atlantic.

It had sounded idiotic when he told her everybody carried a knife.

Like he did!

Cass swam down again, felt until she found the folding knife in Frank's jeans' right front pocket. She cut him loose, wrestled his inert bulk out through the pilot's door, and clawed to the surface.

He wasn't apparently breathing when she dragged him out onto the narrow beach, then turned him on his back. He lay still and serene, as though content to have died trying to do one last thing right.

She pushed on his chest with two hands, as she tried to remember how to give mouth-to-mouth.

Frank stirred. He turned his head to the side, vomited water, then coughed.

She sobbed, and hugged him.

He coughed again, then said, "Landings do need work."

Three minutes later, Cass looked back from the little beach toward the Continental Divide. Beyond the hill to her front, in the place where she thought the tunnel entrance should have been, an orange glow lit the sky. On the near slope, another forest fire roared.

Across the lake, emergency vehicles' flashing lights streaked along a distant road, and sirens echoed across the water.

Frank said, "What's all that?"

Cass said, "Maybe the start of World War III."

Sixty-one

ON THE SECOND MORNING AFTER THE PEDRO CRASHED, CASS SAT with Frank, and with Wilmot Hoffman, around Frank's breakfast table.

All three of them stared at the flat screen mounted on the breakfast room's wall, and at the Denver network affiliate's morning anchor.

The anchor turned from her partner to the camera, then said, "New details on that truck crash, two nights ago, that has closed the Eisenhower Tunnel."

The image changed to video of a forest fire, and she spoke over it. "The explosion of the truck's cargo lit the night sky as far away as Copper Mountain, sparked localized forest fires from the tunnel's portals to near Lake Dillon, and rattled dishes in Silverthorne, fifteen miles away."

Her partner interrupted. "And registered on the Colorado School of Mines seismograph."

She continued, "The truck was reportedly operating under Defense Department contract, and carried highly flammable experimental chemicals."

The male co-anchor said, "Until contamination risks have been evaluated, federal authorities have indefinitely suspended all public access, and overflights, within a ten-mile radius of the tunnel. They acknowledge that the eastbound vehicle's driver failed to heed mandated detour warnings for hazardous material carriers, that were intended to prevent incidents like this. Remotely piloted government vehicles have confirmed that the blast collapsed both the eastbound and westbound tunnel bores, from end to end."

The female anchor said, "The death toll appears limited to the truck's driver, who has not been identified, and possibly a wrong-way motorist, suspected to have caused the accident. The matter is expected to remain under investigation indefinitely."

The male anchor frowned. "After the break: What this means for your ski-area commute." Then he smiled. "But we'll tell you which diner, along which back-road detour, is already offering free coffee, to introduce itself to weary travelers."

Cass set down her own coffee. "This is such bullshit!"

Wilmot muted the commercial as he sighed. "The alternative is acknowledging that a foreign terrorist detonated a nuclear device within the Continental United States. Which would pressure us to get even with somebody."

Cass said, "Wilmot, the government can't get away with covering up a nuclear explosion."

Wilmot shrugged. "As contemporary nuclear weapons go, this one was tiny, and almost completely confined. The tunnel bores collapsed within fractions of a second, so radioactive contamination leakage should have been minimal enough to explain with another whopper, if necessary. Look what governments have already managed to cover up about this bomb for seventy-five years. And who's left to tell the story, now? Mr. Love certainly can't."

Cass looked down at her phone. "Neither can Jimmy Righetti. Merken got a text last night. Jimmy passed away yesterday."

Frank said to Cass, "Jimmy's gone. So now *you* could tell the story. It would make you famous."

Cass shook her head. "The paperwork and the photograph are mush on the bottom of Lake Dillon. Seventy percent of my salary is paid by the same government that says this was a trucking accident. And that lake that plane sits in is owned by the same government that's lying its ass off. Besides, if the alternative to another lie agreed on later is war, I'm fine with having done the right thing even though nobody knows it."

Frank said, "I've gotten accustomed to your face. You don't look fine with it."

Cass stared down at the table. "You're right. It's not enough. I feel a little like Jimmy Righetti and Elliott. I don't need to tell the world. I just need to tell one somebody, somewhere, who will be better off for knowing."

Wilmot adjusted his glasses as he consulted his wristwatch.

"Frank, one thing I know is that, with the detours, you two need to leave now, or Cass will miss her plane."

At Denver airport's curbside drop-off, Frank and Cass sat in his idling pickup, with the windows rolled down in the warm July morning.

He said, "Never thanked you for saving my life."

"I never thanked you for saving mine. So we're even." Cass paused, then said, "No. Not even. I feel like I got the best of the deal, knowing you."

Frank looked out his window. "I think I came out even better, for knowing you."

Cass said, "So, what will you do now, Frank?"

"All the questions that I came to you with are answered. I'll keep teaching fishing, I suppose. After the retirement party there's only one big event left. And I'm not ready for that one."

She smiled.

He said, "There'll be a spot in class reserved for you anytime. On the house. Catch-and-release is vegan friendly."

"Sure. I'll get back to you on the date." She paused. "Frank, when I said your wife was right to give up on you? I didn't mean it. I was wrong. So was she."

Frank said, "I know."

She leaned forward and peered into his face. "Frank, are you *crying*?"

Frank cranked his window closed, as he shook his head. "Nope. Hay fever always gets to me when I come down to the city. Too many lawns and rose bushes."

Cass wiped her eyes. "I guess it's getting to me, too."

She leaned across the cab, hugged him, pecked his cheek, and for an instant he hugged her back.

She hopped from the truck, hoisted her rollaboard from the pickup's bed, then towed it toward the check-in doors.

Frank leaned across the cab and called, "Wrong way!" He pointed. "Flights to Washington check in over this way."

She kept walking, as she called back, "Not going to Washington. Going to Chicago."

"Why?"

"Because there's one question left."

Sixty-two

THE UBER DROPPED CASS IN FRONT OF A CLASSROOM BUILDING, at the University of Chicago campus, as 4:00 p.m. summer-session classes broke. The humid air felt heavy, after Colorado, and she swam upstream against the student tide headed to libraries, dorms, and bars.

The classroom she sought turned out to be an echoing amphitheater, and the last class's last student hurried out past her as she entered.

Below her, on the low stage, the gray-haired, tweed-jacketed prof stood with his back to her. He erased his day's wisdom from the bank of old-fashioned chalkboards that lined the classroom's front.

Cass called, "Professor?"

He moved to the next board without turning around and kept erasing.

"For three more months. Then you can call me emeritus. And the University can replace my chalkboards with touchscreens."

Cass descended the aisle toward the stage, and her voice echoed. "My name is Cassidy Gooding. Could I ask you a few questions?"

"That would be novel. All I usually hear in a 4:00 p.m. class is snoring, and clicking phones."

"Your bio says you were born in 1945."

"Barely. Why?"

"And your middle name is Bergman."

"Yes. My mother's maiden name was Rachel Bergman."

415

Cass felt hair rise on the back of her neck.

"I don't mean to pry. But your online bios are a little light."

"By design. I don't have a Facebook page either. I'm of a generation that minded its own business. But pry away." He stepped to the last chalkboard.

"Could I ask *where* you were born?"

"Manhattan Island. I'm a native New Yorker."

Cass's shoulders slumped. "Oh."

"Also barely. I was born December twentieth. Two days after my mother arrived in the States. From Switzerland, via Lisbon, Portugal, on refugee status. Again, why?"

He turned around and Cass's breath caught.

His hair was thin, his shoulders slimmed by age. But the cleft chin, and blue eyes, were straight out of the photograph that Frank Luck had brought to her, on a morning that now seemed a lifetime before this moment.

The academic stepped down from the shallow stage, extended his hand, and smiled. "Peter Winter." He cocked his head. "You're a little old for an undergraduate, Ms. Gooding."

She smiled. "Cass. Please. And I'm not as old as most of the aircraft and exhibits I curate at the Smithsonian."

He narrowed his eyes. "Aircraft? The Smithsonian? That has something to do with philosophy? And with this course on the moral philosophy of war in particular?"

"If you're comfortable talking about it."

"My curiosity outweighs my discomfort."

"Switzerland? Portugal?"

He smiled again, softer and sadder. "It's complex."

He motioned her to sit in one of the amphitheater's front row seats, then unfolded the seat next to her and sat also.

He said, "Before World War II, my mother's family were Bavarian bankers. And Jewish. Which, of course, complicated their lives greatly. My father, Peter Winter, was not Jewish. That further complicated things. During the war, he was a bureaucrat. Involved in defense production. As most German men not actually in the military were, at the time. Fairly high up apparently.

"My mother was then, and remained for all her life, a most irreverent and secular Jew. Which was ironic, because the Bergmans fared as terribly as all German Jews did during the Third Reich. My great uncle smuggled himself to Portugal, before the war. He later smuggled my mother out of Germany, and eventually into New York. My uncle, her brother, was a devout, practicing Jew. He had also been involved in the German Resistance. The Nazis killed him. My mother and father were able to conceal her background." He paused, then shook his head. "Until, on the day in Spring 1945 that she realized she was pregnant, her identity was discovered. Nazis arrived at the family home to arrest her. My grandfather, who lived there, died resisting them. The house was set afire. My mother was trapped on an upper floor. The floor collapsed beneath her."

Cass wrinkled her forehead. "But you're here."

Rachel Bergman's son said, "It happened like this."

Sixty-three

RACHEL AWOKE IN PITCH DARKNESS, FLAT ON HER BACK, THRASH-
ing, rigid, and sweat-soaked.

She sighed, relieved that she had awakened from the most
terrible nightmare imaginable.

Then she realized that the odor of sulphur and burning wood,
and roaring wind that seared her cheeks, were all still there.

Her next thought was that she was dead, and lay at the gates
of hell.

She raised one hand, touched something rough, but flexible,
inches above her face. Buried alive? She pushed, pushed again,
then again, screaming at the pain in her shoulder that the movement caused. The carpet that covered her moved, and she kicked
and shoved until it rolled away, and she could see again.

Above her, flames leapt and slithered, like living beasts held
back from her by a cage with jagged, black bars.

The situation clarified even as each breath became agony.

When the library's floor had given way, she fell along with it.
The floor's mass and velocity had broken through the weakened
ground floor, and the jumbled debris in which she was entangled
had come to rest in the house's cellar.

The house's outer walls, deprived of architectural support,
had then collapsed inward, an avalanche of stone and timber.

The angled beams and plaster slabs above her held back the
debris and the flames. But the fire seemed to be growing, not
dying. Within minutes, perhaps seconds, the fire would devour
and collapse her coffin-sized refuge.

The hot wind that howled past her was air, drawn in to replace the air that the flames above her consumed.

Where air came in, she might get out.

She twisted, screaming, onto her stomach. One ankle was pinned. She kicked with her free leg until her foot popped free of her shoe.

Coughing and gasping, she laid her burned cheek against the cellar's stone floor, where the smoke was thinnest. She dragged herself on her elbows, away from the grave that fate had dug for her.

The air grew minutely cooler. The flames' roar and glare weakened.

Exhausted, she slept.

She awoke, nauseated, and realized that her peril now threatened not just her life, but the new life she carried within her.

The fire's embers still crackled and glowed twenty meters behind her, but she now lay alongside the house's electric generator. That meant she had crawled down the old mine adit, and lay beneath the airshaft through which the generator drew in its combustion air. The airshaft was a stone chimney, its opening large enough that, as a child adventuress, she had ascended more than once. The shaft emerged at the surface, in her mother's rose garden, between the house and the stables.

She lay still, gathering strength and assessing her wounds, then dragged herself up the stone shaft's walls, by handholds and toeholds, toward the faint rectangle of sky visible three meters above. The shaft seemed narrower, the sky more distant, than she remembered, and the handholds and toeholds seemed both rougher and slipperier.

When she came within one meter of the chimney's exit, she heard a voice, and froze in place.

"Sergeant, how long do we have to guard this rubble?"

The SS sentry sounded so close that he must have been leaning against the shaft's outside wall, less than a meter from her.

A more distant voice said, "Until we're relieved. Straighten up!"

"While I'm here, can I shoot squirrels?"

"If they're Jewish."

"How—?"

"You idiot! Shoot anything that moves except your squad mates! Button that tunic and throw away that cigarette!"

A flicked cigarette butt, its tip glowing orange, tumbled

from above, then lodged on Rachel's already burned and aching forearm. It burned itself out while she clung to the wall, teeth gritted, and as silent and still as a fly.

Four more cigarette butts had fluttered past her, and the stones to which she clung had turned frigid, when the SS detachment finally left, amid shouted orders and truck-engine roars.

Stiff, pain-wracked, and weary beyond remorse, Rachel crawled up the airshaft, into the cold night air, and tumbled into dead weeds and thorny rose stumps. The house behind her was a black, smoking heap, as were the stables.

Her father's remains lay within the rubble of the home he had defended against his own fatherland's soldiers.

Her mind told her that, because the Nazis had come here, Peter surely lay dead in the next valley, too.

Her heart told her to go to him, to be sure, and to sacrifice her life in the attempt to find him, if necessary. But if Peter was alive, *he* would find her, eventually. And there was now another life within her that she had no right to sacrifice, and which might be all that remained of her family.

Except for Uncle Max. She rose to one knee, stood. Then, with one foot bare, she limped west. The Swiss border was four hundred kilometers away.

Sixty-four

PROFESSOR PETER WINTER SAID TO CASS, "MY GREAT UNCLE IN Portugal, who viewed laws as mere suggestions, procured my mother's transit across Switzerland. The war ended in Europe while she was en route to Portugal."

"She didn't return to Germany?"

Professor Peter Winter shook his head. "At that time, no. Germans called the immediate postwar 'Stunde Null,' 'Hour Zero.' The entire country was physically ruined. The Nazi government's eradication left Germany's communications and records infrastructure dysfunctional. From 1945 until 1949, Germany was carved into four countries, the U.S., British, French, and Soviet occupation zones. She clung to the hope that my father was so smart, and so tough, and their love so strong, that he had survived, and would emerge, eventually."

"He *did*?"

Professor Winter shook his head. "She and my great uncle spent years searching for traces of him, unsuccessfully. So, in summer, 1957, my mother took a leave of absence from her job, and returned to what was by then West Germany. With me in tow. We visited the family homestead in the Bavarian Alps—the house where my grandfather had died. It was just overgrown rubble. She expected that."

He stood. "Would you mind if we continue this while we walk back to my office?"

✧ ✧ ✧

Cass and Professor Peter Winter walked side by side through a campus plaza. The students crisscrossing the plaza's stones barely looked up from their phones, or away from their companions. They eddied around an abstract sculpture, which formed the plaza's center point.

Peter Winter's son stopped before the sculpture, then pointed at it. It was a twelve-foot-tall, abstract bronze mushroom.

Winter said, "It's called *Nuclear Energy*. By Henry Moore. It commemorates the squash court, under the football bleachers, that stood on this spot. In 1942, Enrico Fermi's team produced the first nuclear chain reaction here. Some people call Fermi the 'Father of the Atomic Age.'"

Cass smiled. "Do they?"

"Others say Robert Oppenheimer. But I say paternity is less important than morality. Fermi had hightailed it out of Fascist Italy, after he got his Nobel in 1938. Did that make him a courageous moralist? I would argue no. Then he helped build the first A-bomb. Did that make him a cowardly villain? Again, I would argue no. Or did Oppenheimer's leadership of the Manhattan Project make him a worse villain? Or mere flotsam, swept inexorably on history's tide?"

Cass smiled. "According to your bibliography, you've spent your academic lifetime asking questions like that."

He smiled back. "You phrased that correctly. The only hard answers to philosophical questions are the choices we make. War is always a wrong choice. But sometimes history offers only wronger choices. Sometimes the rightest choice is to fight. Sometimes the rightest choice is to walk away from one's enemy. Sometimes the rightest choice is to stay, and treat the enemy of one's enemy as one's friend."

Cass said, "And always to make that right choice. Even if no one will ever know it."

Professor Peter Winter turned to her. "If you wrote that on an exam for me, I'd grade you 'A.'"

Peter Winter's son glanced at the sculpted mushroom cloud as he walked on, and said, "You know, physics was actually my best subject. But my mother steered me into the humanities. She thought the questions that physics answered led to tragedy."

"You were in the middle of telling me about your trip. With your mother, to Bavaria. And what you know about your father."

He looked down at the pavement as they walked, then said, "My mother took me to another valley, near the family home's ruins. Another deceptively beautiful spot.

"Again rubble lay just beneath the greenery. For no reason apparent to me in 1957, or today, either, the valley had been bombed during war. We clambered up a boulder pile, on a hillside. On closer inspection, the boulders were weathered, jumbled building stones.

"She sank to her knees, there, and wept. I was twelve. I didn't understand. So, I hugged her, and she held me, and we just sat there together, until sunset."

He raised his left hand, then grasped its ring finger with his right. "Then she removed her wedding ring, and laid it on a stone. Then we left." Winter looked away.

He said, "I realized later that she had finally accepted that he was dead. And had said goodbye. She never spoke of my father, or of Germany in those times, again." He blinked back a tear, then wiped his eyes.

Cass wiped her own eyes. "What happened to her?"

"Even before that, she had carved out a career. She became a publisher, quite high up, at one of the big New York houses."

Cass swallowed. "Did she ever—?"

"Remarry?" He shook his head. "No. She had numerous suitors. Ernest Hemingway, of whose work she was the greatest fan, asked her to dinner, once. But she turned him down. Because she thought he had other than books on his mind." Winter touched his right shoulder with his left hand. "The fire had left her scarred, here, on her right shoulder and upper arm, which she hid with long sleeves and high collars. But she carried invisible scars, that never really healed.

"My mother always taught me that, no matter what I got myself into, if I kept searching, I would find a way out. But I believe that in this one case she couldn't take her own advice. She never found a way out of what had happened in 1945.

"She loved my father with all her heart, until the day she died. Peacefully, with me, and her closest friends and colleagues, at her bedside. Fifteen years ago."

Cass wiped her eyes with a Kleenex wad from her pocket. "Your mother was a remarkable person. But what else do you know about your father?"

They approached the tree-shaded brick building where Peter Winter officed, and he slowed.

As he stepped into the shadows he frowned. "When I was very young, and knew he had died in the war, I fantasized that he was some sort of hero.

"My mother never would say more about what, specifically, he did. The wounds, I suppose, were too painful to reopen. And perhaps the truth was shameful, or even dangerous. War criminals were pursued well into this century, and their relatives were often shunned. So I only know that he chose to serve the most evil regime in history. Until a random bomb fell on him. That history has been one of the hardest things I've had to accept in my life."

"That's what you think your family history is?"

"I have no reason to think otherwise. Of course, Napoleon said history is just lies agreed on later."

Cass said, "The ring that you saw your mother leave behind on that stone. It was silver. Cast in the shape of two intertwined roses."

His jaw dropped. "How on *Earth* did you know that?"

Cass swallowed the lump in her throat.

Peter Winter's son said, "Please. Let me buy coffee while you tell me. Because I need to know the truth."

"I'm sorry. No."

Peter Winter's face fell.

Cass smiled. "The coffee is on me. Because I need to tell the truth, too."

AFTERWORD

Pineapple Fritters and the Trouble with History

THEODORE VAN KIRK DIED IN 2014, IN STONE MOUNTAIN, GEORGIA, a longish bicycle ride from my house. He was the last survivor, the navigator, of the August 6, 1945, flight during which the B-29 *Enola Gay* dropped the atomic bomb on Hiroshima.

In a vanished America where ethnic references were made with no presumption of malice, Van Kirk's crewmates called him "Dutch." Dutch Van Kirk remembered the event with the humble familiarity to which only those touched by history are entitled. Preflight breakfast was pineapple fritters. Van Kirk hated them.

Decades later, he was invited to address a high-school assembly. The educator who introduced him misread a supplied text, and described Van Kirk to the assembled faculty and students as "a veteran of World War Eleven." Van Kirk said later that nobody in the place, except himself, noticed.

That's startling.

The statistic that two-thirds of U.S. Millennials don't know what "Auschwitz" was is beyond startling. Yet they casually excoriate Mean Tweeters as "Nazis." Nazism has become a pejorative devoid of context. And when everything is "Nazism," nothing is.

And don't even get me started on those whose "knowledge" of history derives from screenplays "inspired by true events."

Which finally brings me to this afterword's point:

The maxim "those who forget the past are condemned to relive its folly" is true only if the past that is not forgotten is true. Whether or not Napoleon actually said it, history is too often a lie built by ignoring inconvenient facts, and by inventing convenient ones.

Now, the lying about which I am ranting is not intellectually honest "revision." Legitimate "revision" reinterprets history by incorporating newly discovered, or wrongly de-emphasized, evidence.

For example, a found shipwreck changes the history of its loss. Or a noble decision is revealed to have been ignoble by a suppressed recording.

Too often, though, history is "revised" not because of supplemental facts, but because of a subsequent agenda, in support of which inconvenient facts are ignored, or convenient facts fabricated.

Even so, the current trouble with history is not intellectually dishonest revisionism. That scourge is as old as less arcane forms of lying. The current trouble with history is that too many people don't know or care about it enough to know whether the next World War will be the third or the twelfth.

Today, America comprises three groups.

The first group includes a minority curious about the past, that informs its thinking about the future from objective facts.

The second group includes those who don't know the past, and are incurious to learn its truths.

Between those extremes resides the most dangerous group. Those in that group invent a past that never was, to justify their insistence on whatever future they prefer.

My Enemy's Enemy aspires only to entertain readers with a past that admittedly never was. But if it turns some few of the ignorant and incurious into curious skeptics, I'd like that.

—Robert Buettner

Acknowledgments

THANKS, FIRST, TO MY PUBLISHER, TONI WEISSKOPF, FOR THE opportunity to write *My Enemy's Enemy*, and for the wisdom and the patience that made it better. Thanks also to my editor Tony Daniel for insight and encouragement, to my copy editor Ben Davidoff for perfection, to the talented Kurt Miller for yet another iconic cover illustration, to Jennie Faries for another wonderfully designed book, to Corinda Carfora for telling the world, and to everyone at Baen Books for their unending support and enthusiasm.

Thanks to the numerous experts, named here and unnamed, who assisted in keeping the many factual aspects of this complex story accurate. Particular thanks to San Francisco law enforcement professional James Griffin Barber for assistance regarding grassroots police procedures, to United States Air Force Major Kacey Ezell, for advice about rotary wing aviation, and about matters aeronautical in general, and to Nate and Tobi Fess for sharing their expertise about the particulars of open water diving. Any errors in all those areas are mine, not theirs.

Finally and forever, thanks to Mary Beth for everything that matters.

About the Author

NATIONAL BEST-SELLING AUTHOR ROBERT BUETTNER WAS A QUILL Award nominee for Best New Writer of 2005, and his debut novel, *Orphanage*, called a classic of modern military science fiction, was a Quill nominee for Best SF/Fantasy/Horror novel of 2004. *Orphanage* and its seven follow-on novels have been compared favorably to the works of Robert Heinlein.

My Enemy's Enemy is his tenth novel, and his first alternate history techno-thriller.

He has been a National Science Foundation Fellow in Paleontology, has prospected for minerals in the Sonoran Desert along the Rio Grande, has served as a U.S. Army Intelligence Officer and as a director of the Southwestern Legal Foundation, has practiced law in Colorado, twelve other states, and five foreign countries, and has served as General Counsel of a unit of one of the United States' largest private companies.

Certified as an underwater diver, he was elected as an undergraduate to the academic history honorary society Phi Alpha Theta, and has climbed and hiked the Rockies from Alberta to Colorado. He lives in Georgia with his family and more bicycles than a grownup needs.

Visit him on the web at www.RobertBuettner.com.